Praise for the
Empires of Armageddon

"This roller-coaster thrill ride will keep readers breathless all the way to a nail-biting cliff-hanger, while the geopolitical premise is plausible enough to make anyone thankful that a sovereign, loving God ultimately holds our safety in his hands, as Terry Brennan portrays so well."

—JEANETTE WINDLE, award-winning author of *CrossFire, Veiled Freedom,* and *Freedom's Stand*

"A simply riveting action/adventure suspense thriller of a novel by an author with an impressive flair for originality and the kind of deftly scripted narrative storytelling style that holds the reader's attention from beginning to end. . . . Especially and unreservedly recommended."

—*MIDWEST BOOK REVIEW*

"A fantastic combination of thriller, historical conspiracy, biblical prophecy, and Middle Eastern complexity—and you're never sure where the line is drawn between fact and fiction."

—IAN ACHESON, author of *Angelguard*

"An engrossing ride into the dark world of political corruption that feels too close to home. In the epic unfolding of biblical prophecy, *Ishmael Covenant* catapults you across a landscape you've only imagined—on both a global and personal scale."

—CHER GATTO, award-winning author of *Something I Am Not*

"Terry Brennan has done it again! This is an epic thriller. The stage is being set for the final parts of history."

—GRANT BERRY, author of *Romans 911*

"Another great biblical prophecy/action novel from Terry Brennan. If you've wondered about the next big events in the Middle East, this book will give you a lot of food for thought. . . . Terry's end-times work will pull you right in."

— **NICK UVA**, Associate Pastor of Harvest Time Church, Greenwich, CT

"Amazing, awesome, powerful, anointed. . . . Will keep you turning pages and praying for the peace of Jerusalem."

— **MARLENE BAGNULL**, director of Write His Answer Ministries

OTTOMAN DOMINION

OTTOMAN DOMINION

Empires of Armageddon #3

TERRY BRENNAN

KREGEL
PUBLICATIONS

Library of Congress Cataloging-in-Publication Data
Names: Brennan, Terry (Novelist), author.
Title: Ottoman dominion / Terry Brennan.
Description: Grand Rapids, MI : Kregel Publications, [2020] | Series: Empires of armageddon ; book 3
Identifiers: LCCN 2020032842 (print) | LCCN 2020032843 (ebook)
Subjects: GSAFD: Suspense fiction. | Christian fiction.
Classification: LCC PS3602.R4538 O88 2020 (print) | LCC PS3602.R4538 (ebook) | DDC 813/.6—dc23
LC record available at https://lccn.loc.gov/2020032842
LC ebook record available at https://lccn.loc.gov/2020032843

ISBN 978-0-8254-4532-3, print
ISBN 978-0-8254-7499-6, epub

Printed in the United States of America
20 21 22 23 24 25 26 27 28 29 / 5 4 3 2 1

To my grandchildren:
Jaclyn, Michael, Jack, Charlie, Zahra, and Khari.
I am hopeful.

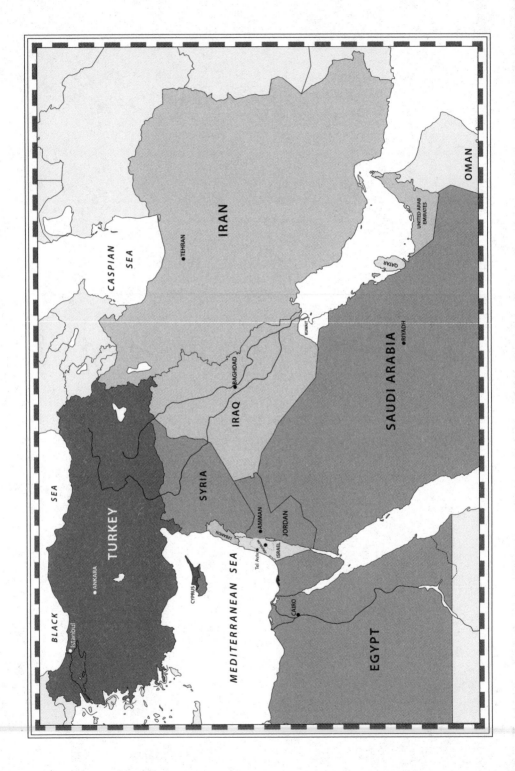

CAST OF CHARACTERS

United States

Brian Mullaney—Diplomatic Security Service (DSS) agent; regional security officer overseeing the Middle East; senior agent overseeing security for Joseph Atticus Cleveland, the US ambassador to Israel

Abigail Mullaney—Brian Mullaney's wife; daughter of Atlanta-based financial giant Richard Rutherford

Joseph Atticus Cleveland—US ambassador to Israel

Palmyra Athena Parker—Ambassador Cleveland's daughter

Tommy Hernandez—Former DSS chief for Ambassador Cleveland's security detail in Israel; Mullaney's best friend; killed in a gun battle with the Disciples in Amman, Jordan

Lamont Boylan—President of the United States

Evan Townsend—US secretary of state

Noah Webster—Deputy secretary of state for management and resources; oversees DSS

Nora Carson—Undersecretary for management; Noah Webster's right hand

George Morningstar—Deputy assistant secretary for DSS; Mullaney's former supervisor

Ruth Hughes—Political officer, US embassy, Tel Aviv

Jeffrey Archer—Cleveland's secretary at the ambassador's residence and the US embassy in Tel Aviv

Pat McKeon—DSS agent in Tel Aviv; interim head of Cleveland's secretary detail after death of Tommy Hernandez

Kathie Doorley—DSS agent in Tel Aviv

Senator Seneca Markham—Former chair of Senate Foreign Relations Committee, now retired

Richard Rutherford—Billionaire Georgian banker and DC power broker

Israel

David Meir—Prime minister of Israel

Moshe Litzman—Minister of the interior of Israel

Benjamin Erdad—Minister of internal security of Israel

Meyer Levinson—Director, Operations Division, Shin Bet—Israel's internal
     security agency
Rabbi Mordechai Herzog—Former head of the Jewish Rabbinate Council
     in Jerusalem
Father Stefanakis Poppodopolous—Greek Orthodox monk; computer
     hacker; code breaker

Turkey: Ottoman Empire
Emet Kashani—President of Turkey
Arslan Eroglu—Prime minister of Turkey
The Turk—Otherworldly pursuer of the box and the prophecy

Iraq and Iran: Persian Empire
Samir Al-Qahtani—Deputy prime minister of Iraq; leader of the Badr Bri-
     gades; orchestrates military takeover of Iraqi government

Saudi Arabia, Egypt, Jordan, and Palestine: Islamic Empire
King Abdullah Al-Saud—King of Saudi Arabia
Prince Faisal ibn Farouk Al-Saud—Saudi defense minister; son of King
     Abdullah
Sultan Abbaddi—Commander of the Jordanian Royal Guard Brigade, per-
     sonal bodyguards of the king and his family

PROLOGUE

Thin and straight like a Popsicle stick in a good suit, Noah Webster stood behind the sofa, a sentry on duty. His eyes never fell to Senator Markham, seated in front of him and in earnest conversation with the chair of the Senate Foreign Relations Committee. No, Webster's eyes relentlessly swept the spacious but crowded room, looking for allies or victims. That was the breadth of his world . . . allies or victims. Not enemies. Senator Markham's enemies were inevitably victims . . . victims of Markham's power and influence. And Webster's ruthless wielding of that power.

Across the room, standing behind one of the columns that flanked the entryway, Joseph Atticus Cleveland took the measure of Webster and recognized a merciless man unwavering in his quest for even greater power. Cleveland broke his gaze away, pivoted through the arched entry, and headed in the direction he hoped would take him to the kitchen and that incredible aroma of mango and sizzling garlic that was causing convulsions in his stomach.

———◦◦◦◦———

"Cleveland, isn't it?"

Turning toward the voice, Cleveland saw Noah Webster emerge from an overfilled dining room as the crowd parted like the Red Sea. His hand was held out, a handshake offering, expecting a response. "Noah Webster . . . Senator Markham's chief of staff."

Trapped . . . make the best of it.

"Joseph Cleveland. It's a pleasure, sir. And I believe most of Washington knows who you are, Mr. Webster. It's kind of you to introduce yourself. But my stomach is demanding I follow this magnificent aroma."

Webster moved closer, his strong hand still wrapped around Cleveland's fingers. The slippery sweetness of gardenia banished the mango and garlic back to the kitchen and nearly overwhelmed Cleveland's outer veneer of composure. Inwardly, every warning siren was wailing.

Great-grandson of a former slave, Cleveland was thirty years old with the build of an NFL tight end, four years into his career with the State Department and well into the lengthy and demanding process of applying for assignment to the US Foreign Service, with aspirations to one day earn a senior consular post overseas. Perhaps Ambassador Cleveland?

"Thank you, Mr. Cleveland. The aroma is captivating, but my duty is to remain by the senator's side should he need me," said Webster, who glanced left, then right, before skewering Cleveland with a look of menacing power. "Joseph, are you aware that Senator Markham is about to open his investigation of Major Lee's unlawful activities at the Defense Intelligence Agency?"

Noah Webster was thirty-one years old, the zen master of Washington politics, notorious within the Beltway. A striking black man—half Caribbean, half African-American, and self-consciously short—Webster was a formidable and forbidding force in the halls of DC political power.

Cleveland's knees felt like the warm mud along the French Broad River that flowed through his homeland in the finger of western North Carolina— they were soft and sinking fast. The sting of acid reflux overwhelmed his hunger. *Steady . . . remain steady. No fear. Please, show no fear.*

"No, sir," said Cleveland, his voice calm and his grip firm. "I wasn't aware of that."

"Yes . . . could be a nasty business." Webster's eyes narrowed, focused like laser-guided weapons. "You worked as liaison between State and the DIA, did you not? In Lee's office?"

"For a short time." Cleveland's voice was steady, but his heart was racing.

For nine months of 1985, Cleveland was on loan to the Defense Intelligence Agency, the organization that provides boots-on-the-ground espionage across the wide spectrum of US military operations. Routinely, twenty-five percent of the president's morning intelligence briefing came from DIA sources. Cleveland was assigned to a project run by Air Force Major Anderson Lee. His task was boring . . . insulting, almost. He was nothing more than an overqualified, highly paid messenger. Until November 26, when subpoenas were served. Lee and his boss, General Isaiah Zimmer, faced the possibility of indictments on illegally diverting Pentagon funding and obstruction of justice. Cleveland had been kept in the dark by Major Lee and was innocent of any wrongdoing. But scandal is a fickle mistress, often condemning the innocent and the guilty with the same brazen impunity.

Without releasing his grip, Webster moved closer and lowered his voice. "The senator knows you are innocent of any complicity in this crime, Joseph. But so often there is collateral damage, and others on the committee may not see, as clearly as we do, the distinction between being simply a messenger boy and a conspirator. I'm trying to convince the senator that you don't even need to be called as a witness. We wouldn't want to jeopardize your pending appointment to the Foreign Service, now would we?"

So there it was. The bait and the trap. Clearly Webster knew exactly what Cleveland's responsibilities were and who he reported to at the DIA. True to his Washington legend, Webster was offering Cleveland a deal—a way out of possible trouble. But what did Webster want in return?

Cleveland tilted his bald head to the right, a question entering his eyes and his voice. "Is there some way I may be of assistance?"

Webster smiled, and Cleveland feared his knees would lose all control. If a smile could threaten annihilation, Webster's smile was nuclear.

"Oh yes. You will be of assistance to me, Joseph." Webster's smile grew wider. "Or you will join Major Lee in a federal prison."

Webster finally released Cleveland's hand. He half turned back into the dining room but looked over his shoulder. "Enjoy your dinner, Joseph." And with a nod of his head, Webster vanished into the crowd.

Cleveland placed his right fist in front of his lips, wrapped his left arm over his stomach and hurried off in search of a restroom. It was bad form to vomit in the midst of a reception for movers and shakers, for allies and enemies.

1

Brian Mullaney's world lurched sideways. The floors and walls of the fortress-like United States embassy in Tel Aviv undulated like a drunken jellyfish. What looked, felt, and sounded like an earthquake had Mullaney's internal threat monitors off the charts. Again.

In the last seventy-two hours, Brian Mullaney's world had raced like an avalanche from the rational to the inexplicable. And through each of those hours, a rising tide of violence had haunted Mullaney's every move—a pervading and relentless carnage that had claimed six American lives, including that of his best friend.

Now to his right, an eight-foot-tall armed angel hovered above the convulsing floor, and to his left, a terrified, bearded rabbi sat flat on the seat of his pants. But after what Mullaney had experienced the last few days, nothing came as a shock.

The angel, Bayard, pulled an immense, gleaming silver sword from the scabbard at his waist. The sword was suffused with light and thrummed like a chorus of heavenly voices; a stiletto sharpness was honed to its edge.

His wings flexing behind his heavily muscled frame, Bayard was prepared to go to war.

"We must hurry," he said, looking toward where the door to Mullaney's office had once stood. "Our enemies are here. They are pursuing the box of power."

It felt as if every molecule in the building had a mind of its own and each was heading off in different directions. Mullaney's office was twisted like a wet rag being wrung out . . . the corners of the room appeared to be melting . . . and the wall opposite was ripped apart.

Regional Security Officer for the Diplomatic Security Service, responsible for the security of all United States diplomatic personnel in the Middle East, Mullaney's six-two frame was still lean and muscled at forty-four. A nineteen-year veteran of DSS, he instinctively placed a hand over his earbud and turned slightly to the mic in his lapel to give orders to his DSS agents and the marines guarding the embassy. "Lock down the building . . . mobilize all security

. . . double the guard at each entry point and do a floor-by-floor, face-to-face accounting of all staff. Stay alert!"

Mullaney stumbled around his desk and grabbed the elderly rabbi, Mordechai Herzog, by the arm. "C'mon . . . you're getting under the desk."

"I don't know if these old bones can squeeze in there," said Herzog, the former chief rabbi of Israel's Rabbinate Council, his eyes darting back and forth, watching the moving walls.

Mullaney pulled Herzog to his feet and emphatically moved him toward the desk.

From across the room, the armor-clad angel called through the groans of a building in torment. "Guardian . . . follow me when you can!" The air seemed to be shifting back and forth as much as the walls as Bayard's form evolved from solid to amorphous to vapor. And he was gone.

Guardian. That was a new title Mullaney needed to absorb. Passed down through generations of rabbis for over two hundred years, the guardian's responsibility was to protect and defend both the prophecy of the Vilna Gaon and the lethal box of power that contained it. Only minutes earlier, Rabbi Herzog had spoken the Aaronic blessing over Mullaney, transferring the mantle of guardian to the DSS agent.

Mullaney hadn't fully grasped why *he* was ordained as the final guardian—Bayard had called him the last in the line of the Gaon's appointed heirs. But after Bayard's warning, he fully suspected that this earthquake was being used by the gang of Turkish terrorists who had relentlessly pursued the box from Istanbul, where it was brought out of hiding only seven days ago. Only the guardian, under the power of the anointing, could touch the box of power without incurring a horrible and instantaneous death. But Mullaney had no doubt that those same murderous thugs were now invading the embassy in order to raid the vault where the Gaon's bronze box was currently secured.

Rabbi Mordechai Herzog was sprawled on the floor under Mullaney's desk, desperately clinging to its legs, as the building continued to convulse in chaotic jolts.

"Follow him?" Mullaney squeezed out of his chest. "How can I follow him?"

Another violent eruption throttled the embassy, and a cascade of concrete crashed into the middle of the floor, missing Herzog and Mullaney by inches.

He looked at Herzog, who was still on the floor, squeezed under the desk, his frail legs pulled up underneath his body. "Stay here. You're safe."

"Where am I going? I can't get up."

"I'll send help."

⎯⎯◆◇◆⎯⎯

Ambassador's Residence, Tel Aviv
July 22, 9:02 p.m.

Palmyra Parker felt as if her shoes were moving across the floor while she was standing still.

Daughter of US Ambassador to Israel, Joseph Atticus Cleveland, and his de facto chief of staff, Parker was in the security office in the north wing of the ambassador's seaside residence in the Herzliya Pitch neighborhood of Tel Aviv, going over the street maps with DSS agent Pat McKeon and the ambassador's driver. In the wake of Tommy Hernandez's death, McKeon was the interim head of the ambassador's personal security detail. In any one week, seldom did the ambassador's vehicles take the same route to the embassy. Cleveland was planning to leave for the embassy early in the morning, so Parker was helping to sketch out a new route. She felt a tingling in her feet.

"Did you feel that?" asked the driver.

Parker had her mouth open to respond when the wall behind the driver appeared to morph into an S shape. Her knees buckled.

One hand grabbed the side of the desk and the other hand went for her phone but . . . everything stopped.

The intercom buzzed. "Did you feel that?" came the voice.

McKeon hit the intercom button that connected her to every phone and every mobile earbud in the residence. "Tremors," she said. "Find the ambassador and let me know where he is." McKeon paused for moment. "Let's take it to code yellow. If there aren't any more shakes in the next half hour, we'll dial it down again."

She released the intercom button and turned toward Parker.

"We used to get these all the time when I was stationed in New Zealand," McKeon said. Turning back to the map, she said, "I can't remember the last time Israel had—"

As if she were on the string end of a mad puppeteer, Parker felt like all the joints in her body were out of her control. Everything was moving, but independently and haphazardly.

Instinctively, Parker reached for the stability of the desk. But her hand grasped only air. The desk was tilting to the left and sliding across the floor. Parker turned to the driver . . . as a piece of concrete fell from the ceiling and sliced away half of his head.

"My father!" screamed Parker. She would have been running for the door. Except she couldn't get one foot in front of the other to run. And because the door to the office had disappeared.

Ankara, Turkey
July 22, 9:02 p.m.

In the red room of the house on Alitas Street, downhill from the Citadel in the old city of Ankara, cryptic golden designs on the crimson painted walls were pulsing with life, glowing brightly in a macabre and random frenzy. The stabbing strobes of light cast cavernous shadows across the face of Arslan Eroglu's body, now occupied and manipulated by the Turk, relentless enemy and pursuer of the Gaon's box, malevolent leader of the Disciples, and servant of evil incarnate—the One. Its eyes closed, the body twitched and jerked as if speeding along a winding road.

The Turk willed his otherworldly power roughly nine hundred kilometers beneath the Mediterranean Sea once more to erupt along fissures, through the bedrock and dirt, colliding with the foundations of both the US embassy and the ambassador's residence in Tel Aviv, thirteen kilometers apart. They were the only buildings in Tel Aviv under assault by the Turk's power to move the earth.

A massive wave of energy hit the two buildings simultaneously. And the Turk felt the collision.

The face contorted in pain, the body violently thrown back into the stone chair, Arslan Eroglu's vocal cords emitted a desperate, keening wail that sounded as if it had risen from the gates of Hades.

"You . . . will . . . die." The voice of the Turk emerged from Eroglu's throat, ripped and raw. But a smile of evil intent bared its teeth.

And a sulfurous vapor hung heavily over the stone table of sacrifice on the far side of the room.

———◦◦◦◦———

US Embassy, Tel Aviv
July 22, 9:04 p.m.

Two jagged fissures tore the rear wall of the US embassy building on Herbert Samuel Street. The new commander of the Disciples stood behind a seawall, the vivid blue water of the Mediterranean only a dark swath of black. The sweeping crescent beach was dimly washed by ambient light, but the commander ignored the beauty behind him. His focus lay on the fortified and heavily protected building across the street. His other teams at the ambassador's residence were well-trained, fervent believers. They had their assignment—swift, merciless slaughter. The commander's target was the embassy and the Gaon's bronze box, held in the embassy's vault.

Surrounded on this side by anti-tank barriers that blocked the only entrance to the rear parking garage, the US embassy to Israel was big, square, solid, and ugly. Situated in the middle of an eclectic downtown neighborhood with a mixture of hotels and restaurants, along with small, local shops topped with apartments on their upper floors, the sidewalks around the embassy building were studded with concrete-filled bollards—four-foot-high steel cylinders embedded into the sidewalks—linked together by a steel beam. The ground floor of the massive building was solid, windowless stone. But now ravaged by the ongoing earthquake, the defenses on the ground floor of the embassy were rent by two huge gashes running vertical to the ground, one to the north, near the corner of the building, another to the south, near the ramp to the underground garage.

Along Herbert Samuel Street, men in civilian clothes, ID lanyards slapping against their chests, raced to the jagged fractures in the embassy's walls. Locally hired security professionals, most of them former members of the Israeli armed forces, they formed the majority of the embassy's security force.

The commander, a young man with a livid pink scar rising from his right ear, along his hairline to the front of his forehead, glanced at the floor plan of the building in his hand. Elevated into his new role by the Turk only hours earlier, he was taking the place of his father—killed in a gun battle with the American agent Mullaney and his allies in Amman. Not only was the new commander determined to fulfill the orders of the Turk and secure the lethal box of power, he was also determined that Mullaney would lose his life in its defense.

With a wave of his hand, as another jolt quaked the ground under his feet, the six disciples to his left began working their way to the gash at the north-western corner of the building. "Keep them occupied."

Then the commander, a finely honed weapon capable of extraordinary vio-lence, turned his piercing black eyes on the growing fissure near the parking entrance. "Follow me," he said, and a dozen black-clad disciples rose from their hiding places.

2

"Brian," squawked his earpiece, "we have intruders. They used huge rips in the walls to pierce the building's perimeter, north and south ends. Looks like we have security and agents down. Response is . . ."

The radio in Mullaney's ear went silent. "Report."

He heard nothing, except for the throbbing headache radiating from his day-old scalp wound and creaking moans as floors and walls continued to randomly shift.

Mullaney stumbled toward where a gash had been ripped in the wall to his office, speaking constantly into the mic pinned to his lapel, whether the comm system was working or not. "Keep the marines at the entrances . . . rally all DSS agents to the incursion sites . . . I'm on my way."

Feeling like he was trying to run on water, Mullaney sloshed to the stairs. Holding on to the railing with one hand, grasping his Sig Sauer 9-millimeter in the other, he bounced down the rocking stairway, inadvertently thumping down two steps at a time. Coming up from below he could hear the sound of gunfire.

———

Palmyra Parker slipped in the gore and crashed to the undulating floor. Next to her, blood was pooling to the side of the ambassador's driver, his body limp on the floor, half his head and a shard of concrete two feet away.

Somewhere behind Parker, Pat McKeon was shouting urgent messages through the microphone in the lapel of her jacket. "Code red . . . Code red! All agents report. Lock down the building and grounds. And find the ambassador!"

What was once the formidable, well-guarded official residence of the United States Ambassador to Israel had quickly dissolved into life-threatening Silly Putty. Another violent tremor shuddered the building from foundation to roof as a rumble and rending filled the air of the north wing with choking dust and the groaning cries of the collapsing structure.

Parker was scrabbling along the floor, away from the bleeding body, but was tossed into the side of the wooden desk. Her determined focus overcoming her terror, Parker twisted to look back at McKeon. "Earthquake? Or something . . . somebody . . . else?"

Sounding like shoes in a spinning clothes dryer, thumping rumbles echoed through the halls of the residence and were joined in a riot of sound by heavy crashes and the shrieks of a building being pulled apart. Another violent rending of the earth knocked McKeon to her knees, but it also opened a jagged hole in the wall of the security office.

McKeon pushed herself to one knee, straining to stand. "Report . . . where's Cleveland?" she shouted into her lapel mic as she staggered toward the opening in the wall. There was no answer. "Where's the ambassador?"

"Unknown," said a voice in her ear. "We've not been able to locate him. He's not in his quarters and he's not in his office. We don't—"

Another voice drowned out the first. "We have a breach!"

———◦◦◦◦———

US Embassy, Tel Aviv
July 22, 9:06 p.m.

The commander knew his time was short, even at the beginning of the engagement. This could not be a prolonged assault. He needed to get into and out of the embassy as quickly as possible, preferably with his two objectives successfully completed: the box of power desired by the Turk would be in his possession and the killer of his father would die by his hands. So even though the private security agents were brave and determined and bolstered by three US Marines, they were no match for the two Herstal MK 48 machine guns that opened up in a crossing pattern on the defenders near the southern breach into the underground garage.

The machine guns swept through the defenders like scythes through wheat, leaving behind a bloody and ravaged harvest. The commander and his nine remaining disciples—two still manned the machine guns to guard their escape—rushed past the wounded and dying and poured through the rip in the embassy's defenses. Running down the ramp, they turned left at the first landing and raced toward a gray, metal door. The bullet-riddled bodies of two civilians, whose defense of the door was short-lived, lay on either side as the commander fixed a rope of plastic explosive around the electronic lock.

Ambassador's Residence, Tel Aviv
July 22, 9:06 p.m.

"Who's this on the line?"

"This is Connors. We—"

Like a rapid cadence on a snare drum, McKeon heard the familiar sound of automatic weapons in her ear.

"Connors?"

"Armed men at the front gate!" His voice was drowned out by a deafening volley of return fire.

"This is surveillance," came another, clearer voice. "We have a breach on the beach wall. Armed intruders are in the garden."

McKeon reached over and grabbed Palmyra Parker under her right arm and lifted her to her feet. "C'mon . . . you stay with me." She pushed herself through the jagged opening in the wall, tearing the shoulder of her suit jacket, and emerged into Brian Mullaney's office which was a labyrinth of tumbled furniture and fallen debris. McKeon looked over her shoulder at Parker. "Stay behind me . . . do what I do." She maneuvered her way into the deserted hallway of the north wing of the residence, stepping around huge chunks of plaster from the ceiling. Continuous gunfire came from both the front and the rear of the residence.

The surface of the earth rolled once again like a wave on the sea, driving both McKeon and Parker into the wall. There was the noise of crashing behind them . . . someone crying in an office to their right. McKeon looked down the hallway in both directions. *Which way to go?*

"We have the ambassador. We're in the kitchen," came a female voice in her ear. Kathie Doorley.

"Stay there, Kathie," snapped McKeon. "I've got Mrs. Parker. We are on our way to you."

—◦◦◦◦—

US Embassy, Tel Aviv
July 22, 9:07 p.m.

The rattling sound of automatic weapons and the steady staccato of the DSS standard issue Sig Sauer 9-millimeter created a stereo effect as Mullaney reached the ground floor. Off to his right, in the direction of the north side of the building and the main entrance, was one source of the fighting. But Mullaney snuck a quick look down the stairwell and into the basement where another battle was raging.

Two of his agents were crouched near the bottom of the stairs, returning fire into the underground space.

Mullaney started down the last flight of stairs just as a new earthquake tremor shook the building. He stumbled and tripped, a headlong fall staring him in the face. But something—an arm?—caught his waist and held him steady until his feet could once again find something solid upon which to stand. He looked over his shoulder but was not surprised that there was no one in sight.

"Behind you, Jack." Mullaney called as he eased down the remaining steps. "Status?"

"Our men outside were slaughtered—machine guns," he said. "Surveillance cameras picked up ten of the attackers when they raced into the hole in the wall by the garage entrance," he said "I figure there are at least four of them, maybe six, down this corridor, minimum of two on each side, hiding behind debris. They were coming this way when we stopped them." He nodded across the corridor toward the door to the armored vault. "Could they have been headed for the vault? I don't know why else they would fight their way down here."

An image of the embassy's basement layout filled Mullaney's mind. *Where could the others be?*

—◦◦◦◦—

Ambassador's Residence, Tel Aviv
July 22, 9:07 p.m.

The kitchen was in the basement level of the residence, in the very middle of the building, a series of dumbwaiters serving into the formal dining room above them on the east side of the building. The open reception area faced the west side, looking out over the gardens and the Mediterranean.

Gunfire came from the front of the building, at the main entrance on the east side, and also at the rear of the building, in the gardens on the west side. On both sides, the sound of the gunfire was getting louder . . . closer.

McKeon had a choice to make. Stairs led to the lower level and the kitchen at the four corners of the building. The northwest corner was the closest . . . toward the garden. *Gotta get her to safety!* Scrambling to the right, keeping Parker tucked in close behind, McKeon skirted some light fixtures that had fallen from the ceiling. As she reached the stairwell, she looked out a broken window into the garden, bathed in the silvery glow of emergency lighting.

At least six black-clad men in black hoods and body armor were deliberately advancing through the garden toward the rear of the residence, firing at targets as they moved. McKeon could see bodies strewn on the grass, some DSS agents in plain clothes, some marines.

McKeon hesitated for a moment. She wanted to engage with the enemy right there, but her primary responsibility was the ambassador's daughter. Get Mrs. Parker safely into the kitchen with the ambassador . . . then the fight. McKeon was about to turn down the stairs when she saw something that brought chills to her blood.

As they inched closer to the residence, despite the withering gunfire that poured forth from its defenders, McKeon could see that the invaders had earbuds and mics pinned to their body armor. One of the men pointed down at ground level with the building, where patio doors opened into the garden. The kitchen was not that far from those doors.

They are monitoring the communications of the residence. They know where the ambassador is hiding!

3

The commander and three of his disciples huddled in a darkened room across the basement corridor from where the American agents were firing down the passageway at his other men. His group, which had led the attackers, split off to the right after getting through the parking garage door and taken a service entrance to a narrow hallway on the east side of the building used primarily by the housekeeping crew and delivery people. After running halfway down the hallway and scrambling over huge pieces of tile floor thrust up into the air by the earthquake, the commander stopped at a door. Having studied the floor plan, he was confident this room had a door on the far side that opened to the corridor right next to the embassy's vault.

Instead of engaging with the enemy he could hear just outside, the commander waited, protected, behind the closed door. He knew what was coming.

Jack's partner, his gun raised, edged himself around the corner and unleashed a burst of gunfire down the corridor. But just as suddenly, he threw himself back behind the wall, his eyes wide. "Grenade launcher!"

Before Mullaney could think of a way to counterattack what was coming, a violent explosion—louder than the rending of the earthquake—ripped through the basement. But the explosion didn't erupt from the impact of a rocket propelled grenade against the door of the vault across the way. The blast originated from down the corridor to their right—where the invaders, with the rocket launcher, were entrenched.

As a wave of smoke, dust, and debris flew past their position, Mullaney edged closer. He wanted to peek around the corner. But Jack's hand on his chest stopped him.

"We'll do this, boss."

Jack turned and stood tall at the corner of the wall to the stairwell, his partner crouched low, near the floor. His partner slid out into the corridor, his gun leveled at the enemy. Jack took a breath, turned, and squared into the corridor.

———◦◦◦———

Ambassador's Residence, Tel Aviv
July 22, 9:08 p.m.

"Go silent," McKeon instructed over the radio. "Invaders are monitoring our comm. And Kathie, get Atticus out of the kitchen. You're spotted."

She had decisions to make and not much time to make them. Fire on the invaders and try to stop their advance? Get Parker to safety? But now the kitchen wasn't much safer than where they were hiding. McKeon looked over her shoulder, back toward where the weapons' locker in the DSS Security Office was located. She pictured the Heckler & Koch MP5, 9-millimeter submachine gun hanging in the closet. The MP5 could empty a thirty-cartridge clip in three seconds. *I sure could use that H&K right now.* But there was no time.

Taking Parker by the arm, McKeon motioned to the opening of the stairwell. "Stay low. Get inside the stairwell, but stay where I can see you."

As Parker scrambled to the right, McKeon turned back to the broken window overlooking the garden. Some defenders were engaging the invaders, but they continued to inch their way closer to the patio doors. They had to be stopped.

McKeon whacked the remaining broken glass with the butt end of her Sig Sauer. The lead invader looked up at the noise. Thrusting her arms against the windowsill, her gun pointed at the lead invader, McKeon pulled back on the trigger, going full automatic, emptying a clip as return fire shredded the metal casing around the window.

———◦◦◦———

US Embassy, Tel Aviv
July 22, 9:09 p.m.

The violence of the grenade's explosion rattled his knees. But the commander knew something was wrong. The explosion came from his left, where the rest of his men were pinned down, and not from his right, where the door to the vault was located—the door that was the intended target for the grenade launcher.

He edged open the door a crack, dust and debris filling the corridor and obscuring his vision. No noise carried from the passageway . . . no guns firing in either direction. On the far side of the hallway, twenty paces to his right, three shadows moved into the billowing dust. The commander shifted his weight toward the opening of the door before a hand on his arm arrested his movement.

"Commander," a voice whispered. "There are no longer enough of us."

Through the slight opening in the door, the commander felt his optimism escaping.

"We don't know how many of them are left," whispered the voice. "And we no longer have the grenade launcher."

The commander was ready to give his life. But not for nothing. They were so close. But there was no way to reach the box. With an impatient swat, he pushed the hand away from his arm, spat on the floor, twisted on the balls of his feet, and led his remaining men in retreat, a burning boil erupting from his stomach and scorching his throat. He hadn't even seen Mullaney.

Moving deliberately, his Glock held in two hands up by his right shoulder, his eyes piercing the doorways and shadowed corners down the corridor, Mullaney emerged from the dust cloud into a scene of carnage and nearly gagged on the smell of burning flesh.

"I don't understand it," said Jack, kicking a handgun away from a smoldering, disfigured body that had been blasted up against a wall.

Where the invaders had taken cover behind fallen slabs of concrete and mutilated walls, an explosion had blown a large cavity in the midst of the debris, gouging out sizable divots from the floor and both walls of the basement corridor. Even though their bodies were mangled and in pieces, it was pretty clear that none of the invaders in this group had escaped the blast.

Mullaney, his eyes continually sweeping the hallway, inched nearer what was left of the damaged grenade launcher lying in the dust and felt the heat coming from the seared metal.

"They must have fired the grenade launcher," said Jack, "otherwise it wouldn't have been armed and able to explode. But it didn't go anywhere. How is that possible? They shot it, but it just blew up right here. Doesn't make any . . ."

Mullaney was thinking of an eight-foot angel wearing a silver breastplate when the DSS station chief and a marine sergeant came running up. "Brian," said the station chief, "we got a call. The residence is also under attack by armed intruders."

Mullaney spun and faced the station chief as Jack and his partner continued inching down the corridor and the sergeant covered their backs. "What do we know?"

"Similar to us . . . invaders front and back pierced the perimeter through the damage from the earthquake."

"Cleveland?"

"Don't know, sir. The gun fight was still going on when we lost the connection."

Mullaney's heart sank. "What's the status here?"

The station chief gave Mullaney a hollow stare. His eyes were open but there was nothing in them. He was seeing something else. "We've been hit really hard . . . especially our local security contractors." His voice was leaden. "Eight to ten are down. Don't know their condition yet. But I do know there will be several DOA. And two marines. So far, none of the embassy staff were harmed."

"Attackers?"

"Two bodies out front, near the hole that was ripped in the corner of the building, another just inside the building, and however many this mess is here. We think we got all of the ones attacking the north side. But I don't feel as confident on this end. There were at least ten that penetrated the garage." He looked down at the body parts sprawled throughout the passage. "This doesn't look like . . ."

The sound of small arms fire ricocheted along the walls of the corridor, coming from the parking garage, followed by the heavy hacking thuds of machine guns.

Without a word the five defenders ran toward the sound of the guns.

4

Al-Yamama Palace, Riyadh, Saudi Arabia
July 22, 9:12 p.m.

He was a deteriorating shell of his former self. Now seventy-six years old, he was stoop shouldered, nearsighted behind wire-rimmed glasses, and still alive only because he kept the best cardiac surgeons in the world on retainer. But behind those wire-rimmed glasses resting on bags of sagging flesh, eyes still burned with fanatical fervor and youthful passion.

Even when rest eluded his weary body.

King Abdullah, sixth in a direct line of the Al-Saud family to rule the oil-rich peninsula of Saudi Arabia, had a vision of the future . . . a future where an Islamic Empire, rooted in the strict Wahhabi sect of Muslim fundamentalism of his fathers, would outreach the global dominance of the seventh century when Islam ruled from central India to the Pyrenes Mountains of Spain. In the quiet of his heart, Abdullah worshiped at the altar of Islamic world supremacy. And the first step, planned on the back of a nuclear weapons arsenal Abdullah was promised from Pakistan, was to impose Saudi rule over the Middle East before the hated Persians of Iran developed their own nuclear weapons.

But his aborted first step remained on the docks of the Gwadar port in Pakistan, molten heaps of irradiated metal that less than two days ago were nuclear bombs waiting to be shipped to Riyadh. Now they were useless to him and a curse to the Pakistanis who were left with the treacherous cleanup.

King Abdullah walked along the dimly lit colonnade that bordered a lavish garden, dappled with subtle, low-level lighting and studded with soothing fountains and man-made waterfalls. He gently massaged his father's prayer beads in the gnarled fingers of his right hand. But no peace filled his spirit or guided his intentions. His mind was aching for a fight he knew the valves of his weak heart could not endure. But his thoughts had remained the same since they got the word from Pakistan. *Someone must pay for this.*

His son and heir, Prince Faisal ibn Farouk Al-Saud, defense minister for the Royal Kingdom of Saudi Arabia, emerged from a side door to the colonnade and strode purposely toward the king.

"Tell me! What happened?" snarled the king, squeezing the beads in his raised fist.

"Father . . . please," said Faisal, the thick, black-rimmed spectacles jostled against his nose as he reached his father. "Please, calm down. Your heart."

The king glared at his son. "Forget *my* heart," he seethed. "I gave you the responsibility for ensuring that shipment reached us safely. You! A simple task."

Abdullah rocked unsteadily on his feet. Faisal reached for his arm and led the king to a bench under the dusky colonnade. Abdullah drew in a long breath as he settled onto the bench, but his voice had lost none of its strength. "What happened? The Iranians? The Israelis? Who?"

Prince Faisal sat down beside his father and took his hand. There was genuine concern in his eyes. A good son.

"Father, ever since we got the call from Islamabad, I've been on the phone with our agents throughout the region," said Faisal, his voice soft, soothing as a night breeze. "There is something we had not anticipated. It appears the Ottoman threat is rising. Kashani cannot be trusted. He may have publicly signed an agreement with al-Qahtani in Iraq that would provide land for the Kurds, but our agent in Turkey says Kashani's real goal is western Syria—assimilating the ancient land of Assyria back into the Ottoman sphere."

King Abdullah's hold on obscene wealth was precarious. The Al-Saud dynasty was only seven decades old and embattled with external opposition and internal disparities. The often-bloody religious conflict between Sunni Muslims and Shia Muslims had been waged for fourteen centuries and continued unabated as the Shia majorities of Iran and Iraq tried to upend the regional economic domination of the Sunni Saudis. Even though over $120 billion a year flowed into the country's treasury from the black gold under the sand of Saudi Arabia, a pipeline of petrodollars that lavished wealth on his entire royal family tree, nearly a quarter of native Saudis lived below the poverty line of seventeen dollars a day. Saudi Arabia had the world's third-highest annual military expenditure and was the world's second largest arms importer, but nearly thirty percent of Saudi young men were unemployed. And most women were banned from economic or political involvement in the nation.

It was just like the Turks, thought Abdullah, to complicate his life even more with another level of intrigue and conflict.

King Abdullah was wearily shaking his head, eyes now closed. "We have long known that Kashani could one day be a problem, but never a problem like the Persians."

Prince Faisal was strangely silent. Abdullah opened his eyes and looked at his son. "What is it?"

Turning to engage his father face-to-face, Faisal revealed the information he had just acquired. "Our agent told me of a rumor. As we were speaking on the phone, someone came to him and interrupted our conversation. It was confirmation of that rumor. There is strong evidence that it was Turkish commandos who raided the docks of Gwadar and destroyed our weapons."

The old king's Machiavellian instincts instantly scrolled through multiple scenarios, like flashing images before his brain, trying to discern the purpose and intent behind the rumors reported by his son. "Kashani is not what he seems? That spineless man who appears to live at the end of puppet strings has a plan of his own? Can Kashani truly be the architect of a rising Ottoman threat? But . . ."

"Yes," said Faisal, completing his father's thought. "But there is Eroglu. A man with unlimited ambition and aspirations. Perhaps a man who pursues unlimited power to accomplish those ambitions?"

King Abdullah narrowed his eyes as he looked into the face of his future. "Tell me."

Faisal leaned closer. "There are whispers. Of a power lurking in the darkness, a power greater than Kashani, greater than Eroglu, a power lusting for the same weapons we seek . . . weapons that will determine the future of the Middle East."

The heart in Abdullah's chest quavered with an unhealthy beat, paused, then quavered back into sporadic action.

He held his breath. Waiting . . . but this was not to be the day.

Abdullah looked at the concern on his son's face and could see his hopes for a Wahhabi empire fading. "There are many nuclear weapons already sitting on the soil of the Turks. Under guard, yes, but still close at hand."

"Much closer than those we hope to receive from Pakistan," Faisal said softly.

Abdullah swore a Saudi oath under his breath. "I should not have listened to the man with the yellow eyes." His words were softer than the drops falling over the edge of the fountain just behind them. "His passion for empire building was contagious. His idea for how to achieve that empire through the Ishmael Covenant . . . well, now I believe he may have been more concerned for his own empire than an empire of Islam."

The king reached out his hand toward the prince. "Contact Islamabad. Tell the Pakistanis that they must replace those destroyed weapons immediately. It was their security that failed so miserably. Tell them we need delivery now . . . yesterday! Tell them!"

———⊰⊱———

US Embassy, Tel Aviv
July 22, 9:24 p.m.

By the time the machine guns went silent, when Mullaney and his agents were no longer pinned down inside the garage by the cross fire, the embassy defenders had lost contact with the remnant of retreating attackers who fled over the seawall opposite the building.

Surveying the damage and carnage around him, Mullaney was faced with two urgent and opposing duties . . . secure the embassy, care for the wounded and cover the dead, and/or rush to the rescue of the ambassador and the staff at the residence.

Mullaney felt only anger about his first duty. Anger at himself for being caught unawares—again—and anger at those responsible for so much bloodletting. On the second urgent duty, he simply felt helpless.

"Any word from the residence?"

The embassy's station chief was standing to his left as they watched medics scrambling to the bodies scattered on the ground. "Nothing yet."

Mullaney pulled out his mobile phone. At least he had to try. "It will take us forever to get through the city after this earthquake. We'll be too late."

The station chief put a hand on Mullaney's arm. "That's just it, sir. The rest of the city wasn't hit by an earthquake. We're monitoring the police bands and there doesn't appear to be any other earthquake activity anywhere else in the city, just the embassy and the residence. We looked out the windows—no other damage anywhere. A few cracks in a building across the street, but everything else is intact. Except for the residence. Weird, eh?"

For a heartbeat, Mullaney stared at the station chief, trying to force comprehension through his battered emotions. "All right, get somebody down here to open the vault. Tell them to hurry and to bring a large diplomatic pouch with them. And I want a car out front . . . now!

5

The Turk willed his body up the stairs toward his bed.

His body? Arslan Eroglu's body, actually. And this body was becoming more ravaged.

Much of the Turk's core, elemental power had been poured into rending the earth's surface in Tel Aviv. Mentally jousting with the winged one earlier, trying to prevent the transfer of anointing to the American meddler, had drained his resources. Creating the earthquakes was an additional and more costly expense of his now dangerously depleted life force.

The Turk was caught in one of the dichotomies of his existence. Like all angels—even those who fell with the great deceiver—he was created with preternatural gifts. The Turk was an immortal created being, free to roam the earth and interfere in the lives of men. He did not possess absolute immortality. No created being is absolutely immortal like the Creator. But he was of the order of angels, who are immortal, unless their Creator chooses to end their existence. But the Turk, and the coven of darkness he served, had forfeited the other preternatural gifts of the created immortals—freedom from sin and ignorance. He and his kind were now subject to sorrow, sickness, and injury. So even though the Turk was immortal and possessed extraordinary supernatural power, he could feel pain. He could suffer. He could exhaust his seemingly limitless strength. Along with whatever strength existed in this body he now occupied.

Struggling up the stairs, in desperate need of replenishing rest, the Turk carried a heavy burden of suffering and pain in the muscle and bones of this assimilated body he had stolen from Arslan Eroglu, prime minister of Turkey. He wondered how much more this body of Eroglu's could withstand. But its purpose was not yet complete. He must restore its strength.

Moving in the dark, the Turk closed the door to his bedroom behind him. He spent little time in this room. Normally, he functioned with little or no sleep. But the body he currently occupied needed to be renewed, refreshed, recharged. He sat on the edge of the bed, rotated on his hip and, like an old tree sliding to the forest floor, lowered himself to the bed, sleep coming before his head came to rest.

⸺⸺◈⸺⸺

US Embassy, Tel Aviv
July 22, 9:31 p.m.

Mullaney was running down the corridor toward the embassy's main entrance on Ha Yarkon Street, the DSS station chief at his shoulder, the reinforced leather diplomatic pouch hanging from its handles and slapping heavily against his left leg, and a cellular phone pressed to his ear as Meyer Levinson relayed what he knew about the unnaturally localized earthquakes and the attacks on both the embassy and the residence.

"I've called every number on my speed dial and nobody's answering," Mullaney huffed between breaths. "What's happening there?"

"Tel Aviv police are converging on the residence," said Colonel Levinson, director of the Operations Division of Shin Bet, Israel's internal security agency. "I had two of my men stationed outside the residence, just as we did at the embassy. I know they were involved in the fight, but they haven't reported in yet."

Mullaney knew what that meant.

"It's not over yet," he said.

"We don't know," Levinson warned. "The police have already locked down your location. They've blocked off both ends of Ha Yarkon Street and Herbert Samuel Street and all the cross streets for two hundred kilometers around the embassy. I know they are trying to do the same thing around the residence. But that situation seems . . . unsettled."

Rounding a corner, Mullaney saw Rabbi Herzog standing in the foyer of the embassy's ravaged main entrance. His eyes were wide and staring into space, his hair disheveled, and his clothes rumpled from crawling around on the floor. He was standing next to the marine who had recovered him from Mullaney's damaged office.

"All right," Mullaney said into his phone as he came to a stop. "I'm on my way to the residence, and I'm taking Rabbi Herzog with me."

"You're going to have a tough time getting there," Levinson warned. "There were street demonstrations—both for and against Meir's government and the

Ishmael Covenant—going on throughout the country, but a couple of the ones here in Tel Aviv have escalated into violent clashes since reports of these earthquakes started circulating. Why are you dragging Herzog with you?"

"Long story . . . not enough time," said Mullaney. "But maybe you should join us. I guarantee you'll be interested."

"Then I'll try to get over to the residence. But stay alert . . . and keep in touch. We're not out of the woods yet."

Mullaney turned to the station chief. "The police have blocked off the street. You need to secure the perimeter as soon as possible with our men. Use the marines to make a thorough sweep of the building to check on our staff and do a damage assessment. Call me with an update when you have one."

He felt a hand touch his right arm. When he looked, Rabbi Herzog was staring at the large bag hanging from his left hand. The size of an oversized canvas boat bag, this heavy-duty style diplomatic pouch was made of leather, banded both vertically and horizontally for strength, with a hasp that came across the top and was secured by a heavy, brass lock that snapped into place and was flush with the surface of the bag.

"Is that what I think it is?" asked the rabbi, his eyes never leaving the bag.

The bag was heavy. Inside were two containers, one inside the other. On the inside was the deadly box of power, a two-hundred-year-old bronze box with kabbalah symbols hammered into its lid, protective home of the Vilna Gaon's second prophetic message. Surrounding that bronze box was the egg-shaped blast container that Colonel Levinson's Shin Bet bomb squad used for containment when the Gaon's bronze box was recovered following a running gun battle in the Old City of Jerusalem.

"Yes," Mullaney answered, hefting the bag. "And right now, I think the safest place I can keep it is right by my side."

Mullaney eased Rabbi Herzog into the back seat of the embassy car, a slightly modified Lincoln with bulletproof windows and armored doors. "What's the fastest route to the residence?" he asked the DSS agents in the front seat.

"North to Rokach Boulevard and then up the Namir Road—it's more direct than the highway," said the driver. "Probably about twenty minutes, depending on traffic."

"You've got ten."

The tires were smoking, the Lincoln flying up Ha Yarkon Street toward the first roadblock, even as the driver said, "Yes, sir."

———◦◦◦———

The commander and one of his men were standing in the midst of a small crowd that had gathered on the far side of Ha Yarkon Street, across from the embassy—those drawn by the sound of gunfire and not frightened off by the roiling eruptions that shook the embassy and undulated the ground at their feet.

"We should leave," said a low voice at his shoulder.

"We wait," said the man with the ponderous scar crossing the right corner of his face.

If I was him, thought the commander, *I would want to reach the ambassador at the residence.* His men had stolen three motorbikes that were watched over and ready on the promenade along the far side of the seawall. His third remaining disciple had recovered their car and was waiting north, beyond the street barricades. If he was correct . . .

An official-looking car skidded to a loud stop in front of the main entrance.

Out of the main doors came his prey . . . with the prize by his side! He was sure of it. In that fat leather bag.

"He has the rabbi," said the voice by his shoulder.

"He has the box!" The commander spit the words into the salt-tinged air. "Quickly . . . I know where they are going."

6

It was only days ago that Nora Carson was totally on board with Noah Webster and all his machinations for ever-increasing power. Though unpredictable and mercurial at times, Webster, her superior at the State Department, appeared to be Carson's best chance for reaching her own desire for influence and riches. Washington, DC, was the capital of influence and riches, and Carson—always stunning in her pin-perfect power suits, her natural red curls falling over her shoulders—was determined to get her share.

But something unforeseen happened. Webster appeared to be coming unglued. The deputy secretary of state for management and resources, Webster spent decades getting himself in position to succeed in his final scheme—buying his way into the highest seats of elected office. During twenty-eight years as chief of staff to Senator Seneca Markham, perhaps the most powerful politician in DC, Webster had carved a reputation for himself: ruthless, heartless, relentless. Nothing was off limits and nothing stood in his way.

Two years ago, when Markham was on the verge of retirement, the senator force-fed the appointment of Noah Webster to his current post at the State Department. During his two years at State, Webster lived up to every unsavory aspect of his reputation.

So Carson wasn't surprised when Webster fell into collusion with the prime minister of Turkey, co-conspirators to derail US President Lamont Boylan's efforts to forge a treaty with Iran. Billionaire banker Richard Rutherford, Markham's money pit, was keeping a closed fist on the confiscated Iranian billions locked up in his banks, money that had spewed forth hundreds of millions in untracked interest over the last thirty years, money Rutherford used to propel his own Machiavellian schemes for power. Money that Noah Webster was promised would overwhelmingly fund his run at a Senate seat from Virginia. If successful . . . well, who knew? That was Webster's big gamble—how far, how high, could Rutherford's nearly limitless pockets take him?

But Webster's grand scheme suddenly appeared to be showing cracks. Two days ago, with the banker demanding the demise of the president's Iran nuclear treaty or he would slap a lid on the flow of his clandestine funding, Webster reverted to extortion, threatening to make public Rutherford's decades of illegal contributions to Senator Markham. A bad idea. Trying to bully the billionaire banker was as healthy as juggling rattlesnakes.

Then this morning, Webster lost his most formidable ally. Seneca Markham was found dead in his DC apartment.

Her boss—her partner in crime?—was playing a very risky game. And the odds were beginning to go against him. Which was not a good thing. Because Webster's reputation for ruthlessness was well earned. And Nora Carson suddenly found herself in a much more precarious position. Over the years she helped Webster execute several schemes that skirted the edges—perhaps overstepped the boundaries—of both ethics and law. A risk-reward equation she was willing to take at the time, as long as Webster exercised the level of power that would hopefully fill her off-shore bank account and shield her from potential harm.

Power that increasingly seemed in jeopardy.

Walking down the fourth floor corridor of the Truman Building in Washington, home to the State Department, arbitrarily summoned to Webster's office once again, Carson was beginning to wonder if she had saddled the right horse. And she was beginning to sweat.

Then there was George Morningstar.

Did Webster know about Morningstar?

Until recently, George Morningstar was the deputy assistant secretary for diplomatic security. Extremely competent, well-liked, Morningstar got too close to Webster's deal with the Turkish prime minister, which got Morningstar banished to a do-nothing job in the bowels of the Truman Building and his right-hand at DSS, Brian Mullaney, bounced out of Washington and into Israel.

Now it appeared that Morningstar, previously the overseer of internal investigations at the State Department, was discretely asking questions about Webster's tenure at State, quietly turning over rocks. Yesterday, Morningstar stopped at her table at the Washington Grill and handed her an envelope. The envelope contained records that hinted to a shady financial link from Rutherford to Markham to Webster and a very preliminary and tenuous outline of what Carson knew were Webster's most nefarious schemes.

George Morningstar was on a hunt. Webster was his prey. And anything that threatened Webster's future threatened Carson's future as well.

So in the pre-dawn hours, Carson called Morningstar and told him they needed to talk immediately. She was desperately looking for a way out. Now walking down this corridor in the Truman Building, she had never been more frightened. Morningstar failed to show up this morning at the remote diner in rural Virginia—and Nora Carson was working very hard to control her rising panic. What were her options? Who could she trust? And what would that trust cost her?

One of Webster's more ludicrous compensations for his height was the raised dais at the far end of his office, close to the windows that looked out upon Washington's splendor, upon which his desk sat in throne-like dominance. As Carson entered, wary and anxious, the wannabe king was seated at his throne. *What does he know?*

━━━━━◦◦◦◦◦━━━━━

Namir Road, Tel Aviv
July 22, 9:37 p.m.

The Namir Road was a long, flat, palm-tree lined, six-lane street through an upscale neighborhood of Tel Aviv. At this time of night, the shopping malls were closed, most people were home, and the traffic was light.

Doors locked according to DSS protocol, the diplomatic pouch sitting on the floor between Mullaney's legs, the Lincoln shot up the Namir Road like a heat-seeking missile. Until . . .

They had nearly reached the intersection with Einstein Road, just to the west of the Tel Aviv University campus, when the driver throttled down dramatically. "Trouble, Brian."

Mullaney looked out through the windshield. Up ahead, closing fast, the intersection of Einstein and Namir Roads was a tumult of people, a swirling knot of humanity, rimmed on four sides by Israeli police cars, their blue strobe lights flashing. "Stop by one of the police cars," said Mullaney. "Let's see if we can we get through."

"I don't like this, sir," said the driver. "That's a lot of people."

"Right . . . but I don't want to lose time and go back unless it's absolutely necessary."

Slowing to a crawl, the driver pulled alongside the nearest police vehicle as Mullaney lowered his window and offered his credentials to the officer who turned in their direction.

"Meir must go," chanted the assembled voices. "Meir must go!"

"Any chance we can get through?" asked Mullaney. "I need to get to the ambassador's residence immediately."

The Israeli police officer looked at the credentials, looked up at Mullaney's face, then turned and looked over his shoulder. "Captain!"

———

"There are two ways they would likely go," said the driver as the commander threw himself through the open door of the car and into the front passenger seat. "Either the Ayalon Highway or up the Namir Road. At this time of night, I would travel the Namir Road. More direct."

"Go!"

———

The police captain looked tired and bored. With Mullaney's credentials in his left hand, he swept it out toward the milling mass of people, some carrying placards, that flooded the intersection and the roads leading into it. "You see this? This is an explosion waiting to happen," said the captain. "There's probably five hundred people crammed into that intersection, and they probably have five hundred differing opinions about this peace treaty . . . some protesting, some celebrating. If I try to drive a wedge through that group to get your car . . ."

"Brian . . ."

Mullaney looked away from the police captain at the sound of the driver's voice. Through the windshield he could see that the tide of the mass protest was heading in their direction, like a wave building to its crest.

"This is not good," snapped the captain. "Keep those people . . ."

But the wave was breaking, protestors washing around and through the policemen and their vehicles, rapidly surrounding the embassy's Lincoln.

"We look too official," said Mullaney, as the first fists started pounding on the car's hood, placard sticks slapping against the roof, a multitude of hands initiating a rocking that was picking up intensity.

"Meir must go! . . . Meir must go!"

The captain and his officer turned toward the crowd, their arms out-stretched, trying to stem the tide, the captain calling for more officers.

"Meir must go! . . . Meir must go!"

"Go faster," hissed the commander.

"We'll get stopped."

"Go faster! If we can catch them on this road . . . what's that?" Up ahead he could see the blue flashing lights . . . then the sea of people spilling out of the intersection . . . then . . . "Stop! Pull over!"

Now that ten, nasty-looking Israeli police officers ringed the Lincoln, the banging stopped, the rocking stopped . . . but the chanting got louder.

"Meir must go! Meir must go!"

And the throng crowding around the embassy car refused to budge.

The commander, one of his disciples at his back, inched his way through the shifting, shouting, chanting crowd that surrounded the black car like a caravan engulfed in a sandstorm. He got to within two rows of protestors, but the people were packed tightly around the car, pushing up against the arms of the policemen who were failing to keep order. Jostled from side to side, he caught only glimpses of the people inside the car. The old man was in the rear seat, on the far side. But his enemy was just in front of him.

The man who killed his father. The enemy of the Exalted One. His enemy. Hate rippled off the commander like heat waves shimmering across the summer desert, his malignant eyes riveted to the man on the other side of the window.

"Meir must go! Meir must go!"

"We could slide a bomb under the car . . . be done with it," said the soft voice from behind him.

"No . . ." he hissed. "We are unleashed to render death upon their heads, but we were also dispatched to retrieve the box. And the box is also within the car. But"—he pushed against the bodies in front of him—"I want *his* blood on *my* hands." He reached behind him for the gun carried by his disciple. His prey was looking forward, the left side of his face visible only on an angle. The commander leveled the wrath of his vengeance like laser beams through the window of the car.

"We'll go. Let us go," snapped the driver.

Mullaney reached forward and rested a hand on the driver's shoulder. "It's breaking up . . . we'll be out of here soon. Don't get jumpy. We don't want anyone hurt."

Settling back into the seat, Mullaney felt heat rising on the left side of his face. He raised his hand to his cheek . . . fever?

Beware! Look to your left.

At the sound of Bayard's voice, Mullaney snapped his head to the left. There, engulfed in malevolent focus, was a young man with Middle Eastern features, dressed in black, the fury of his eyes boring into Mullaney's skull. Tall, clearly muscled, a livid pink scar carved from his right ear across the top of his forehead, just under the hairline, the man was trying to push his way closer to the car. He was reaching behind him for something.

"Look . . ." Mullaney's warning was cut short as the car burst forward.

"Clear!" shouted the driver, muscling the car along an open corridor the police had finally cleaved through the crowd.

Mullaney tried twisting his head, but the car hurtled through the intersection, leaving the crowd—and that vision of unrestrained rage—quickly dwindling in their wake.

The words that burst from the commander's mouth were Turkish, but their foul intent was clear as they were hurled after the fleeing car. He turned abruptly, knocked down a young man and woman who stood in his path, and, once clear of the dispersing crowd, broke into a sprint toward the place where his car was parked, the engine running.

7

US State Department, Washington, DC
July 22, 2:44 p.m.

Noah Webster's pulse was slamming against the walls of his arteries, adrenaline coursing through his blood in a torrent. Even though the covert operators he had hired were outrageously expensive, Webster knew from experience how unearthly effective they could be. That he had received no updates on their surveillance of Richard Rutherford or Abigail Mullaney was disturbing.

And now Markham was dead. Webster wasn't fool enough to believe the initial speculation of a heart attack. Senator Seneca Markham's heart was as strong as a horse. The reports of an apparent heart attack chilled Webster's spine. All his suspicious senses were screaming that Markham didn't die of natural causes. So then . . . what? Or, who? And where was Rutherford?

Too many pieces. Too much could go wrong. Too much at stake.

The world around him was gathering speed, hurtling toward a conclusion he knew was still very much in doubt. If he made a mistake now . . .

I will not fail. I will not falter.

But now he needed every ally he could find. Or frighten.

Carson entered his office. Her steps were . . . hesitant.

Webster kept his eyes on the papers atop his desk. They were blank. But Carson would never know that. He sharpened the razor's edge of his voice, hoping to draw blood. "It's a very short walk from your office to mine," said Webster, his voice hushed. He lifted his left arm and glanced at his watch. "Forty-seven minutes. A new record for sloth. The events of the world will not wait for you, Nora. And neither will I." He looked up and captured her gaze. "Can I depend upon you, Nora?"

Nora Carson may have been three years younger than Noah Webster, but she was just as calculating and ruthless in her desire for the higher levels of power and riches that were the currency of Washington's elite. With the well-sculpted body of a trained athlete, long folds of curly, red hair falling to her shoulders, and arresting jade eyes, Carson was a stunning woman who used her model's good looks as an asset at every opportunity. But Noah Webster never allowed himself to dwell on her beauty. What Webster really needed from Carson, besides a willing accomplice, was someone close enough that—if his plans were thwarted—he could frame for all his crimes.

"That's a question I would ask of you, Noah," Carson responded. "Markham's dead . . . your protector and your link to Rutherford. Where does that leave us? Our plans for the future?"

"We don't need Markham anymore," said Webster. "We have Rutherford . . . and I have Rutherford within my control. I have enough proof of Rutherford's secret dealings to put him in jail for three lifetimes. Our path is still the same. The off-year election for the Senate seat from Virginia. Then use every secret I've uncovered, every debt, every threat of scandal I can muster to—like Markham—build a career in the Senate. Get rich. And exercise a level of power and control that will make me unstoppable."

The dream. Just speaking the words of his dream filled Webster with a euphoric optimism and fueled his passion. It was a singular passion.

"It's right there for the taking, Nora. All those years wheeling and dealing favors for Markham, being his bag boy for the phantom millions that flowed into and out of his office. There is quite a list of elected officials who will wholeheartedly endorse a Noah Webster Senate campaign—or they will risk joining Rutherford in a Federal penitentiary. No . . . the dream is the same, the plan is the same."

And Webster was certain that the result would be the same. One day he would have all of Washington in the palm of his hand as Markham once had. His eyes burned, not with passion, but with revenge.

"Then it's payback time," Webster whispered. "I won't be a benevolent dictator like Markham. There will be a day of reckoning. For every racist insult, for every joke, for every humiliation. I will take their money, and then I will take their dreams and squash them in the dust."

It took all of Nora Carson's discipline and determination to stand steady and unwavering under the brunt of Webster's impassioned words. Thunderheads were roiling in her stomach, droplets of perspiration running down along her spine. What was happening?

This was new for Carson. She thought she understood Webster's drive for wealth, power, and position and his desire to transcend what was the reality for most black men in America, the racism and unconscious bias that still permeates so much of American society. But this . . . this sounded more like vengeance, like the vendetta of a sick and twisted mind. Was Webster losing it? Going over the edge?

Carson felt a new level of fear. She kept her voice neutral, her tone calm. "Not everyone is a racist, Noah. I think you've . . . well, you're not the only black man to feel discrimination. And women are discriminated against all the time. You know that. It's not just you."

Webster jumped to his feet behind the desk on his raised platform. His eyes were wide and staring, the veins in his neck like taut cords, straining against his skin.

"You talk to me about racism? You feel discriminated against, Nora? You feel at risk? Now you know what my world is like," seethed Webster. "It's a world where I will never be your equal, simply because of the color of my skin."

Years of pain, fear, and anguish bubbled to the surface, threatening Webster's grip on self-control. He saw fear in Carson's eyes, alarm at his outburst. *Not now . . . don't you lose it now.* He forced air into his lungs, pressed down on the fury that thundered in his heart. Unclenched his fists.

Webster compelled himself to sit in the chair behind his desk, fold his hands, and lay them on the top of the desk, his eyes never leaving Carson's face. He coerced his lungs to breathe. Then he demanded that they breathe again. And again.

His voice came out calmer, quieter, but with no less vehemence.

"Do you know about *the talk*, Nora? The talk every black father or mother has with their sons as soon as they can understand? How to respond to a police officer so you can walk away free, or at least walk away with your life. How to survive the racism that will confront them in school, at work, in their neighborhoods. How to hold onto your dignity when your character or competence is not only questioned but ridiculed."

His words decreased in volume as they increased in passion.

"The talk is when I decided I would not back down. That I would beat the white man at his own game. That I would take the white man's power, and his money, with one end in mind. To pay back every insult four-fold, to bring suffering to those who have humiliated me. And to grow in wealth, influence, and authority. I will have beaten *the talk*, Nora. Then no one can touch me."

As Webster leaned into his desk, closing the distance with Carson, a memory he had stuffed deep into a hidden place flooded his mind.

When he was at Harvard, a senior from Alabama—Beau Clanton—made his life a hell on earth. They were on the crew team together—Webster the coxswain in a sweep oar eight and Clanton the stroke. Clanton sat face-to-face right in front of Webster and would whisper degradation with every sweep of his oar so no one else could hear him. Call Webster an educated ape. Tell him to go back to the jungle. Call his mother vile names.

One morning before dawn, Clanton took a single out to get in some fast laps. Webster watched from the side of the boathouse. Nobody else was around, and a mist lay heavy on the river. After his first lap, while Clanton was coming back upriver, Webster jumped in a coach's skiff and intercepted him where a bunch of trees were overhanging the river. When Webster got near, he called Clanton's name. Webster came alongside and, as Clanton turned, Webster hit him in the back of the head with an iron bar . . . crushed his skull.

Webster pulled Clanton's body out of the boat, tied it under his, and rowed far down the Charles River. He weighted the body and let it sink to the river bottom, far from where Clanton's boat would have grounded. His body was never recovered. Presumed drowned.

In the few seconds it took for the memory to consume him, Webster felt the same rush of adrenaline as when he had slammed the iron bar into the back of Clanton's head. He could feel the hate rising once again, the fury of humiliation. He must have channeled that hate toward Carson because when his mind returned to the present and his eyes focused, Carson's eyes were wide. Fear pulsated in her pupils.

"Are you worried, Nora?"

She slowly shook her head back and forth, the red curls sweeping over her shoulders. But her eyes were closed, her lips pushed tightly together, her face set in a hardened grimace—signs of resigned frustration that Webster could read easily. "I've been worried ever since you coerced me into altering Joseph Cleveland's Situation Report to the secretary," Carson admitted. "I've felt like there was a bull's-eye on my back ever since. And frankly, Noah, I've wondered who was going to drive an arrow into the bull's-eye first—you or someone determined to take you out."

Now that was an alarming answer. How far had Carson strayed from the fold?

"Many have tried to take me out," said Webster. "None have succeeded. Including George Morningstar."

Ahhh. Carson's eyes broke away at the mention of Morningstar's name. So a traitor in my midst.

Now the death stroke.

"Yes . . . such a shame, though," Webster whispered. "They found George Morningstar's car at the bottom of Bull Run this morning." He paused for effect. "Morningstar's body was still in the car."

Carson looked as if he had slapped her across the face.

"Yes, Nora . . . think well whom you will serve. Do we remain friends, or do you have new friends? Remember, my enemies become my victims. And my victims rarely survive. Which are you?"

Ambassador's Residence, Tel Aviv
July 22, 9:56 p.m.

Mullaney's credentials got their car through a roadblock and onto the street that fronted the residence. But there was no way to get their car near the main entrance. The driveway that curved up to the front door was impassable—huge craters surrounded it with spewed rocks and gravel, the gate to the driveway blocked by a parking lot of police vehicles and ambulances, all with their lights flashing. They pulled to the side of the street and Mullaney jumped out of the car, the diplomatic pouch, unwieldy as a collection of bowling balls, grasped tightly in his left hand. The wound on his head from the gun battle in the streets of Old Tel Aviv screamed in rebuke, but Mullaney ignored the pain and sprinted for the front entrance.

As their car drove away from the embassy, Mullaney called every mobile phone in his residence directory. Only the head chef had answered. He was hiding in a walk-in cooler. And all he knew was that there was still shooting outside. That seemed like an eternity ago. His mind fought against fear as he came closer to the building.

Pat McKeon was just inside the main entrance in the middle of a huddle of DSS agents. McKeon and Kathie Doorley were instructing two agents, emphatically pointing to the southern wing of the residence, two others awaiting their instructions, when Mullaney ran up the steps behind them. McKeon shook herself and faced her boss.

"Cleveland, Mrs. Parker, and Mrs. Hughes are safe and unharmed," she said. "During the fighting we got the ambassador, his daughter, and Ruth into the safe room with a squad of heavily armed marines. They were just escorted back up to the ambassador's study—that room was the least damaged in his suite. We've just completed a sweep of the building. We got the last one about five minutes ago. Kathie and her squad cleared the south wing and the living quarters, we cleared the north wing, the marines are sweeping the basement, and the police are securing the perimeter."

Mullaney waited. McKeon would know what Mullaney wanted to hear . . . how many casualties? How many dead?

"I don't know how many," she said, shaking her head. "But we got hit hard. We've got wounded all over the compound. Some EMTs just showed up and are teamed with the marine medics, doing the best they can. But it's not going to be good."

One of the DSS agents from the Lincoln brought Rabbi Herzog through the front door as Mullaney took a half step forward and put his right hand on McKeon's shoulder. "It's okay, Pat. We all got hit hard. This has been a terrible week. But we've got to keep our focus . . . keep doing our job."

McKeon nodded her head and took a deep breath. "Okay. What do you need me to do?"

Mullaney looked around at the building's damage and glanced out the front door through the bulletproof glass, cracked but still intact. It was a fitting image of the current security condition of the US ambassador's residence—cracked, damaged, but still holding together.

"You and Kathie come with me . . . and bring the rabbi. The first thing I've got to do is check on the ambassador."

With McKeon on his left, Doorley on his right, and Herzog and a trio of DSS agents in his wake, Mullaney convened a very mobile security team meeting as he maneuvered toward the ambassador's private quarters.

"There's no time to make this official—we'll take care of that later," said

Mullaney, as he moved hastily but gingerly over the shards of shattered tile floor just inside the residence's main entrance. "Pat, you will take over for Tommy as interim head of the ambassador's security detail." He glanced to his left. "You will stick to him like glue. Got it?"

"Thanks, Brian," said McKeon. "His shadow won't be as close to him as I will."

"Good."

He glanced to his right. "Kathie, you take point for security here at the residence. Find the construction schematics for the building ASAP and bring them to the ambassador's study. But first, gather every able-bodied staffer who can swing a hammer, pull out all the plywood we have in the maintenance shack, and start nailing closed every break in our perimeter. And I want a structural engineer and a construction crew—all cleared by Israeli security—in here first thing tomorrow morning . . . or sooner. Call Meyer Levinson at Shin Bet and tell him what we need. Use Jeffrey Archer to help you with the phones if necessary . . . wait!" Mullaney stopped at the edge of the reception area. "Do the phones still work?"

"The landlines are still functional, and all the wireless networks are up and running," said McKeon. "But . . . Brian . . . Jeffrey Archer was killed in the earthquake. The ceiling fell on him."

Mullaney closed his eyes. Too many bodies. How much more? He shook himself back to the moment.

"Okay . . . twelve-hour shifts. Nobody gets a day off," said Mullaney, as he turned to his right and into the south wing. "And nobody's allowed to get sick. Got it? We need every hand on deck. And Kathie . . . ask Meyer if he can spare us some contract security agents . . . ex-IDF. We're already short-handed, and I want to double the guard on every shift."

Mullaney stopped at the marine checkpoint and locked door leading into Cleveland's private quarters and turned to face his new leadership team. "Choose your second-in-command and let me know who you've selected. Questions?"

Pat McKeon was a veteran Diplomatic Security Service agent. Her dark hair was cut short, her brown eyes piercing, and she had the athletic build of a triathlete. By reputation and experience, solid and reliable, McKeon had atoned for an earlier lapse in judgment with her selflessly heroic actions during the gun battle in the Nitzanim Reserve that saved Palmyra Parker's life. In her mid-thirties, McKeon gave off the aura of a warrior.

Kathie Doorley had earlier served with Mullaney in Jordan for two years. Even though she was seven years younger than McKeon and with her curly hair and soft blue eyes could pass for a school teacher, Mullaney had no hesitation putting Doorley in charge of the building's security. She was tougher than half of the male agents in his corps. Several years back she had lost two fingers of her left hand to a mail bomb and, following rehab, spent twenty-four months wrangling with the State Department to get reassigned to field work.

Mullaney looked into two pairs of eyes that were anxious but ready. Prepared. Determined.

"We can do this . . . you can do this." Mullaney's voice was less commanding, more comforting. He needed these two to know that he had faith in them. "Follow your training and your instincts. You are both exceptional agents. You are ready for this." He waited for a question . . . some sign of hesitation. There was none. "Okay. I'll find you as soon as I'm done with the ambassador."

8

Baghdad Convention Center, Baghdad, Iraq
July 22, 10:13 p.m.

Samir Al-Qahtani, only two days removed from overthrowing the fairly elected government of Iraq, was not Superman.

Rock solid at six foot five, 250 pounds of muscle, his dark hair cropped close to his scalp, Al-Qahtani dwarfed the fighters of the Badr Brigades, Iraq's infamous Shiite militia. A professional soldier, ruthless, loyal only to his faith and his Shia brothers, even Al-Qahtani's legendary strength and stamina were beginning to erode under the stress-filled days and sleep-deprived nights that followed on the heels of the coup he orchestrated with his battle-hardened militia. He needed some sleep.

The halls of the Baghdad Convention Center, home to Iraq's parliament—the Council of Representatives—and its government, were finally quieting as Qahtani turned off the lights in his office at the end of another grueling day. He walked through the outer reception area and could see the shadows of his Badr bodyguards through the smoked glass of the office door.

"Has the allegiance of your heart changed so much in less than two weeks?"

Al-Qahtani tensed and spun on the heel of his combat boot, his warrior's body quivering with barely restrained aggression as he stared into the dark shadow in the corner of the room.

"Have you forgotten your Shia brothers so quickly and turned your back on our years of support?"

The taut knot at the back of his neck softened as he recognized the voice. Al-Qahtani reached out to the lamp on the desk to his right.

Muhammad Raman, chairman of the Iranian Expediency Council, the Muslim clerics who were the actual rulers of Iran's Islamic theocracy, was reclining comfortably in a cushioned chair. In Tehran, Raman's appearance would have been unremarkable. Slight of build, he was dressed in plain black robes, a round, black, pillbox hat on his head and a long, bushy white beard projecting from his chin. For years, even during the despotic rule of Saddam Hussein, Raman had played the role of banker—the conduit through which

Iranian military and financial support flowed into the hands of the Shia militias who opposed the Iraqi dictator. Al-Qahtani owed much of his success to Raman and the mullahs of Iran.

"You shouldn't hide in the dark . . . you could get hurt that way," said Al-Qahtani, shifting his weight to lean against the edge of the desk. "I won't ask how you got in here, and I won't ask why you're here. The deal with Turkey has nothing to do with you or with the loyalty of the Badr organization to our common goal of a unified Persia. You shouldn't allow a little theater to get you upset."

Raman shifted in his chair and leveled a piercing stare at Al-Qahtani. "You are in power for twenty-four hours and your first official act, yesterday, is to sign an agreement with Turkey for the establishment of a Kurdish homeland? Have you forgotten who your brothers are? Has it slipped your mind how you have come to find yourself in such a position? Was it the Turks who provided the money and weapons to supply the Badr militia? The Ayatollah asked me personally what madness had gotten into your mind. The Ottomans have no love for you nor for the Persian people. And there will be no portion of Iran sacrificed for a so-called Kurdish homeland. We think you have made a grievous error, Samir."

The warrior in Al-Qahtani struggled to escape, to reach across the room and grab Raman by the throat and squeeze him to within an inch of consciousness. Instead, the self-proclaimed prime minister of Iraq turned his shoulders to the wall on his left, upon which hung a huge map of his country and the surrounding nations. His gaze remained fixed on Raman.

"The Turks are not my problem, Chairman Raman," seethed Al-Qahtani, "and the Kurds are not my problem." He slapped his left hand against the map, obliterating most of western Iraq. "My problem is the stain of the Islamic State that controls nearly ninety-thousand square kilometers of Iraq and Syria, stretching nearly from Baghdad to the Mediterranean coast."

He slapped the map once more for emphasis. "Over one million Iraqis have been driven from their homes by this so-called ISIS—oil fields and refineries captured . . . Fallujah, Mosul overrun. And in the midst of this invasion, the farmers of the Anbar are in near revolt because the Euphrates has become a mere trickle and their farms have turned to dust. I don't need the Turks, but I need the water they hoard behind their dams. If my Badr fighters are to turn the tide against ISIS, we need to fight shoulder-to-shoulder with the Kurdish Peshmerga, and we need to rescue the people of the west from these butchers."

Al-Qahtani, still clad in his battle fatigues, pushed off the desk and took one stride toward Raman, who appeared to be sinking into his chair. "Nearly half of our nation is under the control of ISIS, my brother. Baghdad will be next unless we can stop ISIS in its tracks. My respects to the Ayatollah and the other mullahs, but my first concern is saving Iraq. There will be no resurrected Persian Empire if there is no Iraq with whom you can join forces."

Raman's eyes burned fiercely. Al-Qahtani reckoned he had just made an enemy. So be it. Get in line. But he was the man who would determine Iraq's future. He turned abruptly and switched off the desk lamp, throwing the reception area into darkness. "You can show yourself out the same way you came in. And next time—if there is a next time—make an appointment."

The smoked glass in the door rattled as Al-Qahtani slammed it in his wake, three pairs of boots echoing down the hallway as he and his guards exited the building.

<hr />

Ambassador's Residence, Tel Aviv
July 22, 10:18 p.m.

The ambassador's study was one of the few rooms in the less-damaged south wing that was still fairly intact. The inhabitants of the room, Mullaney quickly understood, were much more damaged.

Not only were they shell-shocked from the relentless violence that had filled so many hours of the last week, but the physical damage they had also endured had clearly drained their reserves of strength and optimism.

US Ambassador to Israel Joseph Atticus Cleveland was stretched out on his back on a sofa to the left side of the room. He was in shirtsleeves, his suit jacket tossed haphazardly over the back of a chair, his eyes closed, a wet towel on his forehead. Over the last thirteen days, Cleveland's motorcade had been attacked twice—once in Istanbul and then along Highway One on the route to Jerusalem when his armored limousine flipped through the air and crashed. He was not wounded during the ensuing gun battle in Israel, but he was bashed and bruised from the crash. Now his residence in Tel Aviv was a shattered, vulnerable wreck of a building and he had barely survived a brazen attack from a score of armed invaders.

Kneeling on the floor next to her father, Palmyra Parker was valiantly acting as nurse, tending to a few scratches and cuts while the medics were caring for the most seriously wounded. But Parker looked like she had been through a war herself. Her head was a checkerboard of red, raw skin surrounded by patches of what was left of her dark and once well-coiffed hair . . . compliments of the same murderous thugs who had attacked the embassy and residence and who had kidnapped Parker in hopes of ransoming her for a certain metal box and the prophetic message it carried. Her white dress was ripped and soiled, as if she had been crawling through the debris of the shattered residence, and her left arm was in a makeshift sling, bloodied at the elbow.

Normally unflappable, impeccably dressed, Ruth Hughes, the embassy's political officer who had become Cleveland's closest advisor on the ambassadorial staff, had the thousand-mile stare of a deer in the headlights. A pragmatic and wizened attorney who had mastered Middle Eastern politics during her twenty-five-year career with the Saudi oil behemoth Aramco, Hughes was accustomed to rough-and-tumble negotiations but not with the terror of mortal danger that she had survived twice in the last two days. Her expensive business suit rumpled but not ruined, her pearl necklace askew but still around her neck, Hughes sat on the right side of the room in a cushioned wingback chair, her hands white-knuckled on the end of the arms.

Mullaney, Middle Eastern Regional Security Officer of the Diplomatic Security Service—the armed agents responsible for protecting American Foreign Service personnel overseas—had fired his State Department-issued Glock automatic more in the past three days than in his entire nineteen-year career with DSS. He had been involved in blazing, relentless fire fights along Highway One, in the Nitzanim Reserve when Parker was rescued from her kidnappers, in the tight streets of Old Tel Aviv, in the ancient quarter of Jabal Al Weibdeh in Amman, Jordan—where his closest friend, Tommy Hernandez, had been killed—and in the bowels of the US embassy building just eight miles south of the residence. He had a long, red welt along the right side of his head where a bullet had scraped along his scalp during the gun battle on Malan Street in Old Tel Aviv, deep body contusions from the wreck on Highway One, and a gimpy ankle from where he fell headlong down a sand dune during the gun fight in the Nitzanim Reserve.

All of this violence was ignited when Cleveland accepted a request from Rabbi Kaplan at the Neve Shalom Synagogue in Istanbul to deliver a mysterious—and lethal—metal box and the two-hundred-year-old prophecy it protected to the Rabbinate Council at the Hurva Synagogue in Jerusalem. A box with kabbalah symbols hammered into its lid that a vast, heavily armed gang of Turkish terrorists had attempted to capture or steal from Cleveland and Mullaney at least five times, undeterred even though dozens of their gang had already been killed or wounded. It was a box, they had discovered, that could only be touched by its guardian—a person under the anointing and protection of the Aaronic Blessing. Any unprotected or unsuspecting person who touched the Gaon's box would suffer an immediate and gruesome death . . . their hair would fall out, their tongues swell and turn black, and blood would pour from their eyes as all the organs in their bodies shut down.

None of the others present, Mullaney realized, were sure whether the threat and power of death emanated from the box itself or from the Vilna Gaon's second prophecy that it used to contain. None wanted to find out. And Mullaney didn't feel any compulsion to push his luck and try it, even though he was anointed as the final guardian and was supposed to be able to touch the metal box safely.

The box that now rested inside the leather diplomatic pouch that hung ponderously from his left hand, alongside his leg.

Cleveland's eyes were closed, Parker's concentration on her father. But Hughes was looking at Mullaney wide-eyed, incredulous.

"You brought it here?" she gasped.

Immediately, Cleveland pushed himself up on his right elbow, Parker twisted her head in Mullaney's direction, and all three stared at him with a mix of horror and fear. Mullaney had just brought the plague into their house.

"Where was I going to leave it . . . in the embassy? With the fissures in its walls an open invitation?" asked Mullaney. "No. Too many lives have already been lost, and we still don't fully understand what the box is about or fully comprehend what the message means or its purpose. And those murderers? If they come after anyone, I want them coming after me. No"—Mullaney shook his head—"the box stays with me."

All eyes were on Mullaney, but no one objected. He set the pouch down on the floor at the end of the sofa and took the chair next to Hughes as Cleveland forced himself into a sitting position.

"I've assigned Pat McKeon to head up your security detail, Mr. Ambassador, and Kathie Doorley to take responsibility for security of the residence. We have staff members nailing up plywood sheets over any breaches in the outside security and I've asked Meyer Levinson for more contracted security—ex-IDF—to bolster our defenses. I'll lock the box into the safe room when we're done here. Then we've got to figure out how to deal with this enemy that is right outside our gates."

The ambassador was shaking his head.

"While I don't want the box back in this house," he said, his voice sounding as weary as his body looked, "at the moment I guess there's little alternative. But the first thing we've got to do is call Secretary Townsend. He must be apoplectic by now. Brian, go lock up that box. We've got a call to make."

They crouched behind a huge air conditioning unit on the roof of a seven-story apartment building just south of the ambassador's residence. The commander had a pair of night-vision binoculars pressed up against his eyes as he scanned the rear of the building and the sprawling, well-manicured lawns that spilled down to a cliff overlooking the Mediterranean Sea. He could clearly see the work details nailing up plywood over each of the fractures in the compound's walls. He knew the same work would be going on throughout the complex wherever security had been breached by the earthquake and his raiders.

He set the binoculars onto the roof and looked at his companion.

"Stay here. Watch closely," whispered the commander. "Call me if . . . when you see the American. Especially if he has that leather pouch in his hands. Ismail will watch the other side of the building." He looked around the roof. "Make a low tent with that tarp to keep you concealed."

The commander turned his eyes on the disciple. "The box is in that building. We will get the box. And we will rip the heart out of that American. *Do not sleep!* We must not fail."

9

What felt like the blazing heat of the rising sun gathered in intensity upon his back, luring the Turk out of his sleep—until his memory came alive to recall it was the middle of the night, and there were no windows in this room.

He opened his eyes and saw that his bed was surrounded by fog . . . no . . . smoke assaulted his nostrils with the putrid retch of decay. Fear flashed through his consciousness. He tried to roll on his back to sit up, but he was restrained as if his body were wrapped in massive coils of steel chain. He felt a whisper of breath on his right ear, a breath that contained the essence of every dead and rotting thing on earth.

"You find time for rest? You have accomplished nothing, but still you sleep?"

The temperature of his entire body rose steadily, perspiration soaking his armpits and down the small of his back. Still he couldn't move or see the face that belonged to the voice. But he knew who it was. And he knew what it thought.

The One had ensnared him in a shroud of smoke, but a smoke that did not waft away. It only grew heavier upon his skin, pressing the Turk down into his bed. He had no strength to resist. And trying to resist the One was futile . . . and could prove fatal. Yes, the One could bring an end to the Turk. The One could put to death this new husk the Turk inhabited. Worse, the One controlled the gate to Ghenna—the lake of damnation and fire. A place the Turk was determined to avoid. He did not entertain the thought of spending his immortality in burning agony. So he did not entertain the thought of resistance. At least not at the moment.

"The mantle of guardian has passed," hissed the voice of mayhem. "You failed."

Like thunder in the mountains, the words grew in crescendo. "The American now has the anointing, the box, *and* the message. *You failed!*"

Long, thin, cadaver-like fingers gripped the Turk by the collar of his jubba and yanked him off the bed, bringing him face-to-face with . . . a riot of red, shifting clouds, some swirling maniacally, some circling in place, their ever-increasing speed creating a vortex. In the midst of the vortex pulsed malevolent yellow eyes, harbingers of mayhem, slayers of hope. The diaphanous shape of a face morphed from tortured countenance to flaming rage, a strangled voice rising from the depth of its despair.

"All our work is at risk," bellowed the One. The swirling, red visage floated closer to the Turk, the skin on Eroglu's face crisping under the heat. The voice slewed into a menacing, throaty rasp. "Centuries of planning, and you have failed to do the one thing required . . . to keep our intentions hidden until the prophecy itself has been destroyed.

"We turned the lust of kings to our bidding. That corrupted fool Abdullah was so fearful of losing his family's power that we convinced him to betray his brothers, that now was the time for the sons of Ishmael to enter into covenant with the sons of Isaac. The same lust for enormous stolen wealth corrupted the soul of Rutherford who was our weapon against the Persians. With humans it is always so easy. Almost all worship at the altar of money or power . . . or both.

"But now the reckoning is coming swiftly. There is no time left . . . you must force our plans into position. We need to strike now! While the Persians are handcuffed by ISIS and Abdullah has no weapons to rule or destroy his world. Kashani must be removed. Israel must accept the treaty. And you must unleash our weapons and seize the prize at Incirlik. Tell me, my precious servant, that all of this is happening."

For a heartbeat, the fingers relaxed, the scorching heat abated, and the Turk was able to draw in a breath of sulfurous rank. Hate was boiling over in his heart, where a secret lay . . . a secret he dared not even bring to his mind. *Somehow, the box would be his. He would wield its power. And this One would serve him!*

His larynx nearly crushed, the Turk grasped for his voice. "I will deal with Kashani in the morning. His reign will end. He will end. For the next, most critical days, Prime Minister Arslan Eroglu will be interim head of the Islamic Republic of Turkey and he—I—will ensure the treaty is signed."

The treaty was one important part of their ultimate two-part scheme to obliterate the Mount of Olives, yet it was the most uncertain.

After years of start-and-stop negotiations, Prime Minister Eroglu had finally hammered out an accord between Turkey and Israel that would, through pipelines under the Mediterranean, provide unlimited fresh water to Israel in exchange for unlimited natural gas to Turkey from Israel's vast resources under the sea.

Written into the treaty by Eroglu was a clause that permitted a Turkish consortium to build an ultra-modern shopping mall on the flank of the Mount of Olives to the east of the Temple Mount and Jerusalem's Old City. It would be a mirror image of the soaring, outdoor Mamilla Mall that connected downtown, cosmopolitan Jerusalem with the Jaffa Gate on the western edge of the Old City.

In the middle of a night not far in the future, this consortium, controlled by the Turk, would turn its bulldozers loose on the summit of the Mount of Olives itself. If the Israeli negotiators rejected Eroglu's clause, there was a more desperate and devastating option. Either way, the future would be forever altered.

Why? Because a worthless Hebrew mystic, Zechariah, claimed that a fatherless carpenter from Nazareth bodily left this earth and would one day return to the Mount of Olives as a conquering king. It was that madman Zechariah who promised that the Nazarene's feet would land on the Mount of Olives in his triumphant return, which would inaugurate events that the Jew's book claimed would culminate in the final conflict of good and evil on the plains of Megiddo.

For nearly two millennia, the Turk and the evil incarnate that directed his actions had been intent on one purpose. If they could prevent the fulfillment of just one prophecy from that accursed book, then the promises and possibilities of all prophecies would be invalidated. If there was no longer any Mount of Olives, there would be no place for that illegitimate son to land. He was *not* coming back . . . would never be coming back. And they would change the end of the book. If the bulldozers did not work, they could still unleash the nuclear weapons they planned to steal from Incirlik. That was an option that would deprive the One of a vast swath of his territory. But if it achieved his goals, then so be it.

And to accomplish that, just after midnight on July 24, the Turk's agents would open the valves of annihilation on the people of Incirlik and pillage the B61 nuclear bombs stored on the base by NATO.

Either way, soon the Mount of Olives would no longer exist—either bulldozed into a concrete-covered shopping mall or vaporized and contaminated by one of their coveted nuclear bombs. And then the ultimate battle on the plains of Megiddo would not be the illegitimate son of Joseph leading the Jews to battle. It would be the One pouring out his nuclear wrath against any who dared try to stand against him.

"The weapons will soon be in our hands," wheezed The Turk, "enough pure destruction to destroy the mount and later to eliminate the Zionists, the Persians, and the Arabs, if need be. We are at the brink of ultimate victory."

Did he believe it? Was victory within their grasp . . . his grasp? After so many centuries—nearly two millennium—was the accursed light about to go out? Did he believe it? Did the embodiment of wrath, whose hand was at the Turk's throat, believe it?

How he would spend the rest of eternity hung in the balance.

The yellow eyes, birthplace of mayhem, burned into the Turk's mind.

"Their book predicts the final battle on the plains of Megiddo," hissed the One. "But we will use their book against them. By destroying the Mount of Olives, *he* will have no place to set his feet and will be unable to lead his forces against the kings of the north. We will turn that prophecy upon itself. Unleashed upon the Jew, our nuclear weapons will reverse the so-called battle of Armageddon. No army of earth or heaven will stand against us. The temple will be rebuilt, and I will stand upon its throne in all my glory. The kings and princes of the earth will bow to me. And we shall rule for all time. If . . ."

The skeleton-like fingers at his neck tightened their grip. The Turk was pulled closer and the blast-furnace heat of Sheol roasted his skin. "If you do not fail again," growled the One. "And I can promise you, my friend, that if you fail me once more, you will wail in unrelenting torment as the lake of flames consumes you for all eternity."

The fingers at his throat disappeared, the diabolical red mist evaporated, and the Turk dropped back into the sodden bed, the skin of his face blistered, his clothes awash with perspiration. Utterly exhausted, the Turk collapsed into unconsciousness.

Ambassador's Residence, Tel Aviv
July 22, 11:15 p.m.

"It's about time I heard from you, Atticus."

There was no mistaking the stern rebuke in the words of Secretary of State

Evan Townsend. And Ambassador Joseph Cleveland knew they were fairly deserved.

"I appreciated the text updates," snapped Townsend, "but what in thunder have you been waiting for? I've got federal agents engaged in a gun battle in the streets of Amman. One of our own—*your own*—killed inside a blown-up building. And it takes you nearly eight hours to get on a phone and tell me what's going on? I've got the Jordanian ambassador wearing me out about unregistered armed agents putting innocent Jordanian lives at risk. It's a darn good thing the king is our friend or we—"

Silence. Townsend's voice returned, none too pleased. "And now the ops center tells me there were earthquakes in Tel Aviv, but under *only* our embassy and the residence? Is that true? And I'm just now hearing from my ambassador? You're stretching my patience pretty thin, Atticus. Your story better be good, or I just may have to—"

"Mister Secretary." Cleveland's voice was tempered, his tone insistent, as he interrupted his boss. "I apologize for the delay, but if you give us a few minutes, I believe you will fully understand. Honestly, Evan . . . it couldn't be helped. It's Gang of Four."

Cleveland could hear the long, deep sigh on the other end of the connection. Gang of Four. They were the magic words.

Only thirty hours earlier, Secretary Townsend enlisted Cleveland, Mullaney, and Hughes to join him in a tightly knit group sworn to secrecy. The Gang of Four had the express mandate to track down what they feared was a traitor in the State Department. Evidence indicated a person in State's higher echelons was sharing critically sensitive information that was reaching the murderous gang of thugs who had been relentlessly attacking Cleveland, his daughter, and Mullaney and his DSS agents.

Now Cleveland, Mullaney, and Hughes were huddled in an undamaged corner of the ambassador's study, part of his private living quarters inside the residence. It was one of the few places in the ravaged building where a marine wasn't standing guard with his weapon drawn. They were seated around a low, round, olive-wood table, Cleveland's iPhone on speaker in the middle of the table.

"Tell me . . . fast," said Townsend. "I have a cabinet meeting with the president in twenty minutes and I need to get over to the White House. And

Atticus, I'm sorry I snapped on you. The ship of state is seriously leaking water over here, but it sounds like you and your people are in a war zone. I keep getting body counts. I'm sorry . . . tell me what you discovered."

"It's bad," said Cleveland. "During the earthquakes, both the embassy and the residence came under attack—we believe it's the same gang of terrorists. There are multiple casualties at each location and significant damage to both buildings. We should have a full casualty list within the hour, and we'll find out more about the long-term viability of the buildings in the morning. We *are* in a war here, Evan. But that's not the worst news.

"Ruth and Brian are here with me," Cleveland continued, trying to fill each minute with as much information as possible. "They went to Amman at the urgent request of the Emir of Qatar. He told them King Abdullah holds no hope for Israeli ratification of the Ishmael Covenant but, rather, lusts after a transcendent, nuclear-armed Islamic empire. By the way, the Saudi nukes were intercepted. Somebody melted them on the docks of Gwadar, Pakistan. But Abdullah will try again. And personally I don't believe the Persians will ever relent from their pursuit of nukes and their delivery systems. But there is a third ancient empire poised for resurrection. Evan, the emir said he has seen evidence of an imminent plot by some in the Turkish government to attack Incirlik and steal some or all of the nuclear weapons stored on the airbase."

There was a silent breath. "God help us," whispered Townsend. "Kashani is a fool if he thinks he can get away with—"

"Mister Secretary," Hughes interrupted, "Kashani is a radical Islamic jihadist who thirsts for a reborn Ottoman Empire and the emergence of the last Mahdi. He doesn't care. All that's—"

"Okay . . . okay," said Townsend, trying to quicken the conversation. "I can't take this to the president or the cabinet on the word of the emir of Qatar. He held the US hostage for three hundred million dollars. Said he would not agree to the expansion of the Al Udeid air base unless we sold him another ten F-15 fighter jets in exchange. Then he changed his mind on the expansion once he got the fighters in his hands. He's still dragging his feet on both the base expansion and payment for the F-15s."

"Mister Secretary," Hughes quickly jumped in, "there were reasons for that . . ."

"I hear you, Ruth, but there were three hundred million reasons why the emir should have kept his word," snapped Townsend. "Look . . . I need solid, reliable corroboration before I can take this to the president. It's just too—"

"Evan, there's more," interjected Cleveland. "The emir also informed Ruth that he has firsthand information that someone in our State Department is communicating directly with the same people in the Turkish government who are responsible for this plot to steal the nuclear weapons. It's our guy, Evan."

His psyche frayed and his emotions ripped raw by the terror-fueled anxiety of the last few days, Cleveland still felt sorry for the Secretary of State. He could almost hear Evan Townsend's heart breaking through the connection.

"We need to find him . . . today," Townsend's voice was a whisper. "And I need to know—yesterday—if the emir's assertion is true. We may already be too late."

"Shouldn't we alert the base commander?" asked Cleveland.

"No," snapped Townsend, his voice like a thunderclap through the iPhone. "Not on the word of Sheikh Al Thani alone. His word is toxic around here. I need proof, Atticus, not hearsay. And I need that proof now! Hard facts, first-hand, from somebody I can trust. *And* we need a miracle. Pray, Atticus. Pray like you've never prayed before. But first send a flash report on the earthquakes to my cell phone so I don't look like a fool in front of the president. I must go."

There was a beep and the connection severed.

Cleveland looked up from the iPhone. Mullaney was holding out a thin laptop computer toward him.

"The flash report for Townsend," said Mullaney. "I was working on it while you were talking. It's bare bones, but it should be just what the secretary needs."

"Send it," said Cleveland. "Then we've got to listen to Evan. We've got to pray." He turned to his right, where Hughes was sitting. "You are more than welcome, but you don't have to . . ."

"No . . . I'll stay," said Hughes, turning her chair toward Cleveland and Mullaney. "Prayer sounds like the wisest course of action right now. Even to me." She looked into Cleveland's eyes. "How do we do this?"

10

"Father," Cleveland began, his hands clasped and his forearms leaning on his knees, his head bowed, "we are exhausted . . . mentally, physically and spiritually . . . from the attacks upon us, from the death around us, from the anxiety building in us. We have enemies on all sides and apparently a traitor in our midst. We are tasked with the responsibility of protecting our country and all of its citizens abroad . . . and now tasked with finding this traitor.

"We've also been handed the responsibility for this box and the Vilna Gaon's second prophecy that has been hunted by the agents of evil for two hundred years and which remains important enough that good men and women continue to be killed in its defense. Yet the prophecy is a riddle to us. What does it mean? We still have this lethal box that leaves bodies in its wake. What are we supposed to do with it or about it? Please protect Agent Mullaney into whose care it's been passed.

"Father, we are grieving over all those who have lost their lives and fallen around us," Cleveland continued. "Father, we grieve for Tommy, but we know he is with you and enjoying the fullness of your love in heaven. Tommy was close to our hearts, and we deeply mourn his death. But what about all those others who have died? We pray for all of them, for all of their families, all of their loved ones—those who died from the explosion at the Hurva, those who died from these unusual earthquakes, those who died during the numerous gun battles that have haunted us since the box came into my possession. And we pray for those wounded and injured in all of those incidents."

Cleveland paused, not only to take a breath, but also to listen. Listen for any still, small voice that might be speaking to his spirit, in his spirit. Some word of direction or counsel. Then he continued.

"Father, you know our hearts. You know we need your help. What are we to do? And how are we to do it? We need your help to understand the words of the prophecy. We need your insight and discernment to see the full picture of the Gaon's intentions, of your direction and how you desire this drama to play out to the end. Because, Father, we know you have a plan and a purpose at work here. A plan and purpose for the Gaon to write these prophetic messages, a plan and a purpose as to why they have been hidden so long—and why you are revealing them now. And we ask you, Father . . . please make known to us your plan and purpose."

Cleveland's voice softened. "This is not about us, Father. You have an awesome, eternal purpose in play here. We don't fully understand the why, and we can't see the how, when, or where. But we are honored and blessed that you have called us to join you in this purpose, that you have measured us as worthy . . . faithful to be obedient to carry out your purpose.

"So Father, please help us, show us, lead us. We are lost without you. We don't know what to do. We need you, Father, to lead us into the fullness of your plan so we can accomplish your purpose. Please place your hand upon us and have the Holy Spirit guide us in our every step. And we pray this in the mighty name of your Son, Jesus. Amen."

Cleveland took a deep breath, opened his eyes, and pushed himself back into his chair. Ruth Hughes was looking at him wide-eyed, incredulous, her lips slightly parted as if there were words waiting to be spoken. She started to speak, stopped, shook her head, then looked once more at Cleveland.

"That was beautiful, Atticus. But I don't know if I could ever pray like that."

The ambassador smiled. "You just did. All it takes is to open your heart to him and your words will follow. There's no formula, Ruth. Only intimate sharing of one heart to another. And the remarkable thing is this . . . he talks to us in return. If you listen with your heart and your spirit, you can hear his words. That's how we can know when we hear his answer."

"You spoke . . . you prayed . . . as if he was right here in this room," said Hughes. A look of awe and wonder filled her face. "With the intimacy of an old friend."

Cleveland nodded his head. "That's right. But he is more than an old friend. Through the atoning death of Jesus Christ, I am a son of God. He *is* my father, and I speak to him as a son speaks to a father, with respect and honor, but also with intimacy. And he is right here in this room. Listening to every word we prayed. We prayed, Ruth. Because you were here, you were part of that prayer, participating in lifting up that prayer. And he was listening to you too."

Hughes was clearly beyond anything she had ever encountered before. She stared at the floor, shaking her head. Then she turned once more to Cleveland. "Did you hear anything? I didn't . . . I don't think I . . . but did you get an answer to your prayer?"

A smile as bright and inspiring as a late spring sunrise spread across the entirety of Cleveland's face. "Well, I have some idea—"

A sharp knock on the door of the study interrupted him. Startled, slightly annoyed, Cleveland looked toward the door. "Yes? What is it?"

A marine sergeant stepped into the room. "Excuse me, sir. Please forgive the interruption. But there's a call from Washington. Secretary Webster says he's been trying to reach you, but you're not answering your phone. He said it was urgent."

Cleveland shot a glance at Mullaney, dread filling his heart and suspicion filling his mind. "Please put the secretary's call through, Sergeant. I'll take it in here." Although certainly part of his job description, Cleveland didn't expect Webster to be calling to check on their health or the condition of the embassy or residence. Every part of his intuition and experience were setting off warning signals. He turned to Hughes.

"Ruth, would you mind finding out where they're keeping Rabbi Herzog and make sure he's comfortable. And find out if he's hungry or needs a place to sleep?"

Even though her impeccable suit still carried some dust from the earthquake, even though her normally crisp, white blouse was wrinkled and stained with perspiration, Ruth Hughes rose out of her chair with the confident bearing of someone secure in their own skin.

"Of course, Mr. Ambassador," said Hughes. "And thank you. I don't think I have the patience to sit here and listen to that weasel, Webster. Thank you for releasing me."

———◦◦◦◦———

When the phone rang, Mullaney thought he would take the hint and vacate the office also. He started to get out of his chair, but Cleveland reached out a hand to stop him.

"Please stay, Brian. But don't speak. As far as Webster knows, I want him to think I'm here alone."

Mullaney's eyes narrowed, and his heartbeat increased.

"Yes," said Cleveland, "I want a witness."

Mullaney already had enough good reasons to want to put a significant hurt on Noah Webster. It was clear that Webster was Cleveland's enemy. But a suspicion was growing in Mullaney that perhaps Webster was also the enemy they were seeking inside the State Department. Who else could it be?

But if Webster took off after the ambassador again . . .

"Thank you for the call, Mr. Secretary," Cleveland jumped in as he picked up the phone. Cleveland held the microphone end of the receiver near his mouth, but turned the speaker end toward Mullaney so both of them could hear the secretary's comments. "The staff at the embassy and residence will appreciate knowing you called about their welfare. But some of our staff did not survive the earthquake. I will—

"I know all about your staff, Cleveland, but it's not about your staff that I'm calling . . . although if you and Mullaney did a better job at maintaining security for the mission to Israel I believe a lot of these casualties could have been avoided."

Cleveland's eyes shot daggers at Mullaney, clearly ordering him to remain quiet.

"Well, Mr. Secretary, I think . . ."

"You don't appear to listen to your superiors, do you Mr. Ambassador? They call that insubordination, you know . . . refusal to follow orders. In the State Department, insubordination is a dismissible offense."

Cleveland grimaced and shifted in his seat. He knew what was coming. "And what directive have I failed to follow?"

"Is Mullaney there . . . Hughes?" Webster snapped.

"I'm alone, Mr. Secretary."

"Did I not tell you, specifically, to keep me informed about what's going on in Israel? Me . . . not Evan Townsend. How is it you have time to call the secretary directly, but you don't have time to keep your superior informed? How is it you can have bodies in the streets of Tel Aviv and I hear about it from Townsend's errand boy and not from my ambassador?"

"But Noah—"

"And did I not tell you," Webster continued without break, "to move heaven and earth to get the Ishmael Covenant ratified? And what progress have you made there? None that I can see. I thought my orders to you were clear, were they not?"

Mullaney watched with a sense of grieving, as Ambassador Cleveland sat up straighter in his chair, pushed his shoulders back and recaptured the dignity of his stature as a revered, veteran ambassador for the United States of America—something that Noah Webster was trying to strip from him. "Yes, Mr. Secretary, your orders were clear. But David Meyer's governing coalition is in tatters. At the moment, he doesn't have the votes—"

"Excuses," snarled Webster. "But even worse than that, where did you come up with this sophomoric fable about the government of Turkey plotting to steal nuclear weapons from Incirlik?" Webster's voice was rising in pitch and intensity. "Are you deranged?" There was a loud crash on the other end of the call. Something big and heavy was just destroyed in Webster's office.

The damage reports in Mullaney's hands were twisted into a tight spiral, the outer sheets significantly shredded. If only he could get Webster's neck in his hands . . .

"Is that the level of your intellect?" yelled Webster. "My barber has a better grasp on Middle East reality than you do. That a NATO member and a strategic ally of the United States would commit such an incomprehensible violation of its treaty obligations is ludicrous. Yet you take the word of a dishonorable desert jockey and then go over my head and pass this absurd rumor on directly to the secretary of state as a warning?"

Webster took a breath, but he wasn't done. "Mr. Ambassador, the action you just took in contacting the secretary is gross incompetence and willful insubordination." The words, and their implied consequences, hung in the air between Cleveland and Mullaney. In the following, momentary silence, it felt as if a firing squad was lining up. "I have lost confidence in your ability to effectively fulfill your sworn duty. I can't officially recall you at the moment. That would prove too chaotic. But bear witness, Atticus. You are under notice of recall. One more failure of judgment—or one more attempt by you to directly contact Secretary Townsend—and I will yank you out of Israel so fast you'll leave skid marks in your wake."

That was enough! Mullaney twisted in his chair to look directly at Cleveland, fury erupting through his mind and body, a blast of earthy rhetoric poised on his lips. But Cleveland slapped an iron grasp on Mullaney's wrist, and the pressure of the ambassador's fingers burned through Mullaney's flesh. The fury in Mullaney's heart was reflected back at him through Cleveland's eyes. The ambassador roughly shook his head. No!

Cleveland turned and looked at the phone in his hand as if it was a dagger thrust into his heart. "I serve at the pleasure of the secretary of state and the people of the United States," said Cleveland, his words sounding like an epitaph.

Mullaney heard a muffled laugh from the other end of the conversation. It sounded like the mocking welcome of the gatekeeper to Hades. "You know what I can make happen in a heartbeat. I still have all the documents in my safe. You've had a nice career, Joseph. Too bad it will end with disgrace as your legacy—unless you become invisible and silent. Understand?"

⸺∽∘◆∘∾⸺

Prime Minister's Office, Jerusalem
July 22, 11:37 p.m.

"Kahlon can have the government if he wants it," snapped David Meir.

The prime minister of Israel, tired and cranky from a long day of political arm wrestling and military brinksmanship, was squeezed into the corner of a cushioned patio chair in the middle of his official residence in the center of Jerusalem. Called Beit Aghion, a square, blocky building covered in Jerusalem stone, the prime minister's residence was located at 9 Smolenskin Street in the upscale neighborhood of Rehavia, well away from the government complex containing the Knesset building and his office.

Meir had taken his two closest supporters, Moshe Litzman, minister of the interior of Israel, and Benjamin Erdad, the minister of internal security, into the small, open-air patio in the hopes that he wouldn't wake his family at this late hour. But Litzman and Erdad were almost as argumentative with him as the leaders of the left-wing political parties Yesh Atid and Labor—both pushing for the two-state solution of the Ishmael Covenant—and their polar opposite leaders in the ultra-right-wing Jewish Home and Shas Parties—who railed against giving up any parts of Israel to establish a Palestinian homeland.

"You're going to hand the government to Kahlon without a fight if you push for a vote," Litzman said of Avi Kahlon, leader of the Labor Party. Litzman was sitting close by Meir's right side, his voice low and clipped but still full of urgency and fear. "Kahlon has already built a left-wing coalition powerful enough to sweep you out of office with a no-confidence vote. He will take you down. And Liberman of Shas is trying to build his own coalition, promising everyone the moon if they join up with him. One way or the other, left or right, we'll all be shown the door."

"But the gas-for-water treaty with Turkey has nothing to do with the covenant, which I've said one hundred times today," Meir insisted.

"And . . . it . . . doesn't . . . matter," snapped Litzman, stabbing an exclamation mark at the end of each word. "Bring anything up for a vote in the Knesset—anything—and our enemies will turn it into a referendum on the covenant. And there is no solution on the covenant. Instead of bringing the left and right together, since it has something sacred to each side, the Ishmael Covenant has only ripped our governing apparatus further apart. It's almost as if Yesh and Shas can't abide peace."

His political opposition would condemn Israel to endless conflict with her Arab neighbors and the Palestinians. Bad enough that Hamas ignited running gun battles in the dusty streets of Gaza and that Hezbollah was relentlessly raining rockets across the northern border of the country. But now with the first real possibility of peace for Israel in its seventy-year history, petty politics looked to prevent him from ensuring the safety of Israel's future generations. What a wasted opportunity. But Meir was as determined as he was distraught. Regardless of the consequences—and he knew they were real—he would never be able to live with himself if he didn't at least try to bring peace to his people . . . whether they liked it or not.

"Listen, my friends," said Meir. "It may appear that there are as many options open to Israel as there are points of view, but I can tell you there is only one option for me. I must try for peace. For our children, I must try for peace. What good would—"

The colonel in charge of Meir's security at the residence entered the patio and walked directly to the prime minister's side. "Vigdor Limon is here. He asks for a moment."

It was rare for the director of Mossad, Israel's international intelligence agency, to come to his residence, especially so late at night. Meir knew this would not be good.

Limon was old and stooped, bald headed and stout, leaning on a cane as he slowly crossed the patio. He declined a chair.

"Mr. Prime Minister . . . gentlemen . . . I'll be brief," said Limon, the raspy tone of a lifelong cigarette smoker scraping an edge to the words. He held up a manila folder. "In here are all the details for you to review if necessary. But I'll give you a simple summary.

"Three ancient empires," said Limon, "are poised to resurrect themselves—the Persians, the Ottomans, and the Islamic Arabs. All of them once occupied essentially the same slice of the earth—ours . . . and the rest of the Middle East. All of them want and are plotting to recapture what they believe still belongs to them. And all of them plan to use nuclear weapons to exert their power. There is a race to see who will get there first. The Persians, we know, are avidly pursuing a weapon and delivery system. We have uncovered information that a faction of the Turkish government is hatching an imminent plan to steal some of NATO's nuclear weapons at the Incirlik Air Base. And we have verified reports that King Abdullah has issued an urgent, second request for nuclear weapons from the Pakistanis."

The Mossad director looked carefully at all three men in turn, then moved his gaze back to the prime minister. "Sir, the Ishmael Covenant is a sham. The Saudis have no intention of honoring the covenant. Abdullah's intention is a nuclear-armed Islamic Caliphate. He is as much a fundamental, Islamic jihadist as Kashani in Turkey and the Ayatollah in Iran. They all want our land and they all want us dead . . . nuclear cinders in a scorched desert." Limon held out the manila envelope toward the prime minister. "Sir, ratifying the Ishmael Covenant is a death warrant."

11

Ambassador's Residence, Tel Aviv
July 22, 11:43 p.m.

A nuclear detonation threatened to blow Brian Mullaney's restraint out through the damaged walls of the residence and clear across half the Mediterranean. His Irish was up, his defenses were down from lack of sleep and endless tension, and he was more frustrated than a lottery winner with a lost ticket.

The call ended, and Mullaney jumped to his feet, his fists balled into tight knots that drove fingernails into his palms. He took two paces across Cleveland's study, wheeled around on the ambassador, and was about to launch a broadside, vilifying Noah Webster and berating Cleveland for his timid weakness in the face of such contemptable threats.

But just before he let fly with a stream of invective, Mullaney caught sight of Cleveland's face. And immediately he understood what Tommy Hernandez told him about Cleveland so long ago . . . wait, that was only four days ago. "*But there are times when it seems to me that he's carrying some great weight, something that reaches to the depth of his soul. I want to reach out and hug him when I see it.*'"

Joseph Atticus Cleveland—after three decades of exemplary service in the United States Foreign Service, not far from nomination by the president for the celebratory and coveted title of Career Ambassador, honored and respected by kings, presidents, and prime ministers worldwide—looked like a man who had lost his hope and self-respect. This was not a time to pounce. It was time to be a friend.

Mullaney went and grabbed his chair and pulled it closer to Cleveland, placing a hand on the ambassador's arm.

"Mr. Ambassador . . . sir." Mullaney kept his voice quiet, soft, soothing. "I'm ready to explode. I would beat Noah Webster to a pulp if he was in front of me right now. But I look at your face and I know there is some burden you are carrying, some weight that only you understand, which is the reason behind why you allow that snake to treat you with such disrespect. Shoot . . . to attack you with threats he has no authority to issue. Webster can't recall you from the field. He doesn't have the right or the power. Only the secretary can make that decision.

"But even so, Webster has no right to insult and demean you with such cruel comments. And," said Mullaney, "I keep asking myself why . . . why would a man like you, a man of character and conviction, a man of action and courage, allow a slimeball like Webster to get away with such emotional abuse?"

Cleveland was vacantly gazing down at the floor beneath his feet, as if searching for some understanding.

"Mr. Ambassador, please, let me help you. Let me in. Tommy once told me he saw a great weight pressing against the depth of your soul. But he didn't know what to do about it. Please, Atticus, let me help you. Whatever it is, you can't carry this thing by yourself anymore. And Webster's got to be stopped."

Cleveland's eyes didn't move from the floor. And his voice sounded like it was coming from the depth of the sea. "You think I'm a man of character and conviction, a man of action and courage? Perhaps in my old age. But when I was younger, I was also a man who found himself on the wrong side of doing what I thought was right. I was innocent of any crime but would have supported those who committed the crimes had I known about them. If the truth came out and I was held accountable, I could be charged. It wouldn't stick, but the scandal would end my career in disgrace. It would crush my children, embarrass them before the world. I . . . I don't think I could bear the look in Palmyra's eyes if that day were to come."

It didn't take an investigator's experience to see the truth beneath the surface. Cleveland had made some terrible mistake early in his career, and Webster had the evidence . . . evidence he was using to bully and blackmail Cleveland into silent compliance. Mullaney's inner fury toward Webster increased tenfold. But it was his friend, the man he admired more than any other, who needed his compassion and concern right at that moment. Webster could wait. His day would come. To help his friend, Mullaney drew from the depth of his own painful experience.

"Mr. Ambassador, when you carry secrets deep inside of your heart and spirit for a long time, they get buried, but they don't get solved. There were some secrets I carried for decades in my life, experiences that wounded me deeply, things of which I was ashamed. And as long as they lived in that dark, deep corner of my heart, they helped to define who I thought I was. I was always looking at my life through the lens of those failures, so I thought I was a failure. I was building my self-image based on the guilt and shame and lies of my past.

"Then I met a guy at our church. We used to get together on a regular basis for breakfast and to share what was going on in our lives. One day I told him about the things that had happened to me in the past, the things I was ashamed of, the wounds and circumstances and situations that I had buried deep in my heart. He asked me a profound question. He said, 'What do you think Jesus felt about what happened to you? If Jesus had been there at that very moment, what would Jesus have done . . . what would he have said . . . what would he have felt?'"

Cleveland half-turned his head to the right, his eyes leaving the floor but not quite meeting Mullaney's gaze.

"When I visualized the truth," Mullaney whispered, "I realized that Jesus would have been angry with what happened to me, not angry with me. His heart would have been breaking for my heart, just as my heart was breaking. He would have protected, defended, and encouraged me to look at the truth. The truth that Jesus loved me then just as much as he loves me now. He can't love me any more or any less. And that he would have been outraged at what I experienced."

Mullaney waited, but Cleveland moved no farther.

"I am not the man I thought I was for such a long time," said Mullaney. "Now . . . understand . . . I still have my issues. There is emotional turmoil I'm still trying to sort through, particularly about my relationship with my dad and resurrecting my relationship with Abby. But the past, that past is dead. I'm not that man anymore. And I'm not going to live in the prison of lies that old man built for me. That prison is not a place of safety. It's a place of loss and a place of lies."

Mullaney pushed himself around in front of Cleveland, forcing the ambassador to look into his face. "Sir, whatever happened in the past, that is not the man you are. Palmyra loves the man that you are. I'm sure your sons love the man that you are. We all have mistakes and failures in our past. If we let the past define us, then we're stuck living in the past. But you have a present that is more real than anything that could have happened in your past . . . if you decide to live here, in the now, in this moment. Please, don't let Noah Webster steal from you the truth of who you are."

Cleveland's eyes searched Mullaney's face, a desperate but uncertain hope finding no place to rest. "But you don't know what happened. You don't know what Webster knows."

"Then tell me." Mullaney's words carried the urgency of his heart. "Tell me. Get it out. Bring the lies out of the dark and let's deal with them."

Wavering . . . grappling . . . contending . . . Mullaney watched as Cleveland battled with the demons of his past. For what seemed to be a long time, the outcome was in doubt. Then hope rose as Cleveland's eyes cleared. The ambassador pulled in a long breath.

His voice was an ether in the stillness, a vapor of whisper. "When I was in my second year at the State Department, still trying to qualify for the Foreign Service, I was offered an opportunity . . ."

12

Tragedy came into his life wearing a smile and the uniform of an air force major.

Joseph Cleveland, three bulky files tucked under his left arm, held steady by his right hand, moved like a gazelle running in a herd. His empty stomach dictating thoughts of lunch, Cleveland rapidly navigated through the crowded corridor on the ground floor of the State Department Building, headed for the commissary.

"Cleveland, glad I found you."

Blocking his way was his boss, Norman Fieldstone, assistant secretary of political-military affairs, and a grinning poster-boy for the all-American airman.

"Cleveland," said Fieldstone, pulling Cleveland to the side of the corridor, "I'd like to introduce you to Major Anderson Lee."

Trying to keep his file folders from spilling into the human current, Cleveland managed to accept Lee's handshake, as solid as the spread-eagle insignia on his jacket. "Major Lee, I—"

"Here," Fieldstone tugged on Cleveland's sleeve, steering him into an empty alcove away from the busy corridor. "Major Lee is assigned to the Defense Intelligence Agency," said Fieldstone. "He came to me for help on a project he's shepherding over at DIA, and I thought this might be a good learning experience for you. I want you to help Major Lee in any way you can."

Cleveland felt a tangle of emotions—surprise, because he was in his second year at State and only three months on Fieldstone's staff; encouragement, that he was earning a reputation for reliability; excitement, at doing something more than research and study.

"Thank you, sir," Cleveland said to Fieldstone. He turned to Major Lee. "I'd be happy to help in any way I can."

"Excellent," said Lee. "I'll see you at the DIA office first thing Monday morning."

Without another word, Fieldstone and Lee turned and melted into the moving throng in the corridor. And Joseph Atticus Cleveland wondered what he had just agreed to.

———◦◦◦◦———

Joe Cleveland was twenty-five years old and only two years out of Harvard. Cleveland was proud of his academic achievements—the undergrad degree from Howard University that he earned in between waiting tables and working as a gardener and the masters and law degrees in political science from Harvard that he had sweated blood over to complete. His great-grandfather born a slave in North Carolina, Cleveland revered his accomplishments as a living testament to his family—honoring the sacrifice and aspirations of those who had endured to give him life. The CIA tried to recruit him twice during his days at Harvard. But he nurtured and protected his contacts at CIA even after he decided to sign up with the State Department.

It wasn't long after he joined the State Department that Cleveland applied to the Foreign Service in the consular track. He scored exceptionally high marks in his Foreign Service Officer's Test and his FSO and personal narrative were now being reviewed by a panel of veteran Foreign Service Officers, the Qualifications Evaluation Panel. Cleveland was hoping this new assignment to the DIA might accelerate the lengthy and laborious application process to the Foreign Service.

———◦◦◦◦———

Cleveland didn't have to wait or knock. Major Lee was waiting for him at the entrance to the DIA director's office. "Welcome," said Major Lee, maneuvering Cleveland past the director's secretary, "General Zimmer is looking forward to meeting you."

During his years at Harvard, Cleveland had spent a lot of time in rooms such as this. Aged oak in carved squares covered the walls, except for the wall-length bookcase and the eight-foot-high windows behind Zimmer's desk that were flooded with sunlight. At Harvard, this office would be the domain of a department chair, a man—probably—of significant age and formidable academic influence. Here, behind the flagship of a desk, sat a man who could wield and direct inestimable military power. Same clout, different sphere.

General Isaiah Zimmer was waving a hand at the seats in front of his pro-digious desk. "Mr. Cleveland, a pleasure. Please, gentlemen, take a seat." Look-ing back down at the binder atop his desk, Zimmer let out a sigh and slammed the binder shut.

"Do you think lacrosse sticks are weapons?"

"Sir?"

"Sorry, Cleveland." Zimmer shook his head and pointed at the offensive binder. "Those fools at NSA drive me nuts. Ban lacrosse sticks from airplanes? Sorry . . . let's start again."

The general, short, thick, a buzz-cut fuzz on his head, rose from his seat and came around in front of Cleveland, leaning against the front of his desk, the bright light behind him. "I've known Judge Allord half of my life. Would trust him with my grandkids. The judge asked me to watch out for you. Told me you are a man who can be counted on to do the right thing . . . a man of character." Zimmer folded his arms across his chest, obscuring the medals on his uniform, and tilted his head, looking askance at Cleveland. "Is that true?"

Blinded by the sun behind Zimmer, Cleveland's mind scrambled for an appropriate response. "I . . ."

"Well, that's why you're here," Zimmer continued. "You know what we do—we're the link between the military and the other national intelligence agencies. We provide the boots-on-the-ground espionage that the boys in the suits can't manage on their own. Twenty-five percent of the president's morning intelligence briefing comes from information we gather."

Zimmer stopped talking, but Cleveland didn't know what the general was expecting to fill the silence. So he waited, runnels of perspiration soaking the back of his shirt.

"Right now, Barry Goldwater and Bill Nichols are up to their armpits in crafting legislation that will be the most sweeping change to military structure and intelligence gathering since World War II. We've got some operations run-ning that might not fit under this new structure, operations we may need to bring to a close. And I need a man of character. Somebody that our DIA team can rely on. Somebody *I* can rely on. Is that you?"

Cleveland's mouth opened, but no words had a chance to escape.

"Of course. Listen, Major Lee here needs your help. He's taken on a mission of great sensitivity and importance to this nation's security and its future. It appears we may have gotten ourselves too entangled with that madman in Baghdad. The major is bringing that situation under control, shutting that operation down. But it's gotten too big for him to manage on his own. And it appears our window of opportunity to complete the mission is closing rapidly. He needs help." Zimmer was a black mass surrounded by an orange aura. His shadow leaned toward Cleveland, and his lowered voice sounded like an invitation from the grave. "But Lee needs help he can trust."

Zimmer lowered his hands to the edge of the desk and leaned even closer, his words one notch above a whisper. "There are times, Cleveland, there are missions so crucial to our nation that only men of the highest character have the courage to do the right thing, regardless of the consequences."

Cleveland's stomach suddenly hollowed, and a visceral fear rippled across his skin.

"Do you understand me, son?"

"Sir, I . . ."

"Do you have the courage to do the right thing?"

Across Cleveland's mind flashed an image of a pen scratching his name on a contract that he hadn't read. "If doing the right thing is to serve my country, uphold my oath, and to do my duty, then yes, sir . . . I have the courage to do what's right."

The shadow that was General Isaiah Zimmer's body relaxed, but his voice remained conspiratorial. "Well, Cleveland, the true test of a man is often discerning between doing the right thing and doing what is right." He stood up and extended his hand. "I'm sure Major Lee and I can rely on your loyalty to determine the difference. Welcome aboard."

⸻

"Listen, Joseph . . . what I need most is someone I can trust to carry messages," said Major Lee as they left Zimmer's office. "It has to be done face-to-face, person-to-person. Verbal communication . . . nothing written. And I'll need you to discern and interpret any nonverbal communication as well. It takes too much time for me to try and do it myself. But the communications are critical. I know it's not much of a task, being a glorified messenger. But I can't stress to you how important these messages are."

Washington, DC
Nine Months Later
November 26, 1985

With each document fed into the shredder, Joe Cleveland witnessed his future being mauled and contorted into indecipherable garbage. Another damning invoice was rent to bits, and Cleveland imagined it was his MPA from Harvard that was being destroyed. More letters were shredded into the bin, and Cleveland mourned the death of his dream—a State Department career spanning the world.

"Don't forget that box in the corner."

Major Lee's voice was nearly obliterated by the whirring gears of the two heavy-duty shredders destroying their work of the last year. His uniform jacket tossed over a chair, Lee didn't look up or slow the pace of paper being pushed through his machine. A ribbon of sweat moistened the shirt along his spine as he hunched over the open file box, pulling out documents with no regard for order.

"Sergeant," Major Lee called above the grinding motors, "don't forget the box in the corner! We've got all the Cayman bank account information in there. And we don't have much more time." Lee glanced up at the closed door to his office . . . Cleveland standing just inside. "Joe, I told you to get out of here. This has nothing to do with you."

Across the small office on the second floor of the DIA building on Joint Base Anacostia in the southern tip of the District of Columbia, the overweight sergeant pushed back from the heavy-duty shredder beside his desk. "This is crazy, Major. We're never going to destroy all the evidence. Zimmer's crazy." Cleveland could hear the fear in the sergeant's voice. "This secret is collapsing all around us, but we're the ones who will be prosecuted for obstruction of justice. For God's sake, Major, you know they're just going to hang you out to . . ."

The light on the speakerphone began to flash red. "Major?"

Twisting his neck to the right, Cleveland stared at the blinking light.

"Yes?"

"They're here. Three cars just pulled into the parking lot."

The shredders momentarily muzzled, silence settled into the room with the certainty of a mausoleum. Major Anderson Lee, special assistant to the director of the defense intelligence agency, a decorated combat veteran, pulled himself to his full six-foot height and pushed back his shoulders. "Okay."

Taking a deep breath, Lee crossed the room and picked up the bankers box in the corner, sat it on his desk, took off the lid and grabbed two handfuls of documents, holding one out to his sergeant. "Here . . . we do our duty until the end. We've been instructed to destroy it all. Let's do our best."

Cleveland's emotions were contorted. No, Lee hadn't told him the truth about their "mission." It was only when the subpoena was released this morning that Cleveland had discovered that the money funding their clandestine operations in Iraq had been illegally diverted. But an American hero was about to suffer disgrace for following orders, and Cleveland's heart was nearly as shattered as his hopes. "Major, please let me help."

Lee snapped a half-turn to his left. "Joe . . . I told you to get out of here. You are not responsible for this operation, and if it wasn't for the subpoena you still wouldn't know the truth. Your hands are clean. Keep them that way. I don't want to see your life destroyed before it really gets started. Leave! Go home. And don't talk about this to anyone—anytime. Understood?"

The fatal moment was here. Lee had known what he was doing when he started down this path, long before Cleveland had been assigned to his office. Sure, Lee was only following orders. But the American military held a common standard—no excuses, only responsibility. And Lee had no excuses. Still . . . Cleveland grieved for his short-lived colleague.

"Yes, sir."

Cleveland swept the room once more with his eyes.

"Get out of here, Joe. That's an . . ." The large, heavy oak door closed on Lee's final word.

Cleveland looked to his left, toward the elevators, but ducked quickly to his right, into the antechamber of a meeting room. He crossed the small, cramped room, its shelves stacked with overflowing binders and flanks of map drawers, and pushed through a small door into the closet he used as an office. Two steps to the far door. His ear against the door jamb, Cleveland listened. In the Sunday morning silence there were no footfalls on the marble stairs outside. He scanned the small room, wondering if he would ever be back. He never brought anything personal into this cramped space. But was there anything he should take with him?

No . . . you're not even here. You've got to remember that . . . never even here.

Cracking the door half an inch, Cleveland looked out onto the empty landing. *I guess there was a benefit in having a janitor's closet for an office.* He slipped through the door, closed it firmly and heard the click, then hugged the wall as he quickly descended the stairs. Fleeing. Like a coward. Leaving a hero behind to bear the responsibility.

13

Ambassador's Residence, Tel Aviv
July 22, 2014, 11:58 p.m.

"Two years later, at a DC meet-and-greet power party, Noah Webster stopped me in the hallway," Cleveland remembered as he continued talking to Mullaney. "Senator Seneca Markham, former chair of the Foreign Relations Committee, was about to open hearings into Major Lee's activities at DIA. I was on the cusp of reaching the Foreign Service. Essentially, Webster offered me a deal. He would keep my name out of the investigation . . . I would not be called as a witness. My entry into the Foreign Service would not be blocked. But I would be in debt to Webster until some future moment when he would call for payment."

Cleveland stared off into the distance, perhaps trying to assess his future.

"Webster still has all the documentation, all the records of the DIA operation." His voice had the faraway sound of his faraway eyes. "Should those records become public, I'm sure some law enforcement agency would at least investigate whether I was culpable of a serious crime . . . conspiracy or obstruction of justice. I have no doubt of my innocence. But the damage would be done by the investigation and the association. My career with the State Department would end."

Cleveland paused, as if even the thought of scandal took his breath away.

When Cleveland finished his story, Mullaney was looking at him with the affection of a son. "There is so much I would like to say. The words don't seem enough, but Mr. Ambassador, how do you think Jesus would have felt about what you did? About the situation in which you found yourself?"

Cleveland closed his eyes and composed himself to answer. "I think he would have been angry," said Cleveland. "Angry with how I was manipulated into a circumstance I did not create, into an unethical—illegal—plot. And I think he would have applauded my loyalty."

"And your honor," Mullaney interjected, "you were a victim here, not a perpetrator. And no matter what Webster has in his safe, anybody with half a brain . . . sorry, sir . . . would see the truth clearly. Especially your children." Mullaney waited a heartbeat. "I know I do."

Cleveland tightened his chin, pressed his teeth into his lower lip. Mist glistened in his eyes. He reached out his right hand and gripped Mullaney's bicep. "Thank you, Brian." There was a catch in his throat. "Thank you so much."

"Did Webster ever call in the debt?"

A smile crossed the ambassador's face. "I almost wish he had. Once and done. Instead, for nearly thirty years, he's reveled in reminding me of the sword he holds over my neck."

Palmyra's face . . . the faces of his sons . . . the face of his grandmother . . . flashed through Cleveland's consciousness, each accompanied by a stab of pain. What would they think?

"Webster's probably furious that another black man has earned more honor and prestige than he has," said Mullaney. "I've always thought the man was a rac—"

"Brian."

The ambassador spoke Mullaney's name softly but with such power and urgency that Mullaney's eyes shot up toward Cleveland. What Mullaney intended to say was apparently imprisoned in his throat.

Cleveland looked directly at Mullaney. He kept his voice low but urgent.

"Have you ever considered that Noah Webster may be the source of *all* our problems?" Cleveland asked. "Not just how he manipulated our transfers to Israel, to suit his own designs. But could Webster also be the traitor . . . the insider who's sold us out to the Turks and is in some sort of collusion about this possible raid on Incirlik?"

His gaze never wavering from Cleveland, Mullaney nodded. "He's my number-one suspect. And if I ever get my—"

"Brian . . ." Cleveland waited a beat to get Mullaney's full attention. "I don't have any evidence that Noah Webster has committed a crime. But I have ample evidence of the crimes committed against him."

"What?"

Cleveland leaned back and pulled in a deep, cleansing breath before reconnecting with Mullaney's gaze. "You can understand this, but you will never experience it . . . the reality of being a black man in America. Legal slavery ended in 1867, but racism did not. The myths of racial difference still plague us, shaped by slavery, yes, but reinforced by racial terrorism and legalized segregation.

"There was a reign of terror against people of color—the KKK, bombings, lynchings, racially motivated violence—for nearly one hundred years after the collapse of Reconstruction. That era of violently enforced racial hierarchy was profoundly traumatizing for African Americans . . . a legacy that continues today and is reinforced by random police violence against black men.

"The legalized racial segregation that followed Reconstruction was not simply an issue of inequality in schools," said Cleveland. "African Americans were marginalized by daily humiliations and insults for decades. But segregation also left a lasting legacy of racial presumption: people of color were, and continue to be, constantly suspected, accused, watched, doubted, distrusted, presumed guilty, and feared. As a nation, we can't escape our history of racial injustice. It's a reality black people live with every day.

"While many people of color have thrived in this nation in spite of both inherent and unintentional racism, others have become bitter. Some have fought back . . . some have lost their way and succumbed to the demons of the past. Black men still suffer, but in many ways women of color actually have a much worse experience: fewer opportunities, lower pay, inferior education and health care, and at times even more debilitating presumptions than black men face. Believe me when I tell you that no black American, no person of color alive today, has escaped unscathed from racial injustice. We all carry the scars."

Cleveland laid a hand on Mullaney's arm.

"So Brian, please be careful how you apply labels. I have no respect for the man Noah Webster has become, no respect for the path he has chosen. And personally I would not doubt that there are serious crimes for which he is responsible. But neither of us know what demons Noah wrestles with each night. That's not an excuse. Just a reality."

14

Rabbi Mordechai Herzog, eighty-two-year-old former head of the Rabbinate Council of Israel, was ushered into the ambassador's study by the marine sergeant. "We've tried to feed him; we've tried to get him to rest. But this rabbi just won't give up, Mr. Ambassador. He said he needs to speak to you right away."

"Thank you, Sergeant. That's fine. We'll just—"

Mullaney stood up from his chair, his iPhone in his right hand. "Excuse me, sir, but, since we have a break, can you give me a minute to make a quick call to Abby, to let her know I'm okay—that we're all okay?"

"Of course, Brian. Go ahead." Cleveland turned from Mullaney to the marine. "Sergeant, if Mrs. Hughes is still here, could you ask her to join us? Rabbi Herzog . . . let's sit around this table. There will be more room when the rest of them join us."

———◦◦◦◦◦———

Mullaney stepped out of the study into the formal living room of the ambassador's quarters. The room was a shambles, but Mullaney found a fairly intact corner and hit the speed dial button for his wife's phone.

Abigail Mullaney picked up between the first and second ring. "Brian . . . I'm so glad you called. I was starting to get anxious. We're getting news reports of these earthquakes, but only . . ."

"Abby," he interrupted, "There's no other way to say this. Tommy's dead."

"Oh, dear God." She breathed the words in reverence, like a prayer. But quickly snapped back to the present. "Brian, are you okay? I mean . . . are you hurt? I know you can't be emotionally okay. Oh, God . . . Tommy. How?"

Mullaney bit his lip at the memory. No . . . no time now for emotions. "We were on an assignment in Jordan. We got ambushed. I'm okay . . . a few scrapes. But Tommy didn't make it."

He leaned up against a sofa that appeared to have slid across the floor, ran his left hand through his hair, looked at his watch. When was the last time he got any sleep?

"Brian . . . oh, Brian, my heart is breaking for you," whispered Abby. "I wish I was there so I could hold you, comfort you."

"Thank you, sweetheart. That will have to . . ."

"Wait . . . was it the same men?" Mullaney could almost hear his wife's mind clicking into gear. "The same killers who attacked you and the ambassador before? They came after you in Jordan? Who are they?"

"I wish I had more answers. And I don't have time to get into all the details. Ambassador Cleveland is waiting for me. But I just want to let you know I am okay. And well . . ."

"You don't know when you'll be home, right?" she asked.

Mullaney grimaced. Here it was again. He made a promise to Abby that he was coming home for good, to stay. And now this was another promise that he couldn't keep . . . wouldn't keep. "I'm sorry, Ab. I know I promis—"

"Stop!" Her word was sharp, but her tone was soft, loving. "Brian, I know you love me, and I know you love our daughters, and I know—with all my heart I know—that what is most precious to you is getting home as soon as you can and getting our family back together again. Don't you ever doubt that I know your heart. But Brian, we'll be home and waiting for you when all of this is over. And it won't be over until you bring Tommy's killers to justice. You and I both know that. You have never backed down from a righteous fight in your life. I don't expect you to start now.

"Find Tommy's killers, Brian. Bring the wrath of God down upon their heads. Just, please, stay safe out there, okay?"

<hr>

Ambassador's Residence, Tel Aviv
July 23, 12:20 a.m.

It was well past Rabbi Mordechai Herzog's normal bedtime, but he didn't know when sleep would next be possible. His life had been a blur since Bayard came to visit him while he sat next to the dead body of his son. Bayard . . . the angel. His mind still struggled to grasp the reality of that unreal visitation.

But the angel had drawn him into the midst of this otherworldly conflict, and now he was caught up in its maelstrom. A metal box with a kabbalah warning on its lid and a sentence of excruciating death for the unanointed who touched it; earthquakes that ravaged only two buildings in the entire city of Tel Aviv; determined and desperate terrorists who threatened all their lives; ancient prophecies in elaborate codes with undecipherable symbols. His grieving for his son, Israel, was devastating to his heart, palpable and debilitating. But the grieving was shunted aside for now, as he was enticed into this mystery that was delivered into his hands and could change the future and threaten the lives of millions.

And now he labored under an urgent demand that he deliver a critical message to the United States ambassador to Israel. But who was he to tell this man what he must do? What authority did he have that . . . ?

"Thank you for coming to visit with us, Mordechai. Have you met Ruth Hughes?" Cleveland's tone was welcoming. Herzog's dread began to dissipate. He shook hands with the serious-looking woman in the business suit. "I believe you have something important to share with us, Rabbi? Would you like to wait until Agent Mullaney returns?"

Herzog shook his head and bucked up his courage. "No thank you, Mr. Ambassador. At length have I spoken already to Agent Mullaney. I do not wish to intrude too long on your time. Brian can fill you in with more details if necessary. But some perspective allow me to give.

"The first prophecy of the Vilna Gaon, revealed earlier this year, was a declaration, a herald that predicted Messiah would soon come upon this earth. The Gaon's second prophecy, which was decoded by my son and the Rabbinate Council, was a warning that the prince of this world, the evil one, and his demons were conspiring to prevent the coming of Messiah—or the second coming of Jesus, as Christians believe. The second prophecy read: 'When the times of the Gentiles is complete, when the sons of Amalek are invited to the king's banquet, beware of the Anadolian—he walks on water to offer peace, but carries judgment in his hands. His name is Man of Violence.'

"My belief it is, and I shared this with Agent Mullaney, that the time of the Gentiles' rule over Jerusalem has ended. Our prime minister, the leader of Israel, has broken bread with the sons of Amalek. Entered into a covenant, he did, with the same people that God ordered Moses to wipe off the face of the earth. Amalek is in the tent.

"And now," Herzog continued, "this Man of Violence, who carries judgment in his hands, upon the scene comes. At the same time Ishmael desires to divide the land of Israel, a state of Palestine to create. But the book of Joel the prophet warns that any who try to divide the land God gave Israel will be condemned and punished in the valley of judgment. We are in . . ."

Herzog hesitated as Mullaney came back into the room. "Explaining, I was, what we know about the Gaon's second message," said Herzog as Mullaney took a seat at the table. The rabbi turned back toward Cleveland. "This second message, like the first, is clearly a prophetic warning. Messiah is coming, as the Gaon's first prophecy revealed. And if the time of the Gentiles is complete, as I believe, then the second prophecy confirms the first. Not surprising, then, the ruler of this world has unleashed the full fury of evil to prevent Messiah's coming . . . or his return as others believe." Herzog turned his full attention upon Mullaney. "Only you, Brian, the last of the Gaon's heirs, stand in the way. Anointed and called, you are, to defeat the plans of the devil."

Mullaney's eyes were closed, his head swiveling back and forth in denial. "But why me?" he asked again. "And what role does Bayard play . . . what do the angels have to do with all of this?"

"Angels?" blurted Hughes. She sat up straight in her chair and swept her eyes around the table. "Are you kidding me? Are we really talking about angels? Real angels?"

Herzog reached out a hand in Hughes's direction, a grandfatherly grimace on his face. "I know . . . difficult it is to accept. But I have spoken to him. Agent Mullaney has spoken to him. And he, Bayard, has been protecting the words of the Gaon for over two hundred years. But that is not the important point. It is—"

"We've got angels, and it's not important?" said Hughes. "I . . . I'm stunned. Perplexed. Probably in way over my head here. But okay, let's just say for the moment that the angels are not important. What is?"

Herzog nodded. He reached into the pocket of his black jacket and withdrew a slip of paper, passing it across the table so Hughes could see it. "What is important are these last two lines of symbols from the Gaon's second prophecy."

"What are they?" Hughes looked around the table. "What do they mean?"

"We know not what they are nor what they mean," Herzog admitted. "And that is our quest." He turned toward Cleveland. "And that is my message to you . . . the message I was dispatched to give you, a message I heard in Bayard's own voice, a message he told me was an answer to your prayer. He said your prayer was heard and repeated in the throne room of God. You, Mr. Ambassador, must allow Agent Mullaney to fulfill his mission. And his first task, it is, to discover the meaning of those symbols. That is what Bayard said to Brian and me earlier tonight . . . that in order to understand the message we need to understand the box. In order to understand God's ultimate plan and purpose, in order to fulfill his part in God's plan, Agent Mullaney must decipher two things—the meaning of these unusual symbols and the meaning of the box of power. There is a monumental battle taking place right now between the forces of good and evil. Why, I know not, but Agent Mullaney's assignment is crucial to fulfilling God's plan. You, Ambassador, must release him from his duties so that he may pursue his destiny."

"I still don't understand," said Hughes. "Or maybe I just don't believe what I'm hearing. Brian is the key to the climactic battle between good and evil? Really?"

"None of us understand it, Ruth," said Cleveland. "Who could? Not fully. But of one thing I'm convinced: I may not fully understand what's happening around us, to us, but I do believe the rabbi just presented me with the answer to my earlier prayer. Now I know what I have to do. So I have one question for all of you."

Cleveland looked around the table. "How do we find out what those symbols mean?"

To his left Rabbi Herzog lifted his hand. "An idea I have." He turned to Mullaney. "You said you expected a visit from Colonel Levinson? Tonight . . . er . . . today?"

Mullaney glanced at his watch. "He should be here in the next thirty minutes or so. I'm heading over to my office to check on the status here and at the embassy. If you would like to speak to him, I'll let you know when he arrives."

"Excellent," nodded Herzog. "I can't promise I'll still be awake, but I'll try."

15

Ambassador's Residence, Tel Aviv
July 23, 12:50 a.m.

Looking up from the heart-rending casualty list—five dead, seventeen wounded—and the daunting, preliminary damage report on the residence, out of the corner of his eye Mullaney saw movement at his door. If he didn't know better, he would have sworn that legendary Israeli general Moshe Dyan had just stepped into his office. Wearing the informal and ubiquitous khaki garb of the Israeli military and security services, Meyer Levinson—director of operations of Shin Bet, Israel's relentless and effective internal security division—was lean, muscled, tense, and bursting with energy. Bald, coppered from the Israeli sun, a riding crop in his right hand, the only thing Levinson was missing was Dyan's signature eye patch.

"We've got to stop meeting like this," said Levinson, who leaned against the back of a straight chair in front of Mullaney's makeshift desk. He looked down at the papers in Mullaney's hands. "And we've got to find and crush these . . ." Levinson stopped himself with a sigh. "How many, Brian?"

"Three agents dead, plus two embassy staff," recited Mullaney, the words failing to encompass the enormity of their loss, "including the ambassador's secretary. Seventeen wounded or injured from the earthquake or the gunfight . . . three critical. Don't know if they'll make it."

Levinson was shaking his head. "Too many, Brian. Too many good men and women."

Mullaney had developed a close relationship with Levinson years earlier, when both were stationed in Washington and they discovered a shared passion for the Chelsea Football Club. Educated to be a scientist, a theoretical physicist, Levinson was recruited out of academia into Israel's security apparatus and built a stellar reputation rooting out terrorist cells and leading counterterrorism operations in the West Bank and the Gaza Strip. It wasn't long before he earned elevation to director of the operations division of Shin Bet, the most prestigious and active branch of the anti-terrorism service—the home of fighters and warfare groups that were a scourge to Israel's enemies. At the outbreak of the first intifada, the Palestinian uprising against Israeli occupation from 1987 to 1991, Levinson was handed a list of four hundred targeted terrorists. In two years, that number dropped to less than twenty. Fewer than half were in jail.

"I don't know why this gang of terrorists has brought this war to our doorsteps," seethed Levinson. "But I promise you this. They will pay for these attacks . . . blood for blood. It's gotten personal."

Mullaney looked long and hard at his old friend. He fully understood Levinson's fury . . . it mirrored his own. But they could not allow the desire for revenge to distract them from their first duty—protecting the people still under their care. "I have no doubt a day of reckoning is coming, Meyer. And it's getting closer. I need to bring you up to speed on a number of things."

Even though it was only four hours—but felt like four days—it was difficult to keep a summary short and to the point. Mullaney guided an incredulous Levinson through his encounter with Bayard, his acceptance of the anointing and the role of guardian, and a quick review of what they knew thus far about the second prophecy and the two lines of undeciphered symbols the Gaon included at the bottom of the message.

"Is Rabbi Herzog still here?" Levinson asked.

"The rabbi? I think he's down in the kitchen getting something to eat," said Mullaney. "Why the rabbi?"

"I've worked with the rabbi several times—and his son after him," said Levinson. "I've got an idea and I want to bounce it off him."

"Okay." Mullaney reached for the phone and put in a call to ask Herzog to come to his temporary . . . maybe longer than temporary . . . office.

"While we're waiting," said Levinson, "I've learned a few things about our enemies that might interest you." The colonel finally moved around to the front of the chair and sat down facing Mullaney. "This group calls itself the Disciples and, as we suspected, they are primarily Turkish nationals. We got some information out of the guys we captured at the Nitzanim Preserve, but not much. They wouldn't tell us anything about their structure, or who or where was their leader."

"I sure would like to cut off the head of this beast," mumbled Mullaney.

"Makes two of us," Levinson replied. "But it's a big beast. According to our guests at Shin Bet headquarters, the Disciples are a vast organization. They've got operatives around the globe. Primarily here in the Middle East, but one guy admitted the Disciples even have operatives in the US."

Mullaney sat back in his chair. "How many can there be? How many are left? We've killed or captured, what, a dozen? More if you include the body count in Jordan. How many more can there be here in Israel?"

From the long silence that followed, Mullaney knew he didn't want to know the answer.

"The one guy that would talk, I asked him that question," said Levinson. "He just looked in my face and smiled. Ran chills right down my spine. A big, bright smile. And he says, 'There is no end, no limit, to the power of the Disciples. We are endless. And we do not stop.' You know what, Brian? I believe him. This is evil incarnate that—"

There was a rustle of commotion at Mullaney's door. Standing there, looking a bit disheveled and very weary, was Rabbi Herzog, wagging his finger at a beefy, berated marine. "An old man, a matzo, and a cup of tea can't get by without being disturbed? The time, do you know what is?"

The marine pointed into the office. "Time for you to meet with Agent Mullaney, sir."

Startled, Rabbi Herzog turned and looked into the office. "Oh." He shot a glance back, over his shoulder, at the marine. "Told me, you could have." Then he swiveled his body and entered the office. "Hello, Colonel . . . you are just the man I was hoping to see."

***

Gocuk, Turkey
July 23, 1:02 a.m.

Bayard stood, wrapped tightly in a cloak, among others of his kind amidst the trees on a wind-swept hill nearly two kilometers from the warehouse complex to the east. But even at that distance, he could clearly see every movement around the buildings.

Below him, across a dry plain, men were moving in the stillness and shadows of the bleak night, a frigid north wind blowing down out of the far mountains. Several of the men were dressed entirely in black. To a normal, mortal man the images would be illusory, vague against the metal walls of the warehouse. But this angelic being watched each movement precisely as the men shuttled back and forth from the warehouse to three large trucks. The trucks were stenciled with the logo, name, and contact number for Mirwan's Produce, supplier of tomatoes, cucumbers, and hummus to the dining halls spread across the vast Incirlik Air Base, only fifty kilometers to the east.

Turkish National Police Colonel Fabir Matoush—shorter, rounder, giving out the orders—stood to the side. Commander of the Adana district surrounding Incirlik, Matoush was directing the other men as they hefted wooden crates out of the warehouse and deposited them into one of the waiting trucks. The crates contained weaponized chemical agents, a more effectively lethal form of Sarin gas. Enlisted by his cousin, Prime Minister Arslan Eroglu, Matoush and the elite assault team he handpicked from his command were to unleash the lethal gas at the airbase and steal away with truckloads of the B61 nuclear weapons stored at Incirlik.

A second man, also dressed all in black, came and stood beside Colonel Matoush.

"This is an accursed wind," he said.

Bayard, his cloak snapping in the wind, could hear each word clearly despite the distance.

"How can such a wind be blowing for these many days at this time of year? There is never wind in this season." He looked at his commander. "It is a bad omen."

Colonel Matoush slouched against the side of the warehouse and shrugged his shoulders. "We cannot control the weather."

"But it would be madness to release these weapons into the wind. None of us would escape. And our mission would be a failure."

The fat man in charge turned slowly to his left. "It is not ours to question," said Colonel Matoush. "We've been given our orders. They are clear. We get the canisters in place tonight and tomorrow night. And we release the gas from the canisters just after midnight on the twenty-fourth." Then he looked up at the sky. "Perhaps the wind will cease by then."

The other angelic beings standing on the hill looked in Bayard's direction. He pushed his left arm out from under the cloak, lifted his hand, and cupped it toward the north. "Come, north wind," called Bayard. And he swept his cupped hand down across the dry plain, pushing it out toward the complex of warehouses in the distance.

A steady, strong blast of icy wind roiled out of the snow-capped mountains hundreds of kilometers to the north, accelerated across the plain, and slammed into the warehouses, the vans, and the men in black.

Colonel Matoush stumbled against the wind, then was blown into the side of the warehouse. "Allah, the Merciful . . . curse this wind!" he screamed.

On the windswept hill, the being in the cloak smiled. He looked into the stars. "Praise you, Lord." Then, as a great, dark cloud formed in the north try-ing to block the wind, Bayard joined his brethren, cupped his left hand, and swept it once again over the plain. "Come, north wind."

16

Mullaney felt a cold wind strike his body as he sat behind his desk, and an image imprinted itself on his mind, blocking Levinson and Herzog from his consciousness. Bayard was standing on a hill, his left hand raised into the sky.

"Are you alright, Brian?"

Levinson's voice brought Mullaney back to Tel Aviv, back to the residence, back to this temporary office.

"You look as if across your path some evil walked," whispered Rabbi Herzog. "What did you see?"

Where he had been, what exactly he'd seen, Mullaney did not know.

"I was on a hill. There was a frigid wind blowing. Bayard was there fighting," Mullaney whispered, the vapors of the vision slowly clearing from his mind.

And he had heard Bayard's familiar voice. *"Do not fear, my son. He who is for you is greater than he who is against you. You have time . . . we will protect the innocents."*

Despite the apparent enormity of the conflict he had witnessed, Mullaney felt invigorated. *He* felt ready for battle. "We have time," he whispered.

Mullaney fully emerged to see Levinson and Herzog seated across the desk from him, Herzog nodding and smiling, but Levinson looking more than a little concerned.

"Brian," said Levinson, "you're starting to creep me out."

"Sorry, Meyer, it's been a long day." And he didn't have any other answer to give. He turned to Herzog. "Rabbi, what have you made of the two lines of symbols at the bottom of the Gaon's prophecy? They look similar in style and structure. Letters, or symbols, or ciphers of some kind of communication. Is there any clue in Hebrew text, or kabbalah, or an ancient Semitic language that the Gaon might have accessed?"

Herzog was shaking his head. "At a loss, I am. Nothing in my experience resembles such a thing as this."

Levinson caught Herzog's gaze and held it. A pregnant stillness, like the air before a storm, filled the room.

"I also was thinking of Poppy," said the rabbi. "Why to you I wanted to speak. Didn't you put him in jail?"

Laughter burst out of Levinson as he lifted his hands, palms up. "I've tried . . . several times. But Poppy is confounding. Lucky for him, we know there is no evil intent in Poppy, nothing malicious. He's just . . . curious. A cyber explorer. There are times when he pushes the limits of my patience and the law, but he always seems to have more to offer us than we can refuse. His skills have done more to protect our infrastructure than harm it, which he barters for my continued mercy. But yes, he's the one man I think who could help us."

Some unspoken communication was going back and forth from Herzog to Levinson, but at this time of night, working on very little sleep, Mullaney's patience was evaporating quickly. "Okay . . . so who is this Poppy, how do we find him, and how can we get him to help?"

Levinson turned to Mullaney. "Stephanakis Poppodopolous—hence, Poppy—is a Greek Orthodox monk assigned to St. Archangel Michael Monastery just north of here, along the coast. He's a remarkable scholar and theologian, student of ancient languages, and a gifted code-breaker with a prodigious memory. Unfortunately, Poppy is also an unrepentant and inveterate computer hacker. He's brilliant but indiscriminate. And a few of his escapades have almost earned him time in prison."

"What saved him?" asked Mullaney.

The sly smile of a conspirator creased Levinson's face. "Let's just say he *volunteered* to help Israeli Intelligence with a few very sensitive situations where we needed to break through encrypted firewalls without being noticed. And he still owes us, but I think the pursuit of these strange symbols would be a quest he would take up on its own merit."

"Good," snapped Mullaney. "Let's go . . ." He looked at the watch on his wrist. *Oh, is it really this late?*

"I don't suggest we rouse the monastery at one in the morning," said Levinson. "They are early risers. I'll call first thing in the morning and see if I can get you an appointment. I don't expect it will be difficult."

Noah Webster, rail thin and barely cresting five-six in height, paced back and forth in front of his office windows. The sun was well past its apex, but its heat was still pouring in through the windows, warming one side of Webster's moving body, then warming the other side as he turned and retraced his steps. His head down, his right hand in a fist pounding a rhythm on his thigh, Webster's unscrupulous mind was gathering facts and calculating angles on multiple levels at the same time—building, assessing, and discarding one possible plan after another.

Senator Markham was dead. Webster's voluminous, hidden records of shady political dealings still had the power to ruin a career. But did his threats diminish substantially with the former Senator's demise? Were all the years he spent as Markham's right hand and hatchet man now wasted time and effort? Power fled quickly in Washington. Perhaps all of the favors and promises Webster brokered in Markham's name were just as dead as the senator. There was likely no succor to be had from that quarter. No . . . it was likely that those debtors would now become his enemies. Out for revenge.

Secretary of State Townsend was already withering in his open and obvious contempt for Webster. Two years ago, Townsend was apoplectic when Markham made his final maneuver before retirement. Markham forced Webster's insertion into a senior and critical position at the State Department, deputy secretary of state for management and resources, which brought the Diplomatic Security Service under Webster's command. Even though his appointment was long-ago confirmed and deputy secretaries were not dispatched arbitrarily, Webster knew that if some of his illicit activities became public knowledge, they would surely get him fired, perhaps indicted. Webster could only deduce that his tenure at the State Department had a limited and shortening life span.

And now those ambitious but witless Turks—Kashani or Eroglu, or both—were apparently prepared to unleash a mad scheme that not only threatened NATO's security and unity, but—if successful—could also bring the Middle East to the brink of nuclear confrontation.

How could Cleveland discover this plot and Webster be totally blind to its existence? Had he grossly misread Arslan Eroglu? Was Eroglu, his coconspirator to bring down President Boylan's planned Iranian treaty, really duplicitous enough to withhold from Webster such a desperate and dangerous gambit? If true, did Webster possess enough influence that he could force Eroglu to abandon this perilous plan? And how exposed was Webster, the middle-man in a funnel of money from Rutherford to Eroglu?

Grappling with questions for which he had no answer, Noah Webster turned an about-face and paced back along the windows that looked out over Washington's power centers. He didn't see anything outside his tortured mind. No matter how he juggled the facts or twisted the possibilities, Webster was forced to acknowledge his tenuous grasp on the future for which he had sold his soul. A spear of dread pierced his heart as he imagined life in a jail cell instead of life in the senate. His risks were legion, and his dominion was dwindling. He was playing a hazardous end game that he no longer controlled.

Then there was Rutherford, the billionaire banker. Webster stubbornly held on to a dwindling hope that Rutherford would be compelled to fund his political aspirations. But how dangerous was Rutherford? Had Senator Markham become a liability and outlived his usefulness? Webster suspected that Rutherford could be responsible for Markham's untimely death. Did that mean the twin threats Webster held over Rutherford's head—loss of the Iranian funds now in Rutherford's banks and the ample evidence of illegal dealings between Rutherford and Markham that Webster kept hidden in secret vaults—would no longer effectively coerce the banker's compliance?

"I've waited so long," he mumbled as he paced, drumming his fists into his thighs. "I've worked so hard."

Thud.

He could feel the bruises in his bones. "I've risked so much."

Thud.

The throbbing pain in his legs finally stopped his strides but not the blood pounding through his arteries. "I will not fail!" An empty boast into an empty room.

Thud!

His breathing labored, he pondered his options. He was left with few.

Erase all evidence of his collusion with Arslan Eroglu . . . somehow stop the Turkish plot against Incirlik . . . and control Richard Rutherford. But his time was running out and his enemies were increasing. Everything he had dreamed of, longed for, sacrificed so much to attain . . . all of that was in jeopardy. Cut and run? No, he was long beyond retreat. Now was the time for courage, for bold action. To offset his growing risk with equally drastic action. Something that would stop the men who now threatened everything.

Webster pulled a burner phone from the lowest drawer in his desk and dialed a number that was becoming too familiar. It was only eight hours ago that he had ordered total surveillance on Richard Rutherford from this organization. He was becoming a regular customer of the man in the Panama hat—another point where he was vulnerable but left with few options. At least this man and his organization were top-flight professionals, specialists in black ops, who operated well under the radar of international law enforcement. Arslan Eroglu was now an even greater danger. He needed to act.

"You are impatient," said the voice. "We have no information on Rutherford yet. Our operatives have only just moved into position."

"The mission has changed," said Webster. "I want you to put Mullaney's daughters under surveillance as well. And I want them to know it. I want them to think their lives are threatened."

"You are asking us to increase our level of risk tenfold."

Webster waited for more, but the voice was silent. In that silence, Webster knew the dollar amounts were spinning higher and higher. "And I want Rutherford to know it. And I want Rutherford to know that his granddaughters' safety is in my hands."

"It can be done, for a . . ."

"And I want you to assassinate the prime minister of Turkey," Webster said calmly, as if he was ordering a hamburger. "And that needs to happen in the next twenty-four hours, if possible."

There was no objection from the voice on the phone. Only a pause.

"Do you have one million dollars?" asked the voice.

"Put Richard Rutherford's granddaughters at risk and I'll have two million dollars. If necessary, we'll use his own money against him. But you must act soon."

Tel Aviv
July 23, 1:58 a.m.

"This better be good," said Hughes. "I've lost more sleep in the last two days than I have in the last two years. Why are you keeping me awake?"

Hughes, the US embassy's political officer, was walking along the seafront promenade that extended down a long stretch of Tel Aviv's popular beach area. The night was heavy with moisture from the Mediterranean Sea, a vast, black expanse cloaked in darkness to her right. To her left was a problem.

Boris Vassilev was the cultural attaché at the Russian embassy to Israel. Over the last forty years of service to Mother Russia, Vassilev had filled many positions and carried many titles in far-flung capitals around the world. His duties, however, always remained the same. Spying for the KGB and, after the failed 1991 coup attempt against Gorbachev, its successor, the Foreign Intelligence Service (SVR).

Hughes had first run into Vassilev in 1988 while she was the corporate counsel and board member of Aramco, the former oil partnership between Saudi Arabia and the big three American energy companies—Exxon, Texaco, and Mobile—which the Saudis took over completely in 1980. She met Vassilev at a party thrown by the US embassy in Riyadh, when he carried the unlikely title of undersecretary for tourism at the Russian legation.

Vassilev's long tenure with KGB and SVR was testimony to the fact that he seldom made a mistake, either in how he conducted his espionage or in who he cultivated or blackmailed in the Politburo. Hughes was one of his mistakes. During a dinner meeting she arranged in 1990, Hughes plied Vassilev with a limitless flow of vintage champagne. At the end of the night, Vassilev clumsily tried to both seduce Hughes and recruit her into the service of the KGB. She got it all on a mini-recorder. And Vassilev became her eyes and ears on the wildly vacillating effectiveness and output of the Russian petro-chemical industry.

When Hughes was invited to join the US State Department, she kept Vassilev in her back pocket . . . just in case . . . an asset she had exercised only a few times over the last two decades.

But this was trouble. This time Vassilev called Hughes and nearly demanded to speak with her at once. So here they were, both in their mid-sixties, walking down the promenade as if they were lovers on a late-night date. But Hughes did not like what she was hearing.

"The labyrinthine depth of Turkish politics and power are unexplorable from the outside," Vassilev assured Hughes, "but we are confident of a few things. First, Turkey is double-dealing with both Iraq and Israel. Prime Minister Eroglu has offered the same carrot to both nations—unlimited fresh water. With ISIS carving up his country and his illegitimate coup still a bit shaky, Al-Qahtani jumped at the offer, even though it cost him land to form an independent Kurdistan.

"But the Turks are going to betray Al-Qahtani and his Iranian backers," said Vassilev. They came to a bench overlooking the sea. "Come, let's sit for a moment."

"The Turks are finally going to get in bed with Israel?" said Hughes. "That's logical, but it was a long time coming."

"Yes . . . once the idea of a Kurdish nation takes root in the United Nations, Turkey will scrap its promises to Iraq and enter into a water-for-natural gas treaty with Israel. You know the pipelines were started years ago and the project only lapsed over that Marmora incident." Vassilev turned to look at Hughes. "Our source has read the language in the proposed treaty. Very interesting. In addition to the water-for-gas treaty, Eroglu inserted a clause allowing a Turkish consortium to build an upscale mall on the Mount of Olives. Strange that. And as far as we can discern, the Israelis have not yet expunged that clause. It remains in the treaty."

Hughes's mind was exploring all the nooks and crannies of this new treaty idea. "Eroglu's been a busy boy," she said. "What does our closet jihadist, Kashani, think about playing nice with Israel?"

Vassilev held Hughes's gaze for a long minute. "Funny you should mention that. It appears that Eroglu is pulling many of the strings of the Turkish government these days and not President Kashani. We've known Kashani was pliable, but it seems he's given his prime minister a nearly free hand in some matters. Our source tells us Eroglu is flexing that hand and growing in power."

For many disparate reasons, Hughes was getting uncomfortable—and nervous. Had Turkey suddenly become an adversary and not an ally? And Vassilev was winning hands and gathering chips with all this critical information. He would want something in return.

Vassilev stirred on the bench and started to get more animated.

"I'm sure your CIA and its excellent network got wind of the incursion onto Pakistani sovereign soil?" he asked. "Somebody covertly melted a bunch of nuclear weapons that were bound for the Saudis. Very clever. We thought you did it. You may have thought we did it. We were both wrong. It was the Turks. Eroglu dispatched a corps of Turkish commandos to take out the nuclear weapons before they could ship."

This was not good.

"Yes," Hughes conceded. "We knew about that action."

"Hmmm," Vassilev purred. He was enjoying his moment. "But what you might not know, my dear, is that it is Eroglu's hand that is on the plot to steal your B61 nuclear bombs from the Incirlik Air Base. An attack that is planned for just after midnight on the twenty-fourth . . . less than twenty-four hours from now. An attack that has already been delayed once by a fortuitous windstorm, which is still blowing."

Vassilev allowed the information to drift on the damp, sea breeze. His smile could have greased a pig.

"What do you want?"

Triumph entered his eyes. "Why, I want you, my dear. In my back pocket. Finally, you owe me. And believe me . . . I will collect."

17

"Do you want me to squash that termite?"

Ruth Hughes, arms akimbo, had her clenched fists pressed against her hips. For the alpha dog in Hughes, the next step was to eviscerate the assistant secretary of state and throw his entrails to a pack of coyotes. From the firm set of her chin, her pressed lips, and the scowl of determination that filled her face, Mullaney had no doubt in his mind that she could pull it off.

Three of the "Gang of Four"—Cleveland, Mullaney and Hughes—sat in the ambassador's temporary office. Cleveland had just conveyed to Hughes the essence of Noah Webster's latest and most virulent threat as they tried to figure out their next move . . . especially if Webster had effectively cut off their communication with the secretary of state.

"No, Ruth . . . we'll leave that particular problem for another day," said Cleveland. They sat in the corner of the smaller, more cramped office, three hard, uncomfortable chairs around a small round table. "We don't need to fight a battle in Washington. We need to find allies to fight a battle on the ground in Turkey."

After Ruth's meeting with Boris Vassilev, they now had confirmation that a plot to seize the nuclear weapons at the NATO Incirlik Air Base in eastern Turkey was ready to be implemented. Vassilev even told them when the attack was expected to be launched. But where could they go for help?

With each passing minute, Mullaney's frustration and anger increased. "Even if we managed to bypass Webster and reach Secretary Townsend," he said, "would the word of a KGB spy carry any more weight than the Emir of Qatar? Would Townsend feel confident enough to take these allegations to the president?"

"I doubt it," said Hughes. "Townsend still sees this plot as a rumor. And for him, this rumor is incendiary. If true, it would rip the guts out of the eastern flank of NATO and turn the entire Middle East into a nuclear time bomb. Townsend will demand rock-solid confirmation before he sticks his neck out for this one, probably firsthand corroboration, not hearsay.

"So who are we going to call . . . the French?" snarled Hughes. "They have two non-combatant observers at Incirlik. The Italians? The Spanish? The—"

"The good guys," interrupted Cleveland. "The best good guys. I have a close friend who commands one of the special operations task forces for JSOC."

"Impressive," said Hughes. "I knew you had a lot of connections, Atticus, but to have some pull with the most elite and the most invisible special ops corps in the US military arsenal goes beyond my expectations. But you're right . . . this is what we need. A force that is highly trained, deadly efficient, seldom seen, prepared to strike any time, nearly anywhere in the world."

"Those are the guys you told me about," said Mullaney, "who are ready to move into Pakistan and secure all of its nuclear weapons if the military government were ever overthrown by jihadist radicals. That would be a good bunch to have on our side. And they're close?"

Cleveland was nodding his head but a grimace filled his face. "Yes, they're close. But I don't know if they are available—at least not to us. Let me make a call."

———◦∞◦———

Cleveland was nervously fiddling with a pencil as the speakerphone in the console on his borrowed desk rang for the fifth time. He looked at his watch and cringed at the hour. Was he making a mistake calling Ernie Edwards? Was it a mistake to allow Mullaney and Hughes to be part of this conversation? But an idea had blossomed in his mind, and now Cleveland was mentally sketching the outlines of a high-risk plan that he was growing to believe was his only viable option.

Was he ready to gamble so much—wager his past and his future? Was this the only way?

Would Ernie be willing to take such a risk? He knew the man. How well did he know the soldier?

Colonel Earnest Edwards, United States Army, patiently endured his early school years in Arkansas and the nearly constant harassment he got about his name. But he was the fifth in a long line of Earnest Edwards, all four of his previous namesakes having attained a minimum rank of Brigadier General in the army. The name and the service were a deeply ingrained tradition. Edwards wore his name like a battle ribbon. He *was* earnest . . . and more. He was as tough as cheap steak and as dependable as the sunrise. Colonel Edwards was also a brilliant tactician in the world of clandestine intervention.

After leading the army's Tenth Special Operations Group to stunning successes in Iraq, Colonel Edwards was given a new command within JSOC, the Joint Special Operations Command. JSOC formed the Defense Department's sharpened point of attack against terrorists, hostage-takers—America's most deadly enemies around the world. Tasked with forming one of JSOC's Advance Force Operations teams, Edwards handpicked an elite group of comingled Special Forces units from across the US military spectrum and, through his devotion to operational training and penchant for perfection, forged perhaps the most effective and lethal special ops group in the military. Comprised of battle-tested members of Delta Force, SEAL Team Six, and Ranger Recon, Task Force Black could strike quickly and quietly—and with overpowering force—at any point in the world, although primarily tasked with the Middle East, Southern Europe, or Northern Africa.

Task Force Black was an entire integrated military operation, transported as a package. Not just a bunch of guys with guns, but an elite strike force with the communications, intelligence, and ordinance necessary to fix a problem.

Task Force Black was a ruthless and lethal bludgeon against America's enemies. And Colonel Edwards was the man who brought the hammer down.

The call was answered on the seventh ring. "Atticus, for you to call at this ungodly hour," said Edwards, his voice gathering in clarity and alertness with each word he spoke, "I'm figurin' that you got more trouble than a raccoon sparin' with a pack of pit bulls."

"How's your daughter, Ernie?" Cleveland's question was genuine, but also had a purpose.

"Why, thank you for askin', Atticus," said Edwards, his back-hills Arkansas twang slathering biscuit gravy over every word as he woke to the conversation. "She told me the other day she's as happy as if Brad Pitt showed up on her doorstep with a Publisher's Clearin' House check. Gettin' used to that swamp pit in Washington takes some mighty heavy liftin' after so many years in hippy-dippy San Diego. But she's burstin' proud over that job you wrangled for her in the State Department. I'll never be able to thank you enough, and neither will Maisie."

"Tell your wife that it was my pleasure to help," said Cleveland. "And right now, to be honest, I'm counting on your thanks, Ernie. I need *your* help."

Without hesitation, Edwards responded, "Anythin' less than ignitin' World War III, and you've got my help in a heartbeat. But you've got me on speaker. Who's listenin'?"

"My regional security officer, Brian Mullaney, and the embassy's political officer, Ruth Hughes."

"Ruth, you old war horse. You still got all those desert jockeys in the palm of your hand?"

"Hello, Ernie . . . it's good to hear your voice again," said Hughes, leaning toward the desk. "Send Maisie my love, will you? And tell her I still want her pound cake recipe."

"You got it, darlin'. And Agent Mullaney, I've heard good things about you, lad. Cream always rises, son. Always rises. Now Atticus, what's all the fuss?"

Cleveland took a deep breath. He knew he was getting ready to dive into something that could cost him his career and his reputation. But the stakes were high and getting higher with every breath.

"I need you to gather a strike team from Task Force Black, at the earliest possible moment—as many men as you can muster—and get them to eastern Turkey without drawing notice to themselves."

"Why, I can do that without breakin' a sweat, Atticus," said Colonel Edwards, "within moments after we get off this call. The majority of our assets are operatin' in western Syria. But I've got a cracker-jack team that's just comin' off three days leave. We were tasked with a hostage extraction from ISIS in Iraq. We got there and the place was empty. So my guys are itchin' for action. I could have them boots-on-the-ground in Turkey before the sun comes up, if those were my orders. My first questions are where and why?"

"We have highly credible evidence that a faction of the Turkish military— possibly rogue, possibly directed—is poised for an attack on Incirlik," said Cleveland. "They intend to eliminate the NATO forces guarding our stockpile of nuclear weapons and make off with as many of the B61 bombs as possible."

A low whistle came from the other end of the transmission. "My aunt Martha's bloomers . . . okay, I know it isn't possible, but let's forget for a moment just how stupid that would be," said Edwards. "I fully get the jihadist mindset. They don't care about anythin' except forcin' the ultimate battle. So nothin' they dream up surprises me, stupid or not. But my third question is the most important. Why in heaven's name am I hearin' about this from you—a nice guy, but a civilian—and not from my superior officer, General Claiborne, or the secretary of defense? I can't blow my nose without orders—you darn well know that, Atticus."

"I understand, Ernie, and I'll get you those orders," said Cleveland. "But there are hundreds of American service men and women on that base, couple thousand wives, husbands, and kids. We believe this plot is already moving forward. So all I'm asking on my authority is that you assemble your men and get them prepared to move, and I'll work on getting you those orders."

The pause in Edwards's response spoke volumes to Cleveland. "This is highly unusual, Atticus. You're askin' me to stick my neck out pretty far on your say-so. That's a pretty tenuous plank I'm walkin'. What else can you tell me?"

"It's a long story, Ernie. But I need you to trust me and I need you to get your force together and be prepared to move. Where are you?" Cleveland asked.

"I was in bed, in a pretty swanky officer's billet at the RAF Akrotiri airbase in Cyprus. The Brits have generously loaned us a corner of their base. It gives us and NATO a fairly secret place to use as a stagin' area in the Mediterranean. I've got another officer with me . . . meetings, you know . . . but our main force is on the Turkey-Syria border."

"Okay, I'll be back to you as soon as I can," said Cleveland.

"Not before daybreak, I hope. I'm goin' back to bed. So should you. But don't worry. I can get the wheels movin', and I'm fine with doin' that," said Edwards. "And I understand that American lives are at risk if your information is correct. And I trust you, Atticus. But I can't, and won't, deploy American forces on foreign soil without orders from someone under who's authority I serve. I'm too old an army brat to ignore chain of command. You know that. Get me actionable orders, and I'm at your service."

Cleveland knew he couldn't ask for more. "Thank you, Ernie. Let me get working on those orders."

———⟶∞⟵———

The tension in the room was thicker than Ernie Edwards's homespun drawl. Mullaney had seen Cleveland at work before, a confident man willing to take risks. But this? This could . . .

"This could end your career if it ever got out," said Hughes, a reverence weighing on the solemnity of her words. "Webster would flay the skin off your back if he got his hands on it. Thank you for trusting us so much."

But Cleveland didn't look like a man who was walking in fear. Shoulders back, head up, eyes alive. Mullaney's admiration for the man only increased. But so did his concern. Cleveland was walking a tightrope over alligator alley. One slip . . .

"We can't go through Webster," said Cleveland, "so we've got to look for another way. It's worth a little risk when there are thousands of lives in danger. And it looks to me like we may be the only ones with a chance to stop this madness. I'm ready to do whatever it takes. Are you?"

Mullaney felt the full weight of Cleveland's character.

But he also felt the full weight of his responsibility.

"Sir . . . with all due respect." Mullaney tried to carefully pick his words. "We have bodies here to bury and wounds to bind. We have damaged and vulnerable buildings to repair and a gang of murderous thugs who are a threat to every American life associated with the US mission to Israel. We have a president who is demanding you do everything in your power to get the Ishmael Covenant ratified and a two-state solution a reality. You have a daughter who's been kidnapped and brutalized and has only you to rely on. And you have a body that has been shot at and bashed around in a car flipping end over end. And you—we—have the box."

Mullaney saw that his words were landing—with force. Good.

"Mr. Ambassador, I'll trust you with my life and I trust you with the best interests both of our country and all those who serve her. But sir, before we all suit up with Team Black for an assault on Incirlik—and I'm not opposed to the idea—before we take any further steps in that direction, can we take a deep breath here? What is your most important responsibility? And are we truly the only option?"

Cleveland's eyes were closed, his head nodding in agreement. "You're right, of course," he said. "And I thank you for having the courage to challenge me on this." Then his eyes opened. And they were full of fire. "But Brian, I will tell you this. I swore an oath to serve and protect . . . the same oath you swore. As hammered and harassed as we are here in Israel, as broken as our buildings are, we have a viable and effective security apparatus in place to keep our people and our property as safe as possible. And we have Colonel Levinson and his tenacious soldiers of Shin Bet watching our backs. But who is going to protect the thousands of innocents on and around that air base? We have the knowledge. We believe we know what's coming. Not to act is criminal. Can you live with that? I think not, Brian. I know your heart. And neither could I. So we will do everything we possibly can to thwart this plot."

"Sir?" Ruth Hughes was animated. Her body was rocking back and forth in her chair like an overwound clock. "How are you going to get orders for General Edwards? Secretary Townsend told you to leave it alone. Webster will have you on the first plane to DC if you try to reach the secretary again. You're committing career suicide here, Atticus."

Cleveland leaned back in his chair and stretched his neck. He ran his hands over the shining skin of his bald head.

"Perhaps," he admitted. "But there's got to be a way I can get Ernie to put his men into action." Cleveland appeared to be exploring the ends of his fingers for inspiration. But then he stretched, rotated his shoulders, and let out a vast sigh. "Look, I don't know about you, but I've got to get a couple of hours of sleep. Thanks to Ruth, we know the attack isn't planned for another twenty-four hours—longer if that windstorm continues. I've got to figure out a way to get Ernie his orders, but I feel like my mind is covered in moth balls. Let's take a break for a few hours and come back at this thing in the morning. Maybe we'll see better when we're more clear headed. By the way, Brian, how's the cottage?"

"Amazing . . . a miracle," Mullaney responded. "The lawn on both sides was cleaved like fresh meat, but the building itself came through unscathed. Only now it's become a barracks. I've got three other agents camped out in the living room. But I've got a bed. And I'm going to go find it right now."

Just emptying the pockets of his suit jacket felt like he was power lifting a couple hundred pounds. Mullaney wearily tossed his iPhone on the bureau in his bedroom. Jostled, the screen lit up and he noticed a surprising text message. It was Rutherford.

"Heard about ur troubles. Abby, girls r ok; worried, but won't tell you. Call me. Need to speak. Important. Richard."

Rutherford? Talking to his father-in-law was the last thing he needed at two-thirty in the morning. He was exhausted, in spirit, soul, mind, and body.

But this was very unlike Richard. Mullaney had been married to Abby for nearly twenty years, and this was maybe the third time Rutherford had ever reached out to him. And each of those times it had been bad news. Reluctantly, but with growing apprehension, he tapped contacts, pushed the big RR that could only stand for Richard Rutherford, and put his phone on speaker.

His father-in-law picked up in the middle of the first ring.

"My apologies, Brian . . . it's awfully late over there, and I'm awfully sorry to have roused you at . . ."

"I was up, Richard. Are Abby and the girls okay?"

"They're just fine, Brian. I reached out to you of my urgency, not theirs. At least, not directly."

"What does that mean?"

There was a pause on the other end of the connection, as if Rutherford was taking a deep breath. "My granddaughters want their father home. I know there have been times when I've been a barb in your britches, Brian, but I truly want to help. I can get you home. With honor, and without your career at the State Department taking a hit. But I can get you home . . . quickly."

Now it was Mullaney's turn to take a deep breath. He was so tired his mind was shutting down. He shook his head to clear the cobwebs.

Richard Rutherford was a lot of things, but he loved his daughter and doted on his grandchildren. If Kylie and Samantha were pouring out their hearts to grandpa, it was not surprising that Rutherford was looking for some strings he could pull to answer their prayers. Rutherford liked playing God. *Be fair. Give him grace.*

"Thank you, Richard, I truly appreciate your willingness to help," said Mullaney, searching for a response that would not offend. "And I would like nothing more than to wrap my arms around my girls and hold them close . . . all of my girls."

"But—" Rutherford interjected.

"Yeah . . . but . . . if you know about the problems we've had here, particularly in Tel Aviv, then I think you'll understand why this is not the right time for me to leave."

"Brian, you have always fulfilled your duty to the utmost," Rutherford responded. "And you have been exemplary in your duty in Israel as well. From unimpeachable sources, I understand you've put your life on the line several times in the last few days alone. Protected the ambassador's life with your own, rescued his daughter, been in more gun battles than Wyatt Earp. There is no shame in coming home now."

Mullaney sat down on the side of his bed. He fought the luring temptation to lie back on the soft mattress. *Stay awake. Stay alert!* How could he explain? He was desperate to be home. Where a week ago his marriage was in tatters, the future of his family on life support, now there was more than a spark rekindled between him and Abby. She heard his heart and he felt hers. The emotional barricades that separated them had been broached and banished, never, he believed, to return. His life had been resurrected. Hope restored. His prayers exalted in praise to God.

But . . .

Tommy was still dead. Murdered by these so-called Disciples in an alley in Amman, Jordan. Thirteen Americans had lost their lives—nine DSS agents, two embassy staff, and two marines—plus five of their civilian security team, either killed in gun battles or victims of the earthquakes that targeted the embassy and the ambassador's residence. Another two-dozen people were wounded. And the killers were still at large.

"Brian? Brian?"

Rutherford's voice snapped Mullaney out of a fog. And he realized he had fallen asleep. Sitting up, on the telephone, he had simply shut down.

"I'm here, Richard. Look, I need to get some rest. I'm ready to crash."

"I understand, Brian. But what shall I tell the girls?"

What, indeed. Perhaps the most pressing reason Mullaney couldn't consider going home was something he couldn't even share with Rutherford. It was the box and his new role as guardian. The *final* guardian he was told. And there was the warrior angel, Bayard, who had enlisted and anointed Mullaney into this quest, this calling. There were so many debts waiting to be repaid. And a supernatural assignment waiting to be fulfilled.

And now this crisis in Turkey . . .

Too much. Too much to turn his back on. But how much could he share with Rutherford? How could he justify declining a gift he desired so desperately, in a way that would not insult or infuriate his father-in-law? Richard Rutherford understood the perils of international brinksmanship. Angels he might not understand.

"Richard, there's a part of me that is desperate to get back to Abby and the girls, I won't deny that," said Mullaney. "But right now, I can't entertain that thought. I doubt even you know the full extent of what we're facing over here. I—"

"You're being hunted by a relentless gang of Turkish murderers, for one thing," Rutherford interrupted. "And then there's the oddly localized earthquakes that heavily damaged the embassy and Cleveland's residence. But you make it sound like there is something else, even more formidable, that you're facing. Something that must be pretty closely held, if none of my contacts have heard about it."

Mullaney was fighting to keep his eyes open. Fighting to think through the mush that was his brain. *Yeah . . . something formidable. Formidable enough that Cleveland had to go off the reservation and call in JSOC. Something . . .*

"What was that?" Rutherford's voice snapped Mullaney back to consciousness. "What did you say about Cleveland and JSOC?"

A rush of adrenaline flushed through Mullaney's body, and he was instantly alert, awake . . . and alarmed. What had he said? Wasn't he just thinking? Were those words also on his lips?

"What's Cleveland up to?"

Mentally scrambling, Mullaney was frantic to shut the door he'd just opened. "Look, I told you I was exhausted, Richard. I can't keep my eyes open or my thoughts straight. I must have drifted off to sleep again. I don't know what I was mumbling. Shoot, I don't know if I'm waking or dreaming. So just take no—no thanks—for an answer, okay? We can talk about the reasons another time, okay? Give Abby and the girls my love. Good night, Richard."

His heart beating like a Fourth of July fireworks finale, Mullaney reached over to the top of the bureau and tapped the red disconnect button on his iPhone.

What had he done? Had he revealed the situation in Turkey . . . the mission that Cleveland was cooking up with the JSOC team?

Dread flooded every cell of Mullaney's being. A grimace twisted his face in anguish as he clapped his hands on both sides of his head, trying to deny what he knew was true. He had betrayed Cleveland's confidence, broken his promises. And to Rutherford? *Oh . . . God, help me!*

Mullaney fell back onto his bed. But this time sleep eluded him.

18

The Golden Buddha Chinese restaurant was only five blocks away from the Truman Building, but it existed in a much less rarified atmosphere. On the border of George Washington University, the Buddha was primarily a cheap, take-out joint with paper menus. Its food was common and uninspiring, all of it infused with the overwhelming smell of frying oil. Even the air felt greasy. But it did have a corner booth in the back, dimly lit, alongside the always busy kitchen.

Richard Rutherford had used the back booth before. A stone's throw from the White House, a brisk twenty-minute walk from the action on Capitol Hill, the Golden Buddha was obscure enough to generally be safe for a meeting that needed to be kept quiet.

Rutherford, seated deep in the booth, wasn't wearing the imported suit of a billionaire banker. This evening he wore beat-up jeans, a burgundy L.L.Bean chamois shirt, and a Hoyas baseball cap pulled low over his eyes. He looked like a tired worker at the end of a long day, picking at his steamed dumplings with little interest.

On the inside, though, his anxiety level was just short of boil. Earlier that morning, Noah Webster had left Rutherford in shock. The deputy secretary of state was long a supplicant at Rutherford's altar of wealth. But today he failed to crumble under Rutherford's browbeating demands for action and results in their efforts to scuttle President Boylan's nuclear deal with Iran. Instead, Webster launched his own preemptive attack, threatening to reveal not only the damning details of Rutherford's decades-long collusion with former, now deceased, Senator Seneca Markham, but also rebuffing Rutherford's request to bring his son-in-law home from Israel.

The servant was trying to supplant the master. A southern gentleman, born deep in Georgia, Rutherford's ancestors had bequeathed him a heritage of master over servant. Even though Webster's hidden records could result in Rutherford's conviction on a myriad of charges, the banker's DNA—and his naturally pugilistic personality—was not inclined to yield to blackmail.

It was time to start hitting back.

Rutherford watched Nora Carson bypass the busy take-out counter on her way back to the booth. If there was one person in this world who knew where Noah Webster hid his secrets, it would be Carson. With red hair that fell to her shoulders in a cascade of curls and a trim, athletic figure, Carson was stunning. She was also ruthlessly ambitious and had sold her soul to Webster as soon as he joined the State Department. Rutherford was banking that Carson was now regretting that transaction.

Carson stopped at the edge of the table without sitting in the booth.

"Why am I here?"

"It's a pleasure to see you too, Ms. Carson."

"I don't need platitudes, Mr. Rutherford. I need to know why it was so important that I meet you here"—she swept her hand toward the kitchen—"tonight. What do you want?"

A ripple of resentment coursed through Rutherford's body at Carson's rudeness. But he needed to hold it in check. Rutherford leaned into the table, forcing his gaze upon Carson.

"I want to help you, Nora," he said. "I'm concerned about Noah. He's seemed unusually stressed lately. And with Senator Markham's sudden death, well . . . any indiscretion on Noah's part could place each of us in a very vulnerable position. I want to help. Please"—he pointed to the seat in the booth—"join me."

Rutherford could see the distrust in her eyes, the hesitation in her manner. *I don't blame her*, he thought. *I wouldn't trust me either.*

Carson slid into the booth as if she was having dinner with a python. She sat as far away from Rutherford as possible. And she knew two things: Rutherford was right about Webster coming unglued, and she was now at great risk and needed help and protection. What she didn't know was whether her risk was greater with Rutherford or without him.

"Forgive me for getting straight to the point," said Rutherford. "Noah has all of the records of my dealings with Senator Markham, including those that skirted several federal laws. You already know that, I'm sure. But now he's threatened to leak all of those records to the press unless I commit twenty million dollars to his dream of political campaigns."

"He thinks that blackmailing you will get him to the Senate?" A resigned laugh, lacking mirth, slipped from Carson's lips. "If he tries to burn you, doesn't he realize he'll get caught up in the flames too? He implicates you, he implicates himself."

The smile that creased Richard Rutherford's face froze Nora Carson's heart. It was knowing and malevolent, and it made her skin crawl.

"Do you really think Noah Webster doesn't have an escape plan?" Rutherford shook his head. "Think about it. That's why he has you, Nora, so conveniently close to everything he's done. Who is the perfect fall-guy if the heat on Webster gets too severe? Why you, Nora—the trusted subordinate who committed all these crimes without his knowledge. Now with Seneca Markham dead, Webster can also plead that he was kept in the dark by the senator . . . that he was simply a loyal but innocent pawn in these nefarious dealings I had with the senator."

Carson fought to maintain a tough exterior, but she knew Rutherford was right. "He won't get away with it."

"No, he won't," Rutherford agreed, "not in the long run. Noah's wallowed in too much dirt. Some of it's going to stick to him. And once the cover is off, who knows what an investigation will find. But you and I will already be behind bars, watching Noah's demise from a distance. Personally, I don't want to spend the rest of my life in jail. And I think a beautiful woman like you might not enjoy ten-to-twenty in a women's prison."

The world started closing in on Nora Carson. Originally she had thought George Morningstar was fishing around on his own. But perhaps it was just the opening skirmish in a battle that could consume her hope and turn her future into a train wreck.

Looking down at the table, Carson's voice was soft, the eyes of her mind on the picture of her future that Rutherford had just painted. "George Morningstar stopped in to see me recently. He was asking questions about Noah. And he was not subtle. He wanted me to know that he was looking." Carson looked up just in time to see a flash of alarm cross Rutherford's face.

"Morningstar? I thought he was banished," breathed Rutherford. "Why would he—"

"Townsend," said Carson. "It can only be Townsend. Morningstar was always close to the secretary of state, and his portfolio included internal investigations of the department before he was kicked into the basement by Webster. Yesterday I called Morningstar and asked him to meet me in Virginia. I wanted to find out what he knew . . . and what he wanted. Morningstar never showed up. That was the morning he died."

———◦◦◦◦———

Only the banging of metal pots broke the silence. Rutherford was running the probability calculations through his mind. Morningstar was investigating Webster? And now Morningstar was dead. What else was happening that he didn't know? He felt like shadows were closing in on him, but shadows with weight and substance. He could feel their pressing persistence. And an urgent conviction that Webster's secret records needed to be destroyed.

Rutherford was not a reluctant gambler. He went all-in.

"There's a way we can help each other, Nora," he said, leaning into the table to cut down the distance between them. "I'm sure you know where Noah keeps his secrets."

Carson was good. She didn't flinch. But for just a fraction of a second she dropped her gaze to the table. *She knows!*

———◦◦◦◦———

She wasn't surprised when Rutherford revealed his true motives, but the realization was jarring nonetheless. *I knew I couldn't trust him. All he cares about is saving himself. He's just as much the devil as Noah Webster . . . and almost as unhinged.*

Nora Carson knew her options were dwindling fast. But there was no safe harbor here. She pushed herself out of the booth and stood alongside the table, staring down at one of the richest, most powerful men in the nation.

"You're right, Richard," said Carson, her boldness growing alongside her desperation, "there is a way we can help each other. You just haven't come up with it yet. When . . . if . . . you come up with a plan that will protect us—*both of us*—from Webster's wrath, call me. You have the number." She started to walk away but stopped and looked over her shoulder at Rutherford. "And good luck trying to find out where Noah keeps his secrets hidden. They are legion. And only Noah knows them all."

Rutherford watched Carson maneuver her way to the front door, the human part of him admiring the way her smartly cut suit accented all of her best parts, the survivor in him calculating how much collateral damage would be required to guarantee his freedom. Carson had confirmed for him one critical fact: Webster had several harbors for his secrets. It would be nearly impossible to find and destroy them all. If Richard Rutherford could not erase Webster's secrets, it was time to erase Webster.

Before he left the booth in the darkened bowels of the Golden Buddha, Rutherford pulled out a disposable mobile phone and made two calls. The first was to a number in Miami. The man who answered was told to put the plan in motion. That was all. Richard Rutherford was about to disappear. And he was confident he would never be found, nor would his money ever run out.

The second call was local. It was time to tie up all these messy loose ends. Rutherford recited the number of a secret Swiss bank account. Then he spoke two names: Noah Webster and Nora Carson. Silence those two and cover his tracks. He would miss his daughter, his granddaughters. But he would miss a lot more if he spent the rest of his life inside a jail cell. Perhaps if the prosecutors failed to make the connections, maybe someday he could reappear.

Rutherford swiftly dismantled the phone. He would randomly deposit pieces of it in public trash cans over an eight-city-block loop. As he started to get up from the booth, his eyes fell on the barely touched plate of now-cold steamed dumplings and he realized how hungry he had become. He stabbed two with his fork, pushed them into his mouth, and walked out of the restaurant with every intention to vanish from the face of the earth.

Walking briskly back to her car, Nora Carson started plotting her escape. Webster had a screw loose and was going over the edge. Now Rutherford seemed to be almost as rattled as Webster.

She turned the corner at F Street and Twentieth Street—a container of pepper spray in her right hand, just in case—walked past the nearly full, sidewalk café tables of a Starbucks, and headed for the parking garage where she had left her car.

Carson was always fully aware of her knife-blade existence, walking a very thin, sharp, and dangerous course that could leave her career and her life bloodied, damaged, and discarded.

Carson walked past Rawlins Park, then turned left on E Street to the parking garage. The attendant was not in the closet-sized office. She looked around, but neither saw nor heard anyone. She walked up the ramp toward her car.

For the last two years, with Webster as her cover, pursuing the ultimate goal was worth the risk—a Cayman Islands account that could soon afford to buy its own island. Not now. Now was the time to run. Get to the Caymans, grab the money, and disappear. The only question was how quickly . . .

"Good evening, Nora."

She spun to her left, toward the voice that came from the shadow under the down ramp, her right arm outstretched.

"Please don't use that spray." A shape moved within the shadow and stepped into the half-light. It was the man with the Panama hat. "I have a gift for you."

It had been years since she last spoke with this man, that time as Webster's messenger. A shiver shuddered across her back, and warning signals rattled her already frayed nerves. People simply disappeared at this man's bidding. She kept her arm extended, her index finger on the spray button. "What can you have that I would want?"

The man held up a letter-sized envelope. "Your get-out-of-jail-free card."

Carson's breath caught in her throat. This man could . . .

"We've been doing business with your boss once again," he said, his voice as quiet as the shadows were still. "You know we are discreet and effective in delicate circumstances where others might be . . . morally challenged, shall we say?"

Her arm was getting sore. But she didn't dare lower it. "You and your people are deadly efficient. I'll give you that."

"Yes . . . but even we have our limits," said the man. He lifted the envelope once again. "Webster is desperate. Desperate men make mistakes. Our connection to him could leave us exposed. This," he said, tweaking the envelope, "is everything you need to put Noah Webster in a federal prison and leave a trail that will lead neither to you nor to us. And then you can take the money in the Caymans and buy yourself a life."

Carson was momentarily caught off guard by the man's information. Her hand wavered.

"Why? Why now? Why me?"

She could only see the bottom half of the man's face, the rest obscured in the darkness under the brim of his Panama hat. But she could see his mouth tense in a grimace.

"Well, for one thing, I have daughters, Nora," he said, a slight back-and-forth shaking in his chin. "We draw the line at children."

Carson was surprised, both at the confession and by the silence that followed. "And what is the other thing?"

The man's head tipped up. She caught a glint of light halo his eyes. "We also draw the line at assassinating sitting heads of state. Others have made that mistake and found that it's bad for business. We don't intend to follow in their footsteps. Here . . . what you planned to give Morningstar is not enough. What's in here will bury Noah Webster, once and for all."

The man in the Panama hat placed the envelope on the hood of the car next to him. Carson gazed at the envelope. Was it bait? Was it a trap? She looked up. The man was gone, the shadows under the ramp empty.

Carson lowered her right arm and took a deep breath to cleanse her rattled nerves. Then she picked up the envelope, tucked it under her arm, and turned to find her car. The envelope felt like hope.

19

His mind seemed more fogged, in stall mode, after less than five hours of sleep. Walking down the corridor of the south wing, Mullaney was not refreshed or relieved. He was brimming with frustration and recrimination from his disastrous phone conversation with Richard Rutherford.

The words from his father flashed back through his mind. *"Don't be useless!"*

Mullaney felt worse than useless. He felt as if he had betrayed the one man who most deserved his respect and honor. How could he be so—

He shook his head. Self-pity would be no help in facing the ambassador. Only the truth would help. And the truth, Mullaney believed, would cut Atticus Cleveland to his core. How could he be so—

Palmyra Parker was rounding the corner from the corridor that led to the ambassador's private quarters. Good timing.

"Good morning, Mrs. Parker," Mullaney said as he approached the corridor. "Is your father awake?"

"No." A hand was planted on Mullaney's chest before he could squeeze past Parker. "And you are not going to wake him."

There was challenge in Parker's stance and in her voice. A formidable bulwark. One he had to overcome.

A torrent of words rushed forth from Mullaney's anxious heart. "I'm sorry, Palmyra, but I have to speak to your father. Meyer Levinson is waiting for me out front, I'm not going to be here long and I need to speak to him. It's very important. And . . ."

The hand in his chest pressed more earnestly. "And no, you will not wake him, no matter how important it is that you talk to him."

"But . . ."

"But nothing," she insisted. "Is the building on fire?"

Mullaney tried to summon up his most commanding presence.

"Are there enemies at the gate, killers invading the grounds intent on murder?

He stared at the green eyes that did not flinch.

"Is President Boylan here to play a round of golf with Atticus?"

"Palmyra . . . it is important."

"And it can wait, Brian. My father's had about three hours of decent sleep in the last week. You see him as America's ambassador. I see him as an aging father whose stamina is depleted, who has been terrorized and attacked and is wilting right in front of my eyes. It was only three years ago he had his heart bypass. He needs his rest if he's going to . . . well . . . if he's going to finish this fight."

Finish this fight. Mullaney could see that's what it would take—a fight—to get past this adamant sentinel. He didn't have the time.

He stepped back, relieving the pressure on his chest. "When your father awakes, please tell him I need to speak to him as soon as possible. Rabbi Herzog, Levinson, and I are on our way to the St. Archangel Michael Monastery in the old city to meet with this monk/hacker guy. I don't know how long this will take, but please ask your father to call me as soon as he possibly can." Mullaney did not take well to being outranked. "Okay?"

Mullaney threw himself into the passenger seat of Meyer Levinson's waiting car.

"What makes you so cheerful this morning?"

He was about to respond when his thoughts were speared by a thunderous rutting from the back seat. Mullaney looked over his shoulder. Rabbi Mordechai Herzog was sprawled over the back seat, his black hat over his face, his jacket askew, one leg hanging off the edge of the seat.

"Did he sleep in your car?"

Levinson glanced back. "Looks like it, but no. I pulled him out of a guest room on the lower level about ten minutes ago. Last night, he insisted he wanted to be part of the conversation this morning . . . didn't want you meeting with Poppy without him. So he sleepwalked to the car and immediately collapsed on the back seat. He was snoring before he hit the seat. I threw the hat over his face, but it didn't help at all."

The colonel turned back to Mullaney. "You don't look very well rested either. And something is eating at you. What's up?"

"Forget it," groused Mullaney. "Let's go see this monk. I'm sure we'll all get a lot out of . . ."

"I'm just dropping you off," interrupted Levinson. "I do have other work demands, you know. The State of Israel is paying for my services. I need to show my face at headquarters at least once in a while."

"Then why are you here?" asked Mullaney. "One of my guys could have given us a ride."

Levinson put the car in gear and eased out of the circular driveway. "Because there are a couple of things I wanted to talk to you about this morning, and Father Poppy is one of them."

"He does not have the bag with him."

The commander, in place for only a few days since his father's death, could see the obvious. Mullaney was leaving the residence without the leather bag that he was confident contained the box of power, the box so anxiously coveted by his master. But so coveted by himself as well—as much as he coveted the death of Brian Mullaney . . . preferably under the blade of his knife.

"No . . . we cannot reach the box while it remains held inside that building," said the commander. "But we can reach the Irishman. And I pray that we do. Follow them."

Knesset Building, Jerusalem
July 23, 7:55 a.m.

The Joseph Klarwein–designed Knesset Building was a modern architectural marvel, all stark lines, hard clean surfaces, soaring spaces, and solid stone floors. Even the three colorful Marc Chagall tapestries that adorned the Knesset's entry corridor were hung on a stark, white wall with no embellishments. The seat of Israel's government, both inside and out, was as austere and wrenching as the nation's topography.

Israel was a stark land. There was little comfort for her or in her. She existed in the midst of a desert, surrounded by enemies on all sides, a fortress state trying desperately to survive. And that desperation was fervently displayed in both her government's architecture and her government's structure.

Thirty-four political parties were included on the ballot in Israel's most recent election. The different parties represented ultra-conservative Hassidic Jews and religion-averse secular Jews who never stepped into a synagogue; they represented far left socialists, far right military adventurists, middle-of-the-road pragmatists, and desert-hugging environmentalists. One party stood for Palestinian rights, and another party clamored to annex more land on the disputed West Bank.

Not one of those parties came close to winning a majority of the 120 seats in the Knesset. In the nation's entire history, no party had ever won a majority of Knesset seats in a national election. So in order to build a functioning government, the party that won the most seats in the election needed to entice other parties, enough allies for the moment, to create a majority coalition that could govern the country.

Which is why an Israeli government at any one time could be composed of parties at the opposite ends of the political spectrum, and every shade in between, as long as pragmatism ruled the day—everybody got a little bit of what they wanted.

David Meir had built just such a coalition when he was first elected. And it had worked well, effectively, giving Israel a period of stable leadership. Until the covenant. Ishmael changed everything—again.

As far as Israel's political parties were concerned, the Ishmael Covenant contained something for everyone to despise. Everybody would get a little bit of what they hated.

There was no comfort for Prime Minister David Meir from the building as he strode down the wide hall to the Knesset chamber. Nothing soft, warm, and inviting. No place to sit in comfort for a few minutes before . . .

He was going to kill the Ishmael Covenant today.

Knowing full well that he didn't have the votes necessary to get the covenant ratified, Meir still intended to force the Knesset into scheduling a vote on the proposed peace treaty with Israel's Arab neighbors. Meir's coalition government, already in tatters, would crumble under the pressure of that vote, and his allies would evaporate. The covenant was a document that Meir had signed as Israel's prime minister. When the Knesset rejected the covenant, it would also be rejecting Meir's leadership and his government. A no-confidence vote would follow in short order, and a new election would be called.

David Meir's political career would come to an ignominious end.

So be it. After Vigdor Limon's revelation last night of King Abdullah's duplicity, confirming doubts that Meir would only voice to himself, the prime minister was determined not to allow Israel to enter into a bogus treaty that would bolster its enemies and increase the risk of his nation's demise. The sons of Ishmael remained unwavering in their resolve to destroy the Jewish homeland. Meir was committed to their failure. And the only way to ensure it was to sacrifice himself.

He would throw the Ishmael Covenant at the Knesset today, and at some point in the very near future, the Knesset would trample on and denounce the proposed treaty. He would lose his government, his place in leading the nation he so loved. But Israel would survive once more. Israel must survive.

The covenant never had . . .

Well, yes. There had been a chance. King Abdullah could have been honest and trustworthy. Israeli politicians could have become statesmen, put aside some of their less critical differences, and worked together to give Israel peace for the first time in its existence. But Abdullah was a liar, and Israel was a stark land, full of stark, stiff-necked people.

"The covenant never really had a chance." Benjamin Erdad walked alongside the prime minister. Israel's minister of internal security, one of Meir's staunchest allies, Erdad had been there the day Saudi Prince Faisal first proposed the covenant, a peace treaty between Israel and its Arab neighbors—Egypt, Jordan, Saudi Arabia, Kuwait, the United Arab Emirates, and the other Persian Gulf oligarchy's—along with a mutual-defense pact that would erect a nearly impenetrable barrier both to the fanatics of ISIS and the fanatics in Tehran. It was a stunning attempt at peace. But it was a promise built on sand.

Today that promise would collapse.

"Ah," said Meir, his eyes on the looming doors to the Knesset chamber, "but what if we could have made the impossible a reality, eh?" He turned to Erdad. "I would do almost anything to ensure peace for my children . . . all our children. Even attempt the impossible."

Meir stopped in front of the closed doors and turned to his friend. He held out his hand.

"Thank you, Benjamin. You have been faithful when so many have fled from my side." Erdad's big hand swallowed Meir's more cultured fingers.

"Perhaps history will be kinder to us than our so-called allies." He looked into Erdad's sad eyes. "It was worth the effort, Benji. It was worth the effort."

David Meir released Erdad's hand and turned toward the doors. "Open them, please."

20

Cleveland made this call from his private quarters in the residence. And he made the call on one of the many disposable mobile phones he secretly kept in stock during all of his ambassadorial assignments. Sometimes it was just necessary to talk to someone without the whole world listening in.

"Hello, Ernie, it's Cleveland. Sorry to call you without a caller ID, but I wanted this discussion as private as possible. Are your men ready?"

"The Task Force is on standby readiness, waitin' for orders. We can move whenever we get the green light," said Edwards. "But since I'm talkin' to you and not my boss, my gut tells me those orders have yet to be written."

"I'm working on that," said Cleveland. "There are two—"

"Hold on, Atticus . . . I need you to listen to me closely."

The command in Colonel Earnest Edwards's voice seized Cleveland's attention.

"For the last hour, I've had my guys war-gamin' your scenario. I haven't told them squat about your suspicions, but they are a pretty sharp bunch. They figured it out pretty quick. But here's the thing. Our teams believe the only way to pull off a theft of nuclear weapons from Incirlik is through the use of chemical or biological weapons, and biological weapons will take too long. That base is huge . . . over three thousand acres. If you've got what must be a smaller force, not as well armed, attackin' a fixed, heavily fortified position . . . with airpower at its back . . . you could never expect to overcome the forces currently on duty at Incirlik by conventional means. The attackers would need to take out a whole swarm of people and take them out quickly and effectively. Release a chemical weapon like sarin gas in the right locations, and Incirlik would be undefended within minutes. Do you hear me?"

Cleveland's worst dreams were coming to reality. "That would be a nightmare. How many people are stationed at Incirlik?"

"Includin' dependents—that's wives and kiddies—and civilians, there's nearly five thousand humans servin' or livin' on that base," said Edwards. "You want me to make it worse for you? The base is smack-dab in the middle of an urban area—Adana, Turkey. There are one-point-seven million people within a six-mile radius of the base. There would be a whole lot of hurt goin' on if some fool released chemical weapons on that base. But . . ."

His head came off his chest. "But what?" asked Cleveland.

"This one I don't understand," said Edwards. "Adana sits in the middle of a coastal plain just north of the upper finger of the Mediterranean Sea. It is surrounded on its other three sides by a horseshoe curve of the Taurus Mountains whose peaks are between ten and twelve thousand feet high. That city is better protected from weather than almost any other place on earth. And . . . you know what? There's a windstorm ragin' over that plain right now. It's been blowin' at near gale force for the last few days. And it's projected to keep blowin' like that for quite a while."

"That's good?"

"That's perfect, my friend. Only a madman would release chemical weapons in that kind of wind. First of all, they would blow out of the base so fast they would have only negligible effect. Second . . . Well, who cares a rip about second? The weapons just wouldn't work. So what I'm tellin' you, Atticus, is that a part of the world that never . . . ever . . . has a wind problem, has been throttled by gale force winds for nearly a week. I think I'm lookin' at divine intervention here. But . . ."

Oh, no. "But what?"

"But somebody would still need to go in and find those bad guys and their nasty weapons and neutralize both the weapons and the thugs who have them in hand. Otherwise we could still face a bloodbath. I would like that somebody to be us. So what else can you tell me?"

Here it was. The moment of truth. Either jump in or leave the field of play.

"Ernie, I hope to be on the ground in Cyprus—at Akrotiri—in about ninety minutes. There are some things you need to know that I'd rather share with you personally. And, if . . . when . . . your orders come through . . . well . . . I want to be close by . . . just in case."

There was another of those long, pregnant pauses on the other end of the transmission.

"Atticus, you're tap dancin' in a snake pit—slow down and you'll find fangs in your Florsheim's. I can read your situation between the lines," said Edwards, "but this you've got to know. I'm not goin' anywhere until I get a green light from DOD. So if you want to come visit, I can't stop you. Let me know when you are wheels-up and I'll be lookin' for you at this end."

St. Archangel Michael Monastery, Tel Aviv
July 23, 8:21 a.m.

From the street, Mullaney and Herzog walked down a long pathway between high, Jerusalem stone walls, mostly open to the sky, that ran along the north side of the monastery to the main entrance. The last third of the corridor passed under a deep, vaulted alcove that once again opened to the sky as they reached the striking blue wooden door with a large, white cross on its face, giving access to the building. A Greek Orthodox monastery, St. Archangel Michael's—overlooking the brilliant blue water of the Mediterranean Sea and the seawall of the old port of Jaffa, now Tel Aviv—was built on the ruins of a Crusader castle in 1894 and almost completely rebuilt after a devastating fire in 1994. Its stone facade and clock tower remained landmarks in Old Tel Aviv.

Crossing the round, stone rotunda at the entryway to St. Archangel Michael Monastery, a grave look upon his face, Father Stephanakis Poppodopolous walked purposefully straight to Rabbi Herzog.

"Mordechai," he said, removing his hands from his sleeves and grasping Herzog's, "it's such a tragedy about your son and all his colleagues—please, my heart grieves his loss and your pain. The monks have been praying for you since we first received word of the explosion. I am so sorry, my friend."

"Thank you, Poppy," said Herzog.

Father Poppodopolous was large, round, and covered from his shoulders to his feet by a long, black cassock, its center cinched with a thick hemp rope over the monk's considerable girth. He had an elaborately embroidered black skullcap on his head, covering only a small portion of the long, wavy black locks that were now streaked heavily with silver threads. Though his jowls gave him a succession of chins and his cheeks emulated a chipmunk's—full of acorns—the most striking and memorable facet of his appearance was a pair of piercing, aquamarine eyes that looked like South Sea lagoons—translucent pale green at the surface but deeper, darker blue at the depths. Their color was magnified by small, round, rimless glasses precariously perched on the end of his nose.

"Your prayers are always much appreciated. You have been a good friend to both my son and I, and to all our people." Herzog turned to his right. "Poppy, this is Agent Mullaney, the man I spoke to you about."

Father Poppy's hands were as big as a catcher's mitt, and Mullaney's got lost amidst its folds. A smile crossed the monk's face. "Ah, the man with the secret code. You are a welcome respite from the daily orders of the monastery," he said, his eyes lit with a lively intelligence and mischievous glitter—much like Herzog's himself. "Let's go to my little corner of the monastery where we can speak more privately."

At a surprisingly brisk pace, Father Poppodopolous led the way past the entrance to the church sanctuary, bright with pink marble columns running down each side of the nave, through a low-ceilinged stone passageway, into a warren of corridors, around bends and down stairs that left Mullaney disoriented. The monk slowed at a massive, ancient wooden door from which hung a huge, rusted padlock that could have been used by the Crusaders. Wielding a giant key, Father Poppodopolous unhinged the lock and burst through the door.

Mullaney was expecting a small, narrow monk's cell with a wooden bed, thin mattress, and one chair. What he found messed with his mind.

The room was wide and deep, brilliantly white, sunshine pouring in from a line of windows along the high ceiling. But arrayed under the windows was a large, horseshoe-shaped desk, upon which rested half-a-dozen jumbo computer monitors. In the concave center of the horseshoe's inner arc was a mammoth, deeply padded swivel chair with huge side arms that appeared to integrate some sort of controllers at their flat ends. To the left was an arched alcove that contained a bed big enough to accommodate the monk's considerable size, to the right a modest round table with a banker's lamp in the middle, four chairs arranged around its circumference.

Father Poppodopolous led them to the table, switched on the light, and pointed to the chairs with a sweep of his arm. "Let's have a chat," he said. "What have you brought me?"

21

"Why do you have to go?" Ruth Hughes paced across the small expanse of his temporary office. "What can you do there that you can't do here?"

Cleveland nodded. Good questions.

"First, Kashani is not a madman," Cleveland responded. "Does he have a penchant for stirring up and submitting to the fundamentalist factions in his country? Yes. But in my two years as ambassador to Turkey, Kashani also proved to be candid, as honest as any president could be, and generally a man of his word. We were able to find common ground and strong respect for each other despite our differences. The Kashani I know would never authorize an attack on a NATO facility to abscond with nuclear weapons. If there is collusion in his government or his military, and if I can talk to him without Eroglu or others in the way, I think he'll listen to me.

"Second, if he listens to me, perhaps I can convince him to open the door to Edwards's Task Force Black. It would be a lot better for Kashani if this plot could be stopped before it got started. JSOC's team could come in, snuff out the threat, and be gone without a trace, leaving no knowledge of this disastrous plot within Turkey.

"Third, if the worst happens, if the attack on the NATO base takes place, if nuclear weapons are threatened—or stolen—what do you think the international response will be? Turkey and Kashani's government will be square in the middle of a firestorm. But if I'm there, in country, working directly with Kashani in trying to thwart this attack, capture the perpetrators and their weapons, even if something unthinkable happens, Kashani is off the hook. He's seen as a good guy, an ally. And there's no threat of retaliation against Turkey. That's just pragmatic politics.

"But if I don't get to Ankara as soon as possible, then Kashani is on his own . . . probably under the influence of Eroglu . . . and we have absolutely no chance to avert this catastrophe."

Hughes got up from her chair, walked over to a sideboard, and poured herself a glass of water. Cleveland could tell she was processing, taking the time to think. With the half-filled glass still in her hand, she turned back toward Cleveland.

"Okay . . . you convinced me," Hughes said. "But how do you plan to pull this off? It's not easy for an ambassador to go AWOL."

Cleveland smiled. "Step-by-step," he said. "And that was step one . . . getting you on board with me. Because I'm going to need your help, Ruth. I need a covert ride to Akrotiri Air Base to meet with Ernie Edwards. After that, you don't want to know."

St. Archangel Michael Monastery, Tel Aviv
July 23, 8:28 a.m.

Mullaney placed an envelope on the table in front of him as he sat in a chair. His finger tapped on the envelope. "This is why we've come," he said, "but first I need to give you some background."

The monk leaned against his forearms on the edge of the table and clasped his fingers together. "I can already tell I'm going to enjoy this," he said, raising his right eyebrow and tilting his head in anticipation. "Shoot."

Over the next few minutes, Mullaney retraced the history as much as he could recall: a quick lesson on the Vilna Gaon; the two-hundred-year-old-prophecy he wrote in 1794 that was only revealed recently; the story of the Gaon's second prophecy and the deadly metal box that protected it; how Ambassador Cleveland had been drawn into the story, gotten Mullaney caught up in its mysteries, and been pursued by a murderous cadre of Turkish zealots who had apparently followed the box from Istanbul and were still trying to destroy the Gaon's prophecy and gain control of the box, at any cost.

"Rabbi Herzog's son and the Rabbinate Council successfully deciphered the code of the second prophesy just before explosions destroyed the Hurva synagogue, but both the box and the message survived. So we know what the two prophecies say, even though we're not exactly sure what they both fully mean. But there were two lines of symbols at the bottom of the second message that none of us has been able to decipher. Rabbi Herzog and Colonel Levinson thought you might be able to help since you're . . . a . . ."

"A code breaker and unrepentant computer hacker, right?" said Poppodopolous, a grin stretching across his formidable face. "Who sometimes even stays within the law, right? That's how I first ran into Levinson . . . or more accurately, how he ran into me. I was testing out a new setup to see how deep it could run. I had cruised through the Knesset's backfiles and reports on the IDF's war games results, when there was a knock on my door. It was Levinson and a snarling Shin Bet squad who were ready to throw me into the dungeon of no return. But it was also Meyer who kept me out of jail when I agreed to help with deep web counterespionage. So yes, I love to break codes. What's inside the envelope?"

22

Prime Minister Arslan Eroglu passed through the massive doors leading into the president's private chambers in the Cankaya Palace, acknowledged by the ceremonial guards standing sentinel at the doorposts but essentially ignored by the plainclothes security personnel who lined its hallways. Throughout the time their party had ruled the government of Turkey during the previous decade, Prime Minister Eroglu had been President Emet Kashani's closest and most trusted advisor and confidant. Though absent much of the past few days, Eroglu was a well-known fixture of the palace. But if the creature who now occupied Eroglu's body had been visible to the guards, the prime minister would never have made it close to Kashani's private quarters.

Having assimilated all of Eroglu's capacities, including his memory, while taking ownership of his body, the Turk walked purposefully through the outer receiving rooms and into the study where he knew he would find Kashani.

"Arslan . . . where have you been?" There was a faint challenge to the president's question and the accent of petulant umbrage. "You've been unavailable more in the last two days than you have in the last ten years. The Iraqis are asking almost every hour when we're going to open up the dams on the Euphrates. They see the Kurds taking steps at the United Nations to codify our commitment to an independent Kurdistan but no water reaching their farms. Why haven't the dams been opened?"

The Turk stopped in the middle of the floor and bowed to the president. "Good morning, Mr. President. I hope you are well."

Kashani looked over his shoulder toward Eroglu, a perplexed look on his face. "Are you . . ."

"Yes, I have come to speak to you specifically about our agreement with the Iraqis," said Eroglu. "I believe the time has arrived for us to abandon our agreement with Baghdad and reveal our arrangement with the Israelis. The Iraqis can watch their rivers turn to sand."

Kashani crossed the floor to stand in front of the prime minister, crowding his personal space. "I think you have gotten your priorities confused, Arslan," said Kashani, staring down his nose and punctuating each word with a nod of his head, as if he were lecturing a laggardly student. "We have the Persians where we want them."

The Turk focused Eroglu's eyes on the president and pushed back against his attempt at intimidation.

Kashani blinked, startled, and took a step back. Wrinkles of doubt furrowed the president's brow. Brusquely he turned away and sat in the corner of a leather sofa against the wall, near the door to his bedroom. He tried to look like a man in control.

But the Turk continued to press against Kashani's will.

"We have long planned for this moment, Arslan. The UN Security Council is unanimously in favor of an independent Kurdistan," Kashani said with a wave of his hand, as if the gesture put a stamp of validation on his words. "The agreement with Iraq creates a bulwark for us between Persian ambition and any hopes they may have of western expansion."

"Iraq is not important now," said prime minister Eroglu's body, his words echoing the strength of a command. "The treaty with Israel is imperative. The future hinges on Israel. You must announce the treaty while Meir still has a government that can make it a reality."

<hr />

Ambassador's Residence, Tel Aviv
July 23, 8:29 a.m.

For Cleveland, the direct approach had always been the most effective. So he held the disposable burner phone in his hand and punched in the private number Kashani had graciously given him while he was the United States Ambassador to Turkey for two years. First, he sent a text message, so Kashani would know who was calling his private number.

"Mr. President, this is Joseph Cleveland. I need to speak to you, privately, about a crucial matter. I will call you in a few moments using this same phone. Please accept the call. I cannot overemphasize the urgency of our conversation.

"Remember, I'm the one who got you tickets to the Neil Diamond concert in Washington."

Cleveland shrugged his shoulders. "Well, at least now he'll be certain it's me," he said to Hughes. "Let's see if he bites."

He laid the phone on top of his desk, but almost immediately it buzzed an incoming message. Cleveland checked the screen.

"My wife was delighted with the seats. I'm here."

"Bingo!" said Cleveland. And he made the call, with the phone on speaker.

"Good morning, Atticus," said the voice. "I would make polite small talk but, from the tone of your text, we must, as you say, get down to business. What is so urgent?"

"Thank you, Emet, for taking the time. I'm here with Ruth Hughes, my political officer in Tel Aviv. And I'll come right to the point. Mrs. Hughes and I have received independent, corroborating reports that Turkish nationals— perhaps Turkish military, perhaps Islamic jihadists—have placed in motion a plot to steal some, or all, of the B61 nuclear weapons stored on the Incirlik Air Base."

Cleveland wasn't surprised that there was a period of silence on the other end of the call. His allegation was shocking. In some ways, incomprehensible. Kashani would need a moment to get his head around both the statement and its implications. But the silence didn't last very long.

"That is totally absurd," Kashani blurted. "Who has been feeding you these lies?"

Cleveland sifted Kashani's response through his understanding of the Middle Eastern mindset. It was a denial, but not a categorical denial. Kashani was evading the issue. Why, he didn't know. Not yet.

"At the moment, who, how, when we got this information is immaterial," said Cleveland. "The important thing, at least to us, is that we trust our sources and that both sources reported the same facts: there is a plan, in motion already, to attack Incirlik and steal nuclear weapons. And you've uncovered nothing of this plot?"

Again, a pause. "One moment."

There was the sound of voices, a conversation in the background. Cleveland looked at Hughes and raised his eyebrows in a question. Vassilev had warned them that Eroglu was increasingly pulling the strings in Kashani's government.

"Mr. Ambassador," said Kashani, his words ringing with umbrage, "Prime Minister Eroglu is here with me this morning. I can tell you directly, we have no knowledge of any such plot against the NATO base or the weapons stored there."

Across the room, Ruth Hughes threw up her arms in frustration at Kashani's sidesteps.

"I didn't expect that you would." Cleveland tried to keep his tone neutral. "But in my country as in yours, there are factions, radical groups, unseen forces that can operate without the government's knowledge or approval. You can't control everyone or be conscious of what every group is up to. Even groups you might fundamentally agree with."

"Jihadists, you mean," Kashani snapped. "You know I do not agree with many of the policies or practices of our NATO allies, and yes, I have become more favorably disposed to the grievances of my more fundamentalist Muslim brothers. But an attack against NATO? Only a madman would conceive such a plan. Someone is deceiving you. Or I am a blind fool."

<hr>

St. Archangel Michael Monastery, Tel Aviv
July 23, 8:32 a.m.

Mullaney pulled three slips of paper from the envelope and passed the first one across the table to the monk. "This was the Gaon's first prophecy, kept hidden by the Rabbinate Council for over two hundred years and revealed four months ago by his great-grandson."

Father Poppodopolous quickly scanned the paper:

> When you hear that the Russians have captured the city of Crimea, you should know that the Times of Messiah have started, that his steps are being heard. And when you hear that the Russians have reached the city of Constantinople, you should put on your Shabbat clothes and not take them off, because it means that Messiah is about to come at any minute.

"Right . . . the Messiah message. I remember the announcement. It still has some people jumpy, including my bishop. And?"

"This was the second prophesy that was deciphered only two days ago."

Mullaney looked at the words that had upended his life and passed the paper to the monk:

> When the times of the Gentiles is complete, when the sons of Amalek are invited to the king's banquet, beware of the Anadolian—he walks on water to offer peace, but carries judgment in his hands. His name is Man of Violence.

"Huummmph," grunted the monk as he viewed the second prophecy. "Just as the Ishmael Covenant was signed, eh? That's interesting. And who's this Man of Violence?"

"We don't know," said Mullaney, "but I have a hunch he's the man behind all of the attacks that have surrounded the message and the box since it left Istanbul in the ambassador's care. He . . ."

"Wait!" interjected the monk. "You said this guy and his gang were after the message and the box, right? So why did they blow up the Hurva? Why take the risk of destroying both the box and the prophecy when it's obvious that's what they're still after?"

Ambassador's Residence, Tel Aviv
July 23, 8:32 a.m.

Cleveland's voice stiffened. "Our sources have told us that those behind this scheme are planning to disperse chemical agents into the air around Incirlik."

Now Kashani offered no response.

"There are nearly two million Turkish citizens in the area around Adana," said Cleveland, "thousands of innocent women and children living on the base itself. If these reports are true, and we have high confidence they are accurate, hundreds of thousands of lives are at risk. And if the plan is to use chemical weapons, the attackers would need proper training and equipment. They would have to be professionals."

"Perhaps the Kurds?" offered Kashani. "The PPG could be behind a scheme like this, a scheme to drive a wedge between Turkey and the rest of NATO."

Cleveland jumped at the opportunity. "Which is why I'm calling," he said. "If you agree, I'm on my way to Ankara. Off the record . . . off the radar."

"What? You . . ."

"You need me standing with you, Emet. Between the two of us, we can figure out what is going on . . . is it only rumor, or is there really a clandestine plot that could throw the world into turmoil? If we find a plot and you need outside support, our countries can work together. But most importantly, if something terrible were to happen, the fact that you and I were both employed in an attempt to avert any attack would keep you and your nation in NATO's good graces and protected from any retaliation."

"Wait."

The voices on the other end were still muted but sharper. Kashani and Eroglu were in conflict over Cleveland's involvement. He couldn't hear them clearly, but Cleveland could tell that Kashani and Eroglu were engaged in spirited discussion on their end of the call. Only one word came through . . . "Enough!"

When Kashani came back to the call, his tone was less belligerent. "I do not believe these reports," he sighed. "But . . ."

Cleveland understood the meaning of the *but*. One of the most unsettling realities that all Turkish presidents lived with was the ever-present potential of a military coup against any leader who fell out of favor with the Turkish generals. Since 1960, there had been four military takeovers of the Turkish government, another unproven coup attempt that took the lives of many of the government's leaders, and plans for three other coups that failed to materialize. Kashani, all Turkish presidents, survived on a knife's edge.

"What do you want me to do?" Kashani asked.

Bingo!

Cleveland knew what he needed from Kashani. It was one part of the trip Agent Pat McKeon would not be making.

23

St. Archangel Michael Monastery, Tel Aviv
July 23, 8:35 a.m.

"We wondered about that too," said Mullaney. As he sat there, cataloging thoughts, assessing emotions, probing for the truth and the way, Mullaney felt a quickening in his heart . . . a stirring in his spirit. It was like, well . . . it was like the day of his graduation from the State Police Academy in Virginia, the day he swore his oath of allegiance to "serve, protect, and defend" when he joined DSS. Days when he was on the cusp of a great, new adventure, but also days when he was fulfilling his destiny, his purpose. Today felt like that kind of day.

At this moment, that rising tide of destiny and purpose infused Mullaney with energy, strengthened his resolve, and opened his mind to . . . well, he wasn't quite sure. But he felt like he had just pinned on his badge and strapped on his gun belt. He was more than ready to go into battle. He was looking forward to it.

"Look," he said, spreading his hands before him, "we may not understand it, but we know we are in a battle with the forces of evil—whoever those forces are. And for only God knows why, we have been enlisted into this supernatural fight, at least for this part that is occurring at this time, here on earth. Our best guess is that our enemy's original plan was to prevent the second prophecy from being deciphered and revealed. Now it's certainly possible that these agents of evil have been trying to destroy both of these prophecies since the Gaon first wrote them down. Could be why they were both hidden for so long. Our enemy wants to steal them or destroy them, one way or another."

"Then," said Poppodopolous, shifting his significant weight in a relatively insignificant chair, "why didn't they stop, give it up, when the first prophecy was revealed in March? Game over, right?"

Mullaney jumped at the question, shaking his head. "No! Game changed! Now there was an urgency to prevent the Gaon's second prophecy from becoming public knowledge. There's something in that second message our enemy didn't want revealed. Some clue that will help us try to thwart their plans here. And even though the second prophecy has been deciphered, they still remain violent and deadly in their opposition. Why is that?"

Ever the investigator, Mullaney could feel the excitement of the hunt rising in his spirit.

"We know that touching the bronze box that contained the Gaon's second prophecy was almost instantly fatal for anyone without the anointing of the guardian," Mullaney continued. "Most of us thought it was the prophecy message itself that triggered the lethal zap. But once the original parchment from the Gaon was taken out of the box by the rabbis at the Hurva, touching the box still led to a gruesome death."

Even as the words left his mouth, there was an awakening of understanding in Mullaney.

But Poppy was first to put the idea into words. "You're saying the box has power." It was a statement, not a question. "Even though the message is no longer held within the box, the box itself has the power to kill. So . . ."

"They're after the box," said Mullaney, almost as if he was speaking to himself. "They want the power of the box. They must think they can harness its power, use it for their own purposes."

"Wait," blurted Herzog. "It kills, I think. Anyone who touches that box his own death warrant is signing."

A memory pierced Mullaney's thoughts. "Except for one thing," he said. "Bayard told us that any mortal being who touches the box will die. Well, what about an immortal being? An evil immortal being? Perhaps . . ."

"Eh . . . reconsider that, I would," interjected Herzog. "The Philistines were none too thrilled once they captured the Ark of the Covenant. Something about boils. Without the blessing, maybe the box they can have, eh?"

Ambassador's Residence, Tel Aviv
July 23, 8:37 a.m.

Even in the absence of any official announcement, in the wake of Tommy Hernandez's death in Amman, Jordan, all of the Diplomatic Security Service agents on the duty roster at the US ambassador's residence in Tel Aviv began calling Pat McKeon *Boss* and treating her with the respect and deference owed to the person in charge of the ambassador's personal security detail. She was interim in title only.

McKeon was in her mid-thirties, athletic in build, and wore her dark hair short—less fuss. She was an inch short of six-feet in height and carried herself with the confidence gained from several DSS rotations into challenging conditions. She was solid and reliable by reputation and rarely made a mistake. Four days ago, she made one that could have ended her career. She allowed the ambassador's daughter to leave the residence without a DSS agent at her side. Palmyra Parker was abducted by these Turkish terrorists, held captive, and only rescued after a raging gun battle amongst the sand dunes of the Nitzanim Preserve along the Mediterranean.

But that midnight firefight was where McKeon had redeemed herself. Automatic weapons were still firing from multiple locations when McKeon charged into the midst of the battle and fought her way into the back seat of the SUV carrying Mrs. Parker. It was training, determination, and character that launched McKeon into the rescue attempt, not an attempt to save her job. This *was* her job. Parker was her responsibility.

Now Parker's father was McKeon's responsibility. And Ambassador Joseph Cleveland was not making her life any easier. Cyprus? Now?

"Right," said Cleveland. "Put together a team and we're leaving in five minutes. Mrs. Hughes is coming to the airport with us. She's tapped into her business world connections and arranged a private jet for our use."

"Yes, sir," said McKeon. "But I'll need to reach Agent Mullaney first and let him know you're planning an immediate trip outside Israel. He may not agree with those plans—at least not until he's here to go with us."

McKeon stood inside the door of Cleveland's temporary office in the south wing of the residence, trying to sort through the directive she'd just been given by the ambassador. This trip was awfully sudden, particularly after all that the ambassador—all of them—had endured over the last several days. Brian wouldn't be happy.

Cleveland stood behind the makeshift desk, an imposing figure, his frame leaning toward McKeon and his eyes transmitting a clear message of authority.

"I understand," he said. "But you need to understand this. In five minutes, we will be leaving for Ben Gurion, whether Mullaney is here or not. DSS works for me . . . not the other way around. We're flying into the RAF base at Akrotiri, and it's critical I get there as soon as possible. Mullaney or no Mullaney. Understood?"

"Yes, sir," said McKeon, her anxiety unquenched but her duty clear.

"There will be room for yourself and three other agents on the airplane," said Cleveland.

"Okay. I'll assemble a team and have your car and our escort at the front door in five minutes." McKeon turned and left Cleveland's office, pulling out her mobile phone as she stepped through the door. She tapped the speed dial for Mullaney.

He is not going to like this.

This had been Cleveland's greatest fear, the weakest link in his escape plan . . . getting out of Tel Aviv without Mullaney putting a stop to it. He had hoped to browbeat Agent McKeon into quiet compliance, but not surprisingly, that didn't work. She had tried to reach Mullaney several times, so far with no success. Was this divine intervention?

Just prior to their departure for the airport, as if on business, Cleveland entered the security office of the residence. Lying on top of the unoccupied desk was McKeon's quickly scribbled report to Mullaney, alerting him to this unexpected trip to Cyprus. A report that now was stuffed into the inside pocket of his jacket.

St. Archangel Michael Monastery, Tel Aviv
July 23, 8:43 a.m.

"And there's another question." Poppodopolous gestured across the table. "Why the Aaronic blessing? Why that seemingly innocuous language as a way to protect the guardian from getting zapped? There are hundreds, perhaps thousands of other, more powerful warnings or promises or protections throughout the Bible. Why were these words chosen?"

Rabbi Herzog sat to Mullaney's left. He was leaning forward in his chair, totally engrossed in the conversation. "The Aaronic blessing, Poppy, is anything but innocuous." Herzog, glancing back and forth between Mullaney and the monk, looked wounded—as if someone had declared his uncle Eli was a Black Sea pirate.

"Not that long ago in the valley of Hinnom outside Jerusalem, a burial cave was uncovered," Herzog explained. "Inside the cave were found two silver amulets from the seventh century. For hundreds of years, amulets have been thought to contain magical powers to prevent evil. These two amulets each had the Aaronic blessing etched into their surface."

The monk shrugged his shoulders. "Okay, I concede that Aaron's blessing has been perceived as protection for centuries. But the question we should consider is why? And what does it tell us that the Aaronic blessing was chosen to protect this lineage of guardians from the lethal power of this little box?" The monk shifted in his chair to look at Herzog. "Rabbi . . . this is your territory. I'm sure you understand this a lot better than I do."

Herzog reached out with his right hand, resting it on the left arm of Poppodopolous. "Such a kind man," he said with a smile. "Father Poppy probably knows more about the Talmud and the traditions of Judaism than I do. But . . .

"When Israel was in the desert after the exodus," Herzog explained, "the blessing of Aaron was spoken over the entire people of Israel each morning. The Levite priest Aaron, Moses's brother, would stand in the doorway of the Tent of Meeting, lift his hands, and speak the blessing over the entire people. It was believed at the time that Aaron's blessing had independent power that could be let loose into the congregation by the reciting of his words.

"But the funny thing about the blessing is that it is a singular blessing . . . it's not plural . . . it's not for the massed assembly. It's for each individual person standing there. It was a blessing that each Israelite was expected to take upon themselves, personally.

"And the wording," said Herzog, "is powerful. 'The Lord bless you, and keep you . . .' The word *keep* in Hebrew not only meant to guard or protect. It represented an image of a corral of bushes with long, sharp thorns that shepherds would use to surround their flocks at night to keep them safe. It's a powerful word of protection. And 'the Lord lift up His countenance on you . . .' The word *lift* has the connotation of the Lord lifting you up in his arms, holding you above his head, and smiling up at you. Again, another powerful image of protection.

"So surprising it is not, that the Gaon invoked the power of heaven as protection through the use of the Aaronic blessing," said Herzog. "And my mind believes that invoking a covering this powerful was not only the means of protection, but I believe it was also a key to when the box itself was to fulfill its purpose . . . protect it and the guardians until it was time to put the box to work."

24

The Turk was considering his options even before Kashani disconnected the call. So the American ambassador was coming to plead his case with Kashani. Well, perhaps it would not be Kashani he met with. The Turk had a vision of the box in his hands . . . and Cleveland in a coffin. So be it. He would harness the power of the box and focus its power to achieve his own desires. Then no one could defeat him. No one.

Kashani leaned forward, his hands on his knees, defiance lacing his words.

"You, Arslan? You tell me *I must*? Who do you think you are speaking to, *Mr. Prime Minister*? Don't mistake our years of cooperation as a sign of weakness or as permission to pursue your own agenda. There is only one agenda. Stop the Persians. Rebuild the empire. Syria is a failed state, where anarchy reigns. Soon our troops will pour across that border, slicing through western Syria, bringing the ancient region of Assyria back into the nascent Ottoman Empire. It is the beginning of—"

"It is the beginning of a new order," Eroglu interrupted. The Turk took a step toward where Kashani was sitting. The president saw Prime Minister Eroglu approach. He did not see the malevolent yellow eyes of the Turk behind the mask, eyes that beckoned to bedlam. "The fulfillment of an ancient dream, yes . . . but not your dream."

President Kashani jumped to his feet. "It is not for you to say—"

Eroglu's left hand came up from his side, its fingers splayed out wide. From a deep, primeval well of torment, the Turk generated pulses of power from the tips of his fingers to the neurons of Kashani's spinal cord. As if he was the host of a smoldering volcano, Kashani's body tensed then shuddered involuntarily, spasmodically twitching as it desperately fought against the forces invading his very DNA. Then pain leaped from the fingers of the Turk . . . diabolical shards of torture that flayed Kashani's nerve endings and drove his flailing limbs in disparate directions.

Emet Kashani, President of the Republic of Turkey, fell back onto the leather sofa, his face a contorted portrait of anguish, his eyes wildly searching for hope. There was none.

The Turk sent another pulse of power through his fingers, a laser of molten energy that fried every synapse in Kashani's brain. Terror fled from Kashani's eyes, but so did all consciousness. He was alive. His body still had breath. But there was no one home.

Arslan Eroglu's husk stepped closer to Kashani's limp carcass. He spread both arms over the motionless frame. The Turk inside Eroglu, now brimming with newly absorbed power, spoke words the earth had never heard before. Kashani's body lifted off the sofa. As if he were docking a spaceship by remote control, The Turk guided Kashani's body into his private bed chamber and held him hovering over the bed. At a twist from Eroglu's head, the cover and sheet were thrown back. The Turk lowered Kashani onto the bed and brought the covers back in place.

"They will find you in a coma, and so you will live with the dead," snarled Eroglu, "suspended in the realm of darkness until I call for you once again. But in the days to come, I will be the one who will rule the Ottomans."

The Turk glanced around the room. He walked to the corner and turned on a small table lamp, casting just enough shadowed light so Kashani's body was visible. He closed the door on his way out, passed through the president's study and the reception rooms, and stopped as he crossed the threshold leaving Kashani's private quarters. He turned to the dark-suited man by the door, the lead agent in the president's personal security team.

"President Kashani is not well," said the voice of Arslan Eroglu as he pulled the door shut. "He's running a fever and is fighting a migraine headache. He has taken some medication and is sleeping. And he has ordered me that he is not to be disturbed until he awakes."

The agent turned, glanced at the door, and then back to Eroglu. "Perhaps I should—"

"Perhaps?" snapped Eroglu's voice. "Follow your orders. Let the president sleep, and don't disturb him until he wakes. Understood?"

Without waiting for a reply, the Turk led Eroglu's body farther into the palace. There was much to do—ratify the treaty language with Israel, ensure the raid on Incirlik was successful. But most importantly, prepare for Ambassador Cleveland's arrival, and the great good fortune it brought him.

There was a venomous smile on Eroglu's face and a deepening tint of yellow to his eyes. *The end is near.*

⸻⸻⸻

St. Archangel Michael Monastery, Tel Aviv
July 23, 8:46 a.m.

"So I think our enemy still sees some threat in the message itself," said Mullaney, "but it also appears they now realize the box has significant power of its own, perhaps in the kabbalah symbols hammered into its lid. I still think they want to destroy any of us who have seen the message of the second prophecy. They don't want that message to become public knowledge. But I also think they now want the power of the box. And I think that brings us to this third slip of paper."

Mullaney once again looked at the symbols on the slip of paper, shook his head, and pushed it across the table to the monk.

Father Poppodopolous stared down his nose, through the lens of his glasses, at the paper on the table. Then he pushed it under the light and leaned over the table to take a closer look. Mullaney was waiting for a magnifying glass to pop out of his cassock, but the monk sat back in his chair and looked at Herzog and Mullaney as if they had both started speaking in Lithuanian.

"Do you know what Unicode is?" the monk asked.

"Something to do with computers?" Herzog replied.

"Yes . . . something," said the monk. "In the early days of computers, each computer language or program had its own system for how characters and numbers were encoded so they could be computed or displayed. How a *d* is created on the computer screen, for example. None of the different languages were the same, not in English, and certainly not around the world. It was several years before somebody got the idea that computers should utilize the same character encoding system . . . that how a *d* is created in one system should be the same way a *d* is created in another system. And for our purposes, that somebody invented Unicode."

Mullaney sat there, waiting for the monk to say more. He had to be going somewhere with this explanation. But Father Poppodopolous folded his arms over the large cross that hung from his neck, nodding with satisfaction. "And . . . ?" asked Mullaney.

"And," said Poppodopolous, "when I look at these symbols you've laid before me, what I'm reminded of is Unicode."

Mullaney's mind was spinning like a transmission with a broken gear, trying to absorb and understand what the monk had just said but getting stuck each time where the gear had teeth missing . . . Unicode in 1794?

"I don't understand."

"I don't understand either," said Father Poppodopolous, "I'm just telling you what I see here. Your Lithuanian genius is using symbols that closely resemble some of the symbols of Unicode. Obviously, they are not Unicode. But they are something. His intention is to send us a message. Just as ways were found to decode the previous prophecies, there must be a way for us to decode these lines of symbols. So give me some time and I'll see what I can come up with."

"Time, I think, is something we may not have a lot," said Herzog.

"He's right," agreed Mullaney. "The pace of this conflict has accelerated, and it keeps accelerating more with each passing moment. We've just had a devastating earthquake at the US embassy and a second major earthquake eight miles away at the ambassador's residence—and nothing in between—which would seem to be physically impossible. So it appears that our enemies are getting more determined and more desperate."

"Fine . . . give me some time, maybe a few hours. I'll call or send you an email to let you know how I'm progressing. If you can send me the original messages before they were decoded, that might help. Maybe I can come up with an answer sooner." The monk reached for his phone. "Let me get Brother Jerome to come and show you the way out. It can get pretty confusing." Poppodopolous pounded out a text on his phone then turned back to his guests. "But there is one thing I can tell you now."

"What's that?" asked Mullaney.

The monk pulled the third slip of paper closer to him and tapped his finger on the two lines of symbols. "Regardless of what the previous messages have told you, regardless of their importance or uniqueness, this one," he said, "is the most critical. My intuition and experience tell me there is something here that is the key, the culmination, the reason for all that has gone before. If we don't solve this riddle, gentlemen, I think the level of violence you've experienced thus far will seem like a picnic on a clear spring afternoon compared with what is about to befall us. This time I think it won't just be an isolated earthquake at the embassy and residence. This time, I think the whole world may be shaken."

St. Archangel Michael Monastery, Tel Aviv
July 23, 8:59 a.m.

Disoriented by Brother Jerome's head-spinning traverse through the narrow, dusky corridors of the monastery, emerging into the morning sun of Tel Aviv hit Mullaney like a lightning strike. Momentarily blinded by the intense brightness, Mullaney blinked away the assault on his eyes as he tried to focus on the open-air passageway that spread before them and led to the street.

At the end of the passage a gate stood partially open, the figure of a man standing with the sun at his back.

Mullaney cradled Herzog's left elbow in his hand. "Watch your step," he said as he steadied the rabbi down the two roughly hewn stone steps to the passageway, "until your eyes get adjusted to the light."

"Well, what is it you think of our friend Poppy, eh?"

Herzog was looking for an answer, but Mullaney was looking toward the end of the passage, down by the gate. The shadowed body had moved farther into the narrow, open-air corridor, and light now shone upon his features. Mullaney stopped in his tracks, jolting Herzog to a halt. Even thirty, fifty yards away, Mullaney could see the man clearly. He was a young man, dressed entirely in black, with thick dark hair and Middle Eastern facial features. But two things arrested Mullaney's attention . . . the intense fury of the young man's dark eyes and the livid pink scar that emerged from his right ear across the top of his forehead and disappeared under the hairline.

The street demonstration on the Namir Road. It's the same man who was pushing close to our car, whose eyes were burning holes in my head.

Mullaney assessed the memory and calculated the risk. But then he saw other bodies, also clad in black, moving in the light and shadows behind the young man who relentlessly stared down the passage as if his eyes had locked onto the object of his lust.

His grip on the rabbi's elbow stiffened as Mullaney pivoted Herzog away from the corridor and pushed him up the two steps and back through the door, into the monastery.

"What . . ."

"It's not safe," snapped Mullaney. "We need to find another way out. Stay close to me."

Mullaney paused just inside the door, trying to regain his bearings. He remembered they came up some dark stairs before reaching the round, stone rotunda which led to this door. But there were three sets of stairs leading down from the rotunda, all dark. Mullaney glanced over his shoulder. The young man and at least four or five others were moving cautiously along the open-air passage. *Too many to fight . . . got to protect the rabbi.* He kicked the door shut.

Mullaney tugged on the rabbi's elbow and pulled him into the stairway on the left, gingerly making his way down the well-worn stone steps.

"Who are those men?" Herzog asked between gasps for air as Mullaney hustled him down the stairs.

"The same ones—the Disciples—who have been after us since the ambassador got that box." Mullaney stopped at the bottom of the stairs. Deeply shadowed corridors fanned out in three directions. He tried to remember the layout of the building from when he saw it from the street. Twin towers crowned its front façade, and the blue Mediterranean stretched out behind it. The rest of the monastery appeared to be walled in. He had glimpsed the roof of what looked like a chapel on the left of the building, which is why he took the left staircase . . . hoping to find the chapel and, hopefully, the safety of others.

But there was no chapel in front of them, just three dim corridors. And there were no sounds to follow . . . only muffled voices and scuffling steps above them.

"Which w . . ."

With one hand Mullaney pulled the rabbi into the corridor straight ahead of them and with the other fished out the mobile phone from his jacket pocket. He tapped the screen to bring the phone to life—no bars! They came to a wooden door in the left wall, but it was locked. The voices were closer . . . bottom of the stairs. He got close to Herzog's face. "*Quiet!*" he whispered.

Mullaney pushed forward with the rabbi in tow. Another wooden door stood in the gloom at the end of the corridor. As they came before the door, Mullaney realized another set of stairs led up to the left. There was no light coming from the stairs, only darkness.

He reached for the handle of the door.

"Here!"

Mullaney grabbed Herzog by the arm and pushed the rabbi before him, up the steps to the left. If nothing else, the stairway gave them darkness and the high ground. *Keep the rabbi behind me . . . fire from the darkness . . . downhill.* He reached for the 9-millimeter Glock in the holster at the small of his back and . . .

"Oh . . ."

Rabbi Herzog stumbled on the stairs above him and fell back against Mullaney's legs. As he started to pitch forward, over Herzog's sprawling body, Mullaney reached one hand to catch Herzog and the other hand to cushion his crash into the stone steps. Barely out of the holster, the Glock slipped from his grip and thudded down the stairs.

Reacting simply by instinct and training, Mullaney grabbed Herzog with both hands, yanked him to his feet and pushed him forward, the darkness his only hope, when Herzog ran into something . . .

"Ughhh . . ."

. . . and a door to the outside sprang open before them.

Blinding light poured through the door. A single gunshot echoed, the bullet ricocheting off stone wall, as Mullaney dragged Herzog through the door and hauled his struggling body into the light and slammed the door back into place.

In a heartbeat, Mullaney scanned their surroundings. No other people were in sight, and the windows he could see were heavily barred.

The door they had burst through opened under a buttressed, vaulted stone ceiling that was exposed to the air on three sides. The sea was in front of them, a wall running parallel to the sea behind them. A narrow corridor to the right seemed to lead nowhere. To the left, an outdoor stairway rose to an upper level.

Next to the stairs on the left was a round outcropping from the building—like a shrunken turret, or a hobbit's home—with a humped roof and a miniature-sized doorway at the curved wall's apex.

It took only a fraction of a second for Mullaney to absorb the scene. He wrapped his right arm just below Herzog's shoulder blades and half carried him around the stairs. In a tiny slot between the stairway and the round building, there was a shallow alcove on the far side of the turret door that was barely visible from where they had exited.

Mullaney pressed Herzog into the alcove as far as possible, shielding him with his own body and forcing him down onto his knees. Wishing for a weapon, Mullaney had only his iPhone. He turned off the phone's ringer and started to text when he heard the voices coming closer.

26

McKeon sat in the back seat of the armored limo, Cleveland to her left, her mobile phone pressed against her right ear. Ringing . . . ringing . . . ringing . . . but no answer. She had already left a message for Mullaney with no response.

Cleveland reached into the pocket of his jacket and felt the heft of the small device. Before leaving the embassy, he had flipped its toggle switch to On. The jammer was powerful. It allowed calls to be made. But they would never get connected . . . the impression that no one was answering. It was limited in range. He needed to be fairly near the person to jam their cell phone connection. Limited, but hopefully enough to give him the edge he needed . . . a little more time.

The ambassador's car and its escort were cleared by Shin Bet officers and pulled through one of the back, private entrances to Ben Gurion Airport. It headed for an unmarked metal hanger at the western end of the compound.

"No response from Mullaney?" asked Cleveland.

"No . . . and I'm concerned."

"He's at the monastery with the rabbi," said Cleveland. "Perhaps where they're meeting is outside of normal cell service. I'm sure he'll respond. And you filed your report, so he'll know where we're going."

The line of cars pulled up alongside the hanger, the other three DSS agents taking up positions around the limo before Cleveland could exit. McKeon reached out and placed a restraining hand on the ambassador's forearm. "Sir . . . for the record"—McKeon locked gaze with Cleveland—"I'm not in agreement with you leaving the country without Agent Mullaney. I think you're taking a risk, and I would pull rank on you if I could. Or I would get the green light from somebody in Washington."

Cleveland was shaking his bald head. "I told you, no contact with Washington. You've got to humor me on this, Agent McKeon. As far as Washington is concerned, this visit to Cyprus does not exist."

"Yes, sir . . . and that's another reason I protest," said McKeon. "We're going out of the country with no cover. You need to know how strongly I object to this."

Cleveland gave McKeon a warm, fatherly smile. "Objection noted, Agent McKeon. And appreciated. Ruth," he said to Hughes, sitting to his left, "you're the witness. Make sure Agent McKeon's objections are duly noted in the security log when you get back to the residence. Now please, introduce me to these kind folks who are taking us to Cyprus."

St. Archangel Michael Monastery, Tel Aviv
July 23, 9:06 a.m.

"Which way?" The whispered question came from the other side of the stairs. Mullaney could hear their heavy breathing.

They were trapped. No way to escape . . . no way to defend themselves. He slipped the phone back into his pocket, determined to focus all of his attention on the sounds that were so close. Herzog squirmed behind him, and Mullaney put out his hand to keep the rabbi still.

He listened, straining to hear any sound, his eyes glued to the edge of the stairs around which the attackers would have to come to get to them. The silence was complete, only the cawing of a sea bird in the distance breaking through.

One minute . . . two minutes passed, Mullaney trying to muffle his breathing. Why hadn't they come around the stairs?

He heard steps, coming from the direction of the door they burst through. *They're coming!*

The sound of movement came closer to the stairway. Brian Mullaney made sure Herzog stayed behind him, balled his fists, and balanced his weight over his legs. If he was quick enough . . .

"Agent Mullaney?" came an urgent voice.

Herzog's shoulders jumped and his head popped up, but Mullaney pressed him even harder against the alcove's wall.

"Agent Mullaney?" The voice was more urgent. He could hear someone going up the staircase. "It's Shin Bet."

Mullaney's hold on Herzog never wavered, but he leaned out of the alcove and stole a glance at the stairs. He could see the bottom of khaki uniform pants and brown shoes. No black.

Still wary, Mullaney took the risk. "Down here."

"I've got them," said the voice as the legs turned and the feet descended the stairs. Around the corner came an IDF soldier. "Corporal Lantz," said the soldier. "Are either of you wounded? Here . . . let me help."

The corporal reached down to help Herzog to his feet.

"How did you get here?" asked Mullaney, brushing off his pants.

The soldier turned to Mullaney with a questioning look on his face. "Did you think Colonel Levinson was going to allow you to go anywhere in this city—in this country—that we didn't keep an eye on you? As soon as we heard the gunshot, we had men converging on the monastery."

"The guys dressed in black?"

"Vanished," said the corporal. "Whoever it was that came after you, we didn't see a trace of them."

Mullaney shook his head, frustrated that his attackers should escape again. "Well, I got a good look at one of them. He's not somebody I'm likely to forget." He turned to Rabbi Herzog. "Are you okay?"

"Okay? This life is an exciting one you lead," said Herzog, shaking his head. "But for an old man, it's exhausting. Can I get a nap please before we again take on the enemies of mankind?"

"Sure," said Mullaney. "Do you want us to take you home?"

"Home? And miss all the fun? Not a chance," said Herzog. "We've still got work to do. We need to get the Gaon's original messages to Poppy. I'm sticking with you. Who knows, you may need my help, eh?"

The corporal pointed up the stairs. "We can get out this way. And I've been instructed to escort you, whether it's back to the embassy or the ambassador's residence. Colonel Levinson said he would meet up with you wherever you decide to go."

27

In a plane that flew nearly six hundred miles an hour, it was only forty-five minutes of flight time from Tel Aviv to Cyprus, and Cleveland intended to make the most of the time. His plans were developing on the fly, fleshing out with each step he took. He had two competing objectives: (1) get face-to-face with Emet Kashani in Turkey and attempt to stop the planned attack on Incirlik, and (2) get a JSOC team on the ground in Turkey with the capacity, if necessary, to eliminate the plotters and the threat before a catastrophe unfolded.

Cleveland knew he was on his own, flying solo, in trying to accomplish both of those objectives.

Colonel Edwards would be waiting to meet with him in the officer's mess of the RAF Akrotiri Air Base when he arrived on Cyprus. Cleveland knew he had only one chance to get Ernie Edwards on his side—tell him the truth and all the truth. He planned to unleash an impassioned plea to convince Edwards to activate a JSOC mission to save tens of thousands of lives at Incirlik. Edwards was a man under orders, yes. But he was also a pragmatic warrior in defense of his country and a committed Christian in service to his God. Edwards, Cleveland hoped, would see and understand. Whether he would order his men into defense of Incirlik . . . well, that was one part of the equation Cleveland would have to leave in God's hands.

Despite his hopes, Cleveland didn't really think Edwards would move without orders. Not an incursion onto foreign soil. Which would leave Kashani. But getting himself to Turkey under the radar might be even more difficult.

Cleveland was hunched over his iPhone as the Gulfstream G450, the second-fastest private jet in the world, streaked above the Mediterranean. The ambassador was once again scrolling through the internet. He had already booked an online ticket from Ercan International Airport in Northern Cyprus—the internationally unrecognized sliver of Cyprus still controlled by Turkey—using his own name and personal credit card. Now he made the online connection with Stephanos Car Rentals, right there on the Akrotiri base, just south of the commercial air terminal, and reserved a car.

Cleveland glanced out the window of the Gulfstream as the shadows of puffy white clouds dappled the blue surface of the Mediterranean, but his thoughts were far from the scenery. He quickly surveyed the small cabin. No one was paying him any attention. Good.

He reached into the pocket of his jacket to make sure the jammer was still there. Then he turned his iPhone on its side and found the hole that identified the SIM card tray. He took a paper clip that he had opened and slowly pushed the arm of the paper clip into the hole. It only took a moment for the tray to pop open and for Cleveland to drop the SIM card into his other hand. He pushed the empty tray back into place and slipped the SIM card into the pocket of his jacket alongside the jammer.

Cleveland hadn't been in the Foreign Service for thirty years without learning some things. Like how DSS security would hack the "Find a Friend" app on an ambassador's iPhone, go through a couple of quick steps, and use that app to track the ambassador's location. They would even hide the "Find a Friend" app when they were done. But he wasn't going to allow that to happen today. His phone's SIM card not only contained his identity, phone number, and contacts, but also transmitted his location. The SIM card was not going with him to Turkey.

Too bad about Agent McKeon. She was a good agent . . . reliable. This was going to be another black mark on her record, but there were more lives at stake than just one agent. And if he had any political capital left at the end of this escapade, he would spend it all to ensure McKeon wasn't punished for his willfulness.

He casually surveyed the cabin again. No eyes were on him. Good. Now it got harder.

***

Ambassador's Residence, Tel Aviv
July 23, 10:00 a.m.

Not only did Meyer Levinson, commander of the operations division of Shin Bet, Israel's internal security agency, have the stature and swagger of the dynamic Moshe Dyan, but he also had the well-tanned bald head. As the Shin Bet driver pulled up in front of the ambassador's palatial but severely damaged residence, Mullaney wondered if Levinson has consciously adopted the khaki shirt and shorts to enhance the image. Regardless, Levinson was standing on the steps of the residence, his ever-present riding crop slapping a steady rhythm against his thigh.

Helping Rabbi Herzog out of the car, Mullaney could feel a presence at his shoulder. He turned his head, expecting Levinson. Instead, it was DSS agent Kathie Doorley. "Are you . . . the rabbi . . . injured?" Doorley asked.

Mullaney shook his head. "No, we're fine. What's the situation here? Is security . . ."

"You've been out of communication," said Doorley. "McKeon's been calling repeatedly, trying to reach you. And . . ."

"Awwww." Mullaney reached inside his jacket and withdrew his cell phone. The ringer was still switched off. He clicked the switch on the side. "Turned it off when we were being pursued. What did McKeon want?"

"Don't know. She wouldn't say. But some guy who said he's Father Poppy has also been calling for you."

"Poppy?" chirped Herzog. "Has he discovered something?"

"Let's get inside," said Mullaney, taking Herzog's arm and assisting him up the front steps. "We've got a lot to sort out. Hello, Meyer. C'mon and I'll give you a report on what happened as we walk."

RAF Akrotiri Air Base, Cyprus
July 23, 10:03 a.m.

They were sitting in a far corner of the nearly empty officer's mess, hard against a window that looked out over the green playing fields of the Akrotiri school in the center of the air base, cups of coffee in front of both and a plate brimming with hummus, fresh pita, and three piles of unidentifiable, different colored, mashed something. They were at least trying to maintain the appearance of a social visit.

"By all livin' thunder," Edwards rumbled under his breath, "you've whipped up a wasp's nest for sure. Your keister is in a deep world of hurt, Atticus."

Colonel Earnest Edwards was in his work clothes—the unofficial uniform of a JSOC unit commander: black army boots, camo pants, sleeveless black T-shirt with a unique patch on the left breast—Kandahar Whacker Club, the JSOC Rangers outfit from Afghanistan—and black baseball cap with the beloved "We Love the Night" Special Operations combined units patch. A well-worn, black leather bomber jacket was tossed over the back of his chair.

Edwards, at fifty-years-old still rock solid in physique, devotion to duty, and loyalty to his men, slowly shook his head, peeled off his aviator sunglasses, and pierced Cleveland with a withering stare. "You've got an international disaster waitin' to erupt around your ears. You've got a superior officer who apparently hates your guts and is blockin' your access to the secretary of state. And you believe there is a traitor workin' in cahoots with these yahoos in Turkey somewhere in the upper echelons of the State Department. You, Atticus, are sittin' on top of a land mine with nowhere to go."

Cleveland felt the sting of Edwards's litany. But it wasn't all that bad. He opened his mouth to dispute some of Edwards's claims, but the colonel held up a warning hand.

"And"—Edwards leaned farther across the table—"I'm really afraid you've come here to personally enlist me into climbin' on top of that land mine with you. Please tell me I'm mistaken."

There was no evading Edwards's assessment or his conclusion. Cleveland was operating at a level of risk he had never before encountered during his thirty years of service with the State Department. And he came to Cyprus hoping there was some way to convince Ernie Edwards to sidestep protocol—that was a euphemistic way to put it—and release his Team Black against what Cleveland was certain was a deadly threat aimed at Incirlik and its inhabitants.

At that moment, Cleveland was finally convinced that this part of his plan would fail. Internally, he smacked himself across the side of the head. How could he have been so foolish to think that Edwards would send his men on a perilous mission onto foreign soil without orders from his superior officer. No, there was only one way for Cleveland to prevent this disaster. And it wasn't through intervention with Ernie Edwards.

"I admit . . . it was foolish of me, but I was hoping . . ."

Another halting hand came up. "Atticus, I fully get it. If you and your people are correct, the prospect for a devastatin' loss of life in and around Incirlik is frighten'ly possible. If there are men crazy enough to release chemical weapons in such a heavily populated area—and I know they exist—then thousands of innocent men, women, and children will perish." Edwards tapped the edge of his sunglasses on the top of the table. "Believe me, if it was just me

I had to worry about, I'd be on a chopper to Turkey this very minute. But I can't ask my men to go somewhere—to take on a mission like this in a foreign country—without the direct permission and instruction of General Claiborne . . . probably of the Joint Chiefs. Honestly, I wish I could help you."

Cleveland felt like a kid whose father stopped him from jumping out of a second-floor window into a four-foot high pile of leaves . . . kinda disappointed, kinda relieved. His smile was one of embarrassment. "I was hoping . . ."

Once again, the hand. "That I might call the general . . . off the record, so to speak . . . and run the situation up the flagpole?"

"Well, yes . . ."

Edwards's eyes crinkled at the edges. "Already did that . . . at the margins. I reached out to the general's adjutant. Closer to me than a brother. He was stunned. Said there's been absolutely no chatter about an attack on Incirlik. Said he would keep his ears open. Maybe he plants a seed. But his last words were clear. 'Ernie . . . your guys are not the Avengers. Wait for orders.' So we wait, Atticus. Maddenin' as it is, we wait for orders. I'm sorry you came all the way out here for nothin'."

Reaching his right hand across the table, Cleveland shook his head. "Not for nothing, Ernie," he said, wincing as Edwards's fist engulfed his hand and squeezed it in a vice. "It's just wonderful to see you again. Thank you for your patience and understanding . . . for not confirming that I'm an idiot. Give my love to your wife and daughter, okay? If I get any actionable intelligence, I'll let you know." Cleveland tried to release his hand, but Edwards would not let it go.

"There is a hope we haven't reached out to," said Edwards. "Let's pray, Atticus. It may be the most powerful thing we can do at the moment."

Ambassador's Residence, Tel Aviv
July 23, 10:10 a.m.

McKeon didn't answer his call. Mullaney left a message, then looked at the phone in his hand and wondered if it was damaged at the monastery.

His makeshift office was crammed. He had asked Ruth Hughes and Palmyra Parker to join them . . . there was so much they needed to sort out. Hughes, Parker, and Herzog filled the chairs across from his desk, Levinson and Doorley standing against the wall.

"First, what's security like here? Have we shored up the—"

His phone rang. He looked at the screen. Not McKeon. He tapped the speaker button.

"Mullaney," he answered.

———◦◦◦◦———

St. Archangel Michael Monastery, Tel Aviv
July 23, 10:18 a.m.

In his massive swivel chair, he felt like Star Trek's Captain James Kirk on the bridge of the *Enterprise*.

Poppy's bulk was negated by the snappy maneuverability of the chair. But his Kirk-ness emanated from the swiftness of his fingers on the instrument panels at the end of the chair's two arms and the way he could control a bank of his computer screens with either hand—simultaneously.

Still, beads of perspiration rolled off Father Poppodopolous's forehead and down alongside his pudgy cheeks. He was multitasking at high speed, running a sequential series of algorithms on his computers, the results on the screen for one computer flowing over into the data banks of the next computer, compounding the speed of its calculations. When Poppy watched the seemingly light-speed results flashing across the screen of the fourth computer . . . well, his finite mind had already been left far behind.

For a moment he lifted his hands, stretched his joints, and reached for his mobile phone.

"Mullaney."

"It's Poppy," he said, "but don't get your hopes up. I still don't have a translation of your fascinating little message. But I've got a moment here where I can take a breath, and I thought you might find this update interesting."

"Okay, I'm listening."

"Your guy, Rabbi Elijah Ben Solomon Zalman, was very definitely a genius," said Poppodopolous. "The Gaon was famous for his knowledge of the Jewish Torah, was both prolific and accurate in his written commentaries on the law and the prophets. But his genius didn't stop with Jewish scripture. Did you know he wrote a seminal mathematics textbook? Ages ahead of his time. There's a copy of the book in the library at Columbia University. The university has images of the pages of the entire book up on Google. I was just looking at it a few minutes ago. The last time it was checked out was 1947. It's printed in Hebrew, but it appears to have the Gaon's original drawings and formulas included in it. And guess what? Our Gaon guy understood binary theory."

The monk waited for Mullaney's amazed and appreciative response. All he heard was silence.

"Listen, Father, we're kind of . . ."

"Binary theory?" Poppodopolous said, again disappointed in a lack of response from Mullaney. "Your Gaon understood computers. How they work. How the codes needed to be written." Again, he waited.

"He knew Unicode?" asked Mullaney.

Finally.

"No, not Unicode—at least I haven't found any evidence of that," said Poppodopolous, "but he was a mathematics genius too. He conceived of something very similar to Unicode. A common programming language. I'm running a diagnostic on the entire book now, matching it against the symbols from our message. Nothing yet, but I think I'm on the right track. And there's something else . . . I'm almost afraid to mention it."

There was a short intake of breath on the other end of the call. Father Poppodopolous could tell that Mullaney didn't need any more on his plate. Oh, well . . . nothing ventured . . .

"There is an emerging field called computer learning that is closely allied with artificial intelligence," said the monk. "Not to get too technical with you, but this guy was all over AI and the power of algorithms. Do you understand the concept of the arrow of time?"

Another pause. "I'm lost," said Mullaney.

"Okay, I'll fill you in when I've finally cracked this beast. But I think you're going to be surprised just how much this Gaon guy had under his bonnet. I'll get back to you when I've got something."

"Okay, but you've got to hurry," said Mullaney. "Rabbi Herzog and I almost didn't make it away from your monastery alive. There was an ambush waiting for us. If Meyer Levinson hadn't had his men trailing us for protection . . . well . . . I don't want to think about that."

"My computers are running at warp speed, Agent Mullaney. And so am I. I'll have an answer for you soon."

28

Ambassador's Residence, Tel Aviv
July 23, 10:25 a.m.

"So we've got all the breaches repaired," said Doorley. "Thanks to Colonel Levinson, we have a team of electricians working on any power issues, much needed additional security agents from Shin Bet, and two communications gurus who are working miracles in getting our security apparatus up and running."

Mullaney breathed a sigh of relief. One problem seemed under control. "Thanks, Kathie. Good work." He turned to Levinson. "And once again I'm in your debt, Meyer."

"I think the account is pretty balanced already," Levinson responded.

Clicking off items in his mind, Mullaney turned to Doorley once more. "So where's McKeon and the ambassador?"

"They left"—she looked at her watch—"about ninety minutes ago. Ambassador Cleveland said they were on their way to the embassy."

"Has anyone talked to them since? I can't reach Pat on her cell phone."

To Ruth Hughes, it looked like Mullaney was about to blow a gasket. He pounded the Off button on the phone console on his desk, severing the call to the embassy.

"Ambassador Cleveland is *not* at the embassy," Mullaney thundered. "Neither is McKeon. Neither one has been seen since yesterday."

The tension level in the room had sharpened to a deadly edge.

Cleveland was missing.

RAF Akrotiri Air Base, Cyprus
July 23, 10:28 a.m.

The three DSS agents were seated together around a small table by the doors to the officer's mess, but McKeon was pacing back and forth in the foyer, a cell phone plastered to her right ear and a scowl plastered to her face.

Cleveland had put McKeon in a terrible position, and he regretted the impact his plan might have on her career. But . . . there was no other way.

The ambassador walked through the doors, his escort moving as one to stay on his heels. "Any word from Brian?" Cleveland asked as he passed McKeon and trundled down the steps to the two waiting golf carts and the RAF airmen who were driving them back to the air terminal.

"No," snapped McKeon. "And I'm beginning to worry." The golf carts jerked into motion and careened around a tight corner onto Jacaranda Drive, forcing Cleveland and McKeon to hold tight to the metal struts keeping up the roof. The force of the turn pushed Cleveland's body toward McKeon. He slipped the jamming device into the pocket of her suit jacket.

"I'll call the residence when we get to the terminal," said McKeon.

The performance began. Cleveland squirmed in his seat as they snaked through a roundabout and onto Lightning Lane. He rubbed his stomach, grunting when the golf carts jolted to a stop at the commercial aviation terminal.

McKeon looked sideways at him. "Are you all right?"

Cleveland shook his head. "Don't know. My stomach is rumbling around," he said as they uncoiled from the carts, thanked the smiling drivers, and walked through the terminal doors. "Don't know if it's something I ate or the roller coaster ride we just endured." They walked past an airman on security at the doors. "Where's the men's room?" asked Cleveland.

One hand remaining on his weapon, the airman pointed to his left. "The loo is down the hallway, sir . . . to the left."

"Uuummmhhh." Cleveland bent slightly at the waist. "Might be in there for a while," he said over his shoulder as he walked quickly and turned left into the corridor. The men's room was about halfway down the hallway. He glanced over his shoulder to make sure he wasn't being observed. When he came abreast of the door, Cleveland pushed it open and leaned in. As he hoped, there was a trash can just to the left of the door. He pulled the SIM card out of his pocket, tossed it into the trash can, and continued down the corridor. As his Google searches anticipated, there was an exit door from the terminal at its end.

———————⋙∘∘∘∘⋘———————

Watching Cleveland stagger around the corner, McKeon was battling conflicting emotions . . . respect the man's privacy as his body ejected, one way or another, some foreign ingredient he ingested in the commissary, or send one of the DSS agents in with him and embarrass the suffering ambassador. She reached into the right-hand pocket of her suit jacket and pulled out her iPhone. She switched the phone to her left hand and tapped the "Find a Friend" app with her right index finger. There was Cleveland's icon, halfway down the corridor, inside the men's room . . . a clear signal from Cleveland's phone. Shoot . . . what to do?

One more glance at Cleveland's icon, still in the same place, and McKeon slipped the iPhone into the left pocket of her suit jacket. *Give the guy a break.*

NATO Surveillance Post, RAF Akrotiri Air Base, Cyprus
July 23, 10:29 a.m.

Ernie Edwards was chewing on the mangled end of an unlit cigar stub as he crossed the tarmac to the hanger RAF had assigned to NATO forces in the far, southern corner of the Akrotiri base. He was thinking of his orders. And he was thinking of several thousand women and children . . . American dependents . . . in harm's way on the Turkish mainland. For the moment he had stuffed any possible career concerns into a back pocket of his mind.

His pilot, a US Army Ranger and third in command of Team Black, stepped out of the shade from his airplane's wing and moved toward Edwards.

"Get Traynor on the radio," growled Edwards. His second in command was back in Syria, overseeing the operations of Team Black. "Tell him to pull in every available asset from the Team and get them ready to move out ASAP."

"Where are we headed?"

"Incirlik," Edwards said of the three-thousand-acre airbase on the eastern flank of Adana, Turkey, "just in case. Are we fueled up?"

"Ready to go," said the Ranger.

"Good. Tell Traynor we'll meet him at Incirlik and that I'll call him with the details once we're airborne."

He could cover a transfer of his men to another NATO base. Call it maneuvers or R&R. He could make it stand up. Just in case.

29

Ambassador's Residence, Tel Aviv
July 23, 10:29 a.m.

Mullaney looked at Parker, sitting right in front of him, angry desperation erupting across his features.

"I don't know where my father is," Parker said without prompting. "I thought he was at the embassy. You don't think . . ."

"I'll get my men moving immediately," snapped Levinson, pulling a cell phone from his pocket. "We'll have . . ."

"He's not been abducted."

Mullaney turned slowly toward Hughes, understanding clearing the anger from everything but his eyes.

RAF Akrotiri Air Base, Cyprus
July 23, 10:29 a.m.

Leaving the terminal, Cleveland marched straight ahead along Lightning Lane, about five hundred yards to Flamingo Way and the front door of Stephanos Car Rentals.

Cleveland checked in at the desk using his US Diplomatic Passport— which elicited a momentary glance from the rental agent—and international driver's license. He signed for the compact Ford, which was in a small lot alongside the rental office, and left the rental office just minutes after he entered. He wondered how much time he had. Cleveland got into the Ford, buckled in, and turned right onto Flamingo Way.

DSS Agent Pat McKeon was staring intently at the door to the men's restroom halfway down the corridor. She reached into the left pocket of her jacket to pull out her iPhone and check the app—and felt something else. She pulled them both out.

Cleveland's icon on her phone's screen was in the same place, halfway down the corridor in the men's room. He was there, but was he well?

McKeon looked at the second device. And what the heck was this?

She motioned to the agent on her right. "Get in there and check on the ambassador. Make sure he's okay."

Her anxiety long ago had reached an apex—or so she thought. McKeon turned over the second device in her left hand. A black, plastic square. A small toggle switch on the side. Fear and fury burst up from her gut. *Blast your eyes!* She pulled out her cell phone . . . there were no missed calls; no messages from Mullaney.

Ambassador's Residence, Tel Aviv
July 23, 10:33 a.m.

"He flew to Cyprus to meet with Ernie Edwards," said Hughes. She tried to keep her voice firm, although she now felt like a confessed conspirator. "He ordered McKeon and his DSS detail to go with him and demanded a ban on any outside communication."

The silence in the room had a heartbeat . . . a life of its own. Mullaney's wrath.

"How did he get to Cyprus?" He squeezed the words through clenched teeth.

Caught! "Well," said Hughes, "I helped get him an airplane."

RAF Akrotiri Air Base, Cyprus
July 23, 10:34 a.m.

But Cleveland was not planning on driving the car on the two-hour trip from southern Cyprus to Ercan Airport in the north, where his reservation was waiting. Instead, he drove less than half-a-mile to the east, to the Cost Cutter Car Park near the base post office. Cleveland found an empty slot near the center of the crowded lot. He locked the car, dropped the keys into the postal box in front of the post office, and headed north on foot, winding his way past the soccer field and the cinema, less than a mile, to the base helipad.

———∞∞∞———

Ambassador's Residence, Tel Aviv
July 23, 10:35 a.m.

Anger shimmered off Mullaney like sunshine on asphalt in August. An anger that was now lasered onto her. "You helped Cleveland leave the country without me knowing about it?"

The blade of betrayal sliced in both directions. Hughes was bleeding regret. "He was hoping to convince Edwards—"

"That won't happen," snapped Mullaney. "Edwards is not going to stage a raid on a sovereign nation without orders."

Parker broke into Mullaney's response. "Cyprus is a lot closer to Turkey than Tel Aviv," she said. "And Dad has a long, personal relationship with President Kashani. He may be holding out hope, but he knows in his heart Edwards won't move. I wouldn't be surprised if Kashani is his ultimate target. I'd put my money on Turkey."

"That crazy old . . ." Mullaney's cell phone rang. He looked at the screen. McKeon. *Oh, Lord . . . no!*

———∞∞∞———

RAF Akrotiri Air Base, Cyprus
July 23, 10:35 a.m.

The Turkish chopper with the NATO markings—a massive, twin-rotor Chinook CH-47F—sat on the closest pad. Its rotors started moving as soon as Cleveland walked out of the lee of the hanger and onto the tarmac. At the conclusion of his eleven-minute, roundabout trip through the air base, Cleveland ended up less than fifteen hundred feet from the Akrotiri Terminal where McKeon and the other DSS agents were growing more anxious with each minute that passed. Cleveland slipped through the door of the white, military helicopter.

———∞∞∞———

McKeon began muttering the same Irish epithets she'd heard her grandmother mumble after her third whiskey. She flipped the toggle switch in the opposite direction just as the agent bolted out of the men's room and ran in her direction, holding an object in his right hand.

She knew the truth before he opened his mouth.

"He's not there! I searched every stall. The only window is locked from the inside. And I found this in the trash."

The agent had a small, rectangular printed circuit in his right hand. A SIM card. Cleveland's SIM card. Wiping the memory of her grandmother from her thoughts, McKeon still flogged her psyche with a silent litany of those cutting Irish epithets. Four days ago, she let Palmyra Parker out of her sight, and she got abducted. Now Cleveland? *Not again!*

"Go to the plane," she said to the first agent. "He's not there, but we need to be sure. Call me as soon as you know." She turned to the agent on her left. "Go to the desk and get them to call whoever is in charge of base security. I want this base locked down now!"

McKeon looked at the phone in her hand. Several messages flooded in, one after another. She tapped the speed dial number for Mullaney. This would be painful.

30

Mullaney looked at the ringing phone on his desk and knew to abandon all hope of good news. He tapped the Speaker icon on the screen. "Talk to me, Pat."

There was no evasion from McKeon. "We're on Cyprus, at the RAF Akrotiri Air Base. The ambassador came here to meet with Colonel Edwards," she said. "Their meeting ended. But the ambassador is . . . gone. Not abducted," McKeon was quick to add. "He skipped on his own. He slipped a jamming device into my pocket—why you and I couldn't make contact. He was sick when he went to the men's room . . . probably faked his stomach cramps. But he wasn't there when we checked. And he tossed his SIM card into the trash to keep the locator in the men's room. The base is locked down, and the Brits are looking under every rock—three of our guys too. But so far we have not found him."

As McKeon gave her truncated report, Mullaney felt a profound change permeate his mind and his spirit. The rage he felt moments ago was replaced with peace that reached to his core. He was trained to deal with crises. He'd lived through days when everything that could go wrong, did. Anger and fault-finding would not help them find Cleveland.

"How long ago?"

McKeon looked at her watch. "We last saw him seven, eight minutes ago as he was hustling down the hall to the men's room, half bent over at the waist."

Seven or eight minutes? Mullaney's first thought—he couldn't have gotten far—was trumped by his second thought. If Cleveland was planning this escape, he must have known two things. How he was going to get off Cyprus. And how little time he would have before McKeon would be on his tail.

"I doubt you will find him on the base," said Mullaney. "Find out every possible way Cleveland could get from Cyprus to Turkey and concentrate your attention there. We think his plan all along was to get to Ankara . . . to get face-to-face with President Kashani. Lord willing he's not off the island yet." Mullaney paused. What to say next. "Just find him, Pat. Then don't let him out of your sight."

———◦◦◦◦———

St. Archangel Michael Monastery, Tel Aviv
July 23, 10:41 a.m.

His fingers flying over an ergonomic wireless keyboard, Puccini's *La Bohème* blasting through unseen speakers, Father Poppodopolous was talking to his computer screens as he hammered in a new search code. "Okay, Mr. Gaon, let's run a series of kabbalah symbols against what we've found so far and see what comes up."

Finishing his code, the monk hit Enter and sat back and watched the screens of four of his huge computer monitors whirl like runaway slot machines. Numbers, letters, symbols, and pulsing colors raced across each screen in an accelerating blur. His chair was comfortable, cradling Poppy's significant mass. It wasn't long before heaviness assailed his eyes, and his lids started to droop. He tried to stay awa—

Poppy's head snapped up from his chest and he shook his eyes open. The thought that he must have nodded out stalled in his mind as his eyes stared at a massively muscled, long-haired man sitting on the other side of his desk.

Pinpoints of light glistened across the surface of his silver breastplate.

What?

"I am Bayard, sent to you from the throne room of God."

Bayard . . . Where had he heard that name before? He looked around. He was aware of his surroundings. But he couldn't move. He wanted to move. His body was imprisoned by an invisible heaviness. But his eyes were riveted on the man in silver.

"I have been sent to you with a message." The man stood— and he was no man. He wore the silver armor of an ancient warrior, a great sword in a silver scabbard hanging by his side. But from behind his shoulders, immense pearlescent wings unfurled, filling the width of Poppy's vision. "Watch with me." The man turned, the wings swung away like an immense curtain, and a different room emerged.

Poppy thought he could feel the warmth of a glowing fire on his cheeks. He was looking into an old-fashioned room . . . heavy, rough-hewn wooden furniture; wide-plank wood floor with a well-worn rug before the fireplace; functionally crafted wood shelves, overflowing with books, spanning the walls.

Poppy's eyes followed the sound of a voice. Off to the left, an open window at his back, an elderly man sat behind a desk that was nearly buried—books and Torah scrolls and stacks of paper. He wore a round, black fur hat that looked like a box on his head. The white hair escaping from under the hat migrated down the sides of his face and culminated in a long, full, white beard. Framed by the white hair, two crystalline blue eyes thrummed with the power of joy and wonder.

The huge, winged visitor now knelt on the floor across the desk from the old man, his head and furled wings barely clearing the low ceiling. The tableau was so vivid, it forced Poppy to suspend his state of unbelief. Not only was he looking at an angel, Bayard, but he was confident he was also looking at a room in Vilna, Lithuania. This was the home of the Vilna Gaon. Two hundred years in the past.

"Greetings, favored one," said the angel, Bayard. "I have been sent in answer to your prayer."

The old man lifted a leather pouch from atop a stack of papers. "This pouch is for you to deliver to the last guardian, my final heir, at the appointed time,"

Bayard extended his muscled arm across the desk and took the pouch in his hand.

"And I have a message for our beloved monk," said the Gaon. "Tell him that the truths that rule the world are always the most simple. Faith, love, trust—all simple concepts to the creator of man. It's man who makes them complicated."

The Gaon raised his right hand, palm up. "As simple as on." Then he turned his palm down. "Off."

He turned his palm up. "One." Flip. "Zero." Palm up. "True." Flip. "False."

The Gaon looked up from his hand toward the angel. "Tell

him he is making his search too complicated. He should seek the simple answer."

Poppy felt the warmth of the fire sink deeply into his bones. Heaviness returned to his eyes. He fought to remain in the moment. The simple answer?

"If something is not impossible," the old man said to Bayard, his voice slipping away from Poppy, "it is possible."

Like a curtain closing across a stage, a wash of feathers swept past Poppy's sight.

Father Poppodopolous jolted out of his dream . . . his vision? . . . so abruptly, he almost fell out of his comfortable chair. He scanned the room quickly, then closed his eyes. An angel? The Vilna Gaon? He shook the cobwebs out of his thinking and tried to fix each image, each word into his memory. *A simple answer.*

Opening his eyes, Poppy noticed that all four screens were motionless, the flashing collage of light and color replaced by a single, stationary image of two lines—a string of letters in one line then a sequence of numbers in the second. On all four screens, the sequencing of the letters and then numbers were identical.

He started breaking down the letters into words.

31

The reports came in at almost the same time. A British captain strode through the front door of the terminal at almost the same moment one of the DSS agents slammed down the phone on the far end of the terminal's reception desk.

"The ambassador bought an online ticket on a commercial flight to Ankara," called the DSS agent as he trotted over to McKean's unofficial command post—a table and a few chairs in a corner of the empty lobby. "Out of Ercan Airport, up in Northern Cyprus, east of Nicosia. The only flight connections to Turkey are out of that airport."

"Bloody bad luck, that, but it makes sense," interjected the British officer. "Captain Throwright, base security, ma'am." Ramrod straight, he saluted McKeon. "Ambassador Cleveland hired a rental vehicle—in advance—from Stephanos Rentals, just a short walk from here. A black Ford, signed out just under fifteen minutes ago. Plenty of time to exit the air base and be on his way to the airport."

"Why bad luck?" asked McKeon. "Because we can't allow the ambassador's disappearance to go public? Because we can't get the local cops involved?"

"Aye, that too," said the captain. "But bad luck because Ercan is in Northern Cyprus . . . Turkish controlled ever since the war in seventy-four, you see, but still claimed by Greece. And none of us in the West recognize Northern Cyprus's existence. We have no one on the ground there."

"How far to the airport?" asked McKeon.

"Two hours, give or take."

"Then we may have time to catch him. Can you get us a car?"

"Yes . . . but you won't get past the Turks. You look too much like bobbies on a mission."

"We'll deal with that," snapped McKeon. "One problem at a time." She opened up Contacts on her iPhone.

Only four people were left in Mullaney's office: Mullaney, Herzog, Levinson, and Hughes. Palmyra Parker had returned to the ambassador's private quarters to see if she could find some clues to Cleveland's whereabouts in his study. And Kathie Doorley went back to supervising the resurrection of the ambassador's residence to a viable and safe entity.

Looking like an old man with little sleep, Rabbi Herzog appeared to be taking a nap in his chair. Meyer Levinson was speaking softly into his phone in a corner of the office. And Ruth Hughes was trying her best to be invisible. But Mullaney skewered her with a stare.

"This could go badly for you."

That was obvious. Hughes waited.

"I thought I could trust you."

"You did. You still can. I was helping the ambassador do what he convinced me he had to do. I serve the ambassador, Brian. You know that." Hughes took the other avenue that was available to her. "And we couldn't reach you."

Mullaney shook his head. "No excuse, Ruth. You know what I would have said if you had reached me. This is a fool's errand, a dangerous one. And you gave him the means to do it. This is a big withdrawal from your account with me."

She could hear both anger and hurt in his voice, a hurt that stirred up regret in her emotions but failed to change her mind. "I know, and I'm sorry for—"

Mullaney's cell phone rang. It was still sitting on top of his desk. He tapped the speaker button.

"Pat."

"Cleveland made significant preparation for his escape. He rented a car online at a base car rental agency. He also made an advance reservation on a flight from Ercan Airport, outside Nicosia, to Esenboga International Airport, north of Ankara. It looks like that's where he's headed."

"Can you catch him?"

"We're going to try. The base security chief is willing to send a car after him, and one of our guys can go along. It's about a two-hour drive. Cleveland's got a bit of a start. Hopefully they can catch him. If he gets past the border, it may be tough. Ercan is in Northern Cyprus. Turkish controlled, so I don't know if we want to cross that border. And the Brits don't have anybody on the ground."

"Hold on."

Mullaney put his phone on mute. "What kind of plane did you provide for the ambassador?"

Good idea, she thought. "It was a Gulfstream G450, one of the fastest private jets in the world. Can cruise at nearly six hundred miles an hour. It can beat him to Ankara. And yes . . . it's still there, available to us."

He released the mute button. "Pat, do two things. Yes . . . put one of our guys into a car with someone who speaks Turkish, someone the Brits trust, and have them try to catch Cleveland on the way to Ercan. Then I want you and the other DSS agents to get to Esenboga. Get back to the plane Cleveland used to get you all to Akrotiri. Ruth Hughes will arrange for the crew to be expecting you. The plane is superfast. It can beat Cleveland to the airport. I'll send additional agents from the Ankara embassy, but—if we can't catch him—I want you there when Atticus gets off that plane. Then I want you to stick him in your pocket, if necessary, get him on the Gulfstream, and bring him home." Hughes knew a threat was coming—veiled, but a threat. But it had to be said. "You need this one, Pat."

"Okay, I understand, Brian. I'll stay in touch."

⸻⸺◦∞◦⸺⸻

Güvercinlik Army Air Base, Ankara
July 23, 12:08 p.m.

A nondescript vintage Opel—meaning dented, missing a fender, two red doors on the passenger side standing out from the dusty black of the rest of the car—waited twenty feet from the NATO helipad in a far corner of Güvercinlik Army Air Base in northwest Ankara. As the chopper's rotors slowed down, the Opel pulled alongside. Cleveland—without a tie, his jacket thrown over his shoulder, shirt sleeves rolled up, aviator sunglasses shading his eyes—looked like a tired NATO administrator getting out of the helicopter. No one except the driver noticed his presence.

As Cleveland lowered himself into the passenger seat, he glanced over at the driver. Dressed in black, head-to-toe, he had the look of a professional fighter who had lost more boxing matches than he'd won. The driver shifted into gear and didn't move his eyes from the tarmac in front of him. "He's waiting for you at the palace."

The Opel lurched away from the chopper, a cloud of oil smoke in its wake.

32

Cankaya Palace, Ankara
July 23, 12:37 p.m.

In spite of its looks and condition, the battered Opel was immediately waved through a secluded, rear entrance to the Cankaya Palace, President Kashani's Ankara residence. No inspection and no questions asked. Cankaya was huge, sprawling, and opulent. No Ottoman sultan lived in more ostentatious luxury. But instead of driving toward the massive, pink-stone residence, the driver diverted to the right, wound his way along a narrow garden road, and pulled up alongside an impressive greenhouse complex far from the main building.

Silent as the tomb the entire ride from the airport, the driver nodded toward an idyllic, secluded garden house alongside the greenhouse. "He's in there."

Not surprising. Kashani was an avid gardener. And this was a meeting he would want to keep under the radar. Without response to the driver, Cleveland pulled himself from the sagging bucket seat. He stretched the kinks out of his joints—winced as the pain in his back, from the rollover car crash four days ago, woke out of dormancy. Cleveland tried to erase from his mind all the pain from his myriad bruises and sprains. He would need his faculties on full alert if he hoped to discern Kashani's true intentions and divert him from any foolhardy escapade.

As he walked up the stone path, Cleveland noticed the door to the garden house was slightly ajar. He pushed the door farther open and stepped across the threshold. The house was designed to take in the full grandeur of the spacious and colorful gardens that surrounded it. Floor-to-ceiling windows comprised three walls of a great room off to his left. The windows could open to admit any breeze or be covered by heavy curtains to keep out the heat. Two of the three window-walls were covered by the curtains, leaving the room in a muted state of dusk. Wicker and rattan furniture with luxurious and deep cushions were staged in three seating areas around the room, but the room still had a loose, airy feel to it.

The short corridor before him led to a closed door toward the back of the house. On his right, the one solid wall had a pocket door in its center, closed tightly.

There was no sign of Kashani.

His battered body suddenly aching for rest, Cleveland staggered into the great room to the nearest rattan sofa and lowered himself into an embracing corner of the cushions where he had an open view of the front door, the pocket doors, and the resplendent colors of the garden.

Cleveland jolted. The sun was held hostage behind some thick clouds, deepening the gloom in a room that was designed to celebrate light. The long shadows were the only hint that he must have dozed off. A chill wrapped its arms around Cleveland's shoulders, running down his spine. The smell of compost . . . decayed earth . . . replaced the perfume of the garden.

Like the Red Sea parting, the pocket doors across the hall slowly slid open.

Cleveland shook his head, trying to clear the cobwebs, but the sight didn't change. Standing in the doorway was Arslan Eroglu, prime minister of Turkey, and not Emet Kashani, its president. Whatever Eroglu's presence portended, Cleveland instinctively knew it would not be good. And there was this . . . feeling . . .

"I am ever so sorry to disappoint you, Mr. Ambassador." Eroglu walked across the entry corridor and entered the great room. He walked slowly, his body fairly immobile, his feet barely lifting from the lush carpets. It looked like he was gliding over the floor instead of walking on it.

"I know you expected to meet with our president, but he has been beset by a severe illness." Eroglu's movement stopped about ten feet in front of Cleveland, who was still sitting on the sofa. "President Kashani implored me to meet with you in his place. It is good to see you once again."

While ambassador to Turkey for two years, his previous Foreign Service posting, Cleveland had innumerable interactions with both Kashani and Eroglu. Where he found the president a staunch Muslim, he also found a man of reason with a willingness to listen. But Eroglu? The prime minister was proud, vain, and unscrupulous. Cleveland didn't trust him.

But something wasn't right. Eroglu's voice was the same, but it was different as well. In the past, he had found Eroglu infuriatingly pompous in his speech. But today the arrogance was still there, the condescension, but it was . . . coated . . . polluted? . . . Each word that reached his ears had the feel that it traveled through a sewer before it entered his ear canal. Creepy. And disgusting. A sense of revulsion pushed Cleveland back farther into the cushions.

"How is it I can help you, Mr. Ambassador?"

Cleveland fought a tide of nausea as Eroglu moved closer. He forced himself to speak.

"I need to speak to the president." Cleveland felt like his words were coming from under water. "We are in possession of credible evidence that . . ."

"Incirlik?" interrupted Eroglu. "You believe such nonsense? Is America's State Department so gullible as to believe such cowardly rumors of a NATO ally?" Eroglu took another step forward. It was then, when he pulled his right hand out of the left sleeve of his suit jacket to point, that Eroglu's odd posture finally registered on Cleveland—arms folded over his stomach, hands pushed inside the sleeves of his jacket. It was so very old-fashioned. He had never seen Eroglu . . .

"Are you so arrogant," Eroglu said in rebuke, "is the United States so ignorant of its treaty responsibilities, as to level such an accusation at my country?"

Cleveland felt assaulted. The corruption coating Eroglu's words now spread to a stench in his nostrils. The prime minister's pointing finger seemed to have a power behind it. Cleveland felt it pushing against him. His thinking felt foggy.

"How can you be such a fool as to believe these lies?" Eroglu took another step forward, his voice rose, his eyes widened. Mayhem filled his eyes. And a primal terror swept through Cleveland. His heart skipped a beat, and pain pounded against the inside of his temples. But worst of all, somehow, Cleveland felt his soul shiver.

"You insult our character." Eroglu was little more than an arm's length away, his words an angry and threatening denunciation. "You demean our integrity. You treat us with contempt."

With a blinding certainty, Cleveland recognized two truths. He had never met *this* Arslan Eroglu before. And he was in mortal danger . . . not just to his life, but to his everlasting eternity.

This is the Man of Violence.

The frightening knowledge flooded Cleveland's mind. His spirit cried out. *God, help me!* Caught in their vortex, Cleveland tried to divert his eyes from the one who was searching for his soul.

Father . . . fight for me!

The room was spinning. Those eyes of torment loosened Cleveland's grip on consciousness. Terror gripped him. But he reached deep into himself, to hold onto himself. A word forced itself from his spirit.

"Jesus."

It was little more than a mumble, a croaking whisper that barely cleared his lips.

Eroglu fell back a step. His eyes widened, but now in trepidation.

"Jesus." Cleveland croaked. He desperately grasped onto the word. "Jesus."

"Stop!" Eroglu was no longer concentrating on Cleveland. He was struggling against something that seemed to be opposing him.

Keep fighting, son of the King. Keep fighting.

"Jesus," Cleveland said on a burst of breath.

"Stop!" shouted Eroglu. He threw up his arms and slammed his palms together with a resounding clap. "Stop!"

And consciousness fled from Joseph Atticus Cleveland.

Fairfax, Virginia
July 23, 6:40 a.m.

Though the house was comfortably cool from the central air, Abigail's skin could feel the already piercing heat of the sun's first rays as she walked past the kitchen windows. Raised in Georgia, she lived with the heat and humidity, but she didn't like it. This day was going to be another scorcher. Summer counselors at their church's day camp, her daughters would be wilted and irritable by the end of this day.

"C'mon, girls," Abby called up the stairs as she picked up the pile of mail she had absently tossed on the kitchen island when she got home the night before. "We need to be out of here by seven thirty."

Gutter cleaners . . . mosquito killers . . . basement repairs . . . one envelope after another got tossed into the trash can without a second thought. The "personal" letter from Mr. Basementy was in her fingers, on its way to doom, when her attention was seized by the envelope next in line. It was wrinkled, dog-eared at the corners, as if it had lived in somebody's pants pocket before it hit the postal service. Its condition was not what had arrested her. It was the one word in the upper left corner. *Morningstar.*

Mr. Basementy was banished to the trash, the other mail tossed back onto the island as Abigail Mullaney looked for the second time at the envelope in her hand. It was addressed to her. From George Morningstar? Abby's anxiety ticked up a notch as she slipped her finger under the flap of the envelope and pulled out two sheets of paper. There was a thin memory stick at the bottom of the envelope. For a moment she forgot about the girls. The letter was typed . . . probably a computer printout.

> *Abby,*
>
> *Please forgive me for involving you, but I couldn't trust any-one at State with this information. I tried reaching Brian, but he didn't answer his phone. I just sent him a short text, but I needed somebody else to know what I've discovered.*

Abby flipped over the envelope. The time stamp on the postmark was 8:33 a.m., yesterday, from Manassas, Virginia. But the letter would have been dropped at the post office some time before then . . . where was Brian then? Her eyes jumped back to the letter.

> *Brian asked me to look into Noah Webster, try to find out why Ambassador Cleveland allows Webster to insult and abuse him without reporting Webster to the secretary. Brian also thinks Web-ster could be the one who altered Cleveland's Situation Report before it got to the secretary.*
>
> *While quietly investigating Webster, I uncovered two situa-tions that make me fearful that Noah Webster may be one of the most dangerous men in Washington.*
>
> *First, about six months ago, I assigned Brian to investigate the IT department's suspicions of unauthorized visits to State's HR files. We found hints but nothing conclusive. And then Ankara happened, I got banished to the basement, Brian got transferred . . . end of investigation.*
>
> *In the last week I got a "read only" access to Webster's email account at State and found that he was not only influential in having a young woman added to last year's list of interns, but he*

also made sure she was assigned to Human Resources. When I found that connection, I asked a few questions in HR. Just after Brian was assigned to the investigation, the woman left one Friday afternoon and never came back. I dug a little deeper and found she was renting a condo in the exclusive Skyview Plaza. Either she was independently wealthy or she had some supplemental income to her intern's salary.

What I believe is that Webster paid this woman to scour the State Department HR files for dirt he could use to his advantage.

After leaving the State Department, that woman disappeared without a trace. To me, her disappearance looks like professional work. Like she never existed. We may now know why Brian was expelled to Israel. He was getting too close for Webster's comfort. But we have no clue what happened to the woman.

The second situation could mean trouble for your father.

Just before Webster joined the State Department, Senator Markham introduced him to your father. Everything I've found indicates that a deal was struck—if Webster could help prevent the millions of dollars in confiscated Iranian funds languishing in Rutherford's banks from being returned to Iran, then Rutherford would finance Webster's run for elected office. If true, that plot could mean serious jail time for all three.

The other day, Senator Markham, who never had a problem with his heart, died suddenly from heart failure. That's a technique also used by professionals.

Everything in my gut is telling me that Noah Webster will stop at nothing—like eliminating his risks—to achieve his aims. It's possible Webster may now see your father as a vulnerability. Your father may be in danger. And yes, I think you and the girls need to be careful too.

All of the details, including some troubling contacts Webster's had with the prime minister of Turkey, are on the memory stick in the envelope. But it appears the signs are pointing to Webster at the center of some kind of plot—of what I'm not sure. But I'm getting close.

I've been cultivating Nora Carson, Webster's right hand at State, and finally got her to agree to a meeting in a few hours. I think she knows where all the skeletons are located. With Markham's suspicious death, Webster could be more dangerous than I ever dreamed.

Maybe I'm being paranoid, but I didn't want to be the only one with this information. Please, hold onto this until I get back to you. Maybe we can get Brian home sooner than you think.

George

Abby ran her eyes back to the top of the letter and tried to slow her racing heart while she read through it one more time. She was gnawing on the flesh of her right index finger, her mind flashing from one frightening thought to another, when her intense scrutiny of the letter was interrupted.

"Mom? . . . Mom, are you all right?" Her daughter Kylie was standing beside the garage door. "C'mon, we're going to be late."

33

"Yes," snapped Mullaney.

"Sorry, sir," came the startled voice on his intercom, "but there's a monk out front who says he must see you immediately. Father Poppodopolous?"

For a moment, Brian Mullaney's battered mind stalled, felt it couldn't handle any more. But then . . . the message?

"Sorry for snapping at you. Bring him down to my office. Thanks."

"Yes . . . I think I've figured it out." Poppy was standing behind the chair Mullaney had offered him in his crowded office. Herzog was seated across from him, on the other side of the desk; Hughes in a straight-backed chair to his left; Levinson leaning against the back wall. "But first, I need you to consider something . . . something that will be vitally important if my conclusions are correct."

Mullaney shook his head and looked to the ceiling. "Father, we're in the midst of a couple of crises here. No disrespect, but we don't have a lot of time to be debating your theories."

Poppodopolous glanced over at Rabbi Herzog for support. The rabbi was clearly perplexed. No help there? Well how could he slow Mullaney down for a moment? How could he get his attention and keep it for as long as . . . if he didn't understand, how could he believe?

"Agent Mullaney, I don't know everything that you're facing at present, and I apologize for adding to your burdens," said the monk, "but you need to listen to me. I am convinced that we are at the critical confluence where all that you've been telling me might finally make sense. The lynchpin between all that's happened in the past and what must happen in the future. Please, bear with me."

Clearly in the midst of an internal battle, Mullaney opened his mouth to speak. But Rabbi Herzog reached across the desk toward the agent's arm while he looked up at the monk.

"You have the answer, don't you." It was a statement.

A stillness permeated the room.

"I believe so . . . yes," said Poppodopolous.

Herzog returned his gaze to Mullaney. "To this, I think, you must listen," he said. "I believe Poppy may have uncovered the key, the purpose we've all been looking for." He glanced up again at Poppy. "What is it, Poppy? What have you discovered?"

A lifeline! Thank you, God. The monk seized his chance.

"The Vilna Gaon has been directing this drama from the beginning . . ."

"Yes . . . we know that . . . the messages and the box." Mullaney's tether was tight.

"I'm sorry, I'm not making myself clear," Poppy continued. "The last time we were together, you mentioned the name Bayard. Unfortunately, I did not ask at the time who this Bayard was, so I was knocked off my pins when Bayard showed up in my room at the monastery earlier today."

"Hmmm, yes." Rabbi Herzog nodded. "My first encounter with Bayard nearly stopped this old heart from beating, Intimidating, he is."

"But why . . ." Mullaney stammered. "What was . . ."

"A message." Father Poppodopolous came around the chair and carefully lowered his bulk onto its center, shifting slightly to his left so he could look at both Herzog and Mullaney. "This Bayard," he continued, "has he been a messenger in the past? That is one of the job descriptions of an angel."

"Yes," said Mullaney. "Messenger, ally, protector. All of the above. He's been in the middle of this battle from the beginning."

Poppy nodded his head. "In the middle I don't doubt. But not the orchestrator of events. What I need you to understand is that not only did the Gaon instigate these events over two hundred years ago, but also what he set in motion in 1794 is still playing out today."

No one spoke. All eyes were on Poppodopolous.

"Remember when I mentioned the arrow of time on the phone—everything moves forward?" he said into the silence. "Well, like the prophets of the Old Testament, through divine intervention, the Vilna Gaon was given two prophetic messages that have come to fruition in our time. Bayard clearly has an assignment to help move these prophesies forward, but it was the Gaon who set this game in motion, and the Gaon whose influence continues to be felt.

"A few hours ago, Bayard revealed to me . . ." Poppy shook his head and lifted his hands palms up, the words he was about to speak sounding ludicrous in his own mind. "I don't know if it was a dream or a vision, but I found myself watching an interchange between the Gaon and an angel. The Gaon gave Bayard something to deliver, but then he said to tell the monk—me, I imagine—to look for the simple answer.

"A heartbeat later, I was back in my room, looking at four computer screens whose searches had all concluded at the same place. And the light finally went on in this dull brain of mine. 'Seek the simple answer.'" Poppodopolous scanned the crowded room. "We're not talking about time travel here or bending the arrow of time. The Vilna Gaon is not going to walk in that door and take us all to lunch. But I can tell you this: the prophecy that was given to the Gaon, that Bayard has protected, that has been passed on for two hundred years continues to be revealed in layers and continues to direct our steps today."

There was silence, but Poppodopolous waited for the explosion.

"That's your theory?" The silver-haired woman in the banker's suit wasn't buying it. "Come on now, Father" she said. "That's scientifically impossible. Nobody can warp time to engage the future. You're telling us that a rabbi from two hundred years ago is pulling our strings today?"

Poppy was about to answer when a distinctive ringtone rattled the room, snapping Levinson to attention. "Levinson," he answered. His eyes opened wide as he listened. "Put it in motion," he said into the phone as he turned to the door. "I'm on my way." And he was gone.

Poppodopolous looked around the room. "That was exciting." Then he turned to his right to address the woman. "No, what I'm saying is that what the Gaon set in motion two hundred years ago is still in motion today. It hasn't reached its conclusion, and we appear to be at the crest of its wave."

--- ❦ ---

Esenboga International Airport, Ankara
July 23, 2:27 p.m.

Her body and her mind felt like a sack of wet sand, but adrenaline was pumping through Agent Pat McKeon as passengers began emerging from the Jetway.

She didn't like the feel of this. Cleveland wasn't trying to hide his tracks very well. So if not, what was he trying to accomplish? A wild goose chase?

Without knowing what was going on, Mullaney was wise to keep Cleveland's escapade to himself rather than kick it upstairs. Not yet, anyway. If they could intercept the ambassador, get him back to Israel . . . hey, no harm no foul. But without the resources normally at their disposal, they weren't able to verify if passenger Joseph Cleveland was actually on this flight.

Cleveland was no fool. McKeon didn't like any of this. She thought the likelihood of Cleveland being on this plane was somewhere between slim and none. But what choice did she have? They had to be sure . . . Mullaney had ordered her here . . . and they had to find Cleveland. Soon.

First the flight officers—the captain and the copilot—came up the Jetway, rolling their doubled-up little suitcases behind them, followed by the flight attendants, one male and two female, who all looked bored to death. McKeon stuck a hand out in front of one of the female attendants.

"Nobody else on board?"

The woman looked at McKeon and must have seen the alarm in her eyes.

"No, sorry. The plane is empty," she said, then rolled away down the concourse.

McKeon's stomach sank to her knees. Her career was toast—that was for sure. But more importantly . . . where was Cleveland?

34

Fairfax, Virginia
July 23, 7:29 a.m.

The huge, brown truck from Litchfield Waste Removal strained against low gear as it lumbered past the house. Abby paused in backing out of the driveway. As the truck passed beyond her field of vision, she noticed the dark blue sedan parked farther up the street. Two men sat in the front seat.

I don't like that.

When she backed into the street and drove east, into the rising sun, the blue sedan stayed put. Turning the corner at Lester Street, Abby glanced over her shoulder. The blue car had not moved.

Easy, girl. Don't let yourself get spooked.

———⊙⊙⊙———

Calvary Hill Baptist Church—the church with the garden center on its front lawn—was a low-slung brick building at the corner of the Little River Turnpike and Olley Lane in Fairfax, Virginia. After making a right turn onto Olley Lane, Abby was preoccupied with talking to the girls about pickup time as she closed on Calvary Hill's driveway. But she drove past the driveway, up and over the hill, following Olley Lane south.

"Mom, you missed the church," said Kylie, sitting to her right.

Abby glanced quickly into her rearview mirror. She didn't see it following her . . . the blue sedan that was parked right next to the large, metal clothes collection boxes at the entrance to Calvary Hill. There were two men sitting in the front seat, both wearing sunglasses and both staring in her direction.

"Change of plans." Abby flicked her eyes back-and-forth from the road in front of her to the rearview mirror. "We're going on an adventure."

"But we're going to be late!"

Abby tapped the hands-free phone button on her steering wheel. "Call Doak," she spoke into the embedded mic.

"We're going to see Uncle Doak?"

"Probably . . ."

"Abby?"

"Hi, Doak. Are you on duty?"

"No, I . . ."

"Can the girls and I come visit?"

"Uh . . . sure. Why . . ."

"Doak, it's not safe out here," said Abby, using the same code phrase that Brian, his dad, and his brother used as Virginia state troopers.

There was a heartbeat pause on the other end of the connection.

"How close are you?"

"Ten minutes. I just went past the church."

"Okay. Stay on this call and stay on the main roads. I'll be on the lawn, looking for you."

"Thanks, Doak." Abby took a deep breath and looked once more into the rearview mirror. No blue sedan.

"Mom?" It was Samantha, Abby's younger daughter, from the back seat. Her voice carried the hint of anxiety.

"It's okay," said Abby, trying to sound nonchalant and in control. "We're just going to stop at Uncle Doak's for a while."

Abby's eyes went to the rearview mirror, but she caught Kylie's look out of her peripheral vision—mouth open, eyes wide, a dusting of fear on her face.

"It's okay," she said to herself. And even she didn't believe it.

Georgetown, DC
July 23, 7:33 a.m.

He was pushing down the plunger on his French Press machine when his iPhone came to life on the kitchen counter. Noah Webster recognized the number.

"Yes?"

"It worked. She was taking her kids to the church where they volunteer, but she didn't make it. She spotted our guys and kept on going. She's spooked. If Rutherford isn't the first call she makes, he'll be the second."

Noah Webster knew the risks he was taking . . . full-scale surveillance on Richard Rutherford could backfire badly; a perceived threat to his daughter and grandchildren could trigger an aggressive response. Rutherford was as ruthless as Webster. And he was mega-rich. But Webster held the trump cards—well documented and secure records of every illegal contribution and shady deal ever consummated by Rutherford and former Senator Seneca Markham.

What he didn't hold was an infallible insight into the future. And there were so many variables in play.

———⟡———

Tankhum Street, Old Tel Aviv
July 23, 2:35 p.m.

The white panel van of Joshua's Bakery idled in the dark shade of a building on Tankhum Street, a narrow sliver of alley not more than a stone's throw from St. Archangel Michael Monastery, on the fringe of the random, winding byways of the old city section of Tel Aviv. There was no bread in the truck.

Colonel Meyer Levinson stood in the middle of the van, hunched over a pulsing green screen with several red dots moving across its surface. "How many?"

"Seven on the main floor, four on the upper floor," said the uniformed Shin Bet soldier sitting at the controls. "There's a small basement, but I can't pierce it."

The men in Levinson's Operations unit were battle-tested veterans in Israel's vigilant war against terrorism. They were frighteningly effective in their tracking and pursuit of Israel's enemies. Still, it had taken two days of constant surveillance before they finally got a solid lead on where these so-called Disciples had fled after the gun battle on Malan Street drove them from their original hideout. But find them they did. Now more than thirty Shin Bet soldiers were getting into position for an assault. All were carrying the relatively new Tavor X95 assault rifles which were gradually replacing the formerly ubiquitous Uzi. The Tavors were converted to 9-millimeter submachine guns, and two had been fitted with grenade launchers

Their target was a narrow building sandwiched in the midst of a block of warehouses on Rabi Khanina Street, around a corner and two blocks down from where Joshua's Bakery van was pulled up on the thin sidewalk, no baguettes to peddle.

"Weapons?"

"Yes." The soldier shrugged. "More than I can count. Some large caliber it appears. Explosives also. Unless I'm mistaken."

Levinson gave the soldier a tap on the shoulder. "You are never mistaken, Yoshi. Where shall we hit them?"

The soldier tapped the screen. "There are two doors, front and back, on the main floor. They are secondary. Here"—he pointed to the right rear corner of the building's image—"is a small window into the basement. And here, this window on the main floor leads to a bathroom. Neither appear to be guarded. Those are your first targets."

Levinson squeezed the soldier's shoulder. "Good work, Yoshi." He turned to the officer on his right but was stopped by a hand on his arm. Levinson looked down and saw a depth of longing on Yoshi's face.

"Let me go, Colonel?"

Pulling a stool close, Levinson sat down next to Yoshi. "I have three-dozen fighters staged outside this truck—all of them expert marksmen with a depth of courage that breaks my heart. But"—Levinson pointed his right forefinger—"I have only one Yoshi. You can shoot as well as any of these men. And your courage is well documented. But none of these men can operate this equipment or interpret its data nearly as effectively as you. You're as close to indispensable as there comes, Yoshi."

Older than most of his comrades, Levinson saw the veteran's face harden. He expected an argument. He got a plea.

"My brother was on Malan Street with you. He left his life there, at the hands of these men."

Yoshi's brother had been Levinson's second-in-command. They had served together for sixteen years. Yoshi's brother named his second son Meyer. His death in the Malan Street raid had shattered Levinson's calm veneer and driven him to consider the unthinkable—retirement. Now, Levinson saw the same anguish on Yoshi's face. How could he say no? If Levinson was going to face the life-threatening moments to come . . .

Once again, he pointed a finger at Yoshi. "Okay, you can come. But . . . don't get yourself killed! Got it?"

No smile reached Yoshi's lips. His voice was hard, determined. "I promise. I'll be bulletproof. But . . . I will offer no mercy."

35

Becoming more agitated with each minute that slipped by, Mullaney paced back and forth across the width of his damaged office in the north wing of the residence. "Look . . . we don't have much time. For the sake of argument, let's say the Gaon started this and he's still at the controls. So what do the last two lines of symbols on the second prophecy say? What were the symbols that the Gaon used—the ones that reminded you of Unicode?"

"Actually, they were pictographs," said Poppy. "Images to represent symbols, or phonetic sounds . . . like hieroglyphics. I got a clue from that math book of the Gaon's at Columbia University. He made little drawings of boxes with sections filled in . . . a triangle in one corner of a rectangle, a half circle inside a square. The first trick was breaking down those pictographs and converting them into the correct symbols and phonetics. Plus the Gaon took the symbols and then translated them into a code. He was very thorough."

"But it's pretty simple once you break the code," said Poppodopolous.

"What code did the Gaon use this time?" asked Herzog.

"You know Gamaritia . . . where the numeral one is used for the first letter in the Jewish alphabet, the numeral two for the second letter. He used that Gamaritia sequencing then applied to it an algorithm based on the Aaronic blessing. It was a mass of letters but, essentially, each pictograph devolved into a word. Pretty clever."

"The Aaronic blessing is the anointing prayer for the guardian," said Herzog.

"Doubly clever then."

The monk reached into a slit in the folds of his cassock and pulled a piece of paper from an unseen pocket. "Here, Mordechai, you read it."

Herzog took the sheet of paper and adjusted the spectacles on the end of his nose. His eyes ran back and forth over the paper, as if his mind could not accept what his eyes were seeing. The rabbi looked over at Mullaney. Was there pity on his face?

"It says, 'The last guardian must deliver the box of power into the hands of the Man of Violence.'"

Mullaney felt his mind stop and his stomach turn. He shot a vengeful glance at Father Poppodopolous. No, he wouldn't do that, he wouldn't joke at a time like this.

"But that can't be right," stammered Mullaney. How could he do that . . . just hand the box of power to his mortal enemy, the most specific personification of evil that he'd ever experienced? "After all this, we're just going to hand it over? Are you sure?"

"There's certainly a possibility that I can be wrong," said the monk. "But I don't think so. After the computer program decoded that first line of symbols, the Gamaritia changed sequencing for the second line. It went from a string of letters, what you have in your hand, and became a string of numbers. At first, they appeared random. Then I figured it out."

Father Poppodopolous held up a second piece of paper in his hand. He reached across the table and handed the paper to Mullaney. "I think you'll find this string of numbers more interesting than . . ."

Mullaney didn't hear the rest of what Poppodopolous was saying. His ability to comprehend was obliterated by what he saw on the paper in his hand.

"This can't . . . this isn't possible," mumbled Mullaney, more to himself than to the others in the room. An inflection of absolute impossibility resonated in his voice, overwhelmed by a reverent awe that bordered on a prayer.

Mullaney lifted the paper in his hand, held it out before him, and looked around the room.

"This is my Social Security number."

"Gotcha," said the monk.

Mullaney still had the slip of paper in his hand and a look on his face as if he were told he owed two million dollars to the IRS.

"You are asking me if it's possible?" said Father Poppodopolous. "Is it possible for a man who lived 220 years ago to send a message to you, personally, hundreds of years later, with your Social Security number as the signature?"

The monk spread his large hands before him. "Remember the arrow of time? Well, could God give the Gaon a vision of the future? Could God bend time so the Gaon could have a vision of you? Sure . . . it's possible. Ezekiel saw into the future. So did Isaiah and Daniel. John saw the risen Christ and the final battle of mankind on the plains of Megiddo.

"But you also want to know whether you can trust this message. Not only whether a rabbi in 1794 Lithuania can know what is going to happen in the future, but also whether the steps he put in motion could exert a tangible impact on what is happening today by turning this prophecy into a personal message to you?

"Possible? I think so. But buddy, I just don't know for sure. What I do know for sure is that you are the final guardian . . . that the message you have in your hands says the final guardian must give the box of power to the Man of Violence . . . and that this message is signed with your Social Security number. And I don't believe you have much time to debate or decide what to do."

—∞◊∞—

Rabi Khanina Street, Old Tel Aviv
July 23, 2:48 p.m.

The plan was simple. As the opening salvo of the attack, a squad of soldiers, guns blazing, would advance on the rear window into the basement. Seconds later, a grenade launcher would blow up the front door. But all of that action was only intended to divert attention from the window into the bathroom. A half-dozen Shin Bet fighters would slip through the window and unleash a deadly rain of fire from behind the building's defenders.

Levinson lifted up his right hand, fingers splayed, as he stared at his wrist-watch. *Five-four-three-two*—the fingers of his right hand closed into a fist. At *one* the sound of gunfire erupted from the rear of the building, and seconds later the building was rocked by an explosion.

As the fighting escalated inside the building, the rear door of the van was thrown open. Levinson and his men didn't wait for the dust cloud to settle, running headlong through the front door with their Tavor machine guns rattling out a relentless drumbeat of death.

The seven enemies on the ground floor were already lifeless, bloody hulks as Levinson raced into the building and turned left and led his men to the head of the stairs into the basement. Levinson could hear the thunder of a fierce firefight above him on the upper floor. If there were only four enemies up there, his force was more than capable of extinguishing that threat. But how many were in the basement?

The sound of pitched battle roiled up the stairwell. Going down those stairs they would be vulnerable targets. As those thoughts flashed through Levinson's mind, Yoshi raced past his left shoulder and plunged headlong down the stairs, his Tavor 9-millimeter ready to erupt. Levinson was on his heels.

Each Shin Bet soldier wore body armor with a Star of David emblazoned front and back. Yoshi's Star broke right into the dimness of the basement, sparks bolting from the muzzle of his machine gun. Levinson broke left and threw his body behind a trunk on the floor. A wicked fight was raging to the right of the stairs. Levinson could no longer see Yoshi, but he could see muzzle flashes coming from behind a barricade of boxes in the center of the confined space. His hearing assaulted by the throbbing roar of guns, Levinson buried a full clip into the crate from which muzzle flashes reached out toward the Shin Bet soldiers across the basement. The right side of the crate exploded into a thousand shards of pointed splinters. Someone screamed.

A devastating onslaught of relentless firing inundated the wooden barricade, smoke and splinters filling the air. When Levinson could only hear the unique, crackling thunder of the Tavors, he blew mightily on a steel whistle that was taped to the back of the first two fingers on his left hand.

In the sudden silence, Levinson's ears still echoed with the sounds of battle. A thick cloud of gun smoke hung like a fog under the low ceiling of the basement, burning Levinson's eyes and coating his throat. Ten seconds of silence confirmed there was no longer any enemy threat, and Levinson could finally use the radio mic affixed to his shoulder. "Report!"

Before a voice could respond, out of the gun-smoke gloom emerged Yoshi, who walked directly up to Levinson. "I'm alive," he said, some blood flowing from a bullet hole through his left forearm. "But they're not. No prisoners, sir."

Now there was a smile on his face.

36

The burden of occupying Arslan Eroglu's body was frustrating for the Turk. It left him with so many limitations. But occupying Eroglu had gained him the ambassador. Now it would gain him the box.

The Turk turned away from Cleveland's motionless body. Over and over he had tried, and failed, to access Cleveland's mind, invade and capture his thoughts, find something to use to his advantage. Well he had the ambassador. That would be enough.

"Bring me his phone. This is one call the Irishman will accept."

Assan, a wraith in a dark cloak, moved from the shadows, the ambassador's iPhone in his gnarled hand. "It does not function, master."

Without a word, the Turk held out his left hand and took the phone from Assan. He then leaned over Cleveland's body and picked up his right hand. The Turk wrapped Cleveland's fingers around the phone. He closed his yellow eyes and began chanting. Within moments, the screen was illuminated, the entry code bypassed, and Cleveland's contacts displayed. The Turk tapped on Brian Mullaney, tapped on the speaker icon, and listened as the call rang at the other end.

<hr>

Still sitting on top of his desk, the phone rang and rattled to life. Mullaney looked at the display screen in disbelief.

Cleveland's number?

He tapped the green icon and pulled it to his ear.

"Mr. Ambassador?"

It was as if oxygen had left the room. Herzog, Hughes, and Poppodopolous each sucked in a quick breath. They looked at Mullaney as if he was about to announce a million-dollar sweepstakes winner.

"Oh . . . I'm afraid not."

The voice coming through his phone chilled Mullaney's heart and polluted his hearing. He felt as if some being was whispering to him from inside a tomb. Unconsciously, he reached for a spiritual weapon. *God, please help me!*

Mullaney's mind sped through several scenarios.

"But you have his phone."

"Yes," slithered a sibilant breath. "And I also have the ambassador himself. Perhaps you would like to ensure his safe return?"

"Who is this?"

There was an agonizing pause. Mullaney scrawled on a piece of paper and pushed it toward Hughes. *Parker!* Hughes scuttled out of the room.

"I am your worst nightmare."

Undiluted fear raced through Mullaney's flesh and bones and flooded his mind.

"Across the span of time I've been called many things. I believe you know me as the Man of Violence. An apt but thoroughly incomplete description. More importantly, you have something I want. I have the ambassador. Bring me the box and Cleveland lives. Any delay . . . deny my request . . . in addition to taking Cleveland's life, I will take his soul. And not only will he live the rest of his days in anguish as I torture his daughter and those he loves, but he also will spend all eternity in torment and fire."

Mullaney's fear erupted into fury. "I will find you," he seethed, "and I *will* kill you."

"Hmmm . . . a difficult task on either count. But tell me, Agent Mullaney, are you willing to condemn Cleveland's life and his eternity to agony? Is that what you want? Is that what you would like to explain to his daughter . . . to the secretary of state? Is the box that important to you?"

Within the riot of emotions that thundered through Mullaney, a center of peace beckoned to his spirit. Was the Gaon . . . Poppodopolous . . . right? Was this his mission?

"Be here within three hours, with the box, and Palmyra's father lives."

Mullaney looked up as Hughes, maternally holding her hand, hurried Palmyra Parker through the door to his office. Parker looked devastated.

"Where are you?"

"Ankara. Get to Esenboga International Airport. When you arrive, my disciples will lead you to me. You will come alone. You will bring the box. I will see and know. If you try to deceive me, I will tear out the ambassador's eyes. If you are late, I will begin to dismember the ambassador's body, piece by piece, every ten minutes."

"How do I—"

The phone connection was severed.

Mullaney was furious with himself, with McKeon, with the situation. And especially with this madman who now appeared to have Cleveland in his grasp. The only saving grace was that Parker didn't hear any of the conversation, particularly the final threats. Still . . . if any of so many things had happened differently, Cleveland would not be in such mortal danger.

Ruth Hughes guided Palmyra Parker to a chair to the side of Mullaney's desk and kept a welcoming hand on her shoulder as the DSS agent appeared ready to erupt.

"I told you he would do this one day," seethed Mullaney.

Parker watched him closely. He was angry. Angrier with himself than with her. Still, she should have seen it coming.

"He's known Kashani a long time," she said, "long before he was appointed ambassador to Turkey. They bonded while serving on the Izmet earthquake relief effort, Ninety-nine I think it was. Politics and religion are quickly laid aside when over seventeen thousand have been killed and thousands more are at risk of losing their lives." She looked into his tortured face. "I'm sorry, Brian. I didn't . . . there were no clues. And he never mentioned anything to me. This must have been a hastily concocted escapade. I thought he was at the embassy . . . I'm sorry."

Mullaney turned to face Parker, his countenance softening.

"Not your fault," he said. "If I hadn't turned my phone off, Atticus would never have gotten out of Israel. I can only imagine what Pat McKeon's been through. Her messages as your father ordered her to the airport were more and more desperate for my direction. I'm the one at fault here."

Fault . . . *Fault!* How could this man ever think he was at fault for the tragedies of the last week? If it hadn't been for Mullaney, well, both she and her father would have been dead long ago. He'd risked his life—risked everything . . .

"You won't believe me when I tell you . . . but you are the least at fault of anyone in this nightmare. But let's leave that for another time." She got up and stood in front of Mullaney. "What are you going to do?"

Mullaney pushed back from his desk and his manner became all business. For a flash, a spark of dread filled Parker's heart. US policy was clear: no negotiations with terrorists. Even when lives were at risk.

"The first thing is to make sure that your father isn't somewhere else, safe and sound instead of in the clutches of this monster. The second thing to do is call the secretary and get him up to speed. The Brits are scouring Akrotiri, going over surveillance video. McKeon and two agents are on their way to Esenboga, and I've ordered another half-dozen DSS agents from the Ankara embassy to the airport, just in case, waiting for Atticus to get off that flight from Ercan.

"I'll put in a call to Colonel Edwards, who was the last to meet with him. But we have no idea if, or how, he got off Cyprus, or how he could get to Turkey so quickly. If he isn't on that flight, ditching his tracker at the air base sure makes it look like he had some kind of a plan for escaping Cyprus and getting to Ankara. But we don't know for sure—not yet—whether he's even in Turkey. And I'm not giving up the box on a hunch. We need to be sure."

Parker pulled in a deep breath. Mullaney's methodical approach gave her hope, calmed the storm in her stomach.

"And the third thing . . . I need to figure out a way to get to Ankara, just in case.

"In the meantime, I've got DSS agents and informers trolling the back streets of Ankara, looking for any signs of these Disciples or their leader. Worse comes to worst and we believe Atticus has been captured by this Man of Violence, then the first thing we demand is proof of life before we make any move."

That made her shudder.

Mullaney turned his full attention on Parker. His voice was like sharpened steel. "But you can be assured of this, Palmyra . . . I will get your father back here safely. I promise you that."

Then he turned to Hughes. "We need to call the secretary . . . without Webster getting involved or stirring up a media frenzy."

Hughes looked at her watch. "Let me make a call. I think I know how to get the secretary's attention without raising a lot of red flags."

Rabi Khanina Street, Old Tel Aviv
July 23, 3:04 p.m.

He was leaning against the side of the Joshua's Bakery van, pouring a bottle of water over his head to wash away the gunpowder smell, when an out-of-breath officer rushed to his side.

"Colonel, we found this in the hand of one of the dead guys inside," the officer said, holding up a smudged cell phone. "Before the screen went dark, we could see that he had made a call . . . he hadn't hung up on his end yet."

Levinson spun on his heel and called toward a knot of soldiers who were patting one another on the back. "Yoshi! Over here. I need your magic."

37

US State Department, Truman Building, Washington, DC
July 23, 8:06 a.m.

Evan Townsend sat in a comfortable leather armchair in his place of refuge, a small anteroom to his office at the State Department, off limits to most and as private as any secretary of state could expect. But he was overwhelmed by dread as he disconnected the call from his wife. He was reminded once again of both Ruth Hughes's influence and her discretion. But the unorthodox call to his wife could only mean really bad news. He scrolled through his contacts list and tapped a finger on Hughes's number. He was not surprised when Brian Mullaney picked up.

"Agent Mullaney," said the secretary of state, preparing himself for something tragic, "give my compliments to Ruth . . . that was artfully done. Now this can't be good. What are we facing?"

Townsend heard a deep sigh from the other end of the connection. He closed his eyes and steadied his heart at what must be coming next.

"Ambassador Cleveland is missing."

Physically and emotionally, Townsend winced at the thought. Mentally, he was already weighing probabilities.

"Missing . . . what does that mean?"

"Honestly, Mr. Secretary, at this moment I'm not certain," Mullaney admitted. "About four hours ago Ambassador Cleveland flew to Cyprus and met with the head of a JSOC strike force."

"Incirlik? He's that sure?"

"Yes, sir. But while Cleveland was in Cyprus, he ditched his security detail."

"Wait . . . he went out of the country and you weren't with him?"

Evan Townsend knew he would learn a lot about Brian Mullaney in the next few seconds.

"I take full responsibility, sir," Mullaney said without hesitation, "I should have been there. But here's the problem. We don't think the JSOC commander would send his men into Turkey without ironclad orders. Cleveland probably didn't really think that either. We believe Ambassador Cleveland's ultimate plan was to get to Turkey, talk personally with President Kashani, and try to put a stop to this Incirlik attack before it got started. We were chasing him down when we got a call."

"Now I'm worried," whispered Townsend.

"Yes, sir. We haven't yet been able to confirm Cleveland being in Turkey, but . . . we got a call. A ransom demand. The caller was using the ambassador's phone to make the call. It appears possible Cleveland's been abducted by the leader of this same gang that's been attacking us here in Israel."

Secretary Townsend took a few heartbeats to absorb and assess Mullaney's information. *Not the time to ask questions about how this abduction was possible. There would be time for that . . . after.* "Why only possible?"

Now it was Mullaney's turn to take a moment. Townsend waited.

"Wishful thinking, I'm afraid," he admitted. "The guy called on Cleveland's phone . . . that's not good. But it's possible Cleveland is sitting somewhere on the Akrotiri base drinking a cup of coffee. It's possible he's not in Turkey. It's possible he's still safe. We're running down every possible lead right now, just to be sure."

"What do you think?"

There was a deep sigh on the other end of the call. "I think Atticus tried to do this on his own. And now I think our enemy has him."

Mullaney's assessment rang true to Townsend. "Atticus has always been a doer—when everything is on the line, Atticus doesn't delegate. He acts. I'm not surprised. What do they want?"

Townsend listened as Mullaney gave him a rapid and concise update about the Gaon's prophecies and the box of power. "And where is this box of power now?"

"Not twenty feet away—locked in a safe room," said Mullaney.

"What do you need from me?"

Mullaney's response was out before Townsend completed his question.

"Orders for Colonel Edwards and his Team Black . . . stop the raid on Incirlik and help me rescue Cleveland. It was Edwards who Cleveland met with on Cyprus before he pulled his disappearing act. I know JSOC has a team ready to move, but I doubt Colonel Edwards is going anywhere without orders."

"What about the box . . . the ransom demands?"

"Before time runs out, we make the exchange. With all due respect . . . with or without the JSOC team's support, I'm heading to Ankara to surrender the box. It's my—"

"Help me out here, Brian," Townsend interrupted. "First, you know our national policy . . . we don't negotiate with terrorists. And second, you've warned me about the deadly power of this box. It's Cleveland's life, I understand. But do you really think it's wise to put that kind of power into the hands of a gang that is so ruthless and bent on destruction?

"Look," Townsend pressed, "if I can get Ernie Edwards a green light, why not let JSOC take care of rescuing Atticus. That's what they're trained for. Then there's no question about negotiating or paying a ransom and there's no risk of the bad guys getting the box."

Townsend waited. He could sense Mullaney measuring his response.

"Two things, Mr. Secretary," said Mullaney. "The first is that this whole ordeal here is not only a flesh-and-blood fight. There's a supernatural, spiritual battle being waged over the box at the same time."

"I get that," said Townsend.

"Well, sir," there was a pause, "it would take too long to explain, and I don't know if I could explain it clearly enough even if I had the time. It wasn't my plan or my doing, but I've been drawn into this supernatural battle, and responsibility for the box has been passed down to me. The box is powerful, yes. But we are also fairly confident that the box is a weapon prepared specifically for this battle we're fighting right now. And—you will have to trust me on this—I've been instructed to give the box to our enemy, to hand it over in return for Cleveland's life."

There were a handful of questions Evan Townsend wanted to ask, but he didn't think the answers would help him come to a decision. Clearly, there were forces beyond his control or comprehension in conflict here. Townsend was a believer, a man of faith. He believed he understood what Mullaney was saying. He stepped out in faith.

"Okay . . . what's the second thing?"

"Sir, I took an oath to defend the United States—its people and its property. You are my ultimate boss, so I act at your direction. But Mr. Secretary . . . and I don't intend this to be insubordinate . . . my first responsibility is to the ambassador. To rescue him and protect him, no matter what."

Townsend could hear Mullaney take a breath.

"I feel like I've failed Atticus repeatedly in the short time I've been here. I don't intend to fail him today. It's both my duty and my responsibility to rescue Ambassador Cleveland. I intend to fulfill that duty, hopefully with your permission. And I'm hoping you can find a way to get Edwards a go signal. I sure would like to have him at my back. And yes, sir, I believe the threat to Incirlik is real and imminent. A lot of people, Americans and others, will die if we don't take action."

Entrapped by a cyclone of urgent events over which he had little control—not so uncommon in the secretary of state's job—Townsend had enough wisdom and experience to know when the time for consideration had passed and action was required. It was time to act—and time to pray his actions weren't too late.

"I'll call the defense secretary as soon as we hang up. Colonel Edwards should have his orders for both missions in thirty minutes or less. I pray we're not too late. And Brian . . . I'll be praying for you too. I doubt I fully understand what you're walking into, but I believe you're putting your life at risk also. Please . . . be careful out there. And bring Atticus home."

⁓∘◦∘⁓

Ambassador's Residence, Tel Aviv
July 23, 3:15 p.m.

It wasn't the exact moment Evan Townsend disconnected from the call. Perhaps two or three seconds. But it didn't take long before the enormity of the risk and the weight of responsibility hit Brian Mullaney like a riptide that pulled his confident words under a thundering sea of doubt.

Did he really know what he was doing? Was he seriously intending to put the box of power into the hands of a malevolent and murderous fiend? It was so clear, so simple when he was speaking to Secretary Townsend. But now fear and uncertainty haunted his every thought.

Mullaney scanned the room, looking for help. "How can we be sure this is the right thing to do? If we get this wrong, not only could Atticus lose his life, but then this personification of evil would possess the box and perhaps control the power that resides in it."

"Or the power that comes from the kabbalah symbols that were hammered into its lid," said Rabbi Herzog. "That warning remains . . . it hasn't changed, just because the message is no longer inside. Remember"—he turned to Mullaney—"Bayard told us that we needed to understand the box. That in order to fully understand the message of the second prophecy, we needed to understand the message and the purpose of the box.

"But he also said the meaning was not kabbalah," Mullaney remembered. "The meaning is not what's on the top of the box."

"Then what is the meaning of the box?" asked Hughes. "How can we know?"

Father Poppodopolous stood up and walked over to the reinforced diplomatic pouch which contained both the blast container and the Gaon's metal box. "Well . . . what about this," he said and turned to the others in the room. "Has anyone ever looked at the bottom of the box?"

"What?"

"The bottom of the box," Poppodopolous repeated. "Has anyone ever looked at the bottom of the box? Or inside it, to see what's inside? Rabbi, do you think your son and the Rabbinate took the time to closely inspect the box?"

Herzog shook his head, the reminder of his dead son clearly adding weight to the elderly man's shoulders. "Who is to know? Open it, they did. Inspect it? Did they have time? Those last minutes, I know not what they were like. I wish not to know."

The monk took three steps, stood beside Herzog's chair, and laid a hand on his shoulder. "Forgive me, Mordechai, that was insensitive of me."

The old man shook his head again. "No . . . but you are right. If there is kabbalah on the lid of the box, is there anything else on the rest of the box? Anything that could give us a better understanding of its purpose?"

The other four people in the room turned at once to look in Mullaney's direction. He knew it was coming. There was only one way to find out what was on the rest of the box. He closed his eyes. Took a deep breath. And remembered the feel of the angel's hands on his shoulder and his face. He remembered the words that were spoken over him. And he remembered the light that came with the words . . . the clarity of understanding . . . the new depth of perception beyond the surface into a new realm, one that he now shared with the angel Bayard. And he felt a peace that went beyond his fragile emotions. And he felt duty.

Are you really going to touch it? What if . . .

38

Mullaney stood over the reinforced diplomatic pouch, unlocked the hasp, and opened the bag. Inside was the blast container containing the Gaon's box. No one had come close to touching the box since the IDF bomb squad had maneuvered the box into this blast container in the old section of Jerusalem three days ago, just after Rabbi Chaim Yavod died a gruesome death.

The blast container looked like a stainless steel egg, about a foot long and nine or ten inches high . . . relatively small, for small devices, as opposed to total containment systems that were often carted around on the backs of trucks. It was oval shaped, and one-third of its length was a hinged blast cover. When the cover was closed, completing the egg, a steel hasp pulled the cover tight to the rest of the container. There was a short, L-shaped steel bar on the front of the cover, the short side an integrated part of the blast cover. When the handle was pulled clockwise, it triggered a locking mechanism that clamped hooks over steel bars around the entire circumference of the blast cover.

Mullaney pulled up on the bar in the center of the door, releasing the locking mechanism, and pulled the door aside, freeing the cover from the rest of the container. Inside was a steel shelf on rollers. He pulled out the shelf. On it, wrapped within a steel-mesh cocoon, was the Gaon's lethal bronze box and the shattered pieces of the wooden box that once enclosed it.

Where's Bayard when I need him? Is this going to work? Am I really safe? There's only one way to find out.

Closing his eyes, Mullaney breathed deep. *Lord . . . please be with me.*

Whispering the Aaronic blessing to himself, over and over, with the guarded precision of a glass blower, Mullaney lowered his hands into the blast container, his fingers spread around the steel mesh shroud surrounding the metal box. *Now or never.*

He touched the steel mesh. Then his fingers wrapped around the box itself. He waited.

And his heart leaped with terror. Something . . . was happening. He could feel it.

Mullaney's eyes flew wide open, his mind searching every cell in his body, searching for the harbinger of pain and death.

Something was rising in him.

Oh . . . Abby . . . I'm so sorr . . .

Wait . . . not death!

No. Life.

Or more precisely, beyond life.

His eyes wide open, he no longer needed to see. He could *see*!

Mullaney's mind was exploring a reality he had never experienced before while his emotions were as calm as a day without breeze. He *knew* the box. He experienced its purpose. Then the sounds of mortal combat rushed through his ears.

The crash of metal reverberated, not in his hearing but in every cell of his body. The crash was a thousandfold . . . deep and wide and high. Darkness was on one side. Blinding, life-giving light was on the other. Thousands upon thousands of footsteps moved forward in a clatter of armor and the calls of battle. And the host of heaven was on the march.

The warfare was spiritual. But it was real. Without fully understanding how or why, Mullaney knew he was seeing a glimpse of a spiritual battle going on in the heavenlies. And he was involved. No! He was the reason. An angel army was engaged with the hounds of hell. And all to protect him. The battle still raged in his hearing, but he closed his fingers around the box and lifted it clear of the blast container. Treating it with the reverence of a jeweled crown, Mullaney laid the box on top of the desk. And took his hands away.

Immediately, silence flooded his brain.

Mullaney pulled his eyes away from the box. Herzog, Poppodopolous, Hughes, and Parker were all looking at him as if they were waiting for his head to explode and praying that it wouldn't. His eyes found Parker's.

"You were right," he said. "That Scripture you read to me about us being a part of the spiritual war raging in heaven? You were right. The battle is going on right now. I could hear it."

Parker opened her mouth. But no words came out.

Mullaney turned away, back to the desk. "I'm going to open the box now."

Feeling a little less terrified, yet chiding himself for his remaining fear, his eyes riveted to the kabbalah symbols hammered into the metal, Mullaney placed his hands on either side of the lid and pushed up with his thumbs. After a heartbeat, the lid popped loose on one side. Pressing up on the opening, Mullaney lifted the lid from the box itself. He took the lid and gently placed it on the desk next to the box. Then he looked inside.

"The inside is lined . . . looks like purple velvet," he said, speaking the words so they would carry over his shoulders. He could feel the others inching closer. But he kept his eyes on the box. "I can't see anything else unless I remove the velvet."

Testing the edges of the velvet, Mullaney could feel a slight tug at the corners. He slipped two fingers under one corner and lifted. He could feel the velvet release, so he continued around the inside of the box with his fingers, setting the velvet free. He lifted it out and set the velvet on the lid to the side, but his eyes were on the bottom of the box.

Where another symbol was hammered into the metal surface.

He reached in with his right hand, tracing the symbol with his index finger. And the sounds of heavenly warfare overwhelmed his senses.

Alitas Street, Ankara
July 23, 3:22 p.m.

The room was as dark and as cold as the grave. The smell of human decay filled his nostrils and gagged in his throat. A strip of cloth, bitter and vile to the taste, was wound like a vise around his head and tightened into his mouth. Cleveland prayed that he would not vomit.

As he fully returned to consciousness, it wasn't the only thing he prayed.

Father, help me. I'm afraid . . . terrified. I heard the voice of hell speak my name. He wants my soul. My soul belongs to you, Jesus. Please, Father . . . Holy Spirit . . . release the armies of heaven. Come and do battle for me where I can't fight for myself. Wage warfare for my soul against this demon of wickedness.

Cleveland convulsed. Something frigid, like the hand of perdition, had probed inside him and touched his spine. But the skin of his face, his lips, felt seared, as if the door to a blast furnace had opened in front of him. His senses were flailed by the opposing forces that attacked him inside and out as his body writhed under the malevolent assaults.

"Your God cannot help you here."

The voice violated him, polluted his ears. It was a different voice, more horrible and disgusting than the one he had heard before. But this voice was also more powerful. Its words felt like lightning-fed thunder quaking through his bones.

Filth gnawed at his cells like a spreading cancer. He could smell his clothes smoldering from the ravenous blaze that roared around the outside of his body. Cleveland's grip on who he was wavered as his mind withered under the relentless assault.

Is this hell?

"You will suffer in agony through all eternity. Abandon all hope, you who enter here. Hope no longer exists. Your reality is torture and pain. Renounce him—for he has renounced you. All his lies are worthless. Renounce him!"

At the fringes of his sanity, Cleveland groped for the truth.

You are a liar and a deceiver, the devourer of the just. "I will never leave you nor forsake you."

"You will live in torment and plead for mercy."

I am a child of God. My Father loves me. "As the Father has loved me, so have I loved you."

"You will cry out for rescue through all eternity. Silence will answer you."

My Jesus . . . my Jesus, I am purchased by your blood. I am righteous in your sight: pure and holy and blameless. "For the eyes of the Lord are on the righteous and his ears are attentive to their prayer."

"Fool."

As if a cell door had slammed shut, the heat vanished, the death grip on his spine released. Soaking wet from perspiration, Cleveland's body was racked with violent shivering in the frigid air. A permeating odor of sulfur and burning covered him like a fog.

Cleveland gasped for a cleansing breath and found none. The fiend from the pit of hell had disappeared as suddenly as he had come. But Cleveland's essence, his being—although nearly consumed—had survived. For now.

Thank you.

And he hurtled out of consciousness.

Ambassador's Residence, Tel Aviv
July 23, 3:23 p.m.

Steadying himself against the edge of the desk, Mullaney held the metal box in both hands, its bottom turned up toward the others in the room. Rabbi Herzog had immediately identified the symbol hammered into the bottom of the box.

"It's the shin," he said of the Hebrew symbol for the letter *W*, a tone of reverence in his voice. "The emblem for El Shaddai, the name of God."

"God the All Powerful," whispered Father Poppodopolous. "It's the Birkat Kohanim, the priestly benediction also known as the raising of the hands."

Mullaney looked from one to the other. "The final sign?" he asked softly, almost to himself.

Herzog saw it plainly. In that moment, Mullaney faced the real possibility that his life could end, that he might never again see his wife or his daughters, at least not in this life. The hesitation of a warrior on the threshold of battle. Faithful and determined in his duty, yet only a mortal man.

Fear, yes. But not a coward's fear. This was the overcoming of fear. That moment of decision, the birth of courage from the cauldron of doubt. Herzog's affection for Mullaney only increased.

"It is . . . you are correct." Herzog stood alongside Mullaney but kept a respectful distance from the box. "When Aaron would speak his blessing over the assembled Jewish community in the desert, he would lift his hands over the people. In the Pentateuch Book of Numbers, God speaks to Moses and Aaron and says, 'This is how you are to bless the Israelites. Say to them . . .' And then comes the Aaronic blessing. It was God's blessing for the people through Aaron. When Aaron would speak the blessing, he would take his two hands and lift them, palms down. His thumbs touched each other at the ends and his fingers were spread out, but separated. On each hand, the fingers would spread apart in the middle, like this."

Rabbi Herzog held his hands in front of him, palms down, thumbs touching. His fingers were split apart, two on one side and two on the other side of each hand.

Poppodopolous stepped in front of Herzog's hands. "Looks like Spock's greeting on Star Trek."

"Stolen from the Shin," said Herzog, gazing at his fingers. "Every day that the Aaronic blessing is spoken, in every synagogue around the world, Jewish rabbis will lift their hands in this manner, invoking the Hebrew letter *shin*, the letter *W*. The symbol for El Shaddai. The lifting of the hands for the covering, the protection of God."

Mullaney was nodding his head. "It's the confirmation, isn't it?" he asked. "Confirmation of the last line of symbols in the Gaon's prophecy. That it's time to present the box of power to the enemy. It's time for me to leave."

39

Turning to the desk, Mullaney replaced the velvet lining and covered the box with the lid. Folding the steel mesh over the box, he lowered it onto the shelf, slid the shelf into the blast container, and closed the cover. He pulled the bar clockwise, locking the door in place, then pulled close the outside clasp. For a moment, he rested his hands against the container and took a deep breath.

Hughes was on her phone, pulling more strings. Father Poppodopolous, exercising discretion after a hushed but frantic conversation with Rabbi Herzog, had taken his leave five minutes earlier, just before Mullaney petitioned Palmyra Parker to join him in the sitting room just off Joseph Cleveland's bedroom.

Neither sat.

"He's your father," said Mullaney. "I don't know if this will save his life or put him in even more danger."

"Yes, but he's your ambassador," said Parker. Her words were clipped, urgent, pleading. "And he can't be in any more danger than he is right now. He's not getting out of Ankara alive unless somebody goes and rescues him."

Mullaney knew what he had to do, but every instinct from his experience and his training made him feel like it was a mistake. "But how can I give this box, with all its power, into the hands of the guy who's trying to kill us all? God knows what he'll do with it. I just . . ."

Mullaney could feel the presence before he could see or hear anything. He looked up and around the room.

Parker was startled. "What?"

The molecular structure of a corner of the sitting room warped and morphed and shimmered like tree limbs covered with ice in a blustery wind. A shape began to materialize.

"Oh . . ." Parker's hand covered her mouth, stifling further words.

The top of the wings furled behind his back were as tall as the eight-foot ceiling, and his head, covered with a silver helmet that continued down the back of his neck, just cleared it. His sword was out of its scabbard, held in his right hand, flat against his silver breastplate. It was Bayard. He looked ready for a fight . . . and he wasted no time.

"Guardian, you must fight with the weapon in your hands."

Mullaney wasn't about to argue with an eight-foot angel, but his fear for Cleveland's life and his reluctance to hand so much power into the hands of evil caused him to hesitate. "But—"

"Guardian," Bayard interrupted, "the box of power is a weapon. That has been its purpose from the beginning. While there was divine power in the messages received and written down by the Gaon, the prophecies themselves did not possess the power to hold back and deny the intentions of the immortal evil ones as this box does. You need immortal power to combat immortal enemies.

"That," said Bayard, pointing with his sword to the blast container, "is the box of power. It was anointed from the throne room of heaven and has a mission of its own. No evil shall ever stand against it. It was formed as a weapon against evil . . . this evil . . . and now is the time to unleash that weapon."

A vague thought scratched at Mullaney's memory. Something Bayard once said.

"Wait, I remember you saying that no mortal man can touch the box and live," said Mullaney. "But this Man of Violence, he is . . . was . . . like you, right? He's not a mortal man, is he?"

A struggle was evident in the features of Bayard's face, a tightening in the cheeks, worry lines at the corners of his eyes. He lowered his head, chin to his chest, and pulled in a deep breath. He stuck the point of his sword into the floor and rested his arms against its hilt as he knelt down on one knee, coming to eye level with both Parker and Mullaney.

"Yes, you are correct," he said, a distance to his voice. "My enemy was once my brother. But pride consumed the Prince of Light, and many were seduced into believing his lies. Our enemy is no mortal. And yes, no mortal being may touch the box and live," Bayard agreed. "But the weapons that we fight with are not only mortal weapons. Our weapons are also effective against the immortal. And not everything that is immortal is visible to the enemy. The box of power has a mission of its own. It was made not only to protect the prophecies of the Gaon. That was its original purpose, but not its only one. The box of power is also a weapon that God has designed and ordained to obliterate the enemies of heaven that oppose us and extinguish their evil desires. Its full power will only be revealed as it accomplishes its ultimate purpose. Do not deny the box its intended purpose. The plans of God will not be denied."

"But then why are they doing this?" Parker's frustration, fueled by fear, stoked by exhaustion, spilled into her words. "What are they after? They know the end of the Bible as well as we do. They know what's coming. There's been so much death . . . and suffering. Why?"

Bayard inclined his head toward Parker. "Because death and suffering are his currency. The pride of the evil one exceeds all understanding," he said. "Throughout all time, his intention has been the same, to overthrow the purposes of God. Today, as we move closer to the return of the King, it is to change the end of the book. Prevent the return of the King. Reverse the outcome of the Battle of Armageddon. Emerge victorious against the host of heaven and exalt himself in a rebuilt Temple." Bayard nodded his head. "Those are his plans, and they have changed little over time."

"But that's impossible, right?" Mullaney was stunned. "God's sovereign purpose cannot be overcome."

Bayard shook his head. "But our enemy believes it. Believes he can win. Believes the power of the box will help him. And he has no intention to surrender. He knows his fate if he fails to overturn God's plan. So not only does he continue, his schemes are becoming more desperate as his time shortens.

"We of the brotherhood have been engaged in this battle since our enemies fell from heaven. Our assignment is to disrupt and destroy the plans of the enemy. Do you think this box is the only weapon we have in play, that this is the only time in history when evil has attempted to overthrow the purposes of God? Sometimes, in spite of our efforts—when good men refuse to fight against evil—the plans of the enemy succeed, as they did in Germany seventy years ago. Even now, there are others of my brothers dealing with other threats, forging other weapons in opposing the agents and the intentions of the evil one.

"But this is your time. This is your assignment. For the Father's plan and purpose to be fulfilled, you must deliver the box into the hands of the one who wants to destroy you, the Man of Violence, the man with the yellow eyes. You must leave now, before the enemy can fully discern our purpose."

Palmyra Parker reached out her hand and put it on Mullaney's arm. "How . . ."

Bayard turned toward Parker. His gaze fell on her like an embrace. "Daughter, fear not. Have faith." He turned his head toward Mullaney. "Faith is your shield, Guardian; righteousness is your armor; salvation is your protection. Remain within the armor of God. The enemy will try and lure you into your own strength, for you to rely on yourself. If you succumb to his trap, allow pride to cloud your faith, both you and the ambassador will be vulnerable and at risk. Follow God's plans, not your own. And the brethren will be by your side."

<hr>

Rabi Khanina Street, Old Tel Aviv
July 23, 3:31 p.m.

Once again, Meyer Levinson was hunched over in the middle of the bakery van, peering past the shoulder of his tech whiz, as Yoshi tried to plumb the depths of the iPhone in his hand.

"Child's play to get beyond the passcode," Yoshi mumbled to himself, fully knowing that Levinson could hear every word. "Any rookie could have discovered what number was called. But this . . . now this takes talent."

Yoshi had taken the iPhone apart and gently removed the small chip that contained the phone's GPS identifier. "This is the little buzzard that locates your phone's position on GPS coordinates." He looked over his shoulder at Levinson. "You know, when the screen says, 'Do you want to allow this app to use your location?' Nobody at the manufacturer will admit to it, but you can reverse the application of this circuit."

Comprehension dawned on Levinson as Yoshi removed the side panel from one piece of his equipment. "You mean you can track where that call came from?"

"Maybe . . . maybe . . . maybe," he mumbled softly as he removed and disconnected wires. He took the chip from the phone and slid it into a slot in the equipment. He fiddled with some other internal pieces, then took a small LCD screen and attached it to the wires he had disconnected. He reached for a toggle switch. "Moment of truth."

The LCD screen pulsed, dark-to-light, pulsed again, then cleared. A map emerged, within close proximity to ground level.

"Where's that?" asked Levinson, crowding in closer.

Yoshi tapped the screen several times, pulling back the map's vision to a higher altitude. "Turkey . . . Ankara," he said. Then he tapped the screen a few times again, enlarging the image, moving closer to the surface. A green pointer icon emerged.

"See that?" Yoshi asked, pointing to an irregular shape in the lower left corner of the screen, not far from the location of the icon. "That's the citadel, the castle in the old city section of Ankara. And this"—he pointed to the icon—"is the area where the call came from . . . a couple of klicks northeast of the citadel. Sorry I can't get more specific than that, but that's the neighborhood the call came from." Yoshi heard the click of an iPhone photo being taken. He turned to face Levinson. "Could be the . . ."

But Colonel Levinson was already out the back door of the bakery van, sprinting for a nearby Jeep, his iPhone plastered to his ear. "Brian . . . I think I know where their leader is . . . I'm on my way to you . . . minutes out. Wait . . ."

"We can't, Meyer. I've got to leave now. Cleveland skipped out on us and went to Turkey. Now he's been kidnapped by the leader of the Disciples. It's a straight-up swap . . . Cleveland for the box. I've only got . . . two hours and twenty minutes to get there, and I'm going to need every one of them . . . running for a plane now. But you know where their leader is?"

"We raided the Disciples' hideout," said Levinson, catching his breath. "My IT guru tracked a call that came in on one of their phones. The call originated from the area around Ankara Castle, what they call the citadel, in a neighborhood in the old city. I'd bet my last shekel that's where our enemy is hiding . . . where he's holding Cleveland."

<hr />

Gocuk
July 23, 3:35 p.m.

A door somewhere in the complex of warehouses was snapping shut with the report of a shotgun. Colonel Matoush pulled the wool blanket closer around his body as he stood in the leeway of an entrance and gazed off to the north. "If anything, it's gotten worse."

The wind still slammed into his body and roared past his ears like jet engines at takeoff, even in this partly protected space.

"Only eight hours remain until our orders demand that we unleash the weapons," said the anxious officer to his left.

"I *know* what time it is," snapped Matoush, uttering an age-old Turkish curse. "We can only pray that Allah will calm the wind when it's time. But if it's like this, releasing the weapons could be suicide for us. And questionable what else they will accomplish."

Matoush glanced once more to the north, then turned to go back inside the warehouse building. He felt the fury of the wind, but he failed to see the diaphanous beings on the northern hilltops, swords drawn, swung in sweeping circles above the silver helmets on their heads.

40

Ambassador's Residence, Tel Aviv
July 23, 3:38 p.m.

Mullaney breathed a silent prayer. Finally . . . a break!

"Thanks, Meyer. As we speak, a JSOC special ops unit should be dispatched to Ankara to back me up. I'll make sure your information gets into their hands. Thanks again."

"JSOC? Point of the spear—those guys are the best," admitted Levinson. "Takes a lot for me to say that. Listen. Be careful. Our enemies are blood-lust fanatics. Good luck. I hope both of you get back safely."

"Thanks, Meyer. We're outta here."

⸺◦◦◦⸺

There was no need to be secretive. In fact, he wanted to be seen . . . let them know he was on his way.

All three of them—Mullaney, Hughes, and Parker—hustled down the front steps of the residence and poured into the back of the waiting embassy car, two DSS agents in the front seat. Mullaney placed the leather diplomatic bag on the floor, between his legs, as the car pulled out of the driveway for a quick dash to Ben Gurion Airport.

"Edwards was fast on his feet," remarked Hughes. "But my gut is telling me he already had his men in motion. Didn't take much for him to decide to split his force and tackle both objectives at once."

Mullaney shook his head. "Atticus said JSOC was the best. But I didn't think they had these kinds of resources at their disposal. That Edwards could commandeer a C-130 on the spot is impressive."

"What were the colonel's instructions for you?" asked Parker.

"Just do what the man on the phone said," said Mullaney. "Except when I get to the commercial aviation terminal at the Ankara airport, I'm going to need to use the men's room. Edwards has it all set. I'll touch base with one of his men there and be out before anything looks fishy. I'm sure the man on the phone will have his spies watching my every move at the airport. By the way . . ."

And he turned to look at Hughes on the far side of the back seat. "How many aircraft can you conjure up in one day? You just happened to put your hands on another superfast jet that just happened to be fueled and waiting?"

Hughes stretched and leaned back in the seat. She looked tired. Except for her eyes. "Do you know how much money OPEC nations earn in just one day? About one-and-a-half billion dollars a day . . . six hundred billion dollars this year. The Saudis consume more than thirty percent of the total, nearly two hundred billion dollars a year. My friends in Kuwait earn nearly fifty billion, my former business associates in the UAE earn about sixty billion a year. That money buys a lot of toys for the few guys at the top of the food chain. Those toys are spread out all around the world, and a lot of them are always fueled and ready to go."

"But you made one call," said Parker.

Hughes nodded contentedly. "Yeah, only one. I wrote and negotiated the contracts that are still keeping these good-old-boys in a realm of luxury this world has seldom seen. They didn't ask why I wanted the plane. They asked how many I wanted. Helps to have good friends in high places."

The car rocked around a tight turn, the heavy diplomatic bag tipping over against his leg. It weighed a ton. The box itself was still in the small but heavy-weight blast container that Meyer Levinson's bomb squad used to encapsulate it after it was recovered in the Old City of Jerusalem. Mullaney reached down and righted the bag as the iPhone in his pocket rang. He was going to ignore it, but . . .

⸺◦◦◦⸺

Incirlik Air Base, Adana
July 23, 3:42 p.m.

Under the windows that surrounded three sides of the Incirlik Control Tower, banks of radar screens broadcast the speed, altitude, and relative positions of nearly a dozen military aircraft, both fixed wing and rotary, that were actively engaged with Incirlik ground control. Colonel Earnest Edwards stood at the rear of the control room, his eyes moving restlessly from one particular video screen to a gray smudge in the sky that was gradually gaining in size and defini-tion. But while his eyes continued their vigil, his mind and voice were respond-ing to the men on the other end of this secure telephone line.

"Yes, sir, you can depend on us," said Edwards. "We have enough assets available that we can handle both assignments."

"Time is of the essence, Colonel," said the secretary of defense. "How long before you can muster your forces and get boots on the ground in Turkey?"

Edwards watched as the oncoming bulk of the Lockheed Martin C-130J Super Hercules transport plane bucked like an unbroken bronco, tossed about like a vapor in the torturously unrelenting wind as it entered its final descent onto Incirlik's lone, ten-thousand-foot-long concrete runway. He winced with every convoluted contortion. And with how he was going to explain himself.

"Well, sir . . . by a stroke of coincidence, Team Black is currently runnin' a trainin' operation to see how quickly we can ship men and equipment from one base to another," said Edwards.

"Yes?"

"You asked how long it would take us to get boots on the ground in Turkey?" said Edwards. "Well, sir, they just landed."

There was a protracted silence on the other end of the call. Neither the secretary nor the JSOC commander, Lieutenant General Higgins, who was patched in from Fort Bragg, spoke a word. But Edwards knew their minds were spinning.

"Training exercise? Where are you?" asked the secretary.

"Incirlik, sir."

Once again, silence occupied the airwaves. General Higgins broke it.

"What kind of force is involved in this exercise, Ernie?"

"Fifty fighters, four unmarked, blacked-out panel vans with loaded weapons lockers, and stealth comm equipment in a C-130."

"You just happen to have a ghost unit landing at Incirlik?" asked General Higgins.

"Yes, sir. Very fortunate."

"Ernie . . ."

"With all due respect, sir, I put my men in motion, just in case. General Higgins, not one would have stepped foot outside that plane without orders, sir."

A pause. Edwards wondered who would speak next, what would be said. and whether the birds pinned to his shirt would stay there.

"Well, you've got your orders, Colonel," said General Higgins. "Godspeed."

But . . . it was Abby calling! "Abby?"

"I'm okay." Abby's first words sent Mullaney's anxiety into overload. Her next words blew the meter's gaskets. "And the girls are okay. We're with Doak."

Brian Mullaney tried to slow his heartbeat enough to breathe. "What's going on?"

"Somebody is following me . . . us," said Abby. Her voice was clipped, her words matter-of-fact. Brian could tell she was trying to control her emotions as much as he was trying to control his. "A blue sedan was outside the house this morning, two men in it. The same car, same men were in the parking lot of Calvary Church when I went to drop the girls off at day camp. I kept going and called Doak. We're at his place."

Mullaney ran some time comparisons in his mind. "Day camp this morning? That was hours ago."

"A lot's happened, Brian. Let me explain."

As the embassy car weaved through the streets of Tel Aviv toward Ben Gurion Airport, the heavy diplomatic pouch leaning against one leg then the other, Mullaney listed to Abby run through the events of her morning—the letter from Morningstar and its contents; the men in the blue car waiting for her at church; getting to Doak's safely.

"Doak told me Morningstar had been killed—I'm really sorry, Brian," said Abby. "Then he called his barracks, and they sent some troopers to the church. The car was gone, but they've got an alert out and they're still looking. Doak took photos of Morningstar's letter and sent it to his commander. By the way, I just sent you a text with the letter attached."

Mullaney's mind was spinning, approaching overload. "Okay . . . thanks. But I don't know when I'll have a chance to read it."

"Morningstar's letter said he was headed to a meeting with Nora Carson. He said she was Noah Webster's closest confidant at the State Department. Doak figures that's where George was headed when he was killed. Carson lives over here in Virginia, so Doak went and paid her a visit. When she saw the letter and heard about Morningstar's death, she flipped on Webster. Right now, she's with the FBI. We've only been given short updates, but it appears she's spilling her guts. Supposedly she has documented proof of Webster's misdeeds—no, his crimes—in a safe at the State Department. That will be the FBI's next stop."

"Why has it taken you so long to let me know?"

"That's my fault, Brian," Doak's voice broke in. "I wanted to intercept Carson before she left for the city, and I had very little time. I had two troopers here with Abby and the girls, but I told them no outside communications until I got back. Didn't know if those two in the blue car had trackers on Abby's mobile or could intercept her calls. At that point, caution was the most important element. Sorry."

The embassy car pulled through the side gate at Ben Gurion, waved through by Israeli security, as Mullaney analyzed the new information. "Webster killed Morningstar?"

"Perhaps. Or had him killed," said Doak.

"Where's—"

"Brian," interrupted Abby, "that's not all. I called Daddy on his personal phone and got no response. He didn't answer at home, and he is not at his office. I'm worried. George said Daddy might be in danger too. And I don't know where he is."

The car pulled up alongside the unmarked, white corporate jet. Mullaney looked out the window at the airplane and felt helpless. Useless. Conflicted. He was going off to rescue the ambassador, but he could do nothing to protect his family. Except pray.

"Abby, I'm sorry, but I've got to go. The ambassador needs me. Doak, I'm leaving them in your hands. Keep my girls safe. I love you, Abby."

A Far Corner of Ben Gurion Airport, Tel Aviv
July 23, 3:47 p.m.

The young man with the scar across his face was hidden at a distance, binoculars held to his eyes with one hand, a cell phone in the other, as he watched Mullaney and the accompanying DSS agents board the small, private jet.

"Our tormentor is boarding the plane. Two other agents are with him. There is no doubt they are armed. All the men are in place at Güvercinlik." An F-15 jet with NATO markings but a Turkish pilot was warming its engines not fifty yards from the young man. "I will be waiting for him when he arrives on Turkish soil."

"You will in no way harm or impede the Irishman." The voice of the Turk spewed forth menace. Obedience was the only acceptable response. "You will ensure he gets here directly from the airport, without incident. What he carries is far more important than the man. There will be time to deal with Mullaney."

The young man nodded his head. He was confident Mullaney's neck would be under his blade before this day concluded. In the meantime . . . "Yes, master. It will be done as you command."

As the door to the jet closed across the tarmac, the young man turned off his phone, dropped the binoculars, and sprinted for the open cockpit of the F-15.

——————◆◇◆——————

Incirlik Air Base, Adana
July 23, 3:48 p.m.

Captain Adam Traynor's bald head glowed in the overhead lights of the cargo bay as Colonel Earnest Edwards hustled up the loading ramp of the C-130J super transport.

"Change of plans, Captain," said Edwards. As he closed the distance to his second-in-command, he lowered his voice to a conspiratorial whisper. "We're splittin' the force, Adam. You take the vans and half of the men and fly on to Güvercinlik, the Turkish army's air base in central Ankara. You're on their docket as a NATO trainin' mission."

"Yes, sir. What's the assignment?"

"Rescue operation," said Edwards, drawing the captain away from the loading ramp. "The US Ambassador to Israel, Joseph Cleveland, has been abducted. There's to be a swap in Ankara. You'll meet the DSS RSO at Güvercinlik. We'll get the details worked out en route.

"I'll take the other half of the force and stay here. The base commander is now in the loop, so I'll be able to get on-the-ground logistical support from him. But I want you to handpick your teams . . . yours will be the trickier job. Gettin' in and out of the Turkish capital, with our ambassador, without the Turks knowin' you're even in the country. And I don't anticipate a clean extraction. So hustle up and choose your teams while we offload the necessary weapons."

Edwards looked his second-in-command in the eye.

"I'd be with you, Adam, if I could," said Edwards. "But there's five thousand Americans at risk here, plus all the people of Adana. And if there is anybody who can get our ambassador out of Ankara with his life, it's you. God be with you." He gave Traynor's arm an imperceptible squeeze. "Now, let's get you out of here."

41

Incirlik Air Base, Adana
July 23, 4:12 p.m.

The unused airplane hangar was small, crowded . . . and hot. Closed up tight to keep their presence a secret, the base commander, Edwards, and Team Black's third-in-command were hunched over a map stretched out across a metal table. The twenty-five other JSOC fighters were busy checking weapons, separating ammo and other material, and packing it into four "lockers"—secure areas enclosed by chain-link fence where each of the four squads would keep its supplies.

Everyone was perspiring heavily. And ready to get to work.

"We've doubled the guard and tightened the perimeter," said the commander, "but I've got about eight miles of fence to patrol, a northwest corner bordered by a canal, a mini-suburb crowding right up against our southeast gate, and two major highways bracketing us north and south. We keep a tight fist on security, but in all honesty, this is not Fort Knox. If somebody really wanted to get in, there are a lot of places they could exploit."

Edwards ran his finger around the base perimeter on the map. "And where are the B61 bunkers?"

The commander pointed to a cluster on the western flank of the base and another at the northernmost point. "Two sets, here and here, off the beaten path. Pretty much isolated from the rest of the base."

"Good." Edwards was nodding. "This helps."

The commander, an air force colonel, looked up. "What's your plan?"

"We've war-gamed this," said Edwards, "and we believe the only feasible plan would be to release chemical weapons—wipe out everyone on the base and then steal the nukes. Which gives us a couple of advantages. One, they need to come to us. Two, they need a significant amount of chemical weapons to impact a three-thousand-acre base . . . they can't carry it in a briefcase. Three, it's gonna take a determined effort to properly deploy these weapons so they are effective. And then there is this wind.

"Honestly, I don't think whoever they are can pull off the deployment without us bein' all over them, especially now that we know they're comin'. But—and this is a big but—I don't want to wait that long. I don't want to see chemical weapons anywhere near this base or the city that surrounds it. Chemical agents are too volatile and unpredictable. Too many things can go wrong. We could be right on top of these guys and they could still open enough canisters to kill off a lot of American children. I haven't signed up for that.

"So we need to stop them before they get here," said Edwards. "And that's what we plan to do."

———◦◦◦◦———

While the base commander deployed beefed-up security units to surround both the western and northern cluster of B61 bunkers, Edwards tasked his JSOC units to do what they do best: intervene while unseen. Two Team Black members, spotters, were assigned to each of four helicopter crews. In defiance of the wind, at least three of the four choppers would be airborne at all times, providing constant surveillance from the sky, in concentric circles radiating out from Incirlik. Four other fighters occupied clandestine observation posts, five miles out in either direction on the major highways that bracketed the air base.

That was nearly half his force. Eight fighters Edwards kept in constant reserve, and the other six rotated in and out to give the guys on the surveillance teams a break.

The base commander had a half-dozen, action-ready Bradley Fighting Vehicles staged outside the hanger along with a quartet of unmarked vans. And off to the south of the hanger sat three Sikorsky UH-60 helicopters—the deadly Black Hawk—each with their rotors in a slow but constant spin.

They were ready. They just needed a target.

———◦◦◦◦———

Güvercinlik Army Air Base, Ankara
July 23, 5:01 p.m.

"Güvercinlik Tower, this is NATO heavy on final approach, wheels down, we see your lights. Thanks for your help."

The C-130J Super Hercules with the NATO call-sign descended through the flashes of late-day sun that stabbed through gathering clouds. Its wheels kissed the tarmac, and the big body settled onto the runway. The pilot taxied the jumbo cargo plane along taxiways that took it farther and farther to the right, away from the tower and the primary hangers.

Coming abreast of an isolated hanger near the northwest corner of the airport, the pilot swung the C-130 in a 180-degree arc, its nose pointing out to the rest of the airport, its tail and loading ramp in shadow.

⸺⸻◦◦◦⸻⸺

Flashing his diplomatic credentials, Mullaney bypassed customs in the commercial aviation terminal at Ankara's Güvercinlik Army Air Base, a convenient location for diplomatic traffic, just outside the city's central district. Dressed in a suit and tie, Mullaney carried the heavy diplomatic pouch close to his right leg.

A quick scan of the small terminal's lobby identified the restrooms adjacent to the tiny coffee shop. As Mullaney moved toward the men's room, the other two DSS agents filtered into the terminal from opposite entrances, keeping their distance from Mullaney but their eyes on all those who were in his vicinity.

Mullaney crossed the lobby and paused at a newsstand as one of the agents moved closer to the men's room door. It was a one-person restroom with a door that locked from the inside. A text flashed across the cell phone in his left hand. "Door's locked. I'm waiting."

Stuffing the cell phone in his pocket, Mullaney stepped to the men's room door. He heard the slight click as the dead bolt was released from the inside. In an easy, relaxed motion, he pushed against the door and entered the restroom. As soon as he was inside, Mullaney pushed the door closed and snapped the lock back into place. He looked up.

Across the small room was a bull of a man in a loosely fitting jogging suit, his bald head a gleaming beacon of reflected light from the window above him. "Agent Mullaney," he said in greeting. "Colonel Edwards sends his regards. He's got . . . uh . . . other business."

For the first time in hours, Mullaney drew in a deep breath and tried to calm his anxiety. "Captain Traynor . . . seeing you here makes me feel a little more secure," said Mullaney. He crossed the small room to shake the captain's hand, but without preamble, Traynor held a small, flat, flesh-colored triangular device toward Mullaney.

"Stick this on the skin below your left armpit, near your heart. It's not only a tracker, but it will also monitor your body's vital signs. And it's got a transmitter so we can hear your conversations. It's virtually undetectable."

Mullaney loosened the buttons of his shirt and attached the device to the bare skin under his arm, adjacent to his heart, while keeping his eyes on Traynor. "How many men on your team?"

The captain smiled. "Enough. Most of them are already in position to move with you . . . and thanks to the tip from Colonel Levinson, some are in location down the hill from the citadel."

Mullaney stiffened, a protest on his lips when the captain held up his hand.

"We're invisible, Agent Mullaney," said Traynor. "This is what we've trained for: in and out without being seen or detected. You get the ambassador. We'll get you both out."

"How . . ."

Traynor smiled once more and casually leaned back against the wall, his confidence trumping Mullaney's question. "Sir . . . we've got you covered," he said. "We have multiple scenarios plotted out and multiple points of extraction available to us." Traynor stood straighter. "We know your record, sir. You'll be fine. Follow your instincts. Don't give up the box until you have Cleveland in front of you, close at hand. Find a way to get out of the house alive, and we'll have you and Cleveland out of Turkey in less than an hour. And if we believe the situation warrants, we'll be inside that building faster than a flea farts."

Crude, but it made Mullaney laugh. Which was a welcome respite. And so was Captain Traynor. This was an expert at his trade. Cleveland had shared with Mullaney stories of JSOC's near-perfect effectiveness in seemingly impossible circumstances. Mullaney knew Captain Traynor's lightheartedness was only a thin veneer masking his determination and devotion to duty. But he needed to be sure the captain understood the full parameters of the operation. Mullaney looked into Traynor's eyes.

"Two things will happen in the next few hours," he said, his voice soft but his authority sharpened to a point. "First, I will transfer what is in this bag to the man holding Cleveland hostage. Nothing—*nothing!*—happens until that transfer is complete. Understand?"

The smile was erased from Traynor's features. "Yes, sir. Got it."

"The second thing is that you and I will rescue the United States Ambassador to Israel from his abductor—a man who is responsible for the deaths of more than half-a-dozen federal agents, including my best friend. No matter how much I long for justice . . . revenge . . . for all those dead and buried, you and I will rescue the ambassador and get him back to Israel safely. That is our only purpose here tonight. Make the switch. Rescue Cleveland. Neither one of us can allow anything to interfere with either of those objectives. Understood?"

"Yes, sir." Traynor held Mullaney's gaze without a flinch. "But if Mr. Bad Guy happens to get in my way and takes a stray 9-millimeter slug to the brain, you won't object?"

Mullaney empathized with Traynor's deadly intent but shook his head. "Two objectives, Captain, and only two. And in that order. First the switch, then the rescue. Then we disappear."

———

They were clones. Both dressed in black, head to foot, both bearded, both with the dead eyes of those who kill without fear or remorse. Mullaney had no doubt they were his reception party.

He walked from the airport terminal to the gleaming black Citroen with the smoked black windows. The two men stepped aside and opened the car's back door. Without hesitation, Mullaney ducked into the back seat, placing the leather pouch on the floor between his feet. But his brain was cataloguing every detail.

No words were spoken as a third man in black emerged from the terminal building, gave a meaningful nod to the other two, circled the car, and got into the driver's seat. One of the clones opened the far-side back door and his bulk rocked the car as he sat, his attention riveted on Mullaney. The second clone shut the back door on Mullaney, then got into the front passenger seat.

There was a distinctive *thunk* as the door locks snapped shut. The car pulled out into traffic. Mullaney mouthed a silent prayer as a heavy black hood was pulled over his head.

42

Alitas Street, Ankara
July 23, 6:09 p.m.

After winding through a myriad of streets, cresting and descending numerous hills, perhaps intentionally to throw off any sense of direction Mullaney might have, the car slowed, turned to the right, bumped over a curb, and entered a slow, downward curve to the left. Though he couldn't see anything, Mullaney could almost feel the light leave the car.

He heard the sound of mechanical rollers—a garage door, an opening for the car.

The Citroen moved forward. With each rotation of the wheels, the temperature dropped. And the car drove lower.

The stop was sudden, unexpected. It sounded like all four doors opened at once. Mullaney was pulled out of the car. The hood was removed when he was standing on his feet. The space was black, without light, the only illumination coming from the dome light of the vehicle. Mullaney squeezed and blinked his eyes open. A hand moved past his face, pointing into the back seat of the car.

"Bring it."

Mullaney reached in and hoisted the heavy leather bag from the floor of the back seat. When the doors were closed, darkness reigned. And the hood was put back over his head.

"Bring it."

The voice came through his headset loud and clear. Captain Traynor gave a thumbs-up sign to his tech sergeant with the monitor.

They were seated on benches inside an unmarked, black panel van. Three other, nearly identical, black panel vans, delivered by the cavernous C-130, were scattered throughout the Old City in central Ankara—all of them downhill from the castle. Each van tightly harbored six JSOC fighters, redundant communications equipment, and a small but rigorously vetted weapons locker with all of the tools the assault team anticipated it might need in these circumstances.

"We have audio," Traynor spoke into the mic that snaked in front of his mouth from the receiver in his right ear. A black balaclava was pulled snugly over his bald head. Each member of the team was blacked out: head-to-foot black, no flesh exposed, black body armor, black night-vision glasses that would cover their eyes and the openings in the balaclavas. The only thing they wore that was not black was *JSOC* emblazoned on their body armor, front and back, in ink that would only be visible through the night-vision units.

Each member was armed with a Colt M4A1 carbine, the weapon of choice for US special operations units. A rapid-fire weapon, the M4A1 was fed by a thirty-round, quick-change magazine, and each was equipped with an M68 Close Combat Optic red-dot sight. Two of the soldiers additionally had the M203 underslung forty-millimeter grenade launcher on their weapons. Each soldier also carried two hand grenades and two flash-bangs.

Captain Traynor looked at the circled blip on his handheld receiver. Mullaney's signal had moved underground, but was still strong, about two hundred yards away.

Alitas Street was part of a warren of narrow, winding streets with limited access, a little pocket of low-rise, masonry-and-stucco houses sprawling over the craggy outcroppings along the flanks of the hill crowned by the citadel. The streets of the neighborhood, bounded by Evi Park on the west, a reservoir to the north, a sheer rock butte to the northeast, and the castle on the south, were often little more than glorified alleyways. It was tricky terrain for an assault force to maneuver.

Even though Traynor wanted his units closer to Mullaney's position, they were probably in the best locations possible. One was outside the Ozkan Market and looked like a delivery van; one was farther down the hill, near the reservoir, parked in a little alcove near Tas Bebek Café; and the third was in reserve, tucked into the shadows under an arch of the Ankara Castle. Traynor's unit was in the car park of a mosque to the south, at the foot of Alitas Street. But because Alitas and its adjoining streets were so narrow, with limited, solitary opportunities to park, they weren't going anywhere at the moment.

"Hold your ground for my signal," Traynor directed. Then he waited.

Each step in the dark tested Mullaney's courage. Worse, he found that each step deeper into the clutches of his enemy assaulted his faith, assailed him with doubt. Was he doing the right thing? Was he really the right person for this responsibility? And how was he ever going to rescue Cleveland?

They were still descending a ramp, not stairs. Not only was the cold intensifying, but so was a sulfurous stench that brought heaves of bile out of Mullaney's guts and into his throat. He gasped for clean air, and the cloth from the hood was sucked into his mouth.

A hand grabbed his shoulder and pulled him to a halt. The ramp had flattened out. He heard a clinking of metal—keys?—and the scrape of something against the stone floor. The hood was ripped from over his head. Mullaney was pushed forward. His left shoulder brushed against a corner. A door? He stumbled through the opening.

Into a web of terror. It felt as if silken strands of horrific panic had molded themselves to Mullaney's face, his neck, his hands. Everywhere they touched, frightening alarms raced through every cell of his being. Startled by the assault, fear engulfed Mullaney. He didn't know how to fight, where to fight, what . . .

There, in front of him, boring through the dark and into his consciousness, two pulsing yellow eyes pierced the gloom.

The eyes tugged at his mind, drew on his heart, like life magnets pulling him out of himself. The eyes drew closer. They lured, enticed the life from his body.

While Mullaney rallied his spirit to withstand the attack, he also had no doubt about who he was facing. He was in the presence of pure evil—damnation personified. He stiffened his will against the force that was trying to consume him and reached out for hope.

"God, help me," he whispered.

Cloaked in darkness, standing under an overhanging arch at the mouth of a tunnel in the cavern's wall, the young commander strained his eyesight, trying to keep Mullaney in view. The scar across his face twitched with each beat of his heart.

The man who killed his father was once again within his reach. His master, the Turk, had ordered that Mullaney not be attacked until he had transferred this precious box into the Turk's hands. But after?

The commander toyed with the five-inch-long stiletto in his right hand, narrow yet strong, both sides honed sharp enough to slice a whisper. *After . . . his blood belongs on my blade.*

43

Something stirred in him, a warrior's strength. A warrior's spirit. *The Lord bless you, and keep you* burst into his thoughts. *The Lord make His face shine on you, and be gracious to you; the Lord lift up His countenance on you, and give you peace.* Bayard's voice?

"Your words are empty here. Your hope is dead."

The vile sound of iniquity, the voice on the phone, oozed from the pit of perdition, a slime that coated Mullaney's skin and polluted his heart.

"And your pleas are useless. Just as you have been useless to those you claim to love."

A shape emerged from the dark. A man, shorter than Mullaney, dressed in ancient Middle Eastern garments—his enemy, and the enemy of his soul. His hands were tucked inside the flared sleeves of his tunic. Mullaney tried to register more, but his eyes were continually wrenched back to those yellow orbs that probed his being. Fight . . . he had to fight. Think. Speak! Anything! What was it that Bayard had told him? "The enemy will try to lure you into your own strength . . . remain within the armor of God."

Put on the full armor of God . . . the belt of truth . . . the breastplate of righteousness . . . feet shod with the gospel of peace . . .

Mullaney felt his feet under him, standing firm. Fight!

"Why didn't your men just kill me and take the box when we left the airport?" he blurted out, his words breaking through the fog that had started to infiltrate his brain. "Why didn't you just kill me when we got here?"

Mullaney knew the answers as soon as he asked the questions. This man wanted the box, but he wasn't completely certain if he could touch it and continue to live. And he wasn't ready to kill . . .

"I have something much more interesting in mind for you than a quick death," said his enemy, the man responsible for Tommy's death . . . so many others. His voice sounded like a snake swishing through high grass.

A revelation dawned on Mullaney . . . several in succession.

Before him was a created, immortal being . . . the Man of Violence . . . a fallen angel. Like Bayard, neither omniscient, omnipresent, nor omnipotent. He did not know everything, so he had his doubts. He could not be everywhere at once, so his control and influence were constrained and narrow. And he was not all powerful. This being had limits. Perhaps Mullaney could take advantage of those limits to rescue Cleveland.

Doubt flooded his mind. How was he going to get Cleveland out of here? This being had no intention of releasing either of them. Once he had the box in his control . . . Mullaney knew that would be the end. Neither he nor Cleveland would leave this house alive.

He shook his head, chasing away the tendrils of fear and uncertainty. Stay focused.

Take up the shield of faith . . . Take the helmet of salvation . . . And the sword of the Spirit, which is the word of God.

First, Mullaney needed to find Cleveland. Then he needed time and he needed wisdom. *Please, God . . . No weapon formed against me shall prosper.*

"What has all this been about?" Mullaney asked, a rush of spiritual bravado in the face of death loosening his mind and his tongue. "Why have so many died over this box? And who are you?"

The man with the yellow eyes took a step forward. Mullaney could feel the man's mind trying to force its way beyond Mullaney's will. He pressed back against the force. *The weapons of our warfare are not carnal.* He was surprised when it withdrew.

"Hmmm . . . do not rely on your strength. It's not enough," said the being. "I have been called many things over the ages. Your Gaon knew me as the Man of Violence. My disciples now know me as the Turk. What you call me is not important."

Now that the being had moved closer, Mullaney could see his face more clearly. He was stunned. What he saw before him was not the face of a demented spirit and murderer. The face was like so many Mullaney had seen over the past few days—Middle Eastern in its features, serene, even cultured. It appeared there were wounds on the face. Burns? But it was the face of a businessman or merchant or government official. A face that looked familiar. Only the eyes were those of a madman.

"But what do you want from this box?" Mullaney asked. "It protected the Gaon's prophecy, but what good will that do you now?"

"I seek what all of you mortals seek. Power. The box has great power. I want it."

Mullaney didn't understand. He, others had suffered too much to leave this earth without at least understanding what was the cause of all this violence. "Why? You have the power to move the earth and shake the foundations of just two buildings in a city of thousands. I was there. So increasing your power is not the only reason you made our lives a living hell. What has this really been about from the beginning?"

The being closed his eyes and nodded his head. "Yes, from the beginning . . . it has always been the same, from the beginning."

When his eyes opened again, Mullaney could suddenly see their full fury. The yellow eyes had black irises, but in the yellow of the pupils swirled gray clouds of mayhem and anarchy. Of blood lust.

"At first, it was not the box but the messages of the Lithuanian that we sought," he said. "He had been given insight into the future, insight into our plans. We were determined to destroy those messages before they revealed our plans."

"Failed at that, didn't you?"

Not a good idea.

Thunderclouds of fury that seemed to be spewing lethal lightning hurtled across the eyes. A lance of intense heat pierced the cold, striking Mullaney in the chest, and the putrid decay of death filled the atmosphere. Mullaney staggered before the vehement wrath. The lightning struck his legs and they buckled, driving him to his knees.

The ferocious voice was now a whisper. "Mock me again and the ambassador dies. And I will slaughter his daughter."

Mullaney struggled to find his voice as he stumbled back to his feet, the leather satchel still grasped firmly in his right hand. "Understood."

Chaos receded into the dark.

"I will tell you, so that you will know why you die," said the being. "Since that day, when the death of the Nazarene imposter was stolen from us and we discerned his intention to return and seize our sovereignty over the earth . . .

and over you mortals . . . we have been determined to thwart his intentions, make his return impossible. One of his deranged prophets claims the feet of the Nazarene will land on the Mount of Olives when he returns. Well, what if the Mount of Olives no longer exists?

"You see, all of your book is built on a foundation of prophecies and promises . . . things to come. If we can prevent one of the prophecies from being fulfilled, cause one of the promises to be stillborn, then the integrity of the book is shattered. There is no more truth. And we can change the end of the book."

Mullaney saw the logic but rejected its possibility. He punctuated his words with firm resolve. "You are insane. God's Word is infallible and indelible. You can never change his Word."

The Man of Violence laughed, and Mullaney felt like all the condemned souls in hell laughed with him. Mullaney's body convulsed at the sound.

"Never is a long time," he said. "A length of time that you cannot conceive. But we . . . we have all the time we need to overcome never. Many of us are assigned to the same task but are taking different avenues to achieve the same end. We have the power and the determination to overthrow never.

"Yes, there will be a climactic battle for all the earth," said the man with the yellow eyes. "On the plains of that accursed land that he blessed. But annul a prophecy, reverse the chain of promise, and you reverse the outcome of the battle. Particularly if you have nuclear weapons to destroy your enemies."

It was like a slap across the face. Sudden and painful. Understanding flooded Mullaney's mind. So that was it. Incirlik. Finally, the pieces fit. Not two enemies, not two crises, but one. One plot—that waited to be fulfilled. And the Man of Violence needed the power of the box? Perhaps Mullaney didn't comprehend it all. But he believed he grasped enough. Somehow he needed to stop this creature, he needed to abort this plan . . . lurking tendrils of thievery invaded his mind, once again seeking purchase, clouding his thoughts.

"Do you seriously think you can stop us?" mocked the Man of Violence. "Your efforts to destroy our plans have been useless from the beginning, just as you have been useless since your youth. Just as you were useless in failing to save your father's life."

The sting of past failure, of repressed guilt, bored a hole in Mullaney's resolve. Useless. Was he?

"Face it . . . you are defeated. Give me the anointing."

Wait! The anointing? He believes he needs the anointing? Mullaney's understanding widened.

"You need me," he said, almost to himself. He raised the bag in his right hand. "You need me for this. No mortal man can touch the box and live. Is the same true for an immortal man? Do you have immunity from the protection over the box? Is it possible that the power that protected and filled this box could actually kill an immortal? Is that a risk you're willing to take?"

Mullaney left the question hanging in the gloom. He was beginning to see a way. "Obviously not. So we're here to make a deal. I want Cleveland. You want . . . ?"

"Do not overestimate your importance," said the Man of Violence. "You have caused me a great amount of harm. You have slaughtered my servants. It would give me great pleasure to run this blade"—he withdrew a thin, short, curved scimitar from his sleeve—"across your neck and allow your warm blood to drip through my fingers. But not before I . . . Well let's leave that for later." He pointed at the leather bag. "Bring out the box!"

For the instant the yellow eyes left his face and concentrated on the leather bag, Mullaney felt a surge of strength and clarity, determination. Keep talking. Give Traynor time. And find Cleveland.

"I came here for Cleveland. Cleveland goes free before I hand over this box," said Mullaney. "I need proof of life."

The Man of Violence raised his left hand, the scimitar blade still hanging from his right. "Better yet, I'll give you Cleveland himself." He snapped his fingers. A shaft of light flooded an area off to Mullaney's left, revealing walls. They were in some kind of room. But the light also revealed Joseph Atticus Cleveland. At least it revealed his body.

Cleveland, in a sitting position, was strapped into a straight-backed metal chair. His head was hanging forward, his chin resting upon his chest. His arms were bent back, his hands apparently bound behind his back. Mullaney could not tell if Cleveland was breathing.

"Proof of life!" Mullaney emphasized.

The Man of Violence snapped his fingers once more. Out of the darkness a man entered the light, a dripping cloth in his right hand. He stood alongside Cleveland and laid the wet cloth on the ambassador's neck. Cleveland began to stir, squirm against the restraints. The man stepped behind the chair and released the straps. He took the cloth from Cleveland's neck, tilted his neck back and laid the cloth on his forehead, one hand resting against the ambassador's chest to keep him from falling off the chair.

As if he was emerging from a trance, Cleveland slowly regained consciousness. His face was still blank, his eyes unfocused, but Mullaney could see he was alive and apparently physically unharmed. "Mr. Ambassador?"

A slight jolt passed through Cleveland's body, he sat up straighter, the cloth falling into his lap, his eyes seeking the source of the voice. They reached out to Mullaney.

"Brian?" One word. A lifeline from a drowning man.

"Mr. Ambassador, can you stand?"

Cleveland nodded his head, sucked in a breath, placed his hands on the sides of the seat and struggled to his feet. His stance was wobbly, but the fire in his eyes held conviction.

More light filtered into the space from unseen sources. Mullaney could now see that they were in a large cavern—and he could also see there was another shape, a shadow with a black cowl over its head, motionless and silent against the back wall of the ancient-looking room. Its walls and floors were made of rough-hewn stone blocks, the vaulted ceiling of the same blocks, pillars spaced around the walls to hold up the vault. Though dry, the room still reeked of damp and decay. It contained one door behind Mullaney, where he must have entered. But three archways stood to his right, each with a black maw opening that looked like the entrance to a tunnel passage.

In his quick Google search of the citadel, Mullaney had learned that there were hundreds of caverns and tunnels honeycombed under the thirteen-hundred-year-old castle, many snaking down the hill as routes of escape during a siege. Whether connected to the citadel or not, Mullaney was in the midst of an ancient maze.

As his eyes wandered about the cavernous room, they came once again to the Man of Violence. "I'm not surprised that you dwell underground in ancient caverns," said Mullaney, hoping that Traynor could still hear him. "Where do those three tunnels run, back up to the castle?"

The man ignored Mullaney's question. "The box."

Mullaney returned his attention back to Cleveland. "Sir, I need you to come over here and stand by me."

The man standing beside Cleveland put a restraining hand on his arm. Mullaney turned his attention back to the Man of Violence.

"Enough delays," said the man. "Cleveland doesn't move until I see the Gaon's box. And I want the covering," he said, "the protection that is passed down from father to son. The protection that was transferred to you . . . Guardian."

He needed to buy time. Perhaps Traynor and his men could find a way to reach them. Searching his mind for options, Mullaney came up blank. What else could he do?

"Now," demanded the Turk, "or my disciple will cut off Cleveland's hand."

44

Mullaney turned to his left. He looked more closely at the man who still had a restraining hand on Cleveland's arm. His left fist held Cleveland's right arm in a vise grip, straining the powerful muscles in his forearm and biceps. But as he reached down to the floor, in his right fist he picked up a battery powered reciprocal saw . . . a long, roughly serrated blade made for ripping apart walls. This would be no surgical strike with a lethally sharpened blade. No, the saw would rip and mangle Cleveland's skin, shatter the bones in his wrist, and shred tendons and sinew as it ground its way through his arm.

"If I ever find you again, I'll . . ."

The Turk flicked out his hand and the man squeezed the trigger, bringing the saw blade to life. "Now, Agent Mullaney."

Useless. It was useless to argue, useless to resist anymore.

Mullaney lowered the satchel to the floor and knelt beside it. He flipped the hasp, bent back the sides to open it wide. Reaching in, he felt the stainless-steel blast container that held the Gaon's box. It was a heavy lift. Mullaney got his feet under him, in a crouch, and lifted the blast container using his legs.

He looked around. There was no table on which to put the blast container. So he walked over to the chair where Cleveland had been sitting—the man who had a clamp on Cleveland's arm pulled the ambassador farther away to the left—and placed the container on top of the chair.

Settling the container on the chair, Mullaney pulled the handle on the cover counterclockwise, disengaging the hooks from the steel bars, then released the steel hasp on the side, freeing the cover from the rest of the container. Mullaney swung the cover to the right. Inside was the metal shelf on rollers.

Feeling like he was signing their death warrants, Mullaney drew a deep breath to steady his nerves and reached in to pull out the shelf.

————————

Mullaney felt something large, like an invisible hand, placed over his eyes. The room became an opaque cave. Then a massive, blinding eruption, like the explosion of a supernova star, flooded the cavern with a tidal wave of light so brilliant and intense that it had a sound. The light thrummed. And it scorched.

He felt the heat of the light on his skin. Three voices screamed in unison, the closest one to Mullaney's left, where the muscular man held Cleveland's arm in his grip. Then, as quickly as it had come, the reflection of the blazing light dissipated from around the fingers over his eyes.

Before thought could register, the hand was removed from his face. Mullaney's vision was quickly restored. And he found himself facing the man with the saw. He was screaming, his left hand holding his face, blood seeping through his fingers.

Reflexively, Mullaney took three steps toward the screaming man, reached down with both hands, and grabbed the hand with the saw. He pushed on the trigger as he twisted the man's hand back upon himself, then plunged the vibrating, ripping saw into the man's heart.

Ignoring the blood that burst from the man's chest, Mullaney swung around on Cleveland—who was looking at him strangely.

"Somebody put their hand over my eyes," said Cleveland.

The box! Mullaney turned back toward the chair. The blast container was open, the shelf pulled out. The box was gone . . . and so was the Man of Violence. Fists closed, weight on the balls of his feet, Mullaney turned to where he remembered the two men were standing who had picked him up. He saw both men writhing on the floor. Just as all light vanished from the cavern.

————————

He could feel it coming. A disturbance in the presence around him. A warning. He perceived a lance thrust by an enemy.

In the split second before the blinding light invaded the gloom of the cavern, heavy, hooded lids—like those of a serpent—closed over the yellow eyes of the Turk. Through the heavy folds of skin, the Turk's eyes registered an imprint of the tsunami of light that engulfed the cavern and brought screams of pain

from those around him. He reached out with his other senses, his other powers
. . . where was the box? Where was Mullaney?

Like a receding wave, the blast of light withdrew from the cavern. The
Turk thrust the lids from his eyes. First, he found the box, still on the shelf in
the blast container, then he shifted his gaze to Mullaney. He was attacking the
disciple who held Cleveland.

There was little time to fully assess the situation, his options. A heartbeat.
His enemies, those winged ones who opposed his purposes, had breached his
defenses and pierced the cavern with their light. What else could they do, even
here in his lair? He had no time and no desire to find out. He also did not have
the covering to protect him from the power of the box. Could he force Mullaney to give it to him? Did he need it? No mortal man could touch the box . . .
and he was no mortal man. And then there was the One. Where was the One?

All this flashed through the Turk's mind in an instant. This might be his
only moment. He motioned to the spectral shadow against the far wall as he
sped across the floor and stood in front of the blast chamber, only paces from
Mullaney. He placed his hands above the shelf. The steel mesh that encased the
box of power lifted into the air above the chamber. Without touching the box
or the mesh encasing it, the Turk guided the levitating box before him. He did
not approach the only door, nor did he advance on the three tunnel openings to
his left. He heard the ripping sound of an electric motor behind him, a piercing
scream, as he whispered a word unheard on the earth for millennia. A stone in
the floor slid to the right, revealing stone steps leading down, deeper under the
mountain. The Turk maneuvered the box through the opening, keeping it in
front of him, and started down the stairs, followed by the figure in the black
cape. Speaking the word a second time, the stone in the floor slid closed over
his head, once again surrounding the Turk in darkness.

His left hand locked on Cleveland's wrist, Mullaney stretched his right arm
before him and started inching in the direction he hoped would bring him to
the door. Straining his senses into the dark before him, his fingers outstretched,
Mullaney was distracted by an increasing level of heat he felt on the back of his
neck. He looked back, over his right shoulder. What was back there?

Something red, flaming, was swirling in the midst of the darkness, coalescing into denser folds of red. As the color intensified, an evil presence surrounded him—heavy and oppressive. He felt his body, mind, and spirit probed and violated by a ravenous malevolence that sought to consume his very soul. Fear rising, his heart thumping, Mullaney pushed harder to find the door.

Dragging Cleveland through the dark, Mullaney's hand struck stone, then wood, side by side. The wood vertical. The door jamb?

In that moment, before he could signal to Cleveland, Mullaney heard the whisper of a voice near his right ear. It did not come from the vortex of swirling crimson heat behind him.

"I've been living for this moment. My father's revenge is in . . ."

All his instincts and training triggered without thought. Mullaney ducked low, to his left, put his right hand on the floor for leverage, and pulled Cleveland in a wide arc as far from the voice as his arm would allow.

A face flashed into his memory . . . the rage of the young man with the scar across his face who was trying to reach the embassy car on the Namir Road, who was waiting for him at the monastery.

As he ducked, Mullaney felt more than saw the sweep of a right arm into the space he had just vacated. *A knife.* He couldn't fight, not with Cleveland. But there was no time to flee!

He threw Cleveland to the ground, freeing his left hand, and turned on the balls of his feet. *I hope I'm behind him.* Still crouched low to the floor, Mullaney launched his body forward. His shoulder made contact . . . legs! . . . and he drove his shoulder under the man's body, wrapped his arms around the attacker's legs. In one swift, fluid movement, Mullaney lifted the body off the ground and, with a violent twist of his shoulders to the left, slammed the top of the man's body into the wall he knew was there.

But not before the man, flung to the left, swept his right arm in an arc and buried the knife into Mullaney's left bicep, just below the shoulder.

He was going for my heart!

There was a sickening *thunk* as the man's head smashed into the stone wall and his body went limp. It barely registered. Mullaney dropped the limp body and fell to his knees, his right hand finding the hilt of the knife as an explosion of pain burst down his arm and through his chest.

Cleveland!

45

At the bottom of the stone stairs, the being occupying Arslan Eroglu's body turned to the right and guided the blast container down a stone passageway barely lit by oil lamps attached to the walls at long distances.

Halfway down the passage, the Turk halted.

The specter in the black cape and cowl came forward on his left and turned to a reinforced metal door. He took a key from the pocket of his cloak, turned the lock, pushed the door open, and stepped aside to allow the Turk to steer the box into the room.

The room was painted a deep crimson, the color of blood, on walls, ceiling, and floor. On the walls were a riot of designs in gold paint—a wide spectrum of designs from astrology, occult, Egyptian ritual, and others that no human being could, or would want to, decipher. The room was as cold as a crypt.

To the left was a stone altar of sacrifice, runnels carved into the top of the capstone around all four edges, a chute for drainage at the lower right corner. On top of the altar lay the inert body of the Turk.

But the live Turk, the essence living inside Arslan Eroglu's body, moved the box and its mesh enclosure to the right, away from the altar. He levitated the box over a small, stone table that sat in front of a massive stone throne.

———✦———

Ignoring the pain, holding his left arm close to his body, Mullaney shifted toward his right, the ambassador's name on his lips. "Atticus?"

Distracted by the fear and adrenaline of his short-lived, life-or-death fight, Mullaney's senses revived with a rush. He retched. He was assaulted by a wall of heat and polluted by the putrid stench of festering decay. His repressed fear and anxiety suddenly trebled into terror.

A red glow, like a vibrating emergency sign, colored the darkness and spread a surreal light around Mullaney. In the little he could see, the red swirling, flaming vortex had moved between him and Cleveland. Its shape was becoming more defined. And it appeared to be looking at Cleveland. Mullaney's mind leapt to action. He needed to defend the ambassador. He tried to push off with his right hand, but his body was locked in place. Movement was impossible. Terror multiplied.

And the swirling red menace—it appeared to be growing eyes—turned its attention upon Mullaney.

"Guardian," came a whisper from the halls of Hades.

Mullaney moaned, *Oh, God of heaven, help us!*

A silver sword split the red gloom between Mullaney and this manifestation of evil, its point shattering the stone of the floor and taking root. A silver breastplate reflected the red light. "You cannot have him." It was Bayard's voice. "Neither of them. They are sons of the King, heirs of heaven. He is the anointed of the Creator. No weapon of evil formed against them will succeed."

Mullaney watched the swirling red mist as it jerked wildly in the gloom. In his spirit he realized that, if this demon could form itself, if it materialized here, it would be much more difficult to defeat. A thought flashed into his mind—could he look into the face of pure evil, into the eyes of the evil one himself, and survive? Mullaney didn't want to find out.

Struggling, but now able to stand, Mullaney put Bayard behind his back, between him and his enemy. He reached out with his good arm and pulled Cleveland to his feet.

Which way to go? In the red gloom he could see the outline of the door in front of him. Was it locked? Was it safe? Were there disciples waiting on the other side?

He looked over his left shoulder to where he knew the three tunnel entrances were located. Could they escape that way? But which one?

Cleveland gave voice to his thoughts. "Which way?"

A thunder of fiendish power erupted behind Mullaney. "You are in my domain!" It was a bellow from the abyss. "You cannot—"

Light erupted from two directions at once. Dazzling brightness exploded from behind Mullaney, vaporizing the darkness. He heard a . . . whimper? In the same instant, a fierce burst of sparks melted the lock on the door in front of him.

A dozen black-clad men spilled into the cavern, spreading out in a wide arc, the red beams of their laser sights seeking a target.

Aged and wrinkled, his bald head hidden by the cowl of his long, black cape, Assan, the Turk's spiritually indentured servant, closed the door and turned the lock. He seldom entered the red room. His visits were normally moments of high drama and higher risks, injections of adrenaline that called to Assan like a needle to an addict. Until something went wrong. Then the Turk's wrath transformed thrills into threats he was likely to fulfill.

Assan's eyes avoided the lifeless carcass to his left. The spectacle was unfolding in front of him. He knew the Turk was there, assimilated into and controlling the body of Arslan Eroglu. But it was startling to see Eroglu's shell orchestrating the dark power flowing through the room.

Standing in front of his stone throne, hovered over a low, stone table, Eroglu rotated his hands above the bronze box and the metal mesh that enclosed it. There were things Assan heard in this room, words that were offered as supplication or demand that belonged in the realms of darkness. But in all his many years serving his master, the litany of urgent summonses now spoken into the atmosphere of the red room were both foreign and disturbing to Assan's ears. They carried the weight of pleading petitions. The Turk was begging.

As he watched, the box and its enclosure began to move in a circular pattern following the direction and pace of the Turk's hands. A wave of energy washed across the ceiling and over the red walls, bringing life to the strange golden symbols painted on the walls. Like crazed dancers around a pyre, in cadence with the Turk's incantations over the box, the symbols pulsed, spun, and twisted in upon themselves in fantastic patterns. Startled, Assan looked at the wall to his left then to the wall on his right. Were his ears deceived? The walls appeared to be singing . . . no, chanting . . . to each other. And the volume was increasing.

Captain Traynor swept the scene with a trained eye. Two men writhing in pain in the middle of the cavern; a third to the left with something impaled into his heart; and a fourth a bloody heap on the floor to the left of the door. He saw no threats. But he sensed evil. Powerful evil.

He pointed to Mullaney and Cleveland. "We're moving."

Four of his men stepped forward. Two nearly picked Cleveland off his feet, a hand in each armpit, and hustled him through the open door. One slung his weapon, stepped to Mullaney's right side, and clamped his arms front and back and held on while the other pulled the knife out of Mullaney's arm. He slapped a compress over the wound, wrapped it once with an adhesive bandage, and then they moved Mullaney out with as much dispatch.

Traynor kept his eyes scanning the room . . . the stench was awful, like a garbage truck convention . . . his remaining men exited in pairs. There was a strange taste to the air—metallic and singed, like burning metal . . . until it was only he and the sergeant. He saw no threats, only a dissipating red mist in the gloom. But he knew the presence of evil. He spun on his heel and disappeared through the door, thanking his God to be out of that room.

46

Alitas Street, Ankara
July 23, 6:43 p.m.

Assan's heart jumped in his chest when the wire mesh surrounding the box was rent in two and hurled into the corners of the red room, the Turk throwing his arms wide. The Gaon's accursed box descended to rest on the table, and the chanting filling Assan's ears grew in fervor and tempo.

The symbols gyrating wildly on the walls, a gilded aura—like the gold lust of a buccaneer staring into a chest of stolen treasure—illuminated the face that was not the Turk's, but contained his eyes. The Turk reached toward the box.

Four in front fast-walked up the dimly lit ramp. Then two came with Cleveland in tow; two others moving swiftly in tandem alongside Mullaney who, in fact, could make it on his own. Then four as rear guard . . . the last two trotting backward, up the ramp, their eyes fixed into the blackness below.

Captain Traynor glanced at the myriad-function watch on his left wrist. They had traveled about one hundred meters down the ramp—twenty meters in depth—once they had breached the garage. Another fifty meters remained in the ramp. He had commenced the action at 6:29. It was now 6:41. In his business, time was everything. In. Hit. Out. Before anyone even knew you were there. This was taking too much time. His men at the garage, those on the street, were exposed. Too much time.

He turned and tapped the two men behind him on the shoulder as he spoke to his team and into the mic at the same time. "Gotta move . . . gotta move." Twelve men and Mullaney broke into an uphill run. Cleveland, like the knocker on a bell, careened from side to side between the two soldiers who held him fast.

"We're fifty meters out, hustling," Traynor said into the mic, "on our way to you. Prepare for evac."

Blood racing through his veins, the whirlwind of concentrated power swirling like a tornado around the red room, the Turk licked his lips but fought for discretion. The box was within his reach. But he wasn't fully prepared. Not yet.

He reached inside the container and gingerly grasped the handle on the shelf in the middle.

Just short of the top of the ramp, all but the first four slowed into a trot. The first four soldiers kept running.

"Coming out," Traynor barked before his men got to the ramp's apex.

Mullaney watched as the first four, in two pairs, hesitated at the lip, looked side-to-side, and then broke out in opposite directions. Once all four had disappeared into the garage, Mullaney heard voices from each side of the garage. "Clear." "Clear." "Vans in place."

"Let's move," said Traynor, leading the way.

The first of the JSOC soldiers exited the garage and ran to the two vans in the street. They opened the doors then turned outward, covering the others' approach.

"Get the ambassador in the lead van," ordered Traynor, who grabbed Mullaney by the elbow and guided him to the second van.

As the JSOC team exited the garage and raced into the street, a fusillade of gunfire exploded from rooftops on three sides.

The world became a blur for Mullaney. A rain of bullets tore up the stones in the street, sending lethal shards of rock whistling through the air, and riddled the vans through the sides and the roof. Mullaney frantically glanced to his right to find Cleveland, but Traynor grabbed his arm and literally threw him behind an outcropping of masonry stairs that came down the side of the hill and into the driveway.

"Code red," called Traynor. "Code red . . . above us."

Mullaney could see little from the corner in which he crouched, Captain Traynor kneeling at the edge of the stairs and returning fire across the narrow street. What he saw broke his heart and ignited his blood lust. At least four of the JSOC soldiers were on the ground, bleeding. Only one moved, crawling desperately for cover. And Mullaney could see only the rear half of the lead van. All its windows were shattered by the bullets, the metal body a warren of holes, its engine apparently on fire. But no Cleveland.

The sound of gunfire was relentless and deafening, both from their attackers and from the remaining JSOC soldiers. A grenade erupted above their heads, a second obliterating most of the upper floor of a building across the street.

"Move and advance," roared Traynor, as Mullaney noticed another of the black vans rounding a corner down the street. The van stopped short of the fighting as six soldiers and the driver poured out of the vehicle and rapidly scrambled to higher ground on both sides of the street.

"Where's Cleveland?" Traynor shouted. From his reaction, Mullaney could tell that Traynor had received no answer. Shaking his head, the captain peaked around the corner of the steps and emptied a clip into the far buildings. Then he turned to Mullaney, a puzzled look on his face.

"They're not shooting at us," he said, pulling a 9-millimeter automatic from his holster, two clips, and handing them to Mullaney. "They're shooting at everybody else, but they're not shooting at us." He pointed at the automatic. "Use it!"

<hr />

He withdrew his hand from above the box, turned, and looked to his right. In a stone basin just above the floor was the skinned pelt of a perfect ram, without blemish. He reached down and pushed his hands under the pelt, feeling the still-warm sticky thickness of the ram's blood as it slid through his fingers. The Turk lifted the pelt with care, like it was a gossamer web, and laid it across the top of the bronze box that had eluded him for centuries. Centuries when he chased the prophecy held within the box, unaware that it was the box that held the power of life and death.

Now was the moment, his moment. He hesitated. How to open the box? Was there a pattern, a secret step-by-step method that would assure success? So much he didn't know. But he had waited so long.

The Turk raised his bloody hands into the air, above the box. He focused the power of his eyes upon the ram's fleece and the box beneath. Spells taught to him in the caverns of darkness spilled over his lips while maelstroms of psychic eruptions raged through his yellow eyes and burrowed into the pelt and the box.

The surge pulsing power sped through the red room, expanding in depth and strength. The chanting echoes from the room's walls roiled to a manic crescendo.

The Turk lowered his hands toward the ram's pelt.

———————

Pat McKeon had a formidable force of eight DSS agents with her, heavily armed and wearing body armor, as the flat-lining truck bounded over a curb and careened into the street in front of the Ozkan Market. She heard the riot of gunfire ahead of her. "Faster."

47

Alitas Street, Ankara
July 23, 6:52 p.m.

Mullaney glanced around for a target, then looked over his shoulder. The steps behind him were uncovered. Still in a crouch, he swiveled on his heel, grasped the Glock with two hands, and peeked up the stairs. Two men in black were firing down into the street as they cautiously descended the stairs, one step at a time.

Without hesitation, all his training on the firing range clicked into gear. Two quick, smooth squeezes of the Glock and the head shot dropped the lead man to the stairs. In almost the same motion, Mullaney fixed his sights on the second and, before he could turn his machine pistol down the stairs, placed a three-pattern into his heart.

It was then he saw the young man with the scarred face standing at the top of the stairs. Blood pulsed from the side of his head, falling to his already blood-saturated shirt. Instantly Mullaney knew. *They're not after Cleveland. That one, he's after me.*

Mullaney swung round to Traynor, the words on his lips, "Get Cleveland out. It's me—"

But Captain Traynor was no longer there.

———⊶◈⊷———

The roar of an engine, the wailing screech of tires . . . Mullaney glanced at the street . . . and a garish delivery truck, with a canvas tarp covering the space behind the cab, slid sideways to a stop in the middle of the street, its cab facing Mullaney and the riddled JSOC vans. Before the wheels stopped sliding, two men emerged from a hole cut in the top of the tarp and began inundating the shooters above them, on both sides of the street, with the heavy thump and relentless destruction of .50-caliber machine guns. A bunch of bodies leaped out of the back of the truck, ran for cover while laying down a murderous fusillade on their attackers.

Pat McKeon jumped from the passenger's side of the cab and ran to the front of the burning lead van.

Pat McKeon?

But there was no time to think. He swung around and peeked up the stairs, the Glock held in front of him. Before Mullaney could get off a shot, he caught a quick glimpse of the young man. The machine gun in the scarred man's hands blasted holes in the plaster wall as he descended the stairs, driving Mullaney deep into his corner for cover.

———◦◦◦———

Assan's attention was riveted on the hands of Arslan Eroglu as the Turk reached for the ram's skin over the box.

He was only dimly aware of the heat that built at the back of his neck.

———◦◦◦———

Pat McKeon flew across the narrow street and threw her body in front of the lead van . . . and covered Cleveland's body that was wedged up under the front bumper. He was protected from the gunfire above him by the engine block at his back. And his eyes were open, gazing at McKeon with unreserved shock.

"McKeon?"

"Shut up and stay still," she barked as she pulled her Glock from the holster at the small of her back. She scanned the rooftops, trying to assess the situation. And saw the JSOC soldiers advancing behind parapet walls both up and down and on both sides of the street. The attackers were pinned down by the savage devastation of the powerful .50s pounding out carnage from the back of the truck.

The JSOC pincer was relentless and lethal as they shredded one attacker after another. The roar of the gunfire fell, then rose again.

McKeon looked down at the ambassador. "Are you wounded?"

He shook his head no.

McKeon lowered her face close to Cleveland's ear. "If you ever try to pull something like this on me again, I will personally kick your rear end from Tel Aviv to Jerusalem and back again. Do you copy?"

Cleveland's eyes were wide. But he quickly nodded. "Never again."

McKeon turned her attention back to the remaining shooters, fighting to keep a smile from reaching her face.

He hesitated, uncertain of the next step. How could he bypass Eroglu's body to assimilate the power of the box into his immortal being? Where was the power—on the box, inside? What was the way . . .

The Turk's desire blossomed into overwhelming hunger. He marshaled all of his consciousness, honing his senses, alert to the input of every cell.

Reciting the secret words of the dark lords, overflowing with the ecstasy of triumph, banishing any doubt, the Turk placed his hands on the pelt but pushed his fingers under the pelt until they wedged under the lip of the box's lid. He lifted the lid . . .

The gunfire was shifting in location and dwindling, slowly, in intensity. The tide had turned, but that had little meaning for Mullaney. A flood of bullets continued to rip up the ground and the walls around him. The young man seemed to have an endless feed of ammunition. Mullaney couldn't move. He was caught in a trap, right where the young man wanted him to be.

And the hunter was getting closer.

Eroglu's hands were on it. The Turk was . . .

An intense halo of crimson engulfed Assan, sharpened talons of fire pierced the back of his neck, driving him to the undulating stone floor. Terror pierced his consciousness.

The One!

"Get rid of the gun, or I'll drop you where you are." The young man's voice came from just around the corner, his automatic continually laying down a cascade of bullets.

After all this, he's not going to shoot me. That's not what he's after.

Mullaney played for time . . . and an opening. He threw his Glock down onto the driveway, in front of the stairs.

The young man turned the corner, the red-hot, smoking machine gun in his left hand, a long, serrated knife blade in the right.

Another knife.

"Who are you?" *Play for time!*

The young man smiled. It was the smile of a hungry leopard closing steadily on its dinner.

"I am my father's son." The red, livid scar across the top of his face twitched in anticipation. "You had no mercy for him. I have no mercy for you. And you will pay for his death."

With two lightning steps, the young man advanced on Mullaney and released the gun from his left hand. He turned his shoulders and raised the knife to strike, his left hand snapping out like a striking serpent. With prodigious strength he clamped a vise hold on Mullaney's right shoulder.

The right arm flexed for the lethal thrust. But a stunned look of shock flooded the young man's face and stilled his arm. He opened his mouth to protest something . . . and then uttered a spine-shaking scream. His right fist shook as if he was trying to will the knife blade into Mullaney's throat. But blood began to run like rivers from his eyes. His hair fell out in clumps. And as he gasped for breath, his swollen black tongue erupted in festering sores.

He fell at Mullaney's feet, dead before he hit the stones.

At first, it was an almost imperceptible tingling at the tips of Eroglu's fingers.

The Turk's heart denounced dread and grasped conquest, while increasing the speed and fervency of the occult murmurings crossing his lips—incantations designed to counteract the deadly design of the box. The Turk had seen how his disciples, when they broke into the Istanbul synagogue, and others died once they touched the box—bleeding eyes; black, bulging tongue; hair falling out before life was ripped from them. That fate would not touch him.

His eyes focused on fingers that rested against the box and held the lid. Yes! It *was* warmth that surged into his fingers, warmth that emanated from what he was holding. The Turk's breathing became shallow and faster. He tried to feel into his fingers. What was . . .

Strength. He felt a release of strength, greater power, into his fingers, through the palms of his hands. Not death. Power!

The cresting power coursed up his arms, engorging his muscles with the strength of thousands. A manic smile of triumph engulfed his face as he looked at the rioting madness of the red room's walls. "Yes!"

The Turk could feel an exponential expansion of his strength, through his shoulders, across his chest. Now it was rising up, from his feet through his legs. This was not death. Death had no domain over him. This was power!

The Turk threw back his head and unleashed a roar of triumphant conquest that bellowed off the resounding walls. The power was his! Finally . . . the power and the glory were all his. He would no longer be a slave. He would be the master, master of—

His eyes flashed open and saw the evil, yellow stare of the One, his throbbing red presence on the far side of the room, his devouring mouth wide and a laugh from the pit of perdition erupting into the room.

48

The shooting stopped . . . but not the noise. The two backup black vans raced into the driveway, skidded to a stop, and soldiers from all sides started shouting.

"Move . . . move."

"Nobody gets left behind!"

"Get the wounded in the left van with the doc."

"Move . . . move."

Mullaney looked up from the desiccated body on the driveway beneath him. McKeon was half pulling, half lifting Cleveland in his direction.

"Are you hurt?" Mullaney and McKeon both said at the same time.

But Cleveland was looking down at the body then back to Mullaney. "You still have the anointing of the guardian," he said. "You haven't passed it on. Somehow it saved you."

Captain Traynor raced up, blood oozing from a hole in his thigh. "Get your butts moving," he yelled. "We need to vanish. Move!"

Despite the heat, Edwards was downing his third cup of coffee when he heard the radio squawk from a corner of the hanger.

"Contact!" said a voice nearly drowned out by the thrash of helicopter rotors. "About thirty miles west of the base at thirty-six minutes, seventeen degrees north; thirty-two minutes, forty-six degrees east. An isolated warehouse complex. Three identical trucks parked alongside. Somebody's produce company."

Edwards stood over the shoulder of the radio operator. "What's the tell?" asked Edwards.

"Fenced-in enclosure. Six sentries. All black clad, black hoods, automatic weapons. These guys are not guarding somebody's lettuce."

"Maintain covert surveillance," said Edwards. "We're on our way." He tapped the radio operator on the shoulder. "Recall all of our men. Tell them to get on their giddy-up. We're movin' out."

———◦◦◦———

Alitas Street, Ankara
July 23, 6:58 p.m.

"So my willful one, you finally have in your hands the desire of your lust." The voice of the One was laced with taunting mockery. "You believe you have triumphed over me . . . your master? You believe this is your ultimate victory?"

The Turk sharpened his focus on the One, even as the muscles and sinews of his body physically enlarged, as the reaches of his mind expanded through the universe, as the power of his darkness deepened into ebony dominion. "I have the power!" he bellowed. "It is mine!"

"Yes, it is yours," whispered the vision of the One. "You have finally conquered, completed the work of centuries. What you have in your hands you deserve."

There was something in the One's voice that broke through the Turk's exquisite revelry, something that delivered a warning to the Turk's ever-expanding consciousness. A wisp of doubt? No! It was sovereign power that flowed through him, filled him to overflowing with supernatural strength. He was unstoppable. Invincible.

"You," he screamed at the One, "will now do my bidding. I will—"

The Turk looked down toward the box. His forearms were extended beyond the sleeves of his jubba. The muscles of Eroglu's forearm were thick and throbbing, huge and expanding in strength, pushing against the limits of his skin. Just as his mind was accelerating in perception, new knowledge filling his brain to capacity.

He felt the headache first.

"How does unlimited power feel, my willful one?"

The Turk felt it. Unfettered energy continued to pour from the box, through his fingers and into him . . . body, mind, soul, and spirit. But he was already full.

"Unlimited power," snarled the One, "has no limits. Do you really think I would have allowed you to take what was mine . . . if I wanted it?"

The press of discomfort in Eroglu's body, in the Turk's mind, quickly morphed into an encroaching pain. The Turk tried to pull Eroglu's fingers from the box and failed. He strained with all of his new strength; the bulging muscles of his arms stretched tight with the effort. He failed. And he feared.

He felt it. Like a river unleashed through a broken dam, the overwhelming power and strength gushing from the box was pouring into him unabated. Pushing beyond his limits to contain it. Power being compacted, compressed against the limits of his body, against the confines of his brain. And still it flowed undiminished . . . now unwanted.

Understanding broke upon the Turk like a thunderclap, a punctuation of the pain that began to throb through Eroglu's entire being. He sought the eyes of the One.

"Help me." A penitent's sigh. "Help me!"

The red room was still swirling, the golden symbols gyrating, but now the madness of the red room appeared to have invaded the essence of the Turk. His body began to tremble, slowly at first, but accelerating, and the vibration moved through his consciousness into the depths of his intellectual cortex.

"Help me!"

"Plead!' snapped the One. "I know your black heart. And I've prepared for this day when I knew you would betray me. Another is prepared to take your place. So there is no help for you," he whispered. "And no hope. Enjoy your newfound power. You will need it but will not find it in the lake of fire."

"Help me!" he screamed. The crimson face of the One vanished, but the screams of the Turk increased.

The Turk felt the power grow, expand, push, and the depth of his pain matched the terror of his black soul. He could not stop it. It pressed against every fiber of his body, every cell of his brain. It's force . . .

His last thought was a wail of torture and despair, a keening scream that burst through the walls of the red room, silencing its madness, and rattled the foundations of the house on Alitas Street. And like a dying sun at the edge of the universe, for a shard of a second, the body of Arslan Eroglu . . . home of the malevolent spirit of evil, the Turk . . . collapsed in upon itself like a giant nova. In a final heartbeat, it burst asunder, exploded, erupted, and was vaporized by the outrushing onslaught of unlimited power.

Incendiary devices had consumed the two black vans chewed up by gunfire, leaving only glowing husks as smoke signals for the Turkish police to follow. But they would find nothing in their remains.

The one van was getting crowded with the wounded. Mullaney couldn't see how many, but there were a lot of bodies. McKeon was standing next to him, her arm around the ambassador's waist. She wasn't letting go. The wound in Mullaney's shoulder was starting to throb, but the field dressing the soldier had put on in the cavern was still quenching the bleeding.

Captain Traynor, to his right, was quickly wrapping the wound in his thigh with adhesive gauze. He shoved the remaining gauze in his pocket, picked up his Colt M4A1 with one hand, grabbed Mullaney with the other, and turned him toward the second van. "There's no room for us in that first van. We'll need to . . ."

Whatever blood was remaining in Mullaney's veins turned to ice as both he and Traynor snapped their attention to the open door of the garage. From somewhere out of the pit below, a scream of eternal terror burst into the garage. More than any fear he had faced that day—perhaps in his life—the torment of that wail chilled Mullaney to the depths of his soul, like the howl of a demon at the edge of its grave.

"Now that sounds like evil has met with justice," said Traynor. He pulled on Mullaney's arm and waved at McKeon. "C'mon. There's no time to waste." Traynor maneuvered his way into the second van. He helped Cleveland up into the bed, and Mullaney and McKeon clambered in behind him. "Move out!"

Traynor tapped his sergeant on the shoulder. Grim resignation covered the sergeant's face as he looked back. "All accounted for, sir. But three . . ."

The captain closed his eyes, and his head dropped to his chest. Mullaney knew what the man was suffering in his heart. Traynor took a deep breath. "Okay," he said, looking up. "Where are we headed?"

"Extraction point delta," said the sergeant. "And I give us less than even odds to get there."

49

"Well, I just wasn't sure . . . figured you would want to know, even though you're home with a bug," said Arthur Ravel, the deputy secretary of state.

Sure, thought Noah Webster, *and when was the last time—the first time—you ever called me?* Ravel could barely conceal the glee of sweet revenge in his voice.

"Thank you, Arthur. I appreciate it," Webster said with all the warmth of a cobra's kiss.

"After all," Ravel continued, as if he were chatting with a close confidant, "it's not as if she walks in to see the secretary every day without an appointment. And she had two men accompanying her who I had never seen before. If she were my . . ."

"As it happens," Webster interrupted, "I asked Nora to deliver a very important, personal message to the Secretary. I'm sure that was the reason for her haste. But thank you, Arthur, for thinking of me and being considerate."

Stick the knife in further, if you can, you hypocrite! Two years earlier Webster had sabotaged one of Ravel's pet projects, leaking to the press unreported cost overruns. The storm was short-lived but strong enough that the program was sliced from the State Department's budget. And Arthur Ravel's daughter lost her job.

"Of course, Noah," said Ravel, his voice dripping with barely veiled contempt. "We all need to help each other, watch each other's back. This city is full of unscrupulous scoundrels who would slit your throat for an advantage, or a promotion, or . . . just out of spite."

The deputy secretary of state, Evan Townsend's right hand, let the words sink in. Webster knew this was much worse than Ravel was revealing. He was enjoying himself too much. He had lost all fear of Webster's retaliatory power. Which was Webster's greatest fear. He knew he was staring the end in the face.

"Well, I'm glad it's nothing," said Ravel. "Just thought you would want to know. I hope you are feeling better soon. Good-bye, Noah."

Webster looked at the phone in his hand. Rage roiled his stomach and threatened to cloud his mind. He fought for control and, for the moment, lost.

The phone sailed across the room, smashing into glass shelves behind the bar that held his favorite collection of crystal stemware, as a primal wail erupted from his soul through his throat.

His fists pounding into his thighs, Webster repeated the mantra over and over, "No, no, no, no, no," each time smashing his fists into something—his thighs, then a door he smashed aside as he walked from the dining room of his palatial Georgetown brownstone into his study, a room that exuded and advertised the expanse of his power and influence in this city that lived for power and influence. But today, Nora Carson had not only assassinated his ambition, she had likely sentenced him to life in prison.

A good—expensive—Washington lawyer? Could he plea bargain his way out of this? Doubtful. If Carson turned over all she knew . . . there was no plea bargain for treason. And if they could ever track those bodies back to him? No. No lawyer was that good.

Webster looked around the room, at the treasures he'd extorted from those he held under the threat of his wrath, at the vanity wall of photos with the most powerful men and women in the world, at the pure opulence of the things he'd purchased when money was no object. He walked over to the mahogany bookcase. He lifted the dinged-up wooden bat from its pedestal, the bat from the 1927 Yankees team, the one with the validated signatures of Babe Ruth and Lou Gehrig, the year Babe hit sixty home runs and Gehrig hit forty-seven—both hitting more home runs than any entire team in the American League.

He gazed at the bat with a longing in his heart. One of his most prized possessions. Then he took the bat, swung it viciously above his head, and slammed its barrel into the photo of Webster with Bill Gates. In a continuous fury of destruction, the bat ricocheted off Gates, reversed arc, and obliterated the German chancellor and the French president in one shot. Shards of glass flying, the bat swung high over his head and obliterated the faces of Seneca Markham and Richard Rutherford. Webster's fury and pain were so overwhelming, tears flowing down his face and blurring his sight, that the bat failed to offer mercy on the faces of Rosa Parks and Jesse Jackson.

Twenty minutes later, soaking wet with perspiration from his pillaging rant through the ground floor of his now wasted home, his strength flushed away, Webster's body was thrown into a leather armchair. The bat, its barrel split down the grain, was about to be hurled into the canvas of one of Monet's water lily paintings when Webster's self-pity-fueled blood lust was halted by a racking cough—the result of his continuous wailing as he marched forward in his mission of destruction.

His fingers were bleeding from retrieving his phone from a pile of shattered crystal. He used his other hand to punch in the number he knew by heart.

"I thought I might be hearing from you," said the voice on the other end of the line . . . the man with the Panama hat. "We don't have anything to report on . . ."

Webster's words felt like lead and sounded like despair. "I need to disappear . . . today . . . now."

There was a faint pause. Webster wasn't sure of its source: remorse at a loss of income or a reminder that justice will often have its day. Who was this man to think of justice?

"For you to disappear, it will be expensive," said the man.

"I have the money. My accounts are not compromised."

"Cash transfer," he said. "One-point-five million into our account. In advance. Nothing happens until—"

"Done. When?"

Webster's defeat began displacing his wrath. His body appeared to shrivel in the chair.

"One hour," said the man in the Panama hat. "Walk to the Foggy Bottom station. Casual clothes. One gym bag only. Take the Gray Line to Spring Hill station. A yellow Peter's Plumbing van will be waiting at the station's exit. We'll get you to Dulles and a private jet. You tell the pilot where you want to go."

So this was it. One bag. Exhausted, Webster imperceptibly nodded his head. "Thank—"

There was a beep and the call disconnected.

Hung up on. This was his new world. Until, he recalled, he got to his destination. Where he would live like a king and never be concerned about extradition. Webster pushed himself into a sitting position. Time to go.

The man in the Panama hat disconnected the call and turned to his most-trusted lieutenant.

"Webster."

"Does he know we pulled our men out from Rutherford and the woman?"

"No. But it's over . . . he's over."

"From the information you gave Carson?"

"Hard to be sure. But he's panicked. Wants to disappear today."

"He knows too much."

"Yes," said the man in the Panama hat. "Unfortunate for Webster. Take him to Dulles and find a spot in an empty corner of the long-term parking garage. Tell him he's going to get transferred to a car that will take him to the private aviation terminal . . . just more precaution."

"Will he suspect?"

The man in the Panama hat shook his head. "I doubt it. He sounds physically and emotionally spent. Besides . . . he trusts us."

"Mistake, that."

"Yes . . . but he's not the first. Take his bag. Leave the body in the van. Make sure there's no trace . . . but . . . you know that."

Ankara
July 23, 7:03 p.m.

The two remaining black vans hurtled along the tight lanes below the citadel, completing controlled skids around corners, ignoring all laws and the safety of any pedestrians. The drivers could hear the far-off sirens of the police cars rapidly closing the distance. Too easy to be trapped in this narrow warren of streets, they had only moments to escape.

"How far?" asked Mullaney.

A blur of black as they raced past the Ozkan Market, the vans then careened onto Karaman Street.

"About seven miles to Güvercinlik, once we hit the Istanbul Road," said the sergeant. "The trick is getting off these side streets. We're too visible here."

"We've got an answer to that," said Traynor. He threw his right arm around

Mullaney's midsection and grabbed a metal strut in the ceiling with the other. "Hold on to the ambassador!"

The driver slammed on the breaks at the same time he pulled the steering wheel hard to the right and gunned the engine. The van heeled over hard to the left and almost lost its traction as it bounced over a curb and started to plunge down a steep hill.

"Short cut," said Traynor, keeping his hands glued to Mullaney and the strut.

The vans rumbled down a steep, stone-covered drive surrounded by the trees of Hiskar Park, then burst out into a wide, paved, empty parking lot. They raced through the lot and hurtled past the gates to a large amphitheater to their right. Still they didn't slow and plunged across an access road and down another tight, stone lane as tree limbs pounded against the sides of the vans.

"Tricky part," said Traynor, the muscles in his arms flexing. "Hold Cleveland tight!"

Mullaney couldn't see it, but he could feel it and hear it. The van shot out of the tree-lined lane, bottomed out on something solid, for a heartbeat felt like it was airborne, and then slammed down hard on all four wheels, skidding as the driver fought to keep a straight line. Before he felt the full rush of fear, the van was back on track, barreling down another narrow street.

Whipped left, then right, the vans finally slowed the farther removed they were from Alitas Street and the citadel. They came to a rattling stop.

Held in a bear hug by the sergeant, Cleveland's eyes were wide, but the crinkle of a smile curved the edges of his lips. "Have we come to the end of the roller coaster?"

"Traffic light," said the sergeant.

Mullaney could hear the sounds of increased traffic. The vans eased their way onto what sounded like a well-traveled thoroughfare.

The sergeant turned to Traynor and gave him a thumbs-up. "Past the Ataturk Museum, onto the Mehemet Boulevard, and we're home free."

Traynor pulled his weapon tighter to his chest. "We're home free when we're inside that C-130 and its wheels leave the runway. Find out about the wounded." He pushed a button to activate his radio. "Mother this is baby. Two stillborn. Two for delivery, coming in hot. Lots of bleeding. Be prepared."

Gocuk
July 23, 8:10 p.m.

With the sun slipping behind the mountains to the west, a purple twilight descended onto the plains southeast of the village of Gocuk, Turkey. The wind that seemed to have no end continued to thunder along the flanks of low hills and pound anything standing upright.

Colonel Earnest Edwards believed the conditions were ideal.

His three Sikorsky UH-60 Black Hawk helicopters were being tossed by the force of the gale as they flew in low over the flats south of their intended target. His approach was downwind from the warehouse complex, the noise from the thrashing of the Black Hawk rotors blown in the opposite direction, over the lake to their south. Flying without lights, the Black Hawks were masked by the deepening dusk. They were ghosts.

Leaving one squad to guard the Black Hawks, they came at the warehouse complex in three squads of six, from three directions, cloaked in darkness, each targeting a corner of the chain-link metal fence. All the lights, and their targets, were up at the northwest corner. Edwards whispered into his lapel mic, "Go." A two-man team from each squad approached the three corners, quickly cut through the fence, and slipped through the openings like fog on a wind-swept lake.

Edwards's rules of engagement to his troops were brief. Their targets were heavily armed, trained professionals who intended to unleash inhumane weapons that could cause the death of five thousand American men, women, and children plus countless Turkish nationals. There would be no mercy offered today.

He didn't hear the dull thuds of the 9-millimeter automatics with the sound suppressors that took out all six sentries within seconds of each other. All he needed to hear was "Clear." Without pause, Edwards led his team through the gap in the fence. Weaving through the darkened corridors between the warehouses, each of the three squads had an objective. One squad would open the gate, set up a secure perimeter, and be ready in reserve. Edwards's six-man team would neutralize whatever force was inside the illuminated warehouse. As

Edwards's assault on the warehouse commenced, the third squad would hot-wire the trucks and drive them and the weapons in their cargo holds out of the compound back to the waiting Black Hawks. Securing the chemical weapons was objective number one.

Explosives were out of the question. Canisters of the chemical death could still be inside the building. Edwards and his team knew this would be wet work—close-quarter, rapid annihilation of an armed enemy. They needed to be swift and deadly. But that was their calling card.

There were two doors, front and back. Three of the six soldiers in Edwards's squad were poised at the back door. Edwards, the rest of his squad tucked behind him, had his left hand on the handle of the front door, his right hand pressing the rapid-fire Colt M4A1 carbine to his shoulder. "Go." Edwards slipped open the door and crab-walked through the opening, his team at his back. A short, fat officer with a stunned look on his face and two bullet holes in his chest was the first to drop. Edwards swung his red-laser sight upon a second target as gunfire engulfed the warehouse in lethal thunder.

The Team Black fighters, front and back, moved and fired at the same time, cutting through the dozen black-clad fighters inside the warehouse with surgical precision. Nine died before they could reach their weapons. Only two managed to return fire, their desperate shots wildly off the mark, before their bodies were riddled by the Colt carbines of the JSOC squad. The one who tried to escape behind a row of crates peeked his head around a corner and came face-to-face with the barrel of a Colt and lost half his skull.

The engagement lasted less than a minute.

"Make sure all the chemical weapons were in the trucks," Edwards instructed his men, "then set incendiaries to go off in an hour to melt whatever else may be stored in here. Be quick about it. We're hoofin' it in sixty seconds."

<hr />

Edwards checked his watch as his men finished wrestling the heavy crates onto the three Black Hawk choppers. Time was their enemy. They needed to move. But he looked up over his shoulder to the north. "Wind's stopped," he said, almost to himself. He quickly turned to his second-in-command as the rotors of the UH-80s began to rotate their rotors in earnest. "Burn the trucks . . . timed charges. Then we're out of here."

50

Along the Potomac River, Mason Neck, Virginia
July 25, 1:43 p.m.

Captain Doak Mullaney of the Virginia State Police stood beside two FBI agents and a contingent of Maryland State Police staring at a trio of police boats tied together, floating at anchor in the Potomac River, a little more than seven miles downriver from Washington, DC.

"It takes a while to stabilize the body and collect as much forensic evidence as possible," said the commander of the Maryland Underwater Recovery Team. "They don't want to lose anything in transit."

Doak Mullaney had been contacted by his commander abut thirty minutes earlier after the initial report of the discovery and arrived on scene while the URT divers were still executing their underwater search pattern in the murky, silt-filled Potomac. He was standing along the river bank of Mason Neck, a small peninsula thrust into the river from the Virginia side, in a neighborhood of palatial, secluded mansions. At this point of the river, the Maryland-Virginia border wound tightly along the very edge of the western bank. Jurisdictional cooperation was critical along the Potomac.

"How long has it been out there?" asked one of the FBI agents.

The Maryland URT commander was shaking his head. "Lot of questions . . . not many answers yet," he said. "I don't think it's been in the water that long. But the car's been burned, the body inside the car's been burned, but the inside of the car has not been burned. Figure that one out. And then there's the question of how the car got so far out into the river. The airbags haven't deployed, so it's not likely that it floated. But it sure looks like somebody dumped that car out there hoping that it wouldn't be found."

"How did you make the initial ID?" asked Doak.

"We got lucky," said the commander. "There's absolutely nothing on the body. The license plates were removed, along with the VIN plate just below the windshield and the VIN plate inside the driver's door. But Virginia is one of the few states that requires annual vehicle inspections. Whoever is responsible didn't spot the inspection sticker on the inside of the windshield. The VIN is on the sticker. Gave us a tentative ID of the owner."

"When will we be sure?" asked Doak.

"That it's Rutherford?"

"Or his chauffer," said Doak.

"Couple of weeks," said the commander. "Dental records. It'll take some time."

One of the FBI agents turned to face them. "Two days," he said. "This case is top priority. You'll have the answer tomorrow."

Doak stared back at the FBI agent. "Richard Rutherford is my sister-in-law's father."

"I know that."

He chewed on that nugget for a moment. "So who's behind the top priority push?" asked Doak. "Who is calling in favors?"

The FBI agent was as solid, and as silent, as a rock. "You'll have the positive ID tomorrow."

51

Ambassador's Residence, Tel Aviv
July 31, 8:16 p.m.

Low lighting throughout the expansive gardens of the ambassador's residence added drama to the landscaping without creating enough light pollution to drown out the vast array of stars suspended over the black Mediterranean.

The last week had been nothing but a blur for Brian Mullaney—too much, too fast. And he was much too tired to fully absorb, process, and come to conclusions. But one thing he did know. In two days, he would be going home.

Mullaney didn't know—didn't care—which of the many contributing factors tipped the scales to get him a transfer back to Washington and an airline ticket home . . . whether Cleveland, whose influence in the State Department expanded exponentially after the rescue of Incirlik, had flexed his muscles; whether Mullaney's wounded and battered body was deemed needy enough; whether the injustice perpetrated against he and George Morningstar was finally being recognized . . . too late for Morningstar.

Morningstar. Tommy. Too many others. Too many to mourn right now.

Mullaney closed his eyes and pulled in a deep breath. He could smell the rosemary hedges that circled around the table in a secluded corner of the garden's western edge, the sweetness of the wisteria winding over their heads, and the tangy brine of the sea, just below the cliff upon which they sat. It seemed like forever since the last time he had been able to sit quietly and smell the goodness of God's green earth. He drew in the heady aroma once again.

"Where are you?"

Mullaney opened his eyes. Ambassador Cleveland sat on the far side of the round table, across from him. He had aged.

"I'm here," said Mullaney. "Just in the garden, in the moment, in the peace."

Two white-coated servers appeared out of the shadows around the table and started clearing the table of the remaining appetizers and the dirty plates.

Eight of them sat at the table. Cleveland across from him, Palmyra Parker to Cleveland's right, smiling at her dad and stunning in a bright, orange summer dress that brought a richer glow to her mocha skin tone. Next to Parker sat Rabbi Mordechai Herzog, looking distinguished in a crisp white shirt and impeccable black suit. He still carried a befuddled look on his face, clearly dazzled by the sumptuous setting of silver, crystal, and linen.

Shin Bet Colonel Meyer Levinson had abandoned his ubiquitous khaki shirt and shorts. Stationed between Herzog and Mullaney, Levinson actually looked dashing in a black T-shirt under a peach-colored Calvin Klein blazer. But there was no sartorial salvation for the man to Mullaney's right. Father Stephanakis Poppodopolous had his prodigious girth wrapped in his standard-issue black cassock. Unadorned in his dress, Poppy was nonetheless resplendent in his enthusiasm for the food. He had fork in hand, waiting for the next treat to arrive.

But the woman to Poppy's right made up for any fashion consciousness lacking in the monk. Her short, silver hair styled to perfection and framing her face, Ruth Hughes literally emanated a radiance that shed at least a decade from her age and warmed all those at the table. Hughes wore an arctic-blue, sleeveless dress with a seafoam green shawl draped over her shoulders. The blue in the dress set off fireworks in Hughes's ice-blue eyes, and the shawl drew attention to the marvelous, glimmering pearls around her neck.

But as dazzling as Hughes's presence was to the assembly, the surprise member of the ensemble and true center of attention sat to her right. David Meir, former prime minister of Israel as of earlier that morning, looked more relaxed than Mullaney had ever seen him—black collared shirt, a black sweater tied over his shoulders and hanging down his back, and well-worn blue jeans. Without the weight of a nation on his shoulders, Meir looked like the university professor he once was and planned to be again.

Mullaney looked around the table. They had been through so much, individually and collectively. Their worlds had turned upside down. But here they were, sitting in a quiet garden, in a palatial, safe, and peaceful setting, being served an exquisite meal.

"Peace seems like a lifetime ago," said Mullaney. "Yet now, here, we slip into it like a favorite old shirt that feels like we've never left it." His eyes fell on Cleveland again. "Almost seems like a sacrilege. A lack of respect . . . lack of reverence . . . for those who didn't make it here."

"The poor you will always have with you," said Cleveland, paraphrasing

Scripture. "But I think it's also true of regrets. Things we wish we could change. Things we wish had never happened. All the *if onlys* in our lives."

"But regrets, *if onlys* are all in the past," Hughes interjected. "It's an awfully sad and lonely place to live—the past. We've been born, created to live in the present." Hughes looked down at the clean plate that was put before her, as if examining her own reflection. "I've been thinking about this a lot. Only God lives in the past, the present, and the future, all at the same time. We've been created to live in the present. Not to endlessly grieve the past or constantly fear the future. Live today well. Live today with honor. Let God take care of the rest." She looked up and a girlish smile of embarrassment crossed her face. "I'm starting to sound like Atticus."

"You," Cleveland jumped in, "could do worse, my dear," Cleveland looked to his left, reached out his hand, and placed it on David Meir's wrist. "How does it feel to live in the present, David?"

While Cleveland and Mullaney had been in Turkey, Meir had forced the Israeli Knesset to call a vote on the Ishmael Covenant. After days of political wrangling—nothing ever got done quickly in Israeli politics, with dozens of political parties and constantly evolving power bases to mollify—the vote was finally called yesterday, at Meir's insistence, and the treaty he had hoped would bring peace to Israel for the first time in its short history was soundly defeated. That vote was the death knell for David Meir's government. This morning he had scheduled a general election in sixty days and promptly submitted his resignation.

In the few hours since, a caretaker government repudiated the "fresh water for natural gas" treaty that Meir's government had been negotiating with Turkey. An easy call. Turkey was in a state of crisis.

In a matter of hours several days ago, Turkish President Emet Kashani was found in his bed in a coma. Not only was Kashani still unconscious and incapacitated, but his coma was so severe it was as if the man was dead. The crisis expanded when Prime Minister Arslan Eroglu could not be found to take the reins of the government. In fact, Eroglu remained missing after eight days, with no clues to his whereabouts or fate.

Into that vacuum, Turkey's military leaders gladly pushed their way.

Meir took the linen napkin off his lap, twisted it in his hands, and pulled it hard, apart. Then he snapped it.

"That was my life," he said. "Eight million people, over six million Jewish souls, always living on the edge of annihilation, their fate—and the fate of all who live in Israel or visit here—resting squarely in my hands. Honestly, I doubt whether the Saudis would have honored their promises on the covenant. Abdullah is a treacherous deceiver. But Israel had an opportunity to call Abdullah's bluff. When we had a chance to finally ensure peace for our nation, safety for our children, we threw away the covenant and peace with our neighbors because we grieve for the past and fear the future."

Meir took his napkin, folded it neatly in half, then quarters, and laid it on the table and smoothed out any wrinkles. "That," he said, pointing at the napkin, "is my life today. Clean, neat, at rest. To be honest, the present is very refreshing. The covenant is gone, and I've let it go.

"But I'm more distressed about losing the water-for-gas treaty with Turkey," Meir continued. "That treaty was a win-win for everybody, with nothing in between. But," he said, picking up the napkin, flicking it open, and laying it on his lap, "international treaties are no longer my concern. So yes . . . I'm at peace. Though my nation isn't."

52

Ambassador's Residence, Tel Aviv
July 31, 8:27 p.m.

When the waiter placed a salad in front of Father Poppodopolous instead of a sizzling steak, his disappointment was proclaimed by a pronounced rumbling in his prodigious stomach. He looked across the table at Cleveland. "Please forgive a poor monk who subsists on monastery food, but . . . how many courses are we to expect tonight?"

Cleveland smiled. He had survived the ordeal in Turkey with little more than physical scratches—though his spirit and emotions were profoundly shaken. He was a grateful man. Tonight was a time to indulge in a celebration.

"I'm confident you will be more than satisfied at the end of the evening."

Poppodopolous beamed. "Thank you, Mr. Ambassador." He dug into his salad with a vengeance. "It seems," he said with a mouthful of greens, "that all of us have sidestepped the likelihood of a nuclear confrontation in the Middle East—at least for the moment."

It took Cleveland an instant to circle his mind around the rapid-fire events of the last few days. Somebody, and it had JSOC fingerprints all over it, delivered a clandestine strike force into Baluchistan Province and destroyed Pakistan's nuclear factory—and escaped without a trace.

Two days ago, the alliance between Iraq and Iran was drawn ever more tightly together when the Badr Brigades of Samir Al-Qahtani, backed by Iranian artillery, armored vehicles, and air support, opened a major offensive against ISIS positions in western Iraq and northeastern Syria. The presence of such a massive invasion force operating so close to its border caused the junta ruling Turkey to order a vast military buildup along its eastern border.

And yesterday, as the Israeli Knesset gathered to vote on the Ishmael Covenant, a group of ultraradical Wahhabi clerics stirred up an enormous demonstration through the streets of Riyadh, the chanting mob denouncing King Abdullah for offering the Ishmael Covenant peace treaty to Israel. This morning the size of the ongoing demonstration had doubled, to nearly 150,000 Saudis. Abdullah's reign actually looked endangered.

A lot of growing conflict all around Israel. But nobody was lobbing nukes at each other.

Cleveland's mind scrolled through a Rolodex of the events since he entered Israel as its ambassador less than two weeks ago: the gun battle on Highway One; his daughter's abduction; the deadly earthquakes that shattered only the US embassy and his residence, which were followed by bloody incursions by the disciples of the man with yellow eyes; and that nightmare in the bowels of the building on Alitas Street in Ankara. All triggered by the prophetic messages of an aged rabbi in Lithuania over two hundred years in the past.

Cleveland marveled at the hand of God in the lives of men and was thankful for God's unwavering battle against the powers of evil in both the natural and supernatural realms.

"By the grace of God," Cleveland said. "Only by the grace of God."

Throughout the conversation, Palmyra Parker's eyes had been on Mullaney, who sat across the table from her. He sat there nursing the wounds of battle—with his left arm in a sling, an orthopedic operation on his tendons awaiting him back in the States; a bright red wound on his scalp; and that thousand-yard stare of a warrior who is remembering all those who gave their lives in the battle against evil. It was not happily ever after for Brian Mullaney. He had too many letters to write, too many phone calls to make, too many good men to mourn.

And then there was Noah Webster, vanished off the face of the earth, indictments piling up as the breadth and audacity of his crimes continued to be unearthed.

Even Mullaney's impending return to Washington, to his wife and children, with accolades and commendations waiting for him instead of the manufactured disgrace that had orchestrated his removal . . . even with all that, there was no triumph, or celebration, or joy on his face.

He became aware of the silence around the table, looked up, and was arrested by Parker's gaze.

"We're all going to miss you, Brian."

He just stared at her in return.

"But I am . . . we are . . . very happy for you that you are going home to

Abby and your daughters," Parker continued. "As long as my father behaves himself—"

"Highly unlikely," said Cleveland.

"As long as he behaves himself, I'm confident his safety will be ensured by Pat McKeon and her DSS agents. But . . . I've never known anyone with your courage and loyalty. We owe you much more than our thanks. We owe you our lives. And I, for one, will be eternally grateful."

Mullaney felt all the eyes on him. They expected a response. He gave them one.

"Excuse me."

And he got up, left the table, and vanished into the shadows of the garden.

His prayers had turned to tears, and back to prayers again, when Cleveland found Mullaney on the bench along the path to his bungalow, his home in Tel Aviv. The ambassador crossed the path, sat down on the opposite end of the bench, closed his eyes, and bowed his head. Mullaney waited, but Cleveland said nothing.

So Mullaney continued his prayers. He had already fought through the tortured ones—his long lament for the devastating loss of his best friend, Tommy Hernandez. His battle against the self-pity that came on the heels of the guilt and responsibility he felt for all the DSS agents who had lost their lives, all the children who had lost their fathers. The gnawing hurt that he could have—should have—done something else, something different, and maybe all those lives would not have been lost, all those families would not have been shattered.

He didn't believe all the fine words that were said, the laudatory call from the secretary of state, even the empathy and encouragement from Meyer Levinson. It was his fault. Maybe he was—

"It's not your fault." Cleveland's voice was as soft as the breeze off the Mediterranean.

Mullaney looked to his left, but Cleveland had not moved, was not looking at him. The ambassador's hands were still clasped and resting on his knees, his head still bowed. Then he spoke, to his Father, not to Mullaney.

"Father, I pray for my friend, my son, Brian, and I ask you to bring truth to his heart and peace to his soul."

Mullaney felt Cleveland's prayers like a hug.

"Holy Spirit, help him to reject the lie that the enemy is trying to torture him with, that it's his fault, that he let us all down. Father, please reveal to Brian the truth of his steadfastness and determination. Reveal to him the admiration and honor all of us, all of his men and women, feel toward him . . . how proud they are to serve with him, how confident they are not only in his selfless leadership but also in his integrity and courage. Father, speak to your son and confirm to him how much you love him just as he is . . . who he is . . . a mighty man of God, a warrior of your kingdom, heir of all creation.

"Yes, Father, but more than anything, please fortify in Brian your vision of him, that the words of identification, affection, and affirmation that you spoke to your Son, Jesus, are just as valid for your son, Brian . . . 'This is my Son, whom I love; with him I am well pleased.'"

In the silence, only the leaves in the trees rustled. Tears once again welled up in Mullaney's chest and spilled out of his eyes. Cleveland put a hand on Mullaney's knee.

"I miss Tommy too," said Cleveland. "Not as much, not in the same way you do. But I miss him with all of my being. I ache for his loss. I ache for the loss of all those I didn't know as well but who selflessly gave their lives in the service of their country. In service of me, really."

Cleveland stood up, started out to the path, hesitated, and turned around. "I hurt and grieve from the pain, but I don't own it, Brian." The ambassador's voice ratcheted up a notch in authority and passion. "Their deaths, the reign of terror that engulfed us for so long, is not my responsibility. It's not mine to bear. The enemies of good, the enemies of our country, the enemies of peace are responsible for the deaths of so many good men and women." Cleveland stepped toward Mullaney, stabbing his right index finger into the air. "They will take that burden to their judgment. Not you, Brian!" He turned his finger toward Mullaney. "Not you, and not me. You are a hero. That is the only label that has a right to hang on your heart."

Cleveland turned on his heel and marched back up the path.

Not for the first time, Mullaney thought, *I'd go to war with that man.*

"You already have gone to war with him."

Mullaney knew that voice. He looked left and right . . . swept his eyes across the sky. In a small copse of trees to his right, the rustling leaves began to shimmer and glow, the light swimming and then forming, growing, becoming. Bayard, angel of God, stood once more before Mullaney.

"I didn't think I'd ever see you again," said Mullaney, a little unsettled as to the purpose of Bayard's return. Then he remembered and felt foolish. "Thank you . . . for everything. For saving my life, Cleveland's life, so many others I probably don't even know about. I don't think I'll ever understand the rules of engagement for angels. Zapping all the bad guys before this started would have been . . . well . . . thank you for all that you did for us. I don't entirely know who, or what, we faced in that house on Alitas Street. But I'm confident that neither Atticus nor I would have gotten out of there with our lives, with our souls, without your intervention."

A thought occurred to Mullaney. It startled him. But it also made sense.

"You, or one of your pals, have been standing guard at my house, haven't you? You've been watching over my family while I'm over here."

A beatific smile that lit up the heavens spread across Bayard's face. He stepped closer and got down on one knee so he could face Mullaney eye to eye. "Yes, since the moment you accepted the anointing, one of the brethren—at times, myself—has been stationed by your door. It has been our pleasure. The sweet hearts of your wife and daughters have blessed us."

For a moment, the apprehension returned. "So . . . why are you here?" Mullaney wasn't sure he wanted to hear the answer.

"Your task is complete. This time is complete. Do you recall when Rabbi Herzog spoke to you about the time of the Gentiles . . . when the time of the Gentiles is complete then the end of time may begin?"

Mullaney nodded, now his apprehension spiking. "I remember. Not sure if I understand it all, but I remember. Are you saying that we are now in the end of time?"

Bayard shook his head. "No, not as you imagine it. There is a time for this world and a time when this world, in its present form, will come to an end. In that respect, finite man has been walking in the end of times since Adam and his wife left the garden."

Bayard pushed himself to his full height. "The Creator of all wants you, faithful servant, to know that the times of the Gentiles is not yet complete.

Jerusalem is not about to come under the sword. The days are not yet finished. And you will have time . . . time to watch your daughters grow and prosper. Time to spoil your children's children and go to their weddings. Time to inherit all of the riches of this world that our Father wishes to place into your hands."

He stepped closer. "But this time, your time, has come to an end. The anointing of the guardian I must remove from you. The time and the purpose for that anointing, and the lethal power it harnessed, has passed. But . . ." Bayard moved to within arm's reach. His eight-foot body and furled wings towered over Mullaney. "The anointing of God I leave with you, the anointing on your life."

Bayard stretched out his arms and placed his hands on the sides of Mullaney's head, his wings unfolding and wrapping Mullaney within their furls.

"We remove the mantle of guardian from this man's life. We release him from the responsibility of Aaron's anointing."

Bayard lowered his hands and rested them on Mullaney's shoulders. "No one will be able to stand against you all the days of your life. As I was with Moses, so I will be with you; I will never leave you nor forsake you . . . Be strong and courageous. Do not be afraid; do not be discouraged, for the Lord your God will be with you wherever you go."

53

Ben Gurion Airport, Tel Aviv
August 2, 7:45 a.m.

Sitting in a coffee shop in an empty corner of Ben Gurion's international departure terminal, Brian Mullaney was looking for a diversion completely different than anything he'd experienced in the last month. He pulled a Travel Yahtzee game out of his carry-on for thirty minutes of mindless entertainment before he made his way to the gate. He could do his thinking on the plane to Washington.

He was trying to parlay three fives into five on his third roll when he felt two bodies sit on opposite sides of him. He glanced left. Rabbi Mordechai Herzog was wiping perspiration from the inside band of his wide-brimmed, black hat, a crooked smile on his face. He glanced right. Colonel Meyer Levinson, head of Shin Bet's Operations division, had his legs crossed, tapping his riding crop against his thigh, the same crooked smile on his face.

"The rabbi forced me," said Levinson, as the smile migrated to his entire face. "He said we couldn't let you leave without saying good-bye. Besides . . . he needed a ride."

Without a word, Mullaney swung his attention back to Rabbi Herzog, who was grinning ear to ear. "Left us abruptly, you did," said Herzog. "No chance did you give me to thank you." The old man's face clouded for a moment. "Thank you for avenging the death of my son and the rest of the rabbis at the Hurva Synagogue. You brought them justice, I think."

Mullaney had become very fond of the old rabbi. "I was only doing—"

"No . . . wait." Herzog pushed himself closer and put his right hand on Mullaney's arm. The smile was gone. "Meyer and I are here on very serious business. I found something in the ruins of the Hurva, something that could change Israel's position in history, something that could turn this world upside down. And I want you to take it with you, back to Washington, and give it to the people who will know what to do with it."

Mullaney closed his eyes. *It's not over?* "Meyer," he said, turning to Levinson, "isn't this something you can take care of here?"

A somber frown on his face, Levinson was rapidly shaking his head. "Oh no. I don't think it's possible. The rabbi and I believe you are the only one appointed for this task. Listen . . ." He looked past Mullaney to the rabbi. "Show him, Mordechai. Show him what we've discovered."

The elderly rabbi pushed himself up straight and squared his shoulders. Slowly, he ran his eyes around the terminal. Turning to Mullaney, he pulled a black bag into his lap, started to open it, but stopped to once more face Mullaney. "Promise me, you must never to leave this out of your sight until you can deliver it to the right people."

Mullaney felt a growing anxiety.

"Promise me," urged the rabbi.

"Okay . . . okay. I'll keep it safe."

With another furtive look around the terminal, Herzog reached deep into his black bag. Mullaney jumped when Herzog's entire body shivered violently. The rabbi withdrew his hand slowly.

In his right hand was a snow globe. Inside the globe was the word *Israel*, a star of David, and a street scene. Herzog turned the snow globe upside down, then brought it back to normal. "See, it can change Israel's position . . . and it turns the world upside down."

Rabbi Herzog was giving Mullaney a triumphant smile. Levinson slapped Mullaney on his back. "See . . . you are the only one who can give this to the people who will know what to do with it."

It was beyond Brian Mullaney's comprehension. He didn't think he still had it in him. But he cracked up. The more he looked at Herzog's grinning face, the harder he laughed. The rabbi held out the snow globe in Mullaney's direction. "Here. The weight of the world is once more in your hands."

And the three of them sat in the coffee shop, laughing like schoolboys at a stupid joke, ignorant and uncaring about any eyes that were turned on them, wondering how grown men could get so carried away over a cheap, gaudy trinket.

———————

Mullaney was on his way to clear security for the flight to Dulles International Airport in Virginia. His boarding pass was in his right hand, the snow globe in his left.

"That's an impressive going-away present."

Mullaney turned, the smile still on his face. "It is, but I'm not sure it will clear security. Sad if it ended up in the trash."

"All I brought you was this lousy newspaper." Joseph Atticus Cleveland held out the *International New York Times*. "Something to get you up to speed on life back in Washington."

Mullaney ignored the newspaper. He stepped close to Cleveland, threw his right arm around the ambassador, and hugged him tight. "I'm going to miss you, Atticus."

Cleveland flipped the newspaper into a nearby chair and wrapped Mullaney in a bear hug. "I miss you already, Brian."

They stepped away from each other. Palmyra Parker was behind her dad. Pat McKeon, Kathie Doorley, and two other DSS agents were twenty feet away. Mullaney nodded in their direction. "We made a good team. Thanks."

Cleveland looked at Mullaney as a father looks at his first born going off to college. "Have you made a decision?"

"Not yet," said Mullaney. "Too much, too soon. I've got to get home, hug my kids, talk to Abby, and pray for God's guidance."

"Secretary Townsend really wants you to stay. I think he feels . . . well . . . he's got a lot to make up for. And he needs you. Evan's taking a beating in DC, especially after they found Webster's body in the airport parking lot. He needs some people around him he knows he can trust. Like you."

"I hear you, Atticus. But this time, it needs to be a family decision."

Cleveland nodded his head. "Wise choice. But listen, whatever you decide, you're not getting away from me."

"You're not getting away from any of us," Parker interjected. "We've got a big dining room table at our house in Arlington with plenty of room for you, Abby, and the girls. You've become like family, Brian. And family, we keep close."

Mullaney handed the snow globe to Parker. "Can you look after this?" Then he glanced at his watch. "Gotta go."

"I know, son," said Cleveland. He stepped closer. This time the bear hug was more . . . desperate. "Be careful out there."

54

That Secretary of State Evan Townsend had a car waiting for Mullaney at Dulles was a kind gesture. Brian had told Abby he would take a cab. He wanted his homecoming to be at home.

Now he stood on the sidewalk and looked at the pre-war, center-hall colonial they called home. During the twenty years working his way up through State's Diplomatic Security Service, Brian and Abby—later their daughters— had lived in many places. Seldom did those places feel like home. This one did. This was their home, where they decided to put down roots, where all the two-year assignments to out-of-the-way countries would stop. They had lived in fancier places, bigger places, much smaller places. But this was their place.

He understood completely why Abby had said no to his last transfer. He had promised her a home, this home, and that they would never move again, that Kylie and Samantha could stay in the same school with the same friends— well, they'd see how that developed. Mullaney wasn't able to live up to that promise. Noah Webster had sabotaged those plans when he bum-rushed Mullaney to Israel under an unwarranted cloud of suspicion. Perhaps it was pride, but Mullaney wasn't about to quit his career while under a cloud. So Abby and the girls had stayed here, Brian had gone off to Israel—and all hell had broken loose.

He shook the memories out of his brain. He was home. That was the only place he wanted his thoughts to rest.

Mullaney was halfway up the path when the front door flew open and two bodies with pendulum ponytails burst into the yard. Kylie was the oldest, but Samantha was the fastest. It was Samantha who threw herself into her daddy's arms and Kylie whose flying leap body-slammed them all into the grass. Mullaney hoped his wound hadn't opened . . . but he didn't care. He breathed in the scent of their hair, was buried under an avalanche of kisses, and couldn't get a word in edgewise.

He was home.

Kylie had his carry-on in her right hand, her left hand holding firmly to Mullaney's right. Now conscious of his wounded shoulder, Samantha held Mullaney's elbow as both girls tugged him through the front door, each of them asking questions he had no chance to answer.

Abby stood in the hallway, the light behind her sending dancing flames through her auburn hair. She still possessed the heart-stopping beauty and sensual sizzle of the young woman he first held in his arms twenty years in the past.

The girls stopped chattering at the same moment, looked at their mom, glanced at their dad, and released his hands.

They met in the middle, Brian's good arm wound around Abby's waist, pulling her closer, Abby's longing fingers entwined in Brian's hair. It was awhile before they came up for air.

"Mooommm! Really?" It was a mock complaint from Kylie, but a whistle for a timeout, nonetheless.

Their lips parted. Their eyes met. Their passion vented like steam. Abby leaned her head and rested it on Brian's shoulder. "I'll welcome you home later . . . upstairs," she whispered. She pulled her head back, looked in his eyes, and ran her fingers over his cheek. "It's so good to have you home."

The girls were helping Abby in the kitchen. Airplane food had done little to slake Mullaney's hunger.

His brother, Doak, was sitting opposite him in an identical armchair, flanking the fireplace in the den. Mullaney had walked his brother through a ten-cent tour of his nearly four weeks in Israel, most of which Doak already knew, and Doak was filling in Brian about how Abby was holding up since her father's body was found in the Potomac.

"Do you think we'll ever figure the whole thing out?" asked Mullaney, keeping his voice low in case anyone was listening.

"Doubt it," Doak responded in kind. "That Webster and Rutherford were in cahoots with Senator Markham, that's clear. That Webster got entangled with Eroglu and the Turks—trying to sabotage the Iran nuke deal so Rutherford wouldn't lose all that money in his banks—that's clear too. And it's pretty clear that both Rutherford and Webster knew time was running out on them. Seems like they were both getting ready to disappear. But . . ."

Mullaney nodded. "Yeah, but . . . but Rutherford's burned body is found in a burned car in the Potomac, and Webster's strangled body is found in the back of a plumbing van in a Dulles parking lot. They died within hours of each other, within ten miles of each other."

Only the clock on the mantle disrupted the silence as the brothers each toyed with their thoughts.

"In spite of everything, I feel sorry for Richard," whispered Mullaney.

"What?"

"No, really, I do," Mullaney said. "I mean, my heart breaks for Abby, Kylie, and Samantha. They are the ones really feeling the loss. But Richard . . . there's a man who had everything—and I'm not talking about his money. A daughter and two granddaughters who loved him, thought the world revolved around him, and he threw that most precious gift away for what? More money? More power? And he ends up at the bottom of the Potomac. It's a sad transaction if you ask me."

"Yeah, but who did it?" Doak responded. "Were they both killed by the same person or persons? And why . . . what were the killers covering up? The clues, the forensics we have on either case are slim to none. Whoever did these jobs, they were very good."

"Which leaves us with who and why and no answers," said Mullaney.

Silence descended for a moment. "No answers . . . That reminds me," said Doak as he reached down and picked up something from beside his armchair. He reached across the distance to Mullaney with an envelope in his hand.

"What's this?"

Doak stretched further. "Take it. It's from the superintendent."

The superintendent . . . the highest-ranking member of the Virginia State Police, Mullaney's former employer before he joined the State Department. Mullaney stared at his brother, not at the envelope. "The boss? What does he want from me?"

"It's not what he wants from you," said Doak, shaking the envelope in Mullaney's direction, "it's what he wants to give you."

"Now I'm really getting worried."

A tidal wave of words, drama, and posturing spilled out of the kitchen and into the den as Abby and the girls brought in a tray of food, glasses, and a pitcher of iced tea. Abby stopped, and the girls stopped with her, when she saw the envelope Doak was trying to hand to Brian.

"Do you know what's in it?" asked Brian.

"Yeah . . . I do. They're offering you Dad's job—commander of division seven of field operations. Kinda cool, I think. You would be headquartered right here in Fairfax County."

Mullaney heard a rattle and crash behind him as dishes slipped off Abby's serving tray and collided with the floor. His breathing deepened. His heart skidded a little from one beat to the next. He knew the department wanted him back. He had gotten those signals. But this—Dad's job?

He was trying to sort through so many emotions, wasn't sure how to respond, when he noticed the other item that Doak had lifted into his lap. "What's that?"

55

Fairfax, Virginia
August 2, 9:32 p.m.

Doak stood up. He laid the envelope on an end table beside Brian's chair. Then he brought the other item in front of him. It was a gray metal box, about the size of a shoebox, with something on the top that Mullaney couldn't make out.

"You were already in Israel when I got this," said Doak. "One of the custodians chased me down. It's for you."

Doak reached out and held the box in front of him. For a moment, Mullaney had a flashback to Israel, a stab of adrenaline. But . . . no, Doak was holding it. He was okay. This was different.

Mullaney took the box from his brother. On its top was the decal of the Virginia State Police. Under the decal was stenciled the name John Mullaney. *Captain* was added later, after his name.

"In addition to his locker in division headquarters," said Doak, "which got cleaned out after he left active duty, Dad also had a storage trunk in the headquarters' basement. Nobody realized it was there until a few weeks ago when custodial decided to clean and rearrange the basement. The trunk was full of old uniforms, service manuals—all the stuff Dad accumulated during his decades with the force. But on top of it all was this box."

"What's in it?"

"You should look," said Doak.

Wondering if he had the anointing for this task—wandering down a very painful paternal memory lane—Mullaney flipped up the clasp on the box and opened the lid. Immediately, Brian knew what was in the box. He glanced up at Abby, who put down the tray and came over to stand behind his chair. Mullaney picked up one of the newspaper clippings that filled the box to capacity. It was from his sophomore year in high school, when he had first been elevated to varsity. In his first game, he scored two touchdowns and also played linebacker. The story was something about another Mullaney joining a long line of stellar athletes at Fairfax High. He rifled through the collection of clippings and pulled out another . . . a photo of the day, as president of the student council, senior Brian Mullaney, was introduced to the mayor and . . . *ta-da!* . . . John Riggins, recently retired running back of the Washington Redskins and MVP of Super Bowl XVII. Brian's dad had run a highlighter over Brian's name and that of John Riggins.

Mullaney pulled out another, then another. All of the clippings chronicled Brian Mullaney's life, from grade school sports to honors and promotions with the Virginia State Police. Mullaney's throat grew thicker, his breathing more labored. Abby placed her hand on his shoulder.

All those years, Mullaney had labored under the impression that he had never measured up to his father's expectations. He felt like the personification of John Mullaney's favorite epithet: useless! Brian never knew . . .

Stuffed down along the side of the box was an envelope. Mullaney pulled it out. The only thing written on the outside was one word: Brian.

It was a struggle to keep the tears from flooding his eyes and the regret from tearing at his heart.

The envelope wasn't sealed . . . never had been. As if John Mullaney was planning on adding to its contents. Brian pulled out some folded sheets of paper. And his world turned upside down.

For my sweet son, Brian . . .

"Oh, Brian," Abby gasped from behind, her arms now clasped around his chest as she leaned on the back of the chair. "Oh, thank you, Lord."

> *I was never raised with the love of a father, never taught how to express love as a man. I was taught how to be proud and arrogant; how to be demanding and critical. I am so deeply sorry for that.*
>
> *But I am so proud of you . . .*

Splotches of tears began to dot the paper.

> *. . . All you've done and the fine man of character and integrity you've become. That would be enough . . . to love you for what you've done and who you are. But as my time seems to be slipping away from me, it's more important for me to tell you this. I love you because you are my son—flesh of my flesh, bone of my bone,*

heir of my heart, the best part of me. I wish I had the courage,
or the faith, to believe I could say these things to you personally. I
don't know if I could get the words out right.

So I thought I would at least write these things down, to tell
you that I love you beyond what words can say. And I can leave
you with this, a father's blessing that I recently found. I think it's
in the Bible:

"The Lord bless you, and keep you. The Lord make His face
shine on you, and be gracious to you. The Lord lift up His coun-
tenance on you, and give you peace."

Mullaney stared at the words of the Aaronic blessing. He felt the warmth
of a hand upon his face, the whisper of a voice in his ear. It was Bayard's voice.
Mullaney glanced up, looked around the room. There was no angelic presence.
Only a father's blessing. Mullaney not only felt the cover of protection but also
the fulfillment of affirmation.

He turned the pages over in his hand. There were three, typewritten on
each side. John Mullaney had a lot to say to his son. As Brian turned over the
pages, another newspaper clipping fell into the box. Mullaney picked it up
and opened it. It was a story from the local paper about John Mullaney's son
Brian, who had left the Virginia State Police to accept a commission in the
State Department's Diplomatic Security Service. In the story, the secretary of
state was quoted: "It's an honor to have a man like Brian Mullaney, a man of
character, integrity, and exemplary service with the Virginia State Police, join
the Diplomatic Security Service. You know what the first thing Brian said to
me when we offered him this position? 'My dad will be proud.'"

John Mullaney had run a highlighter over that part of the story. He had
underlined the last quote. And had written in the margins, *"It grieves my heart*
that you would leave the force, because I will miss you desperately. But you will soar
at DSS."

At that moment, the dam on the wellspring of Brian Mullaney's heart
shattered, the regret, guilt, and shame he had carried so long exploded into
vapor, and his lonely longing for a loving father was banished forever from his
life. The tears cascaded down his cheeks like Niagara's famous falls, and his
body wracked in heaves with the weeping of the soul. But Brian Mullaney's

heart was soaring. Through the tears, he saw something on the inside cover of the box. It was in John Mullaney's handwriting. *"Be careful out there, my son!"*

Abby buried her head into the crook of his neck, her tears soaking the collar of his shirt. "Oh, Brian!"

Mullaney couldn't read any more . . . not now. He was awash with a new-found emotion, the blessing of his father's affirmation.

And once again he heard a voice that he recognized. "This is my son, whom I love. In him I am well pleased."

Brian Mullaney was home.

EPILOGUE

Except for one oil lamp burning above his head, Assan sat in the dark, on the stone floor of the red room, the wall at his back. He had lost all sense of time. He had sat there for a day . . . or for a month. He didn't know. He didn't care.

And he didn't know what to do. Or where to go. His whole world lay on the stone altar of sacrifice not four feet away. Cold. Lifeless. Gone.

At the rare time he considered it, Assan assumed he would simply die here in this room. At some point, his body would cease to function without food or water. He didn't need much. But he would not survive on nothing.

Within him, fury raged. Long ago, he had sold his soul to the prince of darkness for a greater infusion of the power of the occult, to which he had already surrendered his life. More power to rule in this world, to seize for himself the things that would satisfy his lust. He became apprentice to the Turk, whom he thought represented the epicenter of power and dominion, to learn how to exercise the dark arts at his command. But all he had become was a slave.

Across the ages his power, like his body, shriveled from atrophy. His heart was still as black, but power? He was impotent. And now the vicarious power of the Turk was vaporized.

He had tried every conjuring, chanted all the words of the dark lords he knew, but the Turk did not resurrect as he had planned.

But Assan's bargain had been struck. All those ages ago, he had received the overflow of evil he desired. But was robbed of his opportunity to wield it. Now he would pay the eternal price.

Assan recalled the bone-chilling scream of the Turk just as Arslan Eroglu's body exploded into subatomic particles. That wail was the harbinger of the endless days during which Assan would endure the torture of the eternally lost. He raged against the injustice but was powerless to change it.

He shivered. Not because it was cold.

Assan gazed once more at the lifeless symbols painted on the walls of the red room. He was free from the Turk's control, free to make his own choices. But where would he go? Whom would he serve? How long before torment claimed him?

It was Assan's recurring lament. He had nothing else to fill his mind. Perhaps he should end—

It was only a perception, the slightest change in the atmosphere around him. Was the oil lamp burning brighter? He looked up at the stone altar of sacrifice.

Two yellow eyes were staring back at him, the mayhem of all that is wicked and condemned swirling through the pupils like frenzied gray clouds in a hurricane. And Assan's lust for dark power was reborn in the maelstrom of the resurrected eyes that burned into his forsaken soul.

Fairfax, Virginia
August 3, 5:15 a.m.

A moonbeam shuddered, as did a window on the western side of Brian Mullaney's home. The molecules that once comprised a solid wall began to sway and shift. Through what appeared to be an impenetrable mass, a shape slowly materialized. Shards of moonbeam danced across the crown of a silver helmet.

Soundless, effortlessly, like fog floating across a moor, Bayard moved through the room to the two chairs facing the fireplace. John Mullaney's metal box of memories rested on the seat of the chair to his left. Bayard knelt down, placed his hands on the box and raised the lid. While his left hand lifted up the stack of documents inside the box, Bayard's right hand slipped under the belt that supported his sword and scabbard. He withdrew a small, leather pouch and slid it under the stack of documents in the box.

The box was closed and Bayard's form was beginning to intertwine with the molecules of the wall when he heard a sound beside him, coming down the stairs.

It was impossible to sleep. Too excited to be home. Too jet-lagged. Too *normal* after all he'd been through. Just couldn't get comfortable.

Brian Mullaney padded into the den in his fleece-lined moccasins, wearing a T-shirt and sweatpants, his iPhone in the back pocket to catch up on the sports pages. A mug of hot tea was steadied in both hands.

He sat in one of the chairs by the fireplace, sipping the tea and enjoying the quiet, wrapped in the cocoon of home. It felt safe.

Mullaney put the mug on a side table and reached for his iPhone. But he noticed the metal box resting on the other chair. He reached over, picked it up, and settled back into his chair.

He felt the same rush of joy and regret wash over him as had earlier. What an amazing gift from his dad. What a heartbreak that they never had a chance to share it together. He opened the box and starting leafing through the clippings. Too many to see adequately.

Mullaney reached into the box and pulled out the whole pile of clippings so he could go through them more carefully.

In the bottom of the box was a flat leather pouch. Curious, he picked it up.

It was more like a leather envelope. On the flap side, the envelope was sealed with stamped wax. Nothing on the front.

He slipped his finger under the seal and broke it. Inside the envelope was a thick, brittle piece of paper. He turned it over. Something was written on it . . . three lines . . . the ink faded and cracked, but still legible:

Brian

Ačiū

Elijah ben Solomon Zalman

His heart racing, Mullaney pulled out his iPhone and googled *Ačiū*. *Thank you* in Lithuanian.

A dark shape emerged from the deep shadows under a vast oak tree on Mullaney's lawn, starlight igniting tiny glints of sparks from a silver breastplate. Through a wide, side window of the house, Bayard could see clearly. A smile brought joy to his eyes as astonishment washed across Mullaney's face, the Gaon's final message in one hand, the leather pouch dangling from his fingers.

With the delivery, Bayard knew his assignment was completed. Still, his immortal heart felt the same emotions as any created man. He experienced a deeply rooted affection for this man of courage and faith, just as he loved the Gaon for his devotion to God and determined stand against the agents of evil. They, all of them together, had fought the good fight. Now, he experienced the bittersweet caress of good-bye.

Well done, my good and faithful servant.

Bayard glanced up at the stars. "Thank you, Father."

As he retreated into the shadows, the molecules at the edges of his form beginning to dance and morph, Bayard looked through the window once more. "The Lord bless and keep you, Brian."

ACKNOWLEDGMENTS

"A cord of three strands is not quickly broken" (Ecclesiastes 4:12).

Or easily broken. Or easy to overcome.

I'm blessed to be in the midst of a cord of three strands . . . the covenant relationship I have with my wife and with our God. That tripart covenant relationship is the source of my life, the joy of my moments, the hope of my future. Our God, the Creator, gave me the gift of writing. My wife, Andrea, gave me the gift of time to write. And both have been cheerleaders in my corner as I've tried to properly exercise that gift and fulfill its calling.

I don't feel worthy of either of them. They willingly enter into my blackest days of doubt to bring comfort, encourage me to stay the course when I falter, and whisper to me "well done" when the last stroke is written. They offer me grace. And I am so much richer for it.

Thanks to our daughter, Meghan, who is always so brilliant in finding ways for me to escape from the corners into which I've written myself. I'm grateful for my agent, Steve Laube, who has helped me become more of a professional. And none of the six books that bear my name would exist without the faith, support, and editorial excellence of the staff at Kregel Publications in Grand Rapids: managing editor Steve Barclift, editors Becky Durost Fish and Joel Armstrong, and marketing manager Katherine Chappell. Also thanks to the three Kregel editors who made it all possible: Miranda Gardner, who opened the door in 2008; Dawn Anderson, who guided the long development of The Jerusalem Prophecies; and Janyre Tromp, who believed there was a diamond in the early versions of *Ishmael Covenant* and who kept on polishing until the Empires of Armageddon was a cord of three solid strands.

In the previous two books, I've thanked Pastor Nick Uva of Harvest Time Church in Greenwich, Connecticut, who first introduced me to the Vilna Gaon, and to Tina Heugh of Bonita Springs, Florida, who permitted me to use her mother's name, Ruth Hughes, as one of the pivotal characters of the series.

I must acknowledge the insight I received from reading Bryan Stevenson's book *Just Mercy* and his thoughts about the impacts of racism in our history and in our present. Stevenson believes America's worst thinking about justice is "steeped in the myths of racial difference" and points to "four institutions in

American history that have shaped our approach to race and justice": slavery; the domestic racial terrorism that plagued black people following the Civil War; legalized racial segregation, racial subordination, and marginalization; and disproportionate mass incarceration of people of color. And I must thank those who are close to my heart who helped me, hopefully, give appropriate and adequate voice to the realities of living as a black man in America.

Some of the ideas about angels and their assignments came from listening to online sermons of Pastor Bill Johnson of Bethel Church in Redding, California.

AUTHOR'S NOTES

With this third book, *Ottoman Dominion*, the Empires of Armageddon series is concluded. But before we get into some of the real events, real places, and real people that are woven throughout this novel, I want to offer you a reward for getting this far.

There are two free opportunities available only to readers of the Empires of Armageddon series:

- Who is the man in the Panama hat? What is his story? I've written an exclusive short story called "Under the Radar" that reveals the origins of the man in the Panama hat and his organization.
- In addition, I'll send you a monthly email post that will expand upon, with greater detail, one of the topics in these author's notes.

If you're hungry to know more about the man in the Panama hat or more about the elements of reality woven into the plot of *Ottoman Dominion*, just send me an email at terrbrennan@gmail.com and I'll respond right away with these two special free offers.

Thanks,

Terry

———⟨∞⟩———

A Personal Note: My wife, Andrea, and I were married in 1979, more than forty years ago. Some years after our marriage, it's so far back I can't remember exactly when, we started to pray together in the morning before the day started and at night before we went to sleep. We don't make it *every* day or *every* night, but we try. At some point over the years, we began the morning prayer and ended the night prayer by me praying a blessing over Andrea—our version of the Aaronic blessing: "May the Lord bless and keep you; may the Lord make his face shine upon you and be gracious to you; may the Lord turn his face toward you and give you peace."

When I started writing this series and had to come up with an anointing to protect the guardian from the lethal effects of the box of power, of course I thought of the Aaronic blessing. Wouldn't that be cool?

What I didn't know was all the history around the Aaronic blessing, how it was administered over the people by Aaron and the priests who followed him, or the depth of the meaning and power of the blessing itself. I was particularly touched by what I found out about the last phrase—"may the Lord turn his face toward you . . ."—that the Hebrew words depict a father lifting his child up above him, at arms length, and smiling up at that child with all his heart.

The dispensing of the Aaronic blessing, and the power of that blessing, became an integral element of the plot for the entire Empires of Armageddon series.

The first book, *Ishmael Covenant*, was released by Kregel Publications on February 18, 2020. Nine days later, Christian singers Kari Jobe and her husband, Cody Carnes, got together with the pastors of Elevation Church in North Carolina for a songwriting session. During that meeting, they composed a new song, "The Blessing." Yup, you got it. The Aaronic blessing. (I doubt they had a chance to read *Ishmael Covenant* by then.)

They debuted the song in a worship service at Elevation Church's Ballantyne campus on March 1 and released the live video on YouTube on March 6. And it took off like wildfire. Here's a link to the YouTube video: https://www .youtube.com/watch?v=Zp6aygmvzM4.

In the first two weeks, the video on YouTube had three million views. In less than a month, it was being sung by church congregations around the nation. At the end of May, it had fourteen million views on YouTube.

On March 6 I had the aortic valve in my heart replaced in a procedure at Mount Sinai Hospital in New York City. I was released from the hospital the next afternoon (I'm fine, by the way). One week later, New York City and the rest of the country were shut down by the COVID-19 pandemic. And our people and our nation were in desperate need of a blessing and hope.

Coincidence? Perhaps. But I prefer to consider it part of God's plan for this time. What does it mean? I have no clue. But I'm anxious to find out. Stay tuned!

———————

While *Ottoman Dominion* is a work of fiction, several plot elements are based on fact.

On the back cover of his 2015 book, *Relentless Strike*, journalist Sean Naylor writes: "Since the attacks of September 11, one organization has been at the forefront of America's military response. Its efforts turned the tide against al-Qaida in Iraq, killed Bin Laden and Zarqawi, rescued Captain Phillips, and captured Saddam Hussein. Its commander can direct cruise missile strikes from nuclear submarines and conduct special operations raids anywhere in the world."

The organization? The Joint Special Operations Command is the United States' super-secret military organization that during the past decade has revolutionized counterterrorism, seamlessly fusing intelligence and operational skills to conduct missions. JSOC is arguably the most potent tactical force on the planet and has performed incredible feats of skill and combat creativity.

JSOC is comprised of over four thousand men and women from the four major armed services. Time and again, the JSOC operations units have proven themselves to be the elite "tip of the spear"—the best trained and most effective members of the US military establishment, engaged in the most highly classified actions around the world. It has assimilated into one formidable strike force, the best operators from the five Special Mission Units of the US Special Operations Command: the army's 1st Special Forces Detachment (Delta Force, Task Force Green), the 75th Ranger Reconnaissance Company (Task Force Red), the navy's Special Warfare Group (SEAL Team 6, Task Force Blue), the army's Intelligence Support Activity (Task Force Orange), and the air force's 24th Special Tactics Squadron (Task Force White), as well as America's most secret aviation and intelligence units.

In *Relentless Strike*, Naylor reveals how an organization designed in the 1980s for a very limited mission transformed itself after 9/11 to become the military's premier weapon in the war against terrorism.

The Diplomatic Security Service is the federal law enforcement and security division of the US State Department. DSS agents are unique in that they are both members of the US Foreign Service, charged with protecting diplomats and embassy personnel overseas, but also armed law enforcement officers who have the authority to investigate crime and arrest individuals both at home and in collaboration with international law enforcement overseas. With nearly twenty-five hundred agents here and abroad, DSS is the most widely represented law enforcement agency in the world. DSS also provides security for foreign dignitaries in the United States, for the annual meeting of the United Nations General Assembly in New York City, and during the Olympics. Descriptions of the State Department's ops center in the Truman Building are accurate to the best of the author's resources.

———

Descriptions of the US embassy and the US ambassador's residence in Tel Aviv are accurate to 2014, before the US embassy was officially moved to Jerusalem in 2018. The US ambassador to Israel did host an enormous, annual Fourth of July party, where over two thousand guests sprawled over the grounds of the residence and feasted on iconic American delights from McDonald's, Ben & Jerry's, and Dominos.

———

The story of the Vilna Gaon—Rabbi Elijah ben Shlomo Zalman (1720–1797)—is accurate in all of its historical elements. He was the foremost Talmudic scholar of his age and a renowned genius in both sacred and secular learning. The story of the Gaon's prophecy about Russia and Crimea, revealed by his great-great-grandson in 2014, is true and led many to believe that the coming of the Jewish Messiah was near at hand. The Gaon did attempt three trips to Jerusalem from his native Lithuania; the last one, only a few years before his death, ended prematurely in Konigsberg, Prussia. The story of the Gaon's second prophecy is a product of the author's imagination.

———

The deeply held enmity and distrust between the Persian Shi'ite hierarchy of Iraq and the Sunni Arab Saudi royal family has raged for centuries. In 1979 when the Arab shah of Iran was overthrown, Ayatollah Khomeini actually declared that Sunni believers were not truly Muslims and demanded the overthrow of the al-Saud family. That conflict continues today with Iran funding and supplying the rebel forces attempting to usurp Yemen, on Saudi Arabia's southern border, while Iran moves inexorably forward in its alliance with its fellow Shia believers in Iraq.

The potential for a nuclear confrontation along the Persian Gulf remains high. Iran continues its development of nuclear power—many believe for the purpose of creating nuclear weapons. And high-ranking US intelligence officials believe Saudi Arabia did in fact finance much of Pakistan's nuclear weapons program, pouring millions of dollars into its development. The intelligence community also believes there exists an agreement for Pakistan to provide nuclear weapons to Saudi Arabia when called for.

In the summer of 2014, the Islamic terrorist army called ISIS controlled more than thirty-four thousand square miles in Syria and Iraq, from the Mediterranean coast to south of Baghdad. The major Iraqi cities of Mosul, Fallujah, and Tikrit were overrun, including key oil refineries and military bases. The Iraqi army was in retreat and disarray. The world expected another offensive thrust from ISIS that could imperil the capital of Baghdad itself. And in late July 2014, ISIS executioners began beheading captives and broadcasting the ghastly videos. It appeared the entire Middle East was at risk of being ravaged by ISIS.

For more than forty years, since 1979, the United States and other countries have frozen Iranian assets in their banks, in retaliation for when fifty-two Americans were taken hostage and held in Tehran for 444 days. Twenty to thirty billion dollars have been frozen in banks worldwide, including approximately two billion dollars in US banks. By 2014, two billion dollars would be earning about one hundred million dollars per year in interest.

The question of accrued interest on those frozen funds and how much interest is owed to Iran continues to be a bone of contention. When four hundred million dollars was returned to Iran by the Obama Administration in January 2016—money the Iranians paid prior to 1979 for US military aircraft that were never delivered—the United States also sent Iran a payment of *1.3 billion dollars in accrued interest.* The money to pay that accrued interest came from the US Department of the Treasury's Judgment Fund, which pays judgments, or compromise settlements of lawsuits, against the government. In 2016, two US senators wrote in *Time* magazine:

The Judgment Fund is a little-known account used to pay certain court judgments and settlements against the federal government. Each year, billions of dollars are disbursed from it, yet the fund does not fall under the annual appropriations process. Because of this, the Treasury Department has no binding reporting requirements, and these funds are paid out with scant scrutiny. The executive branch decides what, if any, information is made available to the public.

Essentially, the Judgment Fund is an unlimited supply of money provided to the federal government to cover its own liability.

The descriptions of the last-days theology of the world's three great religions—Judaism, Christianity, and Islam—are accurate. All three religions trace their roots back to Abraham and claim to be part (though different parts) of the Abrahamic covenant that God established with humanity. And each religion waits for a climactic time in history, birthed in peace, when the long-awaited *One* (either the Messiah, Jesus's second coming, or the Mahdi) will be revealed. While the Jewish Messiah will usher in an eternal time of peace for a world united into one confederation, both Christian and Islamic end times anticipate an ultimate and definitive armed conflict, followed by a "final judgement" of the good and the evil.

Over the course of nearly twenty-five hundred years, the fertile crescent of the Middle East—from modern Turkey into the Tigris and Euphrates valleys in Iraq, down the Jordan valley of Palestine, and across the top of Egypt and the Nile Delta—was but a portion of three vast, evolving, and competing empires: the Persian, the Muslim Arab, and the Ottoman Empires. One of the fundamental beliefs of Islam is, in fact, that once an Islamic group or nation rules any portion of the earth, it rules that portion forever. Even though the Persians gradually converted to the Islamic faith only in the mid-seventh century, following the Muslim Arab invasion of Persia, if those empires were resurrected today, each would claim the same slice of the earth.

Opened in 1955, the Incirlik Air Base—located seven miles east of downtown Adana, Turkey, but still within the city limits—includes NATO's largest nuclear weapons storage facility.

With one ten-thousand-foot runway and fifty-seven hardened aircraft shelters, Incirlik is the most strategically important base in NATO's Southern Region. At one time, the base had over five thousand NATO personnel stationed on its three thousand acres, in addition to two thousand family members. Adana, with a population of over one million, is the fourth largest city in Turkey.

NATO has operated a nuclear sharing program since the mid-1950s. Since 2009, NATO has stationed US nuclear weapons in Germany, the Netherlands, Italy, Belgium, and Turkey. While the United States and NATO maintain a "neither confirm nor deny" posture toward the numbers of its nuclear distribution, the Hoover Institute reported that the United States currently deploys somewhere between 150 and 240 air-delivered nuclear weapons (B61 gravity bombs). It is estimated that twenty-five percent of those weapons are stationed at the Incirlik Air Base in eastern Turkey, with most sources placing fifty B61 nuclear bombs at Incirlik. The B61 is a variable-yield nuclear weapon with an explosive yield of 0.3 to 340 kilotons. The "Little Boy" atomic bomb that destroyed Hiroshima in 1945 had a yield of 15 kilotons.

Other Notes: The exteriors of St. Archangel Michael Monastery, constructed in 1894 over the ruins of a Byzantine fortress and overlooking the old port of Jaffa, are portrayed accurately. The interiors are a product of the writer's imagination.

The Royal Air Force airbase at Akrotiri, on the southern coast of Cyprus, is administered by Britain as sovereign overseas territory. The airbase, now partially used by NATO air forces, was for a time home base for American U-2 spy plane missions over the USSR.

Unicode is a universally accepted computer coding language first implemented in 1987.

The possibility of water wars in the Middle East remains strong. Since 1975, Turkey's dams have cut water flow to Iraq by eighty percent and to Syria by forty percent. Work on a pipeline between Turkey and Israel was suspended in 2010 after an Israeli raid on six civilian ships trying to run the Gaza Blockade resulted in the deaths of nine Turkish nationals.

The Kurdish people, native to the mountainous regions of eastern Turkey, northern Syria, and northwest Iraq, are the largest people group in the world without their own nation.

————⋙⋘————

Other than the basic facts and associated research listed above, the rest of *Ottoman Dominion* is the result of the author's imagination. Any errors of fact are a result of that imagination.

REVISIT THE BEGINNING OF MULLANEY'S HEROIC SAGA

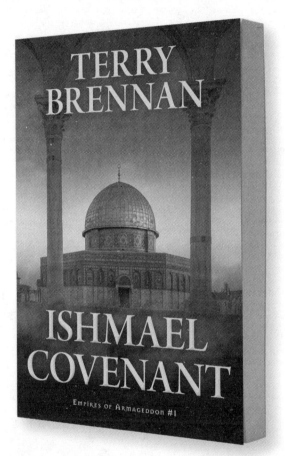

"A simply riveting action/adventure suspense thriller of a novel by an author with an impressive flair for originality and the kind of deftly scripted narrative storytelling style that holds the reader's attention from beginning to end. . . . Especially and unreservedly recommended."

—*Midwest Book Review*

Empires of Armageddon Book Two

"A fantastic combination of thriller, historical conspiracy, biblical prophecy, and Middle Eastern complexity—and you're never sure where the line is drawn between fact and fiction."
— Ian Acheson, author of *Angelguard*

KREGEL
PUBLICATIONS

IS THE ARK OF THE COVENANT HOPE FOR HUMANITY— OR A WEAPON FOR ITS ULTIMATE DESTRUCTION?

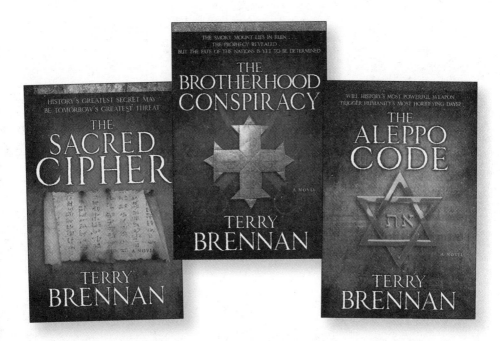

Don't miss Terry Brennan's award-winning Jerusalem Prophecies series—
another epic suspense trek through dangers torn straight from the headlines.
Available wherever books are sold!